glimmers OF YOU

THE LOST & FOUND SERIES

CATHERINE COWLES

Editor: Margo Lipschultz
Copy Editor: Chelle Olson
Proofreading: Julie Deaton and Jaime Ryter
Paperback Formatting: Stacey Blake, Champagne Book Design
Cover Design: Hang Le
Cover Photography: Sara Eirew

For Elle.
Thank you for helping to inspire Grae in all her beautiful badassery and for making sure I found the raw truth in her journey. You are the most amazing and inspiring warrior. I am so grateful for your support and friendship.

glimmers OF YOU

Prologue

Grae
PAST, AGE FIFTEEN

I TWISTED MY NECKLACE BETWEEN MY FINGERS AS I TILTED to the side from my perch on the boulder, straining to get a better view of the trailhead's parking lot. I took in the SUV pulling in, and the air left my lungs in a whoosh of disappointment. *Not him.*

A wet finger snaked into my ear, and I jumped, batting the arm away. "Gross! What is wrong with you?"

My older brother, Holt, laughed as he caught me in a headlock. "Someone's gotta teach you to keep on your toes."

I grabbed for the hair on his arm and pulled. Hard.

"Ow! Shit, G. That hurt."

"That's what you get for playing with fire," our eldest brother, Lawson, said with a grin as he walked up.

"She's like a Tasmanian Devil. Cute but deadly," Holt muttered.

Lawson ruffled my hair, and I shoved his hand away. "But we trained her that way."

I scowled at him, but he wasn't wrong. Having four older

brothers meant three things: One, I was the most overprotected teenager in Cedar Ridge. Two, I'd learned how to fight with the best of them by the time I was five. And three, I wouldn't have a first date until I was approximately thirty.

"You guys are the worst," I grumbled without any heat. The truth was, I loved them like crazy, but they were equally annoying.

"*You* were distracted. Who were you looking for?" Holt asked, suddenly suspicious. "Heard Rance was coming to train with his dad."

Roan walked up then, a frown creasing his brow, and I knew without a shadow of a doubt that my mostly silent brother would be staring my poor classmate down for the entire afternoon during search and rescue training.

I groaned. "No. Rance is a *friend*. Maybe you've heard of those."

I should've just said I was looking for him. It would've been better than the truth. Besides, Holt was a freaking hypocrite since he was dating my best friend, Wren.

Lawson's brows pulled together. "You shouldn't have friends who are boys. You're too young."

"I'm fifteen. Most girls in my class have already lost their virginity," I snapped as I pushed to my feet.

A series of groans and shouts from the three of them filled the air. Our dad crossed to us. "Hey, what's going on? We're about to get started."

Dad had helped run the Harrison County Search and Rescue team for as long as I could remember. The team got a lot of use with the number of tourists who came to our little town a few hours east of Seattle in search of outdoor activities galore. And Dad had gotten his kids involved with SAR early on.

All of us had fallen in love with it. Being in the outdoors, helping people…there wasn't a better combination.

Lawson patted Dad on the shoulder. "Trust me when I say you don't want to know."

Dad looked in my direction. "Pumpkin?"

Heat hit my cheeks. "It's nothing. They're just being annoying."

He chuckled. "What's new?" He surveyed the group that had assembled for one of our training sessions. "Nash."

My youngest brother's head snapped up from looking at his phone. The worried look on his face had my stomach cramping. It had been doing that for the past week. Probably because I knew this day was coming. My fingers found my necklace again, the tiny metal disc imprinted with a compass that had become my talisman since I'd been gifted it on my thirteenth birthday.

"Get over here," Dad called. "We're about to get started." He looked at the rest of us. "I'm going to gather everyone else. Gear up."

Nash moved slowly through the trailhead welcome area, and I met him halfway.

"Have you heard from him?" I asked quietly.

Nash shook his head. "He's not answering my texts."

The cramping in my stomach intensified. "Nothing at all today?"

"No. He said he'd be here, but then…not a damned word." Nash sighed. "Maybe he just needs to be alone."

I worried the corner of my thumbnail. "Maybe." But I wasn't sure Caden really needed that, even if it was what he wanted.

"Come on in," Dad called to our SAR team.

I caught sight of Mom near the parking lot and made a beeline for her instead of following Dad's instructions. The moment she saw me, a hint of concern lined her face. "Everything okay?"

I pressed my thumbnail into the pad of my pointer finger, just shy of pain. I needed to choose my words carefully. "I'm worried about Caden."

Her expression softened. "He was supposed to be here?"

I nodded. "Nash hasn't heard from him, but I think I might know where he is."

My mom's brows rose at that.

"There's a place not far from here. He showed Nash and me one time." Because I'd always been the hanger-on with the two of them and Nash's other best friend, Maddie. But Caden never made me feel that way. He always included me in their shenanigans.

The place Caden had taken us to wasn't the first or the last, but something about how he relaxed when he was there had made me realize it was his *place*. I'd gone there more than once and, if I was honest, did it in hopes of finding Caden there. Sometimes, he was. Other times, he wasn't. But over time, I'd found the peace of it, too.

My mom's mouth slipped into a frown. "I don't know if you should be going on your own."

"I'll take one of the ATVs and text you once I'm there. If he's not around, I'll come right back."

She sighed. "You care about him, don't you?"

"Of course, I do. It's Caden."

He'd been a part of our lives since I was four and he was five, and he and Nash had played soccer together. He should've felt like a fifth brother, but he didn't.

"All right." Mom brushed the hair away from my face. "Text the moment you get there and wear your helmet."

I grinned and gave her a quick hug. "Thanks. I will."

I jogged toward the parking lot and hopped on the ATV I'd ridden over from our property a few miles away. Slipping on my helmet, I started it up. I made a beeline out of the lot before one of my nosy brothers could follow me.

The wind blew my light blond locks away from my face as I rode. Each second that passed wound my insides tighter. If Caden wasn't here, I didn't have the first clue where to look next.

I turned off the access road and onto a path. It wasn't wide enough for cars, but it was plenty big enough for my ATV. I slowed my vehicle as the forest opened to a clearing. As I turned off my engine, my breath hitched.

There he was.

Caden didn't look up at the sound of my vehicle. He kept staring at the creek in front of him, his back to me. Those shoulders had gotten wider this year, his light brown hair just a bit darker.

His hazel eyes were the same, though—except for the sadness I found in them when he thought no one was looking.

I climbed off the ATV and slid off my helmet, leaving it on the seat.

Caden didn't move as I approached. He seemed lost in watching the swirls of deep blues and greens in the water.

"I wondered if you'd show up." His voice was deeper, too—a little gravellier than it had been the year before.

I climbed over the log he was perched on and sat, leaving just an inch or two between us. "Didn't want you to be alone."

"Maybe I wanted to be alone."

"Then you wouldn't have come here."

And there was such relief in that. That Caden wasn't locking me out.

The corner of his mouth kicked up. "I guess you're right. Maybe I just wanted to see if someone cared enough to find me."

I frowned. "A lot of people care. Nash. My parents—"

"But not my family."

I bit the inside of my cheek. "They didn't say anything?"

Caden tipped his head back so he could stare at the sky. "My mom would've if she hadn't taken a ridiculous number of pills and passed out. But my dad and Gabe are pretending like today is business as usual."

I moved on instinct, slipping my hand into Caden's and threading my fingers through his. "She was the best. One of the kindest people I've ever known. And so funny."

Caden's breath hitched, and he stared down at our joined hands. "She took care of everyone. Hell, the only time she raised her voice was if someone was about to kill a bug in the house. She'd insist on catching it and taking it outside."

My heart squeezed. "That's Clara in a nutshell."

"I miss her so damn much." Caden's voice was raw, ravaged.

Of course, he missed her. It was his little sister. He loved her fiercely. Would've done anything for her. But he couldn't stop cancer. It didn't matter how many treatments they tried, she just got sicker and sicker until she left this Earth—two years ago today.

I squeezed his hand harder. "That just shows how much you loved her. She's a part of you, and there's no way you *can't* feel her absence."

Caden shifted his gaze to my face. "She branded me, and it sometimes feels like the wound is as fresh as the day it happened."

My heart rate picked up speed at the intensity in his eyes. "I don't think grief is linear. Some days are easier. Others will take you out at the knees."

He looked back at the water. "Not everyone gets that. Some people just want me to be better. Who I was before."

"But you're never going to be that person again. This changed you."

Caden's gaze jerked back to me. "How do you get that when no one else seems to?"

I shrugged, not wanting to reveal the truth: that I watched Caden with a single-minded fascination. So, I'd seen the change. It had come on slowly and yet all at once. A darkness that hadn't been there before. But it was a part of him, and I couldn't help but love it the same way I loved the rest of him. It just made those glimmers of his light shine that much brighter.

Caden's gaze tracked over my face, stilling on my lips. A second later, he forced his attention away and dropped my hand. "Want to hike with me?"

I tried not to let the disappointment land. For as often as Caden and I spent time together, he'd never made a move to take it further than that. I was used to living in disappointment. I pushed to my feet. "Sure."

I slid my phone out of my pocket and shot off a text to my mom, letting her know what we were doing.

Caden glanced at me. "You got your pack?"

I winced. "I left it back at SAR training."

He lifted his and swung it over his shoulder. "I should have us covered."

"Can I steal some water?"

Caden handed me his bottle, and I took a long swig. "Geez. It's lucky I brought two."

I gave him a sheepish smile. "I was pushing the pedal to the metal over here."

His brows pulled together. "You need to be careful; those ATVs can be dangerous."

I rolled my eyes and handed him the water bottle. "I've already got four older brothers. I don't need a fifth."

Caden chuckled. "Noted. You want to take the north trail?"

I nodded. The views from that one were absolutely stunning. You could see the town nestled next to the lake and everything else for miles around.

Caden started off, heading up the mountainside. The path was wide enough in this first part that we could walk side by side. We were mostly quiet at first, letting the late-summer breeze swirl around us.

I never felt pressure to talk around Caden. I could simply be. There was comfort in just having him beside me. But if I ever did want to give voice to anything, I could do it without fear of judgment. Caden was one of those people who saw all sides of something and knew that things were rarely black and white.

"She loved those," Caden said quietly, inclining his head to the purple flowers mixed in with the other plants.

"They're beautiful. What are they called again?"

"Lupine."

For as privileged a life as Caden had led, he loved nature and consumed knowledge about it like a man starved. The only person who knew more than him was Roan. And that was probably because he spent more time with the mountains than he did with people.

I lifted my phone to take a picture, then jotted it down in my notes app.

"What was that for?" Caden asked.

I shrugged. "I want to remember it. Every time I see it now, it'll remind me of Clara."

Caden's Adam's apple bobbed as he swallowed. "It keeps her alive in a way. Every time we remember."

I wanted to take his hand again, to give any sort of comfort I could, but I held back. "We won't let her be forgotten. I promise."

Caden nodded, clearing his throat. "How was SAR going?"

I got the message. He needed to think about something else and not let himself drown in the grief of today. "Mostly good... Lots of the team was there. My brothers were annoying. The usual."

He chuckled. "What were they getting on you about today?"

I blew out a breath, fluttering wisps of my hair. "Rance Granger."

Caden's footsteps faltered the slightest bit. "What about him?"

"They think I have a crush on him."

"Do you?" Strain wove around Caden's voice.

"It wouldn't matter if I did. They scare off anyone I want to go on a date with."

Caden grunted. "Good. If your brothers can scare a guy away, he's not worth your time anyway."

"I'm never going to lose my virginity," I mumbled.

Caden immediately started choking. "Shit, Gigi. Warn a guy before you say something like that."

Annoyance flitted through me. "I'm almost sixteen, you know. Most girls my age have had boyfriends. I'm not a kid." He was only a year older than me, and I knew he'd messed around with plenty of girls.

Caden halted on the path, looking down at me. "Trust me, Gigi. I know you're not a kid. But you shouldn't rush into that. It should be with someone you care about who cherishes that you're sharing that part of yourself with him."

"And did you wait? Was it special and cherished?"

Caden winced. "You know me. That's not ever going to be something I look for."

Pain lanced my chest. "Why?"

His gaze slipped from me. "It's just not. Don't want to go there."

Caden hadn't always been this way. When he was in middle school, he'd had girlfriends he took on dates and to dances. After Clara died, that had all stopped. There was nothing resembling commitment in his romantic life now.

"Can I have your water again?"

He handed it over. "You okay?"

I nodded but had to admit the first part of this trail had gotten to me more than it usually did. I wanted to lay down and take a nap. "I didn't sleep great last night." I'd been too worried about him.

Caden took the water bottle back. "We can go back if you're not up for this."

I shook my head. "No. The fresh air will help."

We started up the path again, and my muscles protested the movement. I ignored them and kept pushing on. It got a little better, but my vision blurred when we reached the first outlook, the scene in front of me wavering.

I reached out for Caden's arm on instinct.

"Whoa." He immediately steadied me. "Why don't you sit down for a minute?"

Caden helped me over to a boulder, but my legs shook the entire way. He crouched in front of me. "You dizzy?"

"Yeah, and my vision's blurry."

Even through my not-quite-right eyesight, I saw Caden's worry.

"Can I have some more water?" My tongue felt like it was sticking to the roof of my mouth.

He handed me the bottle, and I guzzled the rest of it down.

"How do you feel now?" he asked.

The world tilted again. "Not right. I feel like I'm high or something." Not that I knew what that felt like, exactly, but this was what I imagined it would be.

Caden stood, pulling out his phone. "I'm going to call your dad." He cursed. "I don't have enough bars."

"You don't need to call him." I stood, but it was a mistake. I tipped sideways. It felt like the ground was a moving conveyor belt beneath my feet.

Caden caught me before I hit the dirt. "Shit, Gigi! What's going on?"

"I-I don't know." Pain lanced through my stomach.

Caden's face was a blur above me as he lifted me into his arms. "I've got you. We're gonna get you some help."

"You can't carry me." It was too far back to the trailhead.

"You? You're nothing compared to those massive guys we've had to haul off the mountain."

I might be tiny, but he was carrying me all by himself, and we'd already gone at least a mile or two.

Dark spots danced in front of my vision, and my head slumped against Caden's chest.

"Gigi?" Panic lit his voice.

"Hmm?"

"Stay with me. Stay awake," Caden commanded.

I wanted to. I always wanted to be with Caden. But I was so tired.

The darkness pulled me under, but not before I heard his voice calling after me.

"Don't you leave me, too."

Chapter One

Grae

I ADJUSTED THE BACKPACK ON MY SHOULDER AS I STRODE toward the small cottage on the edge of downtown. My boss, Jordan, had turned the house into his base of operations for Cedar Ridge Vacation Adventures. The company ran day trips for everything from hiking to white water rafting, and Jordan had a bunch of cabin rentals on top of it.

Opening the screen door, I stepped inside. A whistle sounded, and Eddie grinned as he leaned back on one of the sofas. "Back and looking a little worse for wear."

I scowled in his direction. "How would you look if you had two couples who *insisted* they were expert hikers but started moaning and complaining one mile in?"

Noel's lips twitched as he looked up from his desk, flicking his shaggy, dark hair out of his eyes. "Should've turned around."

"I tried, but one of the damn husbands was determined to finish the loop. I'm pretty sure his wife is going to file for divorce when they get home."

Eddie chuckled, his amber eyes lightening with the action. "Nothing like finding out your hubby wants to off you because his man card gets threatened on a hike."

"Love is a con," Noel grumbled.

Jordan popped his head out of his office, his gaze running over me. "That bad?"

I grimaced. "The fact that I'm three hours behind schedule should tell you everything you need to know."

He winced. "Sorry about that. I had a feeling that guy was overstating his experience level."

"I'd be surprised if they'd done more walking than between sample sales in Manhattan."

Jordan chuckled, rubbing the back of his neck. "I'll try to do a little more recon before we send another group on the Upper Ridge Trail."

I sank into my chair and pulled out my phone to check my glucose monitoring app. While on the trail, I'd tried to manage things the best I could, but my clients hadn't made it easy. Opening my desk drawer, I pulled out my peanut butter and some M&M's. I popped a few of the sugary candies and then ate a spoonful of peanut butter.

Eddie pouted at me as he crossed to his desk, and I poured some M&M's onto his stack of papers. The pout turned into a grin. "You always take such good care of me."

I held up the bag in Noel's direction, and he just frowned at me.

"What?" I mumbled around a mouthful of peanut butter.

"He wants to know if you're okay," Eddie said, translating Noel's grumpiness.

I knew the look. I'd become an expert in grunts and grumbles with Roan as a brother, but I hoped that Noel would back off if I asked.

"The hike was longer than I thought. I just need to cover." Otherwise, I'd end up being awake all night with one low blood sugar alarm after the other.

Eddie popped an M&M into his mouth. "You sure about that? We could all take the rest of the week off and go to the hot springs."

"Yes." I stuck out my tongue at him.

He tried to grab it like the weirdo he was.

"Gross. I don't want your germy hands in my mouth."

Eddie snickered. "Then watch where that tongue goes. Although I wouldn't mind it near—"

I smacked a hand over his mouth. "Do not finish that sentence."

Jordan sighed. "Do I need to show another human resources video about harassment?"

"No!" we all shouted at once, but Eddie's was muffled by my palm.

We might give each other hell, but we were our own little band of misfits, and I wouldn't want to work anywhere else. I'd known all of them for most of my life. Had gone to school with Noel and Eddie and was family friends with Jordan, who was a few years older. They had become family over the years, and there was no one I'd rather work with.

My family thought it was crazy and reckless that I wanted to lead outdoor treks after my Type 1 diabetes diagnosis. But that only made me want to do it more. The way I had to fight for it only made the reward sweeter.

But it was more than that. Being out on the mountain reminded me of my fondest memories. The ones before my life changed. The things before Caden had put a wall between us that I hadn't been able to scale.

The door to the office opened, and I dropped my hand from Eddie's mouth. I winced as a familiar figure stepped inside, holding a massive bouquet. I stared at the array of roses and lilies and knew I should have butterflies. Instead, I felt dread.

Jordan cleared his throat. "Hey, Rance."

Rance nodded. "J." He crossed to me, extending the flowers. "Saw your SUV pull in from the station. Wanted to bring these over."

The fire station was next to the police station and within

eyeshot of our little cottage. It wasn't the first time I'd cursed the nearness with Lawson and Nash being able to keep an eye on me from the Cedar Ridge Police Department. I gave him a weak smile. "This really wasn't necessary."

I never should've said yes to the handful of dates with Rance. I'd never felt a spark. But we were casual friends, and he was a good guy, so I'd thought maybe the chemistry would grow. I'd been so wrong. I was always wrong. I'd never felt the buzz of awareness I experienced around Caden with anyone else. But the chemistry with Rance had been especially bad. Like kissing a dead fish bad.

He shrugged, giving me a lopsided smile. "I wanted to see if you could go to dinner tomorrow."

My stomach churned. Why was he doing this in front of the people I worked with? I cast a quick look around the room. Noel was glaring daggers at him. Eddie looked like he wanted some popcorn while he took in every moment of the drama. And Jordan looked…worried.

I pushed to my feet, leaving the flowers on my desk. "Why don't we go outside?" I started moving before Rance had a chance to argue.

I rounded the front of the building, and he came to a stop just a little too close. I took a step back. "I told you before; I think we're better as friends."

Rance sent me a sheepish smile. "I know, but you can't get what you don't fight for. And I think we could be good together, Grae. Just give me a shot."

My thumbnail pressed into the pad of my forefinger. "I did, and I just didn't feel that spark."

A hint of frustration flashed in his expression. "Three dates isn't a shot; it's barely getting to know each other."

I fought the urge to scream. "It's enough for me to know. I'm sorry, Rance. I just don't feel the same."

I hurried back inside before he could argue more.

The screen door slapped behind me, and all three of my co-workers immediately looked as if they were extremely busy. They were horrible actors. Their nosy butts had probably been spying the whole time. I let out a growl of frustration as I headed back to my desk.

Eddie pressed his lips together to keep from laughing, but it only held for so long. His shoulders began to shake, his auburn hair ruffling with the action.

I sent a glare in his direction. "It's not funny."

Eddie leaned back in his chair, locking his hands behind his head. "It's a little funny. He's like a lost puppy just begging for a home."

Noel kicked at his chair. "That shit isn't cool. Grae said no. He needs to leave her be."

The amusement fled Eddie's face, and he glanced in my direction. "He freaking you out?"

I pinched the bridge of my nose to stave off the impending headache. The last thing I needed was to add three surrogate big brothers to the four I already had. "No, it's just awkward. I don't want to hurt his feelings, but I just don't feel that way about him. I tried, but the chemistry isn't there."

It wasn't there with anyone I wanted to find it with. It only flared to life with the last person on the planet it should have.

Jordan leaned against the wall, studying me carefully. "If he's making you uncomfortable, I'll kick him out the next time he stops by."

"Damn straight," Eddie agreed, casting a look across the street as Rance disappeared into the station. "He's a chump anyway. Those teeth are so white they probably glow in the dark."

Noel snorted at that. "The amount of gel in his hair could probably shellac my boat."

"You guys are mean. He's handsome, and he's kind," I argued.

Eddie's lips twitched. "Then why aren't you going to dinner with him?"

That was the million-dollar question.

The parking lot at the local high school was half-full of familiar vehicles. Not many places were large enough for our entire SAR team to meet, but the high school gymnasium was one of them.

I climbed out of my SUV, my body protesting the movement. Today's longer-than-expected hike had done a number on me. As if to punctuate the point, my phone beeped with an alert—my glucose monitoring app letting me know that I was trending upward. I shoved it into my pocket and snagged a granola bar from my cupholder, biting off a piece.

Grabbing my bag from the back seat, I slung it over my shoulder and headed toward the gymnasium. My steps faltered as I caught sight of the familiar Mercedes G-Wagon. My back teeth ground together as a flare of pissed-off annoyance surged to life.

He just *had* to come back here.

Life had been a million times easier when Caden was running one of his family's hotels in New York. I only saw him when I caved to temptation and searched his name. The photos of him with models, socialites, or whatever the flavor of the week was, hurt like hell. But at least I didn't have to see it in person.

Now that he was back and working at his family's fancy resort nestled in the mountains, I had to deal with Caden. But he couldn't leave it at that. No, he had to infiltrate every area of my life. SAR. My friend group. *My* family dinners.

I wrenched open the door and stepped into the gym.

Nash let out a low whistle. "Who pissed in your Cheerios?"

I glared at him. "No one."

He chuckled. "That was real convincing."

His fiancée, Maddie, moved closer, worry creasing her brow. "You okay?"

That was Maddie, through and through. Always wanting to make sure everyone she cared about was all right. Between her and our other friend, Wren, I had an embarrassment of riches when it came to the women in my life. And they'd both be sisters before long.

I pulled Maddie into a hug. "I'm fine. Just exhausted. Long day."

Holt walked up then, frowning. "Are you okay? You don't have to stay. Did you have dinner?"

I fought the urge to scream and instead took one of those deep, cleansing breaths that helped keep me from murdering the people I loved. "I said I'm fine. Just tired."

He stared down at me as if he didn't believe me. "You let me know if that changes."

I made a humming noise that wasn't agreement or disagreement.

"That's Gigi-speak for *go screw yourself*."

That low voice that sounded like it was coated in sandpaper had goosebumps taking flight on my arms. I hated that it had that kind of effect on me. Hated that he somehow still knew me so well.

I straightened my spine, glancing up at Caden Shaw. I would've thought I'd be accustomed to his beauty by now. Those hazel eyes that punched right through you, the jawline covered in stubble that I itched to feel against my palm, the broad shoulders capable of carrying the weight of the world.

He wore his hair differently now. It was cropped close on the sides and long on top. It fit him. The longer strands said *in-control businessman*, but the sides said *rebel*.

"Oh, look what the cat dragged in. The one person no one wants here."

Caden chuckled, and that sound was even worse than his husky voice. It had a smoky heat that wrapped around me, digging in deep. Just that barest hint of sound had my body waking up in ways it never did, even when I searched with all my might for that pull.

"Denial is not just a river in Egypt, Gigi."

Every time my nickname left his lips, I wanted to punch him. It killed—the two syllables that reminded me of a simpler time. One where I was truly happy. Where I thought the world was fair and things always worked out.

My gaze flicked up to his as if of its own volition. "Pull your lip over your head and swallow."

Nash groaned. "Will you two quit it? I thought you were getting along better."

I squirmed in place. There'd been the briefest of cease-fires. A moment in the aftermath of Maddie's kidnapping and Nash's attack where I'd thought that maybe Caden and I were finding our way back to what we had been. But the second we'd known that everyone would be okay, Caden had put that wall right back up.

"I'm going to find a seat," I muttered. I hurried away from the group as fast as I could.

At least two dozen folding chairs were assembled in a semi-circle, leaving an opening for the two EMTs who were requalifying us in first aid tonight. I scanned the people gathered and made a beeline for the one person I knew wouldn't put me on edge.

I dropped my bag to the floor and lowered myself into the chair next to Roan. He glanced down at me, his gaze running over my face, searching the way it always did. He could see more than any of my brothers. Sometimes, I thought it was because he lived his life in the quiet. It made him aware of even the slightest changes in the world around him.

"Bad day?" he asked.

"Idiot tourists pretending they could hike Everest, nosy coworkers, a-hat Caden." I consciously left out the Rance issue. Because while Roan was my most understanding brother, that didn't make him any less protective. And the last thing I needed was my four big brothers thinking they had to step in where my dating life was concerned.

"Tourists," Roan grunted.

He had to deal with his fair share of them while working as a game warden for Fish and Wildlife. Usually, when they didn't store their food properly and attracted bears.

"Summer's almost over," I assured him.

"Not soon enough," he grumbled.

The chair next to me squeaked, and I looked up. The little bit of calmness I'd found from Roan's presence vanished in a flash.

Caden rolled up the sleeves of his button-down, exposing tan, corded muscle. Rage pulsed hotter in my system. Even his forearms were hot.

"Sit somewhere else," I growled.

Caden arched a brow. "You'd think I had an effect on you, Gigi."

"Yeah, indigestion," I snapped.

Roan choked on a laugh.

Caden stretched out his arm and draped it across the back of my chair. "So, what you're saying is I cause deep feelings."

I snarled at him as I pinched the inside of that danged forearm.

"Shit! Sheathe the claws."

"You're the one who wanted to sit here." And now I would be on edge for the rest of the night.

Holt stepped into the center of the semi-circle. "Thanks for coming, everyone."

I glanced at Roan. "Where's Lawson?"

"Couldn't find someone to watch the boys."

Our eldest brother was the world's best dad, but I knew doing it on his own wasn't easy, and he wasn't one to ask for help unless he was desperate.

Holt introduced the two EMTs, and they dove into basic wound care. Between training for my job and growing up in SAR, I could've recited the presentation by heart.

My phone buzzed in my bag, but I ignored it, trying to focus on how to properly wash and sanitize a wound before wrapping it. Heat wafted off Caden in waves. My body was instantly aware of every tiny movement he made. His arm brushed mine, and I jolted as if I'd been shocked by electricity.

Roan sent me a puzzled look, and I crossed my arms, pulling them tight to my body.

My phone buzzed again, and I bent to slide it out of my bag. As my fingers closed around the device, yet another buzz sounded. Tapping the screen, I grimaced.

Rance: *I've been thinking a lot about what you said.*

Rance: *The strongest relationships I've seen started as friendship. The spark came later.*

Rance: *Give us another shot. Let me take you to dinner this weekend. Or we can spend a day out on the lake.*

I toyed with the corner of my thumbnail as anxiety pricked my belly. So much for honest conversations helping close the door.

"What does that jackhole want?"

I'd been so distracted by the texts that I hadn't noticed Caden's nearness until his lips ghosted across the shell of my ear.

I shoved my elbow into his side. "Mind your own business."

"He bothering you?"

There was a strain to Caden's voice that I didn't miss. Because while he had firmly closed the door when it came to letting me in emotionally, he still felt like he had the right to play big brother number five. That fact only poured salt into the wound that was his defection.

"No, he's a friend," I whispered.

Caden's eyes narrowed. "That didn't look like someone who wants to be your friend."

"We went on a few dates last month. It's no big deal."

Caden's jaw hardened, and a tic started in the muscle. "He's not good enough for you."

I wanted to read far too much into those words. I wanted to hear jealousy and desire and a million other things. But they weren't there. Even my traitorous heart knew that.

Because that day when I was fifteen had changed everything. Caden might have saved my life, but he had slammed the door on our friendship, taking away my secret keeper, my resting place, my person, and replacing him with a coolly casual acquaintance. So, when I'd woken up from the coma, I hadn't just lost the normal future I'd planned for. I'd lost everything. Because I'd lost him.

Chapter Two

Caden

I watched as Grae moved through the crowd, her tiny form slipping between team members with graceful deftness until I saw only a flash of white-blond hair before she disappeared altogether. An ache settled deep in my chest the moment she vanished, as if some invisible tether linked us together. It happened every time I watched her walk away, yet I didn't do a damn thing to stop it.

A throat cleared next to me, and my gaze snapped to Roan. His eyes were hard as he took me in. *Shit.* Being away for so many years had dulled my reflexes. I was normally more careful about paying Grae too much attention in front of her brothers—beyond giving her a hard time.

I shouldn't be doing that either, but I couldn't resist. Riling Grae meant getting her attention, even if it was in the form of the sharp side of her tongue. I'd take that over her cool indifference any day of the week.

Nash walked up and cuffed me upside the head. "Stop egging

G on. One of these days, she's going to murder your ass, and I won't be able to do anything to stop it."

I grinned at my best friend as I stood. "What can I say? I like pushing her buttons."

Maddie studied me carefully but didn't say anything.

"She's tiny, but she's vicious," Nash muttered. "I'd watch your back."

He was right. Grae had a fight in her, unlike anyone I'd ever met. It was something innate, burned into her bones as if the Universe had known she would need it someday. It had helped her claw her way back from the brink of death all those years ago, and it gave her the gumption to keep chasing her dreams now.

My gut twisted as an image flashed in my mind: Grae pale and clammy as I ran down the mountain, her breaths shallow. The beep of the heart monitor as I watched her chest rise and fall in the hospital bed that was three sizes too big. Panic clawed at my chest, my ribs tightening around my lungs.

"Caden? You all right?"

Nash's voice jarred me out of my living nightmare. "What? Yeah. Sorry, just spaced."

His eyes narrowed. "Everything okay with your parents?"

Was it ever? But that wasn't something I wanted to delve into here. "As good as they can be."

Which meant they were shit.

Nash opened his mouth to say something, but Maddie squeezed his arm, then turned her focus to me. "Come over for dinner this week. We're finally settled into the new kitchen."

I grinned, and the curve of my mouth was authentic for the first time all day. "A Maddie meal? Twist my arm."

Nash frowned at her. "You gonna make double?"

Holt choked on a laugh as he strode up. "I've never met someone more possessive of food."

Maddie rolled her eyes. "You're one to talk. Wren said you practically called off the wedding when she ate the last of the leftovers."

Holt's face reddened a fraction. "I was saving them for my lunch."

"She's pregnant," Maddie said incredulously.

"It was Wildfire pizza," Holt shot back as if that justified everything.

Maddie threw up her hands. "Men."

Nash wrapped her in his arms and dipped her to kiss her soundly. It started out playful but turned heated in a way that spoke of a level of intimacy I'd never experienced. It made my skin itch as if it were too tight for my body, and I had to look away.

Someone in the crowd let out a whistle, and Maddie broke away, her cheeks pink.

"What was that about men?" Nash asked with a smirk.

She pinched his side. "That you're barely worth the trouble, but you come in handy with the sexual favors."

He snorted and draped an arm across her shoulders. "Want to go home and take advantage of those favors?"

Maddie's eyes softened in a way that had a bit of that panic flaring to life in my chest again. "Always."

Nash gave his brothers and me a chin lift and guided Maddie toward the door.

As I watched them go, I couldn't imagine what Nash had exposed himself to. It was as if his heart were walking around outside his body, and he was completely okay with it. Nothing on this planet could get me to sign on for that. But as I watched Maddie stretch onto her tiptoes to brush her lips across his cheek, I knew it meant my life might be a damn lonely one.

I guided my G-Wagon around the last bend in the road before reaching The Peaks. The resort's beauty struck me as it came into view. It didn't matter that a million dark memories haunted it. This place held my best memories, too: Making cookies with my mom in our kitchen. Racing Clara down to the barn to go on a trail ride. Exploring with her and Gabe. Even softer memories of my father before he turned, but then again, maybe I'd just been blind to the ugliness that lived in him and my brother all along.

I slowed at the massive iron gates as a security guard stepped out.

"Good evening, Mr. Shaw. How was your night?"

"Loaded question, Alex. But at least I've got an ice-cold beer in my future."

He grinned. "Always helps me after a long day. Have a good one."

"You, too. Tell Suzanne I said hello."

"Will do."

Just as I was about to take my foot off the brake, my phone buzzed in the cupholder. I glanced down and grimaced.

Dad: *Come to the house. I need to speak with both of you.*

He'd sent the text to both Gabe and me. *Great.* The last thing I needed was an eight o'clock family board meeting. I wanted a long, cold shower and my bed. But like a good dog, I turned toward my parents' house on the other side of the lodge.

The resort had just about everything you could want in a getaway: five-star dining, an award-winning spa, a movie theatre, and a nightclub. There were facilities for tennis, golf, horseback riding, and every outdoor activity under the sun. And guests were guaranteed a level of privacy that was difficult to find anywhere else. Titans of industry, celebrities, and even royals came to stay.

My father cared about all our properties in our billion-dollar holding company, but this was his crown jewel. Maybe because it was the place he called home for most of the year. Perhaps because it was the resort that got the most press. The reason didn't really matter; what did was that he cared about it far more than his remaining children.

I pulled to a stop in front of the massive private lodge. It nestled into its surroundings nicely, even if it was over the top. I stared at it for a moment, trying to connect to that feeling of home. But sometime over the past decade, that feeling had slipped away.

Forcing myself to turn off the engine, I slid out of my SUV. Gabe's sleek Maserati was already here. Why he needed to drive it when he lived next door was beyond me.

I crossed the circular drive and walked up the stone steps, pausing for a moment. I had the sudden urge to ring the doorbell as if this weren't the home I'd spent my entire childhood in.

Instead, I pressed down on the latch and opened the door. As I stepped inside, I paused to listen. The faint sound of voices came from the living room. I walked in that direction.

I found my father and brother sitting on leather club chairs on either side of the massive stone fireplace, each with a glass of scotch in their hands. My dad looked up. "Took you long enough."

I bit the inside of my cheek. "I was coming home from a SAR meeting."

He scoffed. "What a waste of time."

Gabe grinned as if every insult cast in my direction was a point for him in the make-believe game he had going on in his head.

"Get a scotch," Dad commanded.

"I'm good," I said, taking a seat on one of the sofas. They were hard as stone but had some architecturally significant style.

Dad rolled his eyes. "Such a delicate flower."

My back teeth ground together. *Better than a drunk who let alcohol fuel his temper.* I'd enjoyed my share of beer but never more than one, and had a glass of wine occasionally, but I never touched the hard stuff. I'd seen it ignite the cruelty in my father and wasn't about to let that out in myself.

Gabe swirled the scotch around in his glass and then took a long sip.

My dad leaned back in his chair, taking us in. "It's time for you both to stop pissing around."

I stiffened. I'd gone to work for our family's company the moment I graduated college. A school he'd been adamant about me attending. The same one that he and Gabe had gone to, along with my grandfather on my mother's side. I'd given everything to the company. I'd gone wherever my father asked without argument.

From London to Dubai to Singapore before finally landing in New York. I hadn't complained about leaving my friends behind in Cedar Ridge or only getting to see Mom a handful of times a year. But for him, it was never enough.

Gabe's eyes flashed with his telltale temper, but he kept it in check. "Tell us what you need."

Dad traced the rim of his glass with his forefinger, his gaze zeroing in on my older brother. "I thought I could trust you to handle operations at The Peaks."

Gabe's hand tightened on his glass, his knuckles bleaching white. "I have. We've made a greater profit this year than last."

"That profit will go in the toilet when *Luxury Travel's* issue releases next month."

I braced, the muscles along my spine tensing. It didn't matter how much these best-of lists influenced actual dollars; my father was obsessed with being at the top of them.

Gabe straightened. "What do you mean? That reporter loved The Peaks. I had him drowning in caviar and champagne for his entire visit."

I fought the urge to roll my eyes. Travel and relaxation weren't always about the stuffy amenities. People needed the heart of a place, too. Somewhere they could connect with family and loved ones or get away for a bit of peace in a hectic world.

"There was obviously *something* Lewis wasn't happy with because word is that he put us at number three on the list."

Gabe swallowed. "Maybe the other resorts slipped him a bribe."

Dad scoffed. "Don't blame others for your failures. I've invited him back for the gala and a longer stay in a few weeks. Hopefully, we can sway him before they go to print. In the meantime, Caden will assess the property and see how it might be lacking compared to our others."

I wanted to curse, get up and walk out of here, and never look back. My dad knew what he was doing, pitting Gabe and me against each other. He thought it made us both stronger and the hotels better. In reality, all it did was break our family apart.

Even worse, he was tying it all up in the gala. The one event I actually gave a damn about. Because it raised funds for The Clara Foundation.

My mother had started it not long after my little sister passed, hoping it would help her heal. But it had become something we'd shared over the years. An organization that raised money for childhood cancer research. It was our way of doing what we could to help. We couldn't change our outcome, but maybe we could help other families. My father just saw it as an excuse to hobnob with his wealthy associates.

My gaze caught on the photo wall on the far side of the room. Those snapshots felt like a different time. Sometimes, I thought they were the only soul left in the whole place. I halted on my favorite one: Clara in a field of wildflowers, one hand around her horse's reins, and her head tilted back as she laughed.

"I'll beat you in a bareback race every time, CayCay."

I grinned as I strode toward her. "What do you want to bet?"

She tapped her lips. "You have to do my dish duty for a month."

"No betting," Mom chastised as she snapped a photo of the mountains behind us.

"The betting is just motivation," I argued.

"Come on, Mom. Let me wipe the floor with him and teach him a lesson."

Mom's lips twitched. "He has gotten a little cocky lately."

"Yes!" Clara pumped her fist in the air. Then, before I could blink, she'd grabbed the horse's mane and hauled herself up. "Go!"

"You little weasel." I jumped onto my gelding's back and took off after her, but she'd already left me in the dust. Only our mom's amused laughter carried after us.

I blinked away the memory. Maybe Clara had been our only soul. When she died, she had taken the best parts of all of us with her.

"Don't you have anything to say for yourself?" Dad snapped.

My focus returned to him. "I'll help however I can."

Gabe muttered some choice words under his breath.

Dad took a long drink of scotch, staring at me, assessing. "It takes more than a few smart business decisions to lead a resort like this. You need to quit screwing around and become respectable."

Gabe smiled at that. "Come on, Dad. You know Caden will never be more than a party boy, a different woman every week, rumors always swirling."

Annoyance flickered in my father's gaze. "He's right about your reputation. It's one of the reasons I brought you back here. I'm sick of seeing your face splashed across the tabloids every week."

That was hardly the case. I was occasionally photographed with someone who got that kind of attention, typically a model or an actress. But it wasn't a common occurrence.

"I've never embarrassed our family. I live my life as quietly as possible."

Gabe snorted.

"You need to follow Gabe's example and get serious with an acceptable young woman," Dad argued. "Our colleagues don't trust someone who isn't settled. They think you're reckless, impulsive."

"But my track record proves that I'm not," I pushed back.

"Don't question me. I've been in this business a hell of a lot longer than you, and you'd be smart to listen to me."

I bit the inside of my cheek, wondering for the millionth time why I didn't just quit. And then that damn photo flickered in my peripheral vision. Because of Clara. Because she had always been so excited about working for the company one day. She'd go on and on about all the things she would do, which mostly had to do with horses and pools at her age. But if I let go of this, it felt like I was letting go of her. I couldn't do it.

"I'll be mindful to keep my extracurricular activities under wraps," I gritted out.

Dad glared. "That's not the same thing."

Gabe leaned forward. "Lena and I are happy to fill in on social obligations wherever you need us since Caden isn't capable."

Of course, they were. Lena was a social-climbing bloodsucker, and Gabe cheated on her every chance he got. But I didn't think either of them cared. Lena showed up looking perfect, and Gabe kept her in the lifestyle she was accustomed to.

Dad nodded. "Glad to know I can count on you."

I rose from the couch, unable to take this farce for even one minute longer. "Do you need anything else? I need to get going. I've got an early meeting."

He eyed me. "That's a little more of the gumption I like to see. You can go."

I ignored Gabe's glare and headed for the front door. I stopped short as my mom descended the stairs. She pressed a hand to my cheek. "Hi, honey. I didn't know you were here."

I forced a smile. "Dad just wanted to go over a few things with Gabe and me."

She frowned. "It's too late for that. You should be out enjoying your life, taking some nice girl on a date."

The flicker of hope in her eyes killed something in me. She was itching for me to settle down and give her some grandbabies.

"It's okay. I was on my way home from a SAR meeting anyway."

"How did it go? How's Nash?"

"Good on both counts. Maybe we can meet him for lunch one of these days."

My mom smiled. "I'd love that. And have him bring Maddie. It's been too long since I've seen that girl. I'm so happy those two finally got together. You need someone who keeps you on your toes like that."

"Just haven't found the right person yet," I muttered, hating to lie to her.

She squeezed my hand. "You will. Just give it time."

As she shifted, I caught sight of the dark circles under her eyes. "You doing okay?"

With every year that passed, my mother seemed more and more fragile. I'd thought she would get stronger with time, but it seemed to be having the opposite effect.

She nodded, forcing her smile brighter. "Just fine. I haven't been sleeping great. I think I'll call it an early night."

"Okay. Call me if you need anything."

"I will. Love you."

I pulled her into a gentle hug. "Love you, too."

As she disappeared up the stairs, I stayed frozen. How had we become this? A family so fractured we were ships passing in the night at best. I kept hoping things would change, but they never did.

I stalked out the front door, trying to leave behind the reminders of all our misery. And headed home, where I knew I'd be completely alone.

Chapter Three

Grae

ASPEN SMILED AT MADDIE AS SHE SLID AN ASSORTMENT of baked goods onto our table at The Brew. "You know, when you quit, I was worried I'd never see you."

Maddie grinned as she popped a piece of a scone into her mouth. "With these goodies, you'll never have to worry about that."

Wren rested a hand on her belly, which was just starting to round. "I swear this kid is going to come out asking for orange-cranberry scones."

Aspen chuckled. "We'll have you covered if they do."

A little red-haired girl that was the spitting image of Aspen popped out from behind her mom. "You're gonna have a baby, Miss Wren?"

"I am. I've got some months to go, but they'll be here before we know it."

Cady started bouncing up and down. "I hope it's a girl, and maybe she'll want to do ballet with me. Charlie's my best friend, but he doesn't want to do ballet with me, and some of the other girls in my class are kinda mean. I need a ballet buddy."

I leaned forward in my chair. "Who's mean to you?"

She scrunched up her nose. "Heather Beasley's the worst. She always says I'm not good and my tutus are ugly."

Fury lit through me. "What the heck? That little—"

Maddie squeezed my arm, silently reminding me I was talking to a five-year-old.

"That's not cool," I adjusted.

Aspen crouched so she was eye-to-eye with her daughter. "And what does it mean when someone is unkind to us?"

Cady's lips pressed together. "That they've got some sadness in them. It's not about us."

"That's right. There's something going on with her, and we should feel bad."

Cady nodded, her expression serious. But as quickly as the look filled her face, it was gone. "Can I go help Zeke make the cookies?"

Aspen laughed and ruffled her daughter's hair. "Sure. But only one spoonful of dough, or you'll get a stomachache."

"Okay!" Cady was already off.

"Promise?" Aspen called after her.

"Cross my heart!"

She sighed. "Kids are not for the faint of heart."

"You are so good with her," Maddie said. "Most kids wouldn't be able to see the reason behind someone's actions at that age."

"I think someone needs to give ole Heather Beasley a swift kick in the booty," I grumbled. "What's wrong with people?"

Maddie chuckled. "She's five. Are you going to take her on?"

"I'd like to at least threaten her a little."

"Trust me, I've thought about it," Aspen said. "She's awful. And her mother's even worse."

Wren groaned. "Katelyn, right? She picked on Grae and me like crazy in middle school. And I'm pretty sure she tried to hook up with Holt in high school."

I gaped at my best friend. "Are you serious?"

She nodded. "Holt's given her a wide berth ever since."

Aspen leaned against a chair. "I don't think she's changed much since then, so I'm taking Holt's approach as much as I can."

Wren squeezed her hand. "I hope I can be half the mom you are to this little one. You're amazing."

Aspen's eyes glistened. "Thank you. Some days I wonder if I'm enough. It's tough doing it alone."

Maddie stood and wrapped her in a hug. "You've always got us. Whatever you need."

Aspen took a shuddering breath. "Thank you. I swear I'm not usually this emotional. It's just been a long week."

"You need a girls' night. Drop Cady with Lawson for a sleepover with Charlie, and we'll do something fun."

Maddie arched a brow at me. "The last time you called for a girls' night, you got wasted, and I got cracked over the head with a tree limb."

I winced. "Quiet girls' night?"

Aspen laughed. "That sounds like a plan. I'll let you know when I can get off for an evening."

She headed back behind the cash register, and I turned to Maddie and Wren. "Has Aspen told you anything about Cady's dad?"

They both shook their heads, and Maddie worried the corner of her lip. "I get the sense that he wasn't a great guy, but she hasn't opened up any more. I just hate that she hasn't had help all these years."

"I can't imagine how hard it must be. But Cady's amazing, and it's because of Aspen," Wren said.

I watched as Aspen smiled warmly at a customer, but she had shadows in her green eyes that told me her life hadn't been easy.

"So…" Maddie began. "Caden certainly seemed to be needling you last night."

I grimaced at the reminder, but Wren perked right up. "What was he doing?"

Maddie leaned back in her chair. "He's like a little boy pulling G's pigtails at recess."

I snorted. "Hardly. He just gets extreme pleasure out of annoying the hell out of me and suggesting I make horrible life decisions."

Wren frowned at that. "I've seen him tease you, but I've never seen him be mean."

"It's not mean, exactly." It was as if Caden were assessing me every moment, certain I would screw something up. "It's like he doubts me. I can't explain it."

Maddie nodded. "And that hurts because you two used to be so close."

"He used to be the person who believed in me the most." Saying the words out loud lit a burn along my sternum. "Enough about him. Tell me about the new house," I said to Wren.

She filled us in on her and Holt's new build, Maddie told us all about her new dog training clients, and I recounted the tourist trip from hell yesterday. Before I knew it, we'd been there for over an hour.

"I need to run, or I'm going to be late for work," I said, pushing to my feet and throwing some cash onto the table.

"Hope there aren't any delusional tourists on your trips today," Maddie said with a laugh.

"Me, too." I pressed a hand to Wren's belly. "Take care of my bestie in there."

She grinned up at me. "I will."

With a wave at Aspen, I headed out the door. Laughter caught on the air from the kids playing at Dockside Park across the street, and the sun streamed down in a way that made me want to hold on to summer for just a little bit longer. I took a deep breath of fresh, pine-scented air. Days like these made me certain I'd never want to move away from Cedar Ridge.

"Grae," a masculine voice called.

I stiffened as I turned my gaze to the figure hurrying down the street in his navy firefighter slacks and tee.

Rance came to a stop in front of me, but just a few inches too close. "You didn't text me back."

I bit the inside of my cheek. He was right. I hadn't returned the three texts I'd gotten while at my SAR meeting or the four he'd sent after that. "I've been busy. And I honestly didn't think there was anything else to say."

Annoyance flickered in his brown eyes. "That's a little extreme, don't you think? We're friends. We've been dating."

"We went on three dates over a month ago. That's not the same as dating."

He waved me off. "You know what I mean."

But I didn't. I had no idea what Rance was fighting so hard to hold on to.

"You weren't home until late last night. Is everything okay? I was worried."

A chill skittered down my spine. "How do you know that?"

Rance scoffed. "We live in the same neighborhood. I was out for a late jog."

My stomach churned. That much was true. Rance lived about half a mile from my cottage on the outskirts of town. But feeling like he was checking up on me had me on edge.

"Where were you?" he pressed.

Maybe it was growing up with four older brothers and never wanting to answer to them, but I had the urge to dig in my heels. "That's not really any of your business."

Rance's eyes narrowed. "It's a simple question."

It didn't matter that it was simple; I didn't owe Rance any information about me.

He sighed, but a smile played on his lips. "Your stubbornness is one of the things I love about you."

Oh, schnitzel. We were heading into stage-five clinger territory.

A flash of movement caught my attention. It was as if my body had some finely honed radar for Caden Shaw, no matter how far away he was. I blamed my desperate, short-circuiting brain for the word that popped out of my mouth next.

"Babe!" I called in Caden's direction.

His gaze snapped to me so fast it made my head spin.

I widened my eyes at him, pouring every bit of silent pleading into the look. He was the last person I wanted to ask for help, but he was all I had.

Caden's brow furrowed for a moment, but then he caught sight of Rance and glared. He crossed toward us in five long strides, wrapping an arm around me and pulling me close. "Hey, *babe*."

The gleam in his eyes told me I'd be paying for this one in the form of teasing torture for years to come.

"Babe?" Rance gaped. "But you hate him."

Caden chuckled, the sound wrapping around me, along with the heat from his body pressed against mine. "Love, hate, two sides of the same coin, right?"

"Love?" Rance spluttered.

Caden squeezed my shoulder. "She's got me wrapped around her little finger. I'd do anything for her."

My heart hammered against my ribs, and it became painful to breathe.

Rance's gaze ping-ponged between the two of us. "You're *dating*?"

"Oh, I'd say it's more than dating. Wouldn't you, Gigi?" Caden asked, glancing down at me.

I let out a tiny squeak. "Yup. It's pretty serious."

"Since when?" Rance demanded.

"I've had my eye on her since the moment I got back, but I'd say the last couple of weeks really took things to the next level," Caden said, toying with a strand of my hair.

Rance's face reddened. "The next level?" His gaze snapped to me. "You can't think that's a good idea. He's a total manwhore."

Caden stiffened. "I was just waiting for the right woman to come along, and she has."

Rance scoffed. "I'm sure. Do your brothers know?"

My hand fisted in Caden's shirt. "My brothers have nothing to do with this."

He arched a brow at that.

"She's right," Caden said, his voice going hard. "Not a damn thing on this planet could keep me from her. And I'll be honest, it pisses me the hell off that you won't stop texting her."

"She didn't tell me she was dating anyone," Rance said, clearly flustered by the intensity in Caden's tone.

"Well, you know now, don't you?" he growled.

The ferocity in Caden's words had me glancing up at him and pressing my hand harder against his abs.

Rance scoffed. "This is nothing. It'll fizzle out in a few days, and then Grae will come to her senses and see who she really needs."

Caden's jaw clenched, anger flaring in his expression. Then he looked down at me, those hazel eyes swirling into a mix of greens, browns, and golds that hypnotized me. He lowered his head slowly and quickly, all at the same time. My heart hammered against my ribs as time slowed.

I should've moved, given him my cheek, *something*. But I didn't. I was held captive in the spell that Caden wove with his presence alone.

At the first touch of Caden's lips, I was lost. Heat and need swirled around me as my lips parted on instinct, and his tongue slipped inside, stroking. A buzz lit low in my belly—one I'd never felt with any other kiss, no matter how much I'd searched for it. That buzz deepened into a hum that spread through my muscles, making my knees weak.

When Caden finally pulled back, I blinked up at him and could only think one thing.

He'd completely ruined me.

Chapter Four

Caden

I WAS SO UNBELIEVABLY SCREWED.

As I looked down at Grae, her cheeks flushed to a deep pink, her blond hair mussed, and her blue eyes shining, I knew that I'd made a fatal mistake. I'd seen the gleam in Rance's eyes, one that said he had no plans of giving up. I had heard the challenge in his words. I'd just wanted him to back off, and this seemed like the easiest way to do that. But I'd been so incredibly wrong.

Kissing Grae was like downing a shot of whiskey set on fire. She burned through my system in a way that would leave scars in its wake. It was hard enough to ignore her pull on a good day. Now that I'd tasted her? It would be nearly impossible.

Rance cleared his throat, his eyes flaring with anger. "I'll be here to pick up the pieces when you take off for who knows where with some model."

Temper surged in my gut, and I bit back the snarl that wanted to escape my lips. "Can't imagine why I'd leave when I have everything I want right here."

I hoped he read the truth in my words, even though I knew I

was playing a dangerous game. But something about Rance had always put me on edge. Maybe it was because he'd been staring at Grae with need in his gaze for as long as I could remember. Maybe it was just because I thought the guy was a douche. Whatever it was, I wasn't about to leave Grae open to his clearly unwanted advances. But it would've been a hell of a lot safer to just deck the guy and be done with it.

"We'll see about that," Rance muttered. "I'll talk to you later, Grae." And with that, he took off back toward the fire station.

Grae's shoulders slumped. "What is wrong with him?"

I forced myself to release my hold on her, but it was like pulling away from the sweetest heat I'd ever experienced. "Tell me what's really going on."

Grae worried her thumbnail with her forefinger. "It's not that big a deal."

"Clearly, it is," I snapped.

She clamped her mouth shut, and I sighed.

"Please, tell me."

"I don't want to," she said quietly.

The timidity in her voice had my skin prickling. It was so unlike her.

"Why not?" I struggled to keep my voice gentle, something deep inside clawing at me to find out what had her shrinking in on herself.

Grae's gaze dropped to the sidewalk between us. "I hate the way you look at me when you think I've screwed up."

My spine snapped straight. There was such defeat in her tone, though it was mixed with something else—grief, maybe? "What are you talking about?"

Her head snapped up, a little more fire in her eyes now. "You look at me like I'm a moron who can't handle her own life."

My jaw dropped as a slideshow of memories flowed through my mind, and I tried to see them through her lens. I'd needed emotional distance from Grae like I'd needed air, but I hadn't been able to let her go entirely either. It was a shit thing to do, but sticking around and needling her was the best option I had. Her annoyance and frustration had guaranteed the distance I'd so desperately needed, but I still got to be in her presence. Only now, I saw that my selfishness had done real damage.

"Gigi, the last thing I think you are is a moron."

She scoffed. "Sure."

"I don't. I know I give you a hard time, but—"

Grae held up a hand. "It doesn't matter. I shouldn't care what you think anymore, anyway. It's not like we're friends."

Each word cut like a carefully placed blow designed to cause maximum damage. I could argue, but she was right. I hadn't let her into my life because I was too damn terrified of her pull. What a chickenshit that made me. "Tell me anyway? Even though I don't deserve it."

She blinked back at me, surprise filtering through those baby blues. Then she sighed. "Rance and I have always been decent friends. Not close or anything, but we ran in similar crowds. Days on the lake, nights at the bar, those kinds of things, ya know?"

I nodded.

"Every year or so, he asked me out. I was never interested, but last month I figured I should give it a shot. He's a nice guy and has a good job helping people. I thought maybe I could grow to like him as more than a friend."

"I don't think chemistry works that way."

She winced. "You might be right there."

"So, you went on a couple of dates…" I wanted to ask so many more questions, but I was terrified of the damn answers.

"It wasn't anything crazy. Drinks, a hike, one dinner. But I just didn't feel anything. Kissing him was like kissing a dead fish."

I choked on a laugh. "You certainly paint a strong mental image."

The corner of her mouth kicked up. It was the first hint of true amusement I'd seen in her eyes since I'd walked up. "Too much tongue." She shivered.

Jealousy coursed through me like an inferno, and I suddenly wished I had gone the decking route with Rance.

"Now, he won't leave me alone. I've told him I don't feel more than friendship for him and that I'm not interested, but he thinks I'm not giving us a proper shot. He shows up at work with flowers, texts me all the time, and today he was asking why I wasn't home last night. It freaked me out a little, and I just…"—she gestured at me—"panicked."

Ice slid through my veins. "He showed up at your house last night?"

"We live in the same general neighborhood. He said he was on a run and saw that my car wasn't there."

Wariness pricked at my gut. "I don't like the sound of that."

"Me either, hence the stroke that was me calling you *babe*. Like it's believable that we're dating."

"I don't know. I think that kiss sold it pretty well."

Pink hit Grae's cheeks. "Maybe."

"Why don't you just have Lawson have a talk with him?"

Her hand snaked out to grab my arm, her nails digging in. "Don't say a word to him."

My brows lifted. "Why not?" Her brothers would send lover boy packing so fast his head would spin.

"You don't know what it's like. They just—things changed after my diagnosis. They were always protective, but now it's like an extreme sport. I don't want them involved. I know I never should've roped you into this. It's not exactly going to be believable when you pick up some tourist at the bar this weekend. But—"

"Gigi," I said, squeezing her hand. Aw, hell. This was beyond stupid. It was reckless, but the words slipped out anyway. "I'll help you."

"You will?"

My thumb slid along the inside of her palm, and I relished the feel of her skin. I was playing with fire. "I think I've got something that can solve both of our problems."

She looked up at me skeptically. "What?"

The corner of my mouth kicked up. "Be my girlfriend."

Chapter Five

Grae

M Y JAW WENT SLACK, AND I GAPED AT CADEN. I CLEARLY needed to get my hearing checked because those words could not have possibly come out of his mouth. Caden's hand lifted, and his fingers skated along my jaw to my chin, where he gently closed my mouth. "Wouldn't want any bugs to fly in there."

I shook off his touch—the feel of those roughened fingertips against my skin. "Did you get hit on the head this morning?"

He arched a brow.

"We can't be in each other's presence for longer than two minutes without fighting."

Caden shrugged. "We can play it off as passion."

"My family and friends know you're the bane of my existence."

I swore I saw a flicker of pain in his expression at that, but it was gone so quickly that I figured I must've imagined it.

He shoved his hand into his pocket, gripping something tightly. "Like I told the jackhole, love and hate are two sides of the same coin."

I snorted. "Well, when it comes to you, murder is my love language."

The corner of Caden's mouth kicked up. "See, we're making our case already."

I studied him for a moment. His years away from Cedar Ridge had only made him more handsome. His jaw was sharper, his hazel eyes more hypnotizing. "Why would you want to do this?"

Caden met my gaze. "I hate that he's bothering you. It's crossing a million different lines. You shouldn't have to constantly look over your shoulder, wondering when he might show. If we make everyone believe we're all loved up, I know he'll eventually back off."

"You said this would help both of us."

His focus flicked across the street to the lake for a moment before he spoke. "My dad is on my case about not being respectable enough. Wants me to settle down. If he thinks I'm serious about someone, it should buy me some time without him criticizing every move I make."

"Your dad is a total prick," I grumbled. Harrison Shaw had never been warm and fuzzy, but it had gotten so much worse after Clara passed away. Instead of letting his remaining children know he loved them unconditionally, he'd made it his mission to berate them and point out every part of them he saw as a weakness.

Caden grunted. "And that's never going to change. Best I can do is get him off my case while I'm home."

"And you think pretending to date me will help?"

"My mom has always loved you and your family. And as much of a douche as my dad is, he has a begrudging respect for the business your father built."

My dad had created an outdoor gear company in his twenties that had taken off. He sold it when we were kids, giving him—and us—more than enough money so we didn't have to work. But all of us kids had wanted to, and that was largely due to the work ethic my dad instilled in us.

I shifted my weight from foot to foot. Agreeing to this would be the dumbest thing in the world. Just seeing Caden around town was hard enough—remembering all I'd lost when he walked out of my life. Being near him and knowing I'd never really have him, even as a friend, would be like throwing acid on the wound.

"It wouldn't be for long," Caden hurried to say. "I'm hoping my dad will send me back to New York after The Clara Foundation gala in a few weeks."

A heavy weight settled over me like one of those lead blankets they put on you when you get an X-ray. I knew that Caden loved Cedar Ridge and that he felt the most connected to Clara here, but because of his dickhead father, he didn't want to stay. "Okay."

The agreement was out of my mouth before I knew I'd consciously decided. Worries about Rance were forgotten, but the idea that Caden had to put up with his father's vile criticism was more than I could take.

Caden's mouth split into a grin that hit me low in the belly. *Schnitzel.* I was in such trouble.

"We can tell your brothers it's just an act—"

"No," I cut him off. "If we tell them, they'll want to know why, and they know I wouldn't just help you out of the goodness of my heart."

Caden choked on a laugh. "Right. That whole murder-is-my-love-language thing."

They would see through any supposed altruism in a flash and want to know why I needed a fake boyfriend. If they found out that Rance was paying me a little too much attention, they'd jump all over protecting weak, little Grae. They'd try to move me in with one of them, and I'd never have a moment of peace to just…be.

My throat burned. I loved all four of them and knew I was beyond lucky to have them in my life. But their love was stifling sometimes. I couldn't breathe under the weight of it.

"They can't know. Not even Nash."

I knew that was asking a lot of Caden. Nash was his best friend. And I didn't think he'd be crazy about Caden dating his baby sister. None of my brothers would be when Caden had never dated a girl for longer than a weekend since middle school.

Caden frowned at me. "This could come back to bite us both."

"Not if we amicably break up when you move back to New York. My family knows I'd never leave Cedar Ridge. It would make complete sense."

He toyed with something in his pocket that I couldn't see. "Okay." Then his smile was back, the one that had me wanting to lean just a little bit closer. "Let's do this, girlfriend."

I kicked my feet onto the porch railing as I took another sip of my beer and cracked my neck, trying to alleviate some of the pressure there. The day had been long. Too long. Usually, sitting out on my tiny cottage's front porch and watching the sun go down was enough to melt away my troubles. Not this time.

Anxiety churned in my stomach as I thought about what I'd agreed to. But maybe this was exactly what I needed. I'd get to spend time with Caden and see who he truly was and not who I remembered him to be. We likely weren't compatible. This could be the ticket to finally moving on.

My fingers ghosted to the empty spot on my chest. The place where the necklace Caden had given me on my thirteenth birthday had always lain. It had disappeared the same way Caden had, lost in the shuffle at the hospital the day I'd ended up in a coma. But there were days I still reached for it the same way I wanted to reach for Caden.

Footsteps on my front stairs had my gaze shifting. Roan's large form lumbered up the steps, day-old scruff dotting his jaw and his light brown hair in disarray.

"Hey," I greeted, lifting my legs off the railing so he could pass and take the second chair on my porch.

He grunted and sat.

"Want a beer?"

Roan shook his head.

I put my feet back on the rail. I was used to Roan's silence.

It was a balm of sorts when the rest of my family had incessant questions.

We sat there for a while, watching as the sun disappeared over the horizon and left us in gorgeous twilight. This time of day always reminded me of Wren. She'd dragged me out to sit in it more than once, and I wondered if she and Holt were looking at the same sky.

"You okay?"

The question had me jolting out of my musings, and I glanced at Roan. He wasn't looking at me, but I knew he still somehow tracked every flicker of my reaction. "Sure."

"You've been edgy lately."

Of course, Roan had picked up on that. Rance's attention had made me jumpy, and Caden being back only made things worse. "You know how summer is. I'm crazy-busy and ready for that fall break when all the tourists leave."

Roan was quiet for a moment. "You don't have to tell me."

I pressed my thumbnail into the pad of my forefinger. Of course, he'd known that wasn't the whole truth. He was like some sort of human lie detector.

I went for changing the subject instead. "What about you? How's work?"

Roan grunted. "Tourists are morons."

A laugh bubbled out of me. "Bears and campers?"

He nodded. "Got these hysterical girls who thought a serial killer was after them when their tent was slashed to bits."

"But?"

"But they left chips and candy inside when they went for a hike. They're lucky they weren't attacked in their sleep. Read the damn signs."

I grinned. "Bet they were all over asking you to protect them from the vicious killer."

Roan scowled. "Not interested."

I couldn't help but stare at my brother. I'd never known him to date a single soul. He'd always been a loner, preferring the outdoors to large groups. But he changed after becoming a suspect in a horrible attack that had left Wren and a handful of others injured or dead. He didn't truly trust a soul other than his family. And that made for a lonely existence.

"I could set you up with someone," I suggested.

That scowl turned in my direction. "No."

"Could be fun. There are lots of women around who like the outdoors and wouldn't be moronic enough to leave food in their tents."

"G…"

"Why not?"

Roan's eyes narrowed on me. "I'll tell you why if you tell me what's going on with you and Caden."

I snapped my mouth closed.

"That's what I thought."

Too danged perceptive for his own good.

We both opted for silence as darkness descended. Sometimes, I wondered if Roan showed up here just to get a little dose of human connection before returning to his cabin in the woods.

As if my brother had some invisible timer, he stood. "See you at dinner tomorrow."

My stomach twisted. Family dinner. They were a regular occurrence. I both loved and hated them. I loved being around my siblings, nephews, and parents, but I hated that I had to be on guard for the countless check-ins I received.

"Drive safe."

He grunted again and disappeared with a wave.

I stood from my chair, stretching and grabbing my now-empty bottle. I headed inside, making a pit stop to toss the bottle into the recycling bin, and then headed for my bedroom and bath. I'd read for a bit, but I was hoping for an early night. I still needed some recovery from the hike from hell yesterday, and sleep was one of my best tools for keeping my diabetes in check.

I took a quick shower and brushed my teeth, but fatigue already had my bed calling. I opened a drawer and pulled out silk sleep shorts and a matching tank. As much as I lived in workout gear during the day, I loved having silk to sleep in. I shucked my clothes and tossed them into my hamper. Then I pulled on my pajamas, hooking my insulin pump to the waistband. I crossed to my bed, yanked back the brightly colored comforter, and climbed inside.

My bedroom was just like the rest of my home, full of color and character. I had an array of photos and tchotchkes from travels or special moments. Together, they formed a décor that was only mine.

A rustling sounded outside my window, and I stilled, listening. There was nothing for a moment, and then it sounded again.

I flicked off the light and let my eyes adjust for a moment. Then I pulled back the gauzy window covering so I could peek out. I caught a flash of movement, but it was so quick I didn't have a chance to pin down what it could be. An animal? A person?

A chill skittered down my spine as I remembered Rance and his late-night runs. I instantly got up to set my alarm.

Chapter Six

Caden

A KNOCK SOUNDED ON MY OFFICE DOOR, AND I straightened in my desk chair. "Come in."

It was probably for the best that I'd been interrupted because I was about ready to pull out my hair. I'd spent all morning going over the changes Gabe had put in place at The Peaks. He was sucking the life and soul out of my favorite place on Earth. He'd canceled the weekly field games where families could partake in competitions like potato sack races and cornhole. He'd ditched our outdoor movie showings for a wine-tasting event that cost a fortune. And, worst of all, he'd suggested switching our trail rides for polo. Clara would've been beside herself.

My assistant, Jalen, walked in. He smiled, and his perfectly straight, white teeth gleamed against his tanned skin. But we'd been working together long enough for me to know that the smile he wore meant bad news.

"What happened now?" I grumbled.

Jalen winced. "I've been working on getting eyes and ears in all the helpful places."

I nodded.

"And a little birdie at The Terrace told me your father made a lunch reservation at one for your family."

I grimaced and checked my phone. No texts or missed calls. I opened my email. Nothing. "I take it you didn't get a call from his assistant."

"Nope." Jalen popped the P on the word.

I let out a growl of frustration. "He probably told Gabe to tell me."

"Good thing I've got us covered, and you're already looking dapper enough for a casual family lunch that is actually anything but."

I chuckled. "Have I told you yet how damned glad I am that you came out here with me?"

Jalen waved me off. "Like I would leave you to deal with these vultures alone. You can thank me with spa credits and introductions to rugged mountain men."

My lips twitched. "I'll see what I can do."

"Come on, up you go so you're not late."

I shoved back from my desk. "Can you do me a favor and have the stables pull the logs for the past several months? I want to gauge interest in the trail rides. And set up a meeting with Juliana so we can talk about their programming."

"I'll get on it right now."

"Thank you."

I strode out of my office and down the hall toward the lodge's main entryway. The space was massive, with thick, dark wood beams overhead and stone walls. Guests milled about, planning their afternoon activities. Each staff member greeted me with a dip of the head and some version of *hello, sir*. I hated the term, but it was one of my father's requirements. It felt stuffy, forced, and antiquated to me. I wanted the respect I got to be earned, not required.

Weaving through the lobby, I found my way out to the back patio, where a gorgeous terrace overlooked a pool and the mountains. A young hostess beamed up at me. "Mr. Shaw. Good afternoon, sir."

"Hi, Anna. I believe my father made a reservation for lunch."

She nodded. "Right this way, sir."

I followed her through the array of tables. Almost all of them were full, this being our busy season. "How are things going here?"

She cast a look over her shoulder, confused. "In what way?"

"Just wondering how everything's running. Is there anything you would change in how we're operating?"

Anna stopped in front of an empty table, flicking her auburn hair over one shoulder nervously. "You want to know if *I'd* change anything?"

I nodded. "You're the boots on the ground and have a better idea of what's working or not than I ever will."

Her eyes flared. "Wow, that's not what your brother thinks." She immediately flushed. "I'm so sorry. I shouldn't have said that."

I held up a hand to stop her. "No apologies needed. I have met my brother before."

Anna stifled a laugh and then worried her lip. "I think keeping a handful of tables free for walk-ins would be good. Guests get annoyed when they learn that reservations are often made weeks before. They don't always think of that when going on vacation."

"That's a great idea. Might even be better to make the more casual restaurants not require reservations at all."

She nodded eagerly. "Most people don't plan out their vacation schedules. It ruins the spontaneity you have when you get away."

"So true. Thanks for the insight, Anna. I appreciate it."

She smiled widely back at me. "Anytime. Can I get you something to drink while you wait?"

"I'd love an iced tea. Thanks."

She headed off as I slid into one of the empty chairs. A minute later, another server hurried over to me. "Here you go, sir. Can I get you anything else?"

"No, thank you, Henry. I'm good."

He nodded. "Just flag me down if that changes."

I leaned back in my chair, taking in the view. There was nothing like the Cedar Ridge mountains. It didn't matter what amazing sights I saw in my travels; nothing compared to this. There was a calmness about the range, an unparalleled peace.

"Nice surprise, you being on time."

And my father could ruin that serenity in a second.

I looked up at him, my mother and brother in tow. "Good to see you, too."

A muscle in Gabe's cheek ticked, and I knew he was annoyed that I'd made it to our little family gathering.

My mom maneuvered around my father and bent to kiss my cheek. "You're looking handsome today."

I was surprised she hadn't remarked on the circles under my eyes. Ones there because I'd tossed and turned all night reliving that damned kiss with Grae. It would take time to burn her out of my system and memory, and having her play the dutiful girlfriend wouldn't help. Yet, I wasn't bailing on our bargain. There was too much at stake.

"Thanks, Mom. You look beautiful." The truth was, she looked exhausted, but I couldn't say that. I stood and pulled out the chair next to me.

She took it and patted my hand. "Such a gentleman."

Gabe grumbled something under his breath that I couldn't make out.

"I'm so sorry I'm late," a high-pitched voice called.

I fought the urge to groan as Lena bounded up to our table.

Gabe's fiancée beamed at us, but the smile was as fake as her tan. "My appointment at the spa ran late. Baby," she cooed, kissing Gabe's cheek. "I missed you."

Gabe's arm encircled her waist in a proprietary hold. "I keep telling you that you need to keep a better eye on the time."

She pouted. "I know, but I wanted to make sure I was looking my best for our lunch."

Dad chuckled as he took the seat next to Mom. "Can't complain about that, Gabe."

"I guess not."

Lena hurried to take the chair next to me before Gabe could pull one out for her. She fluttered her eyelashes in my direction. "How are you settling in, Caden?"

"Fine."

She laughed. "So verbose."

Gabe took the last remaining seat. "You know my brother doesn't have much of a vocabulary."

Mom frowned at him. "That's not very nice, Gabriel."

Gabe waved her off. "Caden knows I'm kidding."

My brother could slit my throat and still say he was kidding.

Thankfully, Henry approached at that moment to take all our orders. When he finished, Dad leaned back in his chair. "I just had a meeting with Erika about the gala."

I bit the inside of my cheek. Dad would try to suck all the vitality out of an event that was supposed to be life-giving. He'd turn it into a stuffy affair that was just a bunch of rich people showing off their wealth with extravagant outfits and vehicles.

Mom beamed at him. "She always does such a lovely job."

"She needs to step it up this year if Lewis will be here. We need to be number one on that *Luxury Travel* list. And Clive Jones will be here, as well."

I fought the groan that wanted to surface. If there was one person my father would want to impress, it was Clive. As the head of one of the top banks and investment firms in the country, Clive had every power player on speed dial.

Mom's lips tipped down. "Isn't it enough to just be together as a family and enjoy the event?"

Dad reached over and patted her hand. "Of course, we'll enjoy it. But success is important, too."

I swore I saw my mom deflate at those words. I knew she longed for the family we'd had before Clara passed away. My sister had a way of bringing out the best in all of us, and losing her had taken away our North Star in many ways. But even when she was with us, my father had always had a vicious need to be the best, and Gabe had followed in those footsteps.

"I've been combing through all the latest lines out of Paris and New York, looking for the *perfect* dress," Lena cooed. She shifted so she gave me a shot of her cleavage, and I leaned toward my mom.

"I'm sure you'll look beautiful," Mom said, but her words had no heart.

Lena beamed at Gabe. "Have to look perfect for my baby."

I had the sudden urge to vomit.

"What about you, Caden?" Dad asked, zeroing in on me. "You can't bring some random floozy."

Gabe scoffed. "You know he will. It'll probably be some girl who looks more like a stripper than anything else."

"Actually, I've been seeing someone. I'll be bringing her."

Dad arched a brow. "This is the first I'm hearing of this."

The urge to roll my eyes was so strong. "It was new, and we have a shared history, so I wanted to tread carefully until we were sure it was going somewhere."

Mom's eyes brightened, and I saw color in her cheeks for the first time in months. "Now you're just teasing us. Who is it?"

"Grae Hartley."

The pure joy on my mother's face had guilt churning in my stomach. "Oh, Caden. That's wonderful. She's just the partner you need. She's kind but strong enough not to take any flack from you. And a beauty on top of it, which I'm sure doesn't hurt."

Lena scrunched up her nose. "Isn't that Nash's sister? The one who leads the hiking trips? She's probably constantly covered in dirt."

I cleared my throat to hide my laugh. "She does lead several outdoor excursions."

Dad lifted his drink and took a sip as he studied me. "At least she comes from a respectable family."

Gabe's jaw worked back and forth. "But Lena's right. That's not exactly a job fit for someone of our station."

Mom waved him off. "Grae is doing something she loves and

making a living at it. I think that's incredibly honorable, especially given she doesn't need to work. And she's always been willing to lend me a hand with things at the foundation."

I didn't miss how her gaze shifted to Lena when she said that. Lena had lived off her trust fund in San Francisco until she met Gabe, and he started footing the bill. She'd gone to college, but I thought it was more in the service of finding a husband than anything else.

Her cheeks flushed. "I guess I just have different priorities. I want to make sure I'm available to support Gabe however he needs me."

Gabe lifted her hand to his lips. "And I appreciate that, baby."

Dad ran a finger over the rim of his glass. "This could be good. The Hartleys are well thought of in the local community and beyond. Sharing the news of your settling down with a local girl whose family has been through so much might be just what our colleagues need for them to trust you a bit more."

My grip on my iced tea tightened. Of course, my father would only see Grae as a pawn in whatever power games he played. "What I care about is that I've met an incredible woman. She cares about the people around her and challenges me in ways no one ever has."

He waved me off. "Sure, sure. But I know Clive will be glad to hear you've settled down."

Gabe's grip on his glass tightened. "When does he arrive?"

"A few weeks. He'll be hosting his company's annual retreat here this year, and we need to wow him. I want both of you to draft plans. We'll let Clive choose which one he likes best."

Gabe's jaw worked back and forth in irritation, but there was a glint in my father's eyes that I knew well. He loved pitting Gabe and me against each other. This was just another chance to do it.

By the time we'd finished lunch, I was about ready to punch someone. My mom could sense it because she pulled me into a hug and whispered in my ear, "So pleased for you and Grae. This would make Clara so happy."

My gut twisted. What would my sister have to say about this charade? She'd probably issue a warning about how it would all come back to bite me.

"Love you, Mom." It was all I could say that wouldn't be a lie.

"Jocelyn," Lena began. "Why don't we go check out the aesthetic design options for the gala? I want to make sure whatever dress I get doesn't clash."

Mom smiled, but it was strained. "Sure, that sounds like a good plan."

As they left, Dad turned to Gabe and me. "I expect you to make sure we are prepared for Lewis's and Clive's visits. Do whatever it takes."

He didn't wait for an answer. He simply left, expecting that Gabe and I would bow to his dictates.

I headed out the moment he disappeared into the lodge. I didn't have any desire to listen to whatever bullshit Gabe would spew. I strode through the grand lobby and out into the sunshine, needing to go for a drive. Maybe I could disappear to my spot for an hour and rein in my temper.

Footsteps sounded behind me as I headed for my SUV. "What the hell was that all about?" Gabe snapped.

"You mean why did you forget to tell me about lunch?" I asked without stopping.

"A sudden girlfriend won't keep you off Dad's shit list."

I shrugged. "Not worried about what he thinks." That would be true if it didn't affect my mom. Whenever there was tension between us, it sent her spiraling, and she'd been through enough.

Gabe scoffed. "I guess I don't blame you. Grae always was a hot piece of ass. Wouldn't mind having a little taste—"

I moved so fast that he didn't have a chance to react. I slammed Gabe up against my SUV. "Say another word, and you will live to regret it."

Gabe laughed, but it had a maniacal and hysterical quality to it. "Well, I'll be damned. Caden Shaw has a weakness, after all. Good to know."

Chapter Seven

Grae

I PULLED INTO A MAKESHIFT PARKING SPOT IN FRONT OF MY parents' house and let out a long breath. There was always a mixture of emotions when coming home. Their property was truly one of my favorite places on Earth, with its acres of forest and magical mountainside views of the town and lake.

The house itself felt like it blended in with the landscape—a mix of dark wood and stone that stretched across the slope. A glass walkway joined the two halves of the structure. My mom always used to joke that having so many kids meant they needed a kids' house and an adults' house. But the truth was, she had always been right in the middle of the mayhem because she loved us so much.

Turning off the engine, I climbed out of my SUV and took in the other vehicles. It looked like I was the last one here. Then, my gaze caught on a familiar G-Wagon, and my stomach flipped.

I hadn't known Caden would be here. Why hadn't he texted me? I needed time to come up with a plan. Would he act as if nothing had changed? Or were we supposed to pretend to be a couple?

I cursed him seven ways to Sunday as I walked up to the house.

Suddenly, the front door flew open, and my six-year-old, bundle-of-energy nephew barreled out. "Aunt G!"

I laughed as he launched himself at me. I had to shift so he wouldn't knock either my glucose monitor or insulin pump free on contact, but I managed to avoid a fatal blow. Lifting him onto my hip, I ruffled his hair. "How's my favorite kid?"

He threw his arms around my neck and hugged me tightly. "Better not tell Luke or Drew that."

I chuckled. "It'll stay our little secret."

I let Charlie down, and he immediately took my hand. My heart squeezed. How many more months of this did I have? Time when Charlie wasn't embarrassed to show his aunt affection. However long it was, I didn't want to miss a second.

Drew and Luke had grown up way too fast. The best I got out of Luke now was a grunt on a good day, and Drew was thirteen going on twenty-one. I missed when I could cuddle them close and read them bedtime stories. I couldn't imagine how Lawson felt. His eldest would be driving before long.

Charlie tugged me toward the front door. "Grandma made Boston cream pie for dessert, me and Uncle Nash's favorite. Uncle Nash already tried to steal some, but Grandma smacked him with her spoon."

"Why am I not surprised about that?"

Charlie smiled up at me with his gapped-tooth grin. "Gotta get it while you can."

"Sounds like a Nash-ism."

Charlie bobbed his head up and down.

As we stepped inside, voices sounded from the living room. That cacophony of chaos always warmed my heart. Moving into the space, I took in my family scattered about.

Luke sat in the corner, entranced by his phone. Drew shamelessly flirted with Maddie while Nash scowled at him, and Maddie laughed. Wren was pressed to Holt's side as they talked to Dad. Lawson was helping Mom chop veggies for a salad in the kitchen.

And Roan sat off to the side, staring out the window as if he longed to be back in nature.

"Aunt G's here! Can we freaking eat already? I'm starving."

An array of heads popped up, and people began to laugh.

"My man!" Nash agreed. "Let's get this party started." Then he turned to Drew. "You do *not* get to sit next to my girl."

Drew grinned. "I told you that you were gonna have to bring your A-game if you wanted to keep a babe like Maddie."

Nash wrapped an arm around Maddie and kissed her hard and deep. "How's that for A-game?"

Charlie made an exaggerated gagging noise. "No kissing around the food! That's illegal. Right, Dad?"

Lawson chuckled. "I'm afraid that's not in our town's bylaws, bud."

Charlie's brows furrowed. "Who do I talk to about that?"

Everyone laughed.

I jumped as an arm slid around my shoulders. Looking up into mischievous hazel eyes, my heart hammered against my ribs. Caden grinned down at me. "Hey, babe. Missed you today."

As his lips brushed my temple, everyone froze.

I counted from one beat to two, and the entire room erupted.

"What the hell?" Nash barked.

"Why are your lips touching my sister?" Holt growled as he pushed to his feet.

Lawson strode out from the kitchen. "This is a joke, right?"

But Roan stayed sitting. He simply stared, a thoughtful expression on his face.

Caden didn't seem especially worried and showed no signs of releasing me as three pissed-off guys charged toward him. I, on the other hand, immediately started sweating.

"Explain," Nash growled.

Caden rubbed a hand up and down my arm. "Gigi and I are dating."

Lawson's jaw dropped open, then closed, then opened again. "You two hate each other."

Caden shrugged. "I think that was really just flirting."

Holt's gaze narrowed on him. "Grae said she was going to murder you. Repeatedly."

My fingers twisted in Caden's shirt as the panic set in.

"Murder is apparently Gigi's love language," Caden explained.

Wren let out a strangled laugh as her eyes went wide.

Holt whirled on her. "Did you know about this?"

She held up both hands. "I certainly did not." Her eyes narrowed on her fiancé. "But if I did and G swore me to secrecy, I would've been well within my rights not to tell you a danged thing."

"Of course," Holt quickly backed down.

Nash snorted. "Whipped."

"Like you aren't?" Holt snapped. "You can't even handle your thirteen-year-old nephew flirting with Maddie."

"Enough," Lawson barked. "When did this start?"

Schnitzel. Schnitzel. Schnitzel. Caden and I hadn't come up with a backstory to tell people. They were going to see through us in two seconds flat.

Caden's fingers tangled in my hair as he gazed down at me. "I've always known Gigi was special. It only takes a second in her presence to realize that. But when I came home this time, I just couldn't stay away. She has this pull. Makes you want to lean in and get as close to that light as possible. Makes you want to do better. Deserve her. I'm just lucky she gave me a shot."

My throat tightened. Had Caden gone to acting school while he was in New York? That performance deserved a freaking Oscar.

My mom shoved through the wall of my brothers and beamed at us. *Oh, crud on a cracker.* She looked so dang happy. "Caden." She pulled him into her arms. "I've always thought of you as one of mine. This just makes it official."

Red danger lights flashed in my mind. My mom would be planning a wedding before we knew it.

"Mom, it's new. Don't go crazy," I said, panic digging in deep.

She released Caden and turned to me. "Don't you tell me not

to be excited when my girl hasn't ever once brought a guy home before."

"Technically, he brought himself," I argued.

Nash choked on a laugh. "Burn, dude."

Maddie smacked him.

"You guys set the table," Mom called. "I need a few minutes with my girl."

"But—"

She cut me off with a look. And I didn't protest as she dragged me toward Dad's office. I glanced over my shoulder to see my brothers descending on Caden with what looked like murderous intent. He just grinned at me and winked. Freaking winked. Who winked when they were about to get murdered? I was starting to think that Caden had a bizarre death wish.

Mom pulled me into Dad's office and shut the door behind us.

"It's really not that big of a deal. It's new and casual," I said, hoping to stave her off.

"Sit," she ordered.

I knew that tone and immediately sat on the sofa. My mom lowered herself to the seat next to me and just studied me for a moment. "Are you happy?"

I swallowed hard, trying to come up with an answer that wouldn't be an outright lie. "There's been a lot going on. Between the attacks on Holt and Wren, and then Nash and Maddie, the craziness at work, Dad still recovering from his heart attack…"

Mom's expression softened as she took my hand. "We've certainly had our fair share of drama lately."

"Understatement," I muttered.

"But are you happy with Caden?"

I fidgeted with the edge of the sofa cushion. "He's not what people think."

My mom's brows pulled together.

"He'd do anything for his family, even though his brother and dad don't deserve it. He has this gentleness with his mom unlike anything I've ever seen. He cares about the people around him and wants to make their lives better." I'd known that just by the way he'd stepped in with Rance when he didn't have to.

"You've always had a way of seeing the best in people."

I shrugged. "Not always, but I think I see him. The good and the bad." That was why it had hurt so badly to lose Caden. I just had to hope that spending time together now would get us to a new place—one where I could appreciate him as a friend but let him go as anything more than that.

Mom's mouth curved. "I always knew you were half in love with him growing up."

I jerked. "You did not."

She laughed. "A mother knows these things. Your eyes would light up whenever he came around, and he just had this way with you. He could calm you when you were pissed off or upset, make you smile when you were hurting." Her amusement melted into a hint of worry. "I could never figure out what happened between the two of you that your friendship fell apart the way it did, though."

My mom looked at me as if expecting an answer. But I didn't have one. Because I had never been able to figure out why Caden walked right out of my life without a backward glance. All I knew was that it had left me in pieces that had never fit right again.

Chapter Eight

Caden

"Now, boys," Nathan said as he stood from the couch. "Don't make the poor guy piss himself."

I snorted at Grae's father's words. "They'll have to try a little harder if they want to do that."

Nathan chuckled. "You *did* grow up with these knuckleheads."

Nash glared at me. "Which means he owed me a conversation. That's the minimum of best-friend code."

I winced. He had a point there, and this was making me feel like the worst kind of asshole. "It happened without me planning it. I wanted to tell you from the beginning." That much was true. I wanted to let them in on everything. But I knew how much holding on to control meant to Grae, and I wasn't about to take that away from her.

"Does that mean you saw our little sister as a hookup?" Lawson growled.

"Oh, shit," Drew mumbled. "Run now, Caden. That is not his happy tone."

"Of course not," I said, hurrying to defuse the situation. "It's just that I never thought she'd give me the time of day."

"A couple of months ago, you were joking about how a weekend was a long-term relationship," Holt challenged.

Oh, crap. I needed to watch my mouth. "Obviously, Gigi is different."

Nash glared at me. "Why should we believe you?"

I shrugged. "You don't have to. Grae's an adult who's smarter and stronger than all of us put together. Pretty sure if I messed things up between us, she'd have me out on my ass before I could blink."

"That's true." Roan's voice cut across the room. He hadn't moved, but he stared me down with a lethal gaze. "But her heart's more tender than you'll ever know. And if you hurt her? I know lots of places to hide your body where no one will find it."

I grabbed the flowers from my passenger seat and slid out of my SUV. I stared down at the array of blooms. Wildflowers would forever be tied to Clara—and to Grae because I'd shared that ache with her. As I looked at them, I wondered if this was the world's stupidest idea.

Roan's words echoed in my mind. *Her heart is more tender than you'll ever know.*

I had known that once. I'd seen how she struggled to stand on her own in her family. How she worried about finding her place. I had a feeling that had only intensified after her Type 1 diagnosis.

Just thinking about that time had my ribs tightening, making it hard to breathe. Memories battered at the walls of my mind, but I shoved them down.

They were just flowers. I was only playing the role of the dutiful boyfriend as we'd agreed. I crossed the parking lot to the small cottage that housed Cedar Ridge Vacation Adventures. Voices sounded through the screen door. Grae's laughter caught on the air and froze me to the spot.

How long had it been since I'd heard that sound? Years? Because when I'd put up the walls between Grae and me, she'd become guarded. She laughed but not freely or fully like this.

A stranglehold overtook my chest. I wanted that sound directed at me again.

I forced a smile and opened the door. The entire room went silent. Grae's coworkers were scattered around the room. Her boss, Jordan, lounged on the couch. Noel sat behind his desk, scowling at me. And Eddie kicked back in one of the overstuffed chairs, taking my measure.

Grae was perched at her desk, her legs crossed in some sort of knot that made her look like a pretzel. "Caden," she squeaked. "What are you doing here?"

I strode toward her. "I'm taking my girlfriend to lunch." I bent, the pull of her lips so strong, but I forced myself to brush my mouth against her temple instead. But I didn't miss the shiver that ran through her at the contact.

Eddie's mouth opened, closed, then opened again. "You're dating the suit?"

I scowled at him. "Don't give me that shit. You know I can hang with the best of you."

Noel scoffed. "I didn't think you could get that Armani wrinkled."

Grae sent them both looks of warning as she took the blooms from me.

"Gonna be able to open a florist shop around here before too long," Jordan muttered.

I arched a brow at that.

Grae frowned. "Rance brought some the other day."

"Why am I not surprised?" I grumbled.

"These are beautiful," she said, pushing to her feet and crossing to the kitchen on the opposite side of the space.

Noel's gaze roamed over me. "How long are you in town?"

His words had no warmth, but that wasn't anything new. I swore he'd been prickly since kindergarten.

"Not sure yet."

"Think it's wise to take up with G when you don't even know if you're sticking around?" he challenged.

"Noel," Grae warned from the kitchen as she put the flowers in a mason jar. "I'm fully capable of making this one's death a slow and painful one if he messes up."

Noel's lips twitched. "Just lookin' out, G."

Eddie kicked his feet up onto the table. "Just remember, she goes for the balls if you mess with her."

I choked on a laugh. "I'm well aware of Gigi's proficiency in ass-kicking."

She'd taken down a guy more than twice her size in high school and left him crying for mercy.

Grae placed the flowers on her desk and glanced at Jordan. "It okay if I take lunch?"

Jordan hesitated for a long moment, and I thought he might say no. But then he nodded. "Sure, just make it quick. We've got that kayaking group coming in at two, and it's bigger than originally planned, so I'll need Eddie and you."

"You got it. I'll go quick and then grab my swim stuff from home." She glanced at me, suddenly looking a little nervous. "Ready."

I couldn't stand the unease I saw in Grae, and I moved before I'd even consciously made the decision. I curled my hand around her smaller one, threading my fingers through hers. "See you guys."

They all grunted a series of farewells, but none of them were especially warm. "Not sure your coworkers are all that fond of you dating," I said once we were outside.

Grae scowled. "Sometimes, they're as bad as my brothers. Not about my work but definitely about boys."

"Boys?"

She grinned, and that flash of pure amusement hit me somewhere in the chest.

"Pretty sure you're all boys until you hit seventy. I think that's when the troublemaker phase ends."

I chuckled. "You might be right there."

Grae glanced down at our joined hands. I should've released

her. That would've been the safe thing to do. But I argued with myself that this was all part of the game we were playing.

"Why are we going to lunch?"

There was an adorably confused look on Grae's face that had me fighting the urge to kiss her.

"If we're dating, people will expect to see us together occasionally," I reasoned. But the truth was, after a shitty morning dealing with Gabe and my father, she was the person I'd wanted to see.

"I guess that's true," she said, her fingers fidgeting in mine.

"I told my family about us."

Grae's fingers jerked as her gaze snapped to my face. "How'd that go?"

"My mom was thrilled. Dad was begrudgingly happy. Gabe was an ass."

She searched my eyes. "It's still bad?"

It had been so long since I'd talked to Grae about my family. I used to lay all those burdens at her feet. When I no longer had her, I'd started shoving them down and locking them away.

"It just gets worse and worse. Dad seems determined to tear us apart in his quest to make us his version of the best."

Grae was quiet for a moment, but she kept a tight hold on my hand. "I wonder if it's his twisted way of protecting you."

My steps faltered. "Protecting us?"

She toyed with the hem of her shorts before answering, seeming to mull over her words before setting them free. "He couldn't protect Clara from what happened. It had to make him feel powerless. I always wondered if he wanted to make his remaining children as strong as humanly possible so they could face anything."

Grae's theory took root in my mind as memories swirled— Dad's obsession with us being the best in all things. School, sports, work. "I don't know. He seems to like pitting Gabe and me against each other. Gets a thrill out of us being at odds."

The scowl that took root on her face would've sent anyone running. "God, why does he have to be such a prick?"

But even though she thought that, Grae sought to understand him and show empathy. That was just who she was.

I let out a long breath. "I kept hoping things would get better, but I'm not sure that's the case."

Grae looked up at me. "What does that mean for you?"

I shrugged as I opened the door to Dockside Bar & Grill. "Nothing."

She frowned as she stepped inside. "You could always go work for another company. I mean, they're your family, and you'll still have to deal with them, but not working with them would change the dynamic."

I shook my head. "I can't."

"Why?"

This was one of the things I both loved and hated about Grae. She was never afraid to boldly ask whatever questions she wanted answered.

"Clara always wanted all of us to work for the company. She painted this picture of all of us being there together with family lunches and all the amazing things we'd plan for the hotels. And now there's her foundation, too. I can't give up on that."

"Well, look what the cat dragged in," said a feminine voice laced with humor.

I grinned at the waitress who'd been working at Dockside since before we were in high school.

"Hey, Jeanie."

Her smile widened as she took in our joined hands. "I heard rumors, but I didn't believe it." She glanced at Grae. "You gonna make an honest man out of him?"

Grae snorted. "I hardly think that's possible."

Jeanie barked out a laugh, then sent her a wink. "But it'll be fun to try, won't it?"

Grae's face flamed.

I dropped her hand and wrapped an arm around her shoulders. "You got room for two?"

"You two? Always."

Jeanie led us through the maze of patrons toward a booth by the windows overlooking the water. I felt heat on my face and glanced to the side, seeking out the source. Rance sat at a table with two other firefighters, glaring in our direction.

"He looks pissed," Grae whispered.

I squeezed her shoulder. "Just ignore him. This is what he needs to move on."

"God, I hope so."

Something about her words had me stilling. "He still hassling you?"

She shook her head. "Just a couple of texts. He couches it as a friend checking in, but…"

"It doesn't feel that way."

Grae nodded, defeat filling her expression.

I bent, pressing my lips to her forehead. "He'll start to get the picture." And if he didn't, I'd have some strong words with the guy.

The screeching of a chair against the floor had me looking up to see Rance shoving back from his table and stalking out of the restaurant.

Grae bit her lip. "I can't tell if that's good or bad."

"I'm going with good. He'll go from pissed off to moving on in no time."

We sat at the booth, and Jeanie took our orders. The tourists ignored us, but we were an afternoon show for the locals.

Grae squirmed in her seat as she nervously picked at her club sandwich. "I hate people staring."

"Ignore them."

"Easier said than done."

"Eyes on me, Gigi."

Her gaze snapped to mine.

"There's no one here but you and me."

Grae's breath hitched, and her attention dropped to my mouth as she swallowed hard.

Shit. Shit. Shit.

"Just you and me," she whispered.

"Eat," I commanded, my voice gruff.

That broke the moment. Whatever lust swirled around us melted away as Grae scowled at me. "Don't take that tone with me. I'm not some employee you can boss around."

The corner of my mouth kicked up. "A little role-play might be fun, though…"

Pink hit Grae's cheeks. "Whatever."

She looked down at her insulin pump and hit a few buttons.

Any remaining amusement fled my system. "What are you doing?"

Grae didn't bother looking up, just kept at what she was doing. "I'm covering for what I'm about to eat so my blood sugar doesn't spike."

"But this is okay, right? You don't need something else?" Panic edged my voice.

"I can eat whatever I want. I just have to plan accordingly."

A little of the tension in my chest eased.

Grae lifted her gaze to me. "I'm not going to combust. I've been living with this for a long time. I know how to deal."

But I knew better than anyone that things could go sideways when we least expected it and send our worlds spiraling. And Grae was at higher risk for that than most.

The reminder of that fact had my appetite vanishing, but I forced myself to choke down the burger and fries. To answer Grae's questions and ask some in return. But I was somewhere else. Not truly here with her.

Grae stood as I signed the check. "I need to run back to my house to get my swim stuff."

"I'll come with you."

"You don't have to."

I shoved out of the booth. "It would look weird if I didn't," I said quietly.

Her nose scrunched. "Fine." But she was already heading out of the restaurant.

"Hey." I hurried to catch up with her as she stepped out into the sunshine. "Why are you leaving me in the dust?"

"You always get weird with my diabetes. Like what I have to do is gross or something."

I jerked upright. "I don't think it's gross."

Her hands went to her hips. "Then what?"

My heart pounded against my ribs, and my palms dampened. "It reminds me of that day, okay?"

Grae stilled. "When I got sick?"

I nodded. "It's not one I like reliving. Sorry if that means I go weird on you."

Empathy filled her face. "I'm sorry."

"Don't be."

She let out a breath. "But if we're going to do this, you're going to have to get used to Isla and Dex."

My brow furrowed. "Isla and Dex?"

Grae grinned and patted her insulin pump. "Isla." Then she lifted her shirt sleeve to show a small device the size of a Bluetooth earpiece taped to her arm. "Dex."

"What's the second one?"

Her finger ran over the tape surrounding it. "It's a Dexcom continuous glucose monitor. It checks my levels and sends alerts through my phone."

I frowned at the device. "So, there's a needle in there?"

Grae nodded. "It sends continuous readings to the app. I'll share the info with my mom if I'm going on a long hike or something. Just in case."

My mouth went dry. "Does it hurt?"

"Only when I don't get it in right or if it's been in the same spot for too long."

I hated the idea of Grae hurting for any reason. But because some random disease had picked her to attack? It pissed me the hell off.

Her mouth kicked into a smile. "It isn't that bad. It only really sucks when I hit Isla on something, and she gets yanked out."

I grimaced. "That sounds painful."

"It's not rainbows and kittens."

"I'm sorry, Gigi."

She scowled at me. "I don't want your pity."

"It's not pity." I squeezed the back of her neck. "But I hate that you have to deal with this. It's not fair."

"No, it's not. But I don't think anyone on this planet gets the promise of fair. We all have our shiz; it's just different for each of us."

A smile played on my lips. Grae had always had a pretty foul mouth, the byproduct of growing up with four older brothers. But when Lawson had his first kid, she'd made a vow to clean up her act so Luke's first word wasn't an F-bomb. She'd replaced all those curses with non-curse variants.

"I guess we do all have our *shiz*."

Grae stuck out her tongue at me. "Come on, or I'm going to be late, and I really don't want Jordan reaming me out."

"Okay, Gigi." We started down the sidewalk, and I had the bizarre urge to take her hand again. There was no reason for it. We'd made our public displays. Rance had seen us, and so had what seemed like half the town. Yet my fingers flexed at my side, wanting to get to her.

What the hell was wrong with me? I didn't hold hands with women. I'd open doors and guide them with a palm on their back but not take their hands in mine.

I needed to rein it in. To find a way to put some emotional distance between Grae and me. I'd never make it through the next month if I didn't.

Grae turned up the steps to her cottage. The tiny bungalow fit her, with its welcoming porch and pots of brightly colored flowers on the front steps.

As she came to the door, she pulled up short. "That's weird…"

"What?" I looked over her shoulder and saw that the door was wide open.

Chapter Nine

MY HEART PICKED UP SPEED AS I TRIED TO PEEK INTO my living room, but Caden pulled me back.

"No way."

I scowled up at him. "It's my house."

"And you're one hundred pounds soaking wet. If someone is inside, they could take you down in two seconds flat."

My scowl only deepened at that. "I've taken several self-defense courses. I know how to use someone's body weight against them."

Caden let out an exasperated sigh. "Fine, you're a badass. But will you let me go in first anyway?"

I shrugged. "I don't mind using you as a human shield. Just don't get blood on my carpet if someone shoots you."

He glared at me.

"If you want to play all macho protector, you get the bullet holes."

Caden shook his head but stepped inside.

The moment he did, my stomach twisted. Humor was my default armor, but the idea of someone actually hurting Caden made me physically ill. I'd call the police to check it out, but that would mean my brothers showing up in full force to bulldoze my life.

The seconds ticked by exceptionally slowly, each one twisting my insides tighter. When Caden reappeared, the tightness in my lungs finally released so I could breathe again.

"No one's here, and it doesn't look like anything was touched."

My brows pulled together. "That's bizarre."

"Did you lock the door this morning?"

I rolled my eyes. "I did grow up with Lawson, Roan, Holt, and Nash. What do you think?"

Caden held up both hands. "Just asking. Most people around here don't bother with it."

But many had started the practice again after two twisted people had fixated on Wren and Holt, and Maddie's ex had come after her and Nash. People were realizing a little community like this didn't guarantee safety.

"Why don't you come in and make sure nothing is missing? Do you keep cash or prescription meds anywhere?"

I shook my head as I stepped inside. "The only medicine I have is insulin. If someone stole that, I'm going to be pissed because it's freaking expensive."

Caden grunted.

I moved around the living room, taking in the space. I stopped at my bookshelf, frowning.

"What is it?" Caden asked.

I bit the inside of my cheek. "Nothing."

"It's something."

I stared at the shelf littered with books, trinkets, and framed photos. "I thought that picture was on a different shelf."

It was a photo of me, Maddie, and Wren on paddleboards in the lake. We wore bathing suits and held the paddles over our heads triumphantly.

"Maybe I'm wrong, though. I think I'm just paranoid since the door was open."

Caden was quiet as he stared at the picture. "Let's call Nash. He can dust it for prints."

I whirled on Caden, shaking my head. "No police. No brothers. Just, no. Not unless something is missing."

"Gigi, this could be Rance escalating. He didn't seem thrilled to see us together earlier."

Nausea swept through me at that. "I didn't set the alarm this morning. I usually only do that at night when I'm home. I'll set it from now on. I promise."

A muscle in his jaw ticked. "This isn't playing things smart."

"It's my decision. Don't take that from me. It's not like someone's boiling baby bunnies and leaving them in my kitchen. It's one photo out of place that I might have just forgotten I moved."

Caden sighed. "You swear you'll set your alarm at all times now?"

"I promise." And it was the truth. The idea that someone broke into my home gave me the creeps.

He scowled, clearly not liking the decision, but he didn't argue further. "Let's check out the rest of the house."

I nodded. We surveyed the rest of the living room and then moved into the kitchen. "If this jerk stole my leftovers, I'm going to be really pissed."

Caden's scowl deepened. "It's not funny."

I widened my eyes at him. "I never joke about sausage risotto and roasted asparagus."

"Gigi…" he growled.

"Sorry. I get punchy when I'm anxious. Someone possibly breaking into my house qualifies as anxiety-inducing."

The annoyance on Caden's face melted away, and for a second, I thought he might reach out and pull me into his arms. My traitorous heart wanted nothing more.

"We're going to figure this out," he promised. "But it would be a lot easier with police manpower."

My annoyance was back. "No."

Caden sighed. "Come on. It doesn't look like anything is out of place here. Unless you keep cash in the freezer."

"I keep ice cream in the freezer like a normal person."

I peeked to make sure my insulin was still in the fridge, then headed out of the kitchen and down the hall. I looked in the bathroom—nothing out of sorts there. Then I made my way to my bedroom.

I fought the urge to squirm as Caden and I stepped into the space. Something about having the two of us in such a small place, one where I slept, did funny things to my insides.

He looked around the room, seeming to take in more than just possible burgled spots. His gaze landed on each photo and knickknack as if it gave him some invaluable piece of information about me.

He used to have a place among those things. When I was growing up, photos of him with my brothers and me had littered my room. The goldfish stuffed animal he'd won me at the fair one year. The movie stub from when he and Nash had snuck me into a PG-13 movie when I was still eleven. A million memories I'd shoved away in boxes in my closet.

I forced my gaze away from Caden and moved around my bedroom. As I approached my bed, my stomach tightened. The comforter was rumpled in a way that almost looked as if someone had lain on top of it.

I swallowed hard as I studied the bed. I'd sat on it to put on my socks that morning. Maybe that had caused it. I opened my bedside table drawers. Nothing was missing.

Moving to the closet, I opened the door and flicked on the light. All the clothes seemed to be in place. I glanced at the shelves above. All the boxes were there. My gaze caught on my hamper at the bottom of the closet, and my stomach bottomed out.

Something was missing. When I'd gotten up that morning, I'd tossed my pink silk pajamas on the top of the pile of dirty clothes. But they weren't there now.

I crouched, pawing through the contents of the hamper. My heart hammered against my ribs. Nothing.

"What is it?" Caden asked, coming up behind me.

I pressed my thumbnail to the pad of my forefinger, almost hard enough to draw blood. If I told Caden my PJs were missing, he'd call Lawson and Nash for sure. I pushed to my feet and turned to face him. "Nothing. I can't find anything out of place. Maybe it was kids doing something on a dare."

That could very well be the case. We'd had a series of prank wars and vandalism this summer. Graffiti on the dock, bizarre items stolen from stores, houses egged. Someone even left a toilet on one of my neighbor's front lawns.

Caden grabbed my hand and lifted it, gesturing to my thumb and forefinger. "You do that every time you're freaked. What gives?"

A dozen mental curses flew as I tugged my hand free. "I'm just skeeved out that someone might have been in my house. I'm going to have to clean everything. Who knows what they got their cooties on?"

That much was true, at least. It was dumb to hide the rest of it from Caden. I knew that much. But what good would it do to worry him and my brothers? Everyone knew Nash and Lawson worked for the police department. I was sure whoever had broken in had been smart enough to wear gloves. But the fact that they'd left the door open made me wonder if they wanted me to know they had been here.

Caden studied me for a long moment and then pulled out his phone and tapped the screen a couple of times. "Hey, Jordan."

My eyes flared.

"Yeah, we're at Grae's right now and a pipe leaked under her bathroom sink and made a mess. Any chance you could get someone else to cover that kayak trip while we clean it up?"

There was a pause for a moment. "Thanks, man."

Another pause.

"No extra hands needed. I've already got it fixed. We just need to clean up, and she didn't want to be late."

I glared at the interfering bastard as he talked to my boss.

"Sounds good. Appreciate it." Caden ended the call and then looked at me. "What?"

I arched a brow in his direction. "Did you get a plumbing license that I don't know about?"

He chuckled. "I can fix a leaky pipe. I'm not totally helpless."

"I don't know. Those hands look pretty pampered to me."

It was a lie. I'd felt the calluses when Caden took my hand as we walked to Dockside. It made me wonder what they were from these days. He used to horseback ride weekly with Clara and go rock climbing with Nash—plus a million other things that would leave those kinds of marks behind. But I wasn't sure what they were from now, and I hated that.

Caden just shook his head. "You want my help cleaning or not?"

I groaned when I thought about scrubbing this place from top to bottom, even as small as it was. "Yes."

"Then be a little nicer."

I stuck my tongue out at him. "Help me strip the bed."

Caden's brows furrowed.

"Possible cooties in the vicinity. The sheets must be sanitized."

Caden laughed but moved to the mattress and started pulling the comforter back. We worked in tandem and surprisingly well. Caden didn't make fun of me when I asked him to wipe down every touchable surface with alcohol wipes or when I burned incense around my room to clear the air.

I wiped down everything in the bathroom twice and then headed back to the living room, only to pull up short. Caden had his sleeves rolled up and a mop in hand. He systematically worked it from one end of the living room to the other, his drool-worthy forearms flexing with every swish.

He looked up, his gaze locking with mine. "What?"

I forced a smirk to my lips, hoping it would cover any lust in my eyes. "Never thought Caden Shaw would be helping me scrub my house."

"Gigi, I'm full of surprises."

That was exactly what I was worried about.

Chapter Ten

Grae

CADEN NEEDED TO LEAVE. RIGHT NOW. ONE MORE MINUTE of him with those freaking rolled-up sleeves, putting up with my germaphobe self, cleaning my whole house from floor to ceiling, and being all sweet and understanding, and I was going to jump him.

"I think that's everything," I said, trying not to meet his gaze. Because those hazel eyes were just as lethal as the forearms. I needed to start finding things about him that I hated—and quickly.

"You going to be okay here by yourself?"

That low, rumbly voice forced my gaze up to Caden's. "I've lived alone for a long time."

"But not after a break-in."

"We don't even know if it was a break-in. Maybe I forgot to lock my door, and the wind blew it open." All these lies were going to send me straight to the fiery pits.

Caden frowned. "I hope to hell you lock your door every day."

I grabbed hold of the surging flicker of annoyance at his words.

"I'm not an idiot. I don't choose *not* to lock my doors. But everyone can be forgetful sometimes."

"Not about stuff like this they can't."

My back teeth ground together. "I already promised I'd be more careful from now on. I'm going to lock my doors and set the alarm. Do you need me to take a blood oath or something?"

"Always so dramatic," Caden grumbled.

"Not dramatic. Human. But you always seem to think I should be perfect. Newsflash, Caden, no one is. Not even you."

His jaw clenched. "Trust me, I know I'm far from perfect."

"Then maybe cut the rest of us some slack."

He sighed. "I'm sorry. I just want to make sure you're safe."

The worst of my frustration melted away at the honesty in his tone. "I will be. Locked doors—"

"And windows."

I rolled my eyes. "And windows. Alarm set. Two police officers, one Fish and Wildlife game warden, and one ex-security specialist on speed dial."

A hint of humor flickered in his eyes. "Your brothers sound like the start of a bad bar joke."

The corner of my mouth kicked up. "Don't tell them that."

"Never."

Caden twirled his keyring around his finger.

"I really will be okay. Promise," I assured him.

"If you don't want to call your brothers, but something seems out of place, call me."

Damn him for being all understanding and worried. "Okay."

He made his way to the door. "Lock it behind me."

"I will."

Caden looked at me one more time, then opened the door and stepped outside. I closed it behind him, locking it immediately.

"Set the alarm, too," he called through the door.

"I'm doing it," I groused, pressing the *arm* button on the keypad.

I waited a handful of seconds until I heard Caden's footsteps on the porch. Then I did what any woman in this situation would do. I sank to the floor and buried my face in my hands. My brain was in danger of short-circuiting. Between a break-in and all that proximity with Caden, everything was going haywire.

I needed a strong drink. Except that didn't seem like the smartest idea if someone really *was* lurking around and creepily stealing my pajamas. That was the bucket of ice water I needed.

Climbing to my feet, I strode toward my bedroom. Maybe I'd just missed the bin this morning. I opened the closet and pulled out the hamper altogether. There were no pajamas accidentally shoved behind it. I dumped the contents of the hamper onto the floor. Pawing through them, I searched every item. No pale pink silk.

Frickety frack. This was not good. I thought back to the figure behind my house last night. What if it hadn't been an animal but the same person who had broken in today? Suddenly, I wished I'd asked Caden to stay.

"Don't be an idiot," I scolded myself. The last thing I needed was more one-on-one time with him.

I threw all the clothes back into the hamper and took it to my laundry room. I poured them into the washer, added soap, and turned the cycle to hot. I didn't care if I shrank things, at least there would be no cooties on my clothes.

I left the basket by the washer and headed back to the living room. The sun was already setting, and I knew darkness would soon be upon us. I moved around the space, double-checking the window latches.

I'd stayed alone in this house what seemed like an infinite number of times, yet that felt like a slightly terrifying prospect all of a sudden. The sensation sparked a flicker of anger. Whoever this asshole was, they didn't get to steal my haven.

I pulled out my phone and hit a number on my favorites list. A second later, someone picked up.

"Wildfire Pizza, this is Sheila. How can I help you?"

"Hey, Sheila. It's Grae."

"Hey, Grae! How are you?" the bubbly teenager asked.

"Good. I'm hoping you guys aren't too slammed, and I can order a pepperoni pie for delivery."

Chances were the tourists had them in a rush. I could hear the din of customers in the background.

"I'll slide you to the front of the line," she said.

"You are an angel."

Sheila laughed. "Us locals gotta look out for each other."

"Dang straight."

"It should be about thirty minutes."

"Thanks. I'll be here."

"See you later," she called and hung up.

"Pizza will cure all," I muttered. I looked around the space for something to occupy me while I waited. I didn't want to watch TV, and there was no way I could focus on a book. I worried the inside of my cheek until an idea hit me, and I grinned.

Crossing to the hall closet, I opened it wide and pushed aside the array of jackets. I grabbed hold of the kickboxing dummy and hauled it out into the living room, panting by the time I was done. Then I grabbed a plastic case from the shelf in the closet and set it on the coffee table.

I opened the lid and took in the set of throwing knives. Pulling one out, I tested the weight in my hand. I straightened, took a deep breath, and let it fly. The blade hit center mass, and I felt just a little bit better.

I grabbed the second knife and then the third. I threw blade after blade until I regained a little bit of the control I so desperately needed.

The doorbell rang, and I set the last knife back in the case, crossing to the front door. Whoever was running delivery had made good time.

I unarmed my alarm and opened the door to six feet three inches of pissed-off male. He'd changed from his more formal attire into gray joggers and a tee that clung to his muscled chest.

"You didn't even ask who it was," Caden said, glowering.

"It was supposed to be pizza."

"But it wasn't, was it?" he snapped.

"No, it's a grown man who looks like he's about to throw a tantrum."

Gold flashed in Caden's hazel eyes. "Forgive me if I don't want your ass to get murdered."

"Murderers don't usually ring the bell."

"I'm sure some do, just waiting for naïve women to answer."

"I'm not naïve," I snapped.

"The events of today don't really prove that."

"You, you—"

A throat cleared behind Caden, and we both whirled toward the sound.

The delivery driver, who was in his early twenties, held out a pizza box. "Sorry to interrupt the lovers' quarrel, but I've got your pizza, Grae."

"Thanks, Tim," I said, moving forward. "Sorry about this."

Tim shrugged. "I get it. My girl and I can get into it, too." He grinned. "But the makeup sex is always out of this world."

I nearly choked on my tongue.

Caden pulled out his wallet and handed Tim two twenties, taking the pizza box. "Keep the change."

Tim's grin morphed into a megawatt smile. "Thanks, man. See you two around."

I glared at Caden. "What are you doing here?"

He shrugged, and the action bringing attention to a duffel bag hanging off his shoulder. "I didn't want you here alone."

Some of the annoyance slipped away. This was how it always was with Caden. He'd piss me off ninety percent of the time, but then I'd get a glimpse of the guy I used to know. The one who always had my back and made me feel understood. Safe. Those glimmers of him were like daggers to my chest because they reminded me of just how much I'd lost. But I still hungered for them all the same. I was a masochist that way.

I didn't say anything, just stepped back so Caden could enter.

He strode into my space as if he owned it. But that was how he entered every room, his presence bleeding out into the ether and taking over.

I closed the door, flipped the lock, and set the alarm. Then I headed into the living room. I came up short as Caden stood in the middle of the room staring at the dummy with my knives embedded in its chest and head.

"Gigi…"

I took the pizza box from his hands and moved to the kitchen. "Yes?"

"Why is there a mannequin in your living room that looks like it just got ax murdered?"

"It's not a mannequin. It's a martial arts dummy, and his name is Bob."

Caden slid his bag off his shoulder and set it next to the couch. "What did Bob ever do to you?"

I pulled two plates out of the cabinet and loaded up a piece of pizza on both. "Bob is the best man in my life because he lets me take out all my aggressions on him."

Caden snorted. "Bob's screwed." He crossed the small space, his gaze sweeping over my face. "When did you pick up knife throwing?"

The question had a deep ache taking root in my chest. Caden used to know everything about me. If I picked up some random new hobby, discovered a new book or band, or found a new hiking spot, he would've been the first one I told. But that couldn't be further from the truth now.

"A couple of years ago." I opened a drawer and pulled out two brightly colored placemats and napkins, handing them to Caden. "Set these out on the coffee table?"

He tore his gaze from my face and studied the items in his hands. "You eat at the coffee table?"

I shrugged. "It's got the view. I like it."

Even as the sky was turning dark, the moon illuminated the water below and created a sparkling canvas you could get lost in.

"You need a real table and chairs," Caden grumbled as he set the coffee table.

I grabbed a regular Coke and a diet from the fridge. "And you need to remove the stick shoved where the sun doesn't shine."

Annoyance flickered in Caden's expression. "I'm not in preschool, and this isn't snack time."

I handed him the sodas and took the two plates to the table. "Are you so old that you can't get up and down anymore? Do I need to get you a cane?"

Caden's lips twitched. "If I break a hip, it's on you."

I pulled out two of the meditation cushions I used for seats. They were both jewel-toned with rich gold embroidery. "Here, this should help your delicate disposition."

Caden had set us both up on the same side of the coffee table so we could lean against the couch. I lowered myself to my cushion and mentally calculated the carbs in my meal, then adjusted my insulin pump.

"What are you doing?"

Caden's gravelly voice skated over my skin. He was close—too close—but I couldn't let that show.

"I told you before; I'm just giving myself insulin to cover my carbs."

"I know, but how do you know how much to give yourself?"

My back teeth ground together at his doubt. "I've lived with this disease for a while. I know roughly how many carbs are in everything I consume on a regular basis."

Caden studied me as if he weren't totally convinced.

The annoyance burned brighter. "I have been keeping myself alive for the past eleven years."

Pain streaked across his eyes, and I instantly felt like a jerk.

I gentled my tone. "I just mean, I've been doing this for a long time. I've got it down."

Caden nodded, taking a bite of his slice. "Damn, I always forget how good this is."

"Better than New York?"

He chuckled. "Nothing's better than New York pizza. But this reminds me of home. How many times did we order more pies than I could count?"

A million different memories flitted through my mind. My house had always been the gathering spot growing up. Holt, Wren, Nash, Maddie, Caden, and I would pile into the movie room with half a dozen pizza boxes. Or we'd order after playing an epic round of Ghost in the Graveyard around our property. Or after a day of swimming in the creek or four-wheeling around the mountains. There was nothing like those exhausted summer nights when we'd laugh until my parents forced us all to go to sleep.

I missed it. How simple things were. The belief that things would always work out.

"Gigi?"

I shook myself out of the memories, my gaze locking with Caden's. "I miss it."

"Miss what?"

"Those days. How easy everything was before life got complicated."

Caden's eyes bored into me as if they could read all my secrets. "I know what you mean."

Our lives had been torn apart in one way or another after those blissful summer nights. But I guessed that was what happened when you grew up. Everyone had their baggage.

"How are things at the resort?" I asked, trying to steer us away from conversations that reminded me just how much I'd lost.

A flicker of something passed over Caden's expression. It was so quick that I likely would've missed it if I didn't know him.

"What's wrong?"

Caden took another bite of pizza, seeming to mull over his words. "Just more of Gabe being an ass."

"I'm sorry." Caden's older brother had always been a piece of work. The guy honestly gave me the creeps. He had no sense of personal space whenever I saw him, and he stared in a way that made me want to shower.

Caden leaned back against the sofa. "I think he sees me coming back to Cedar Ridge as some sort of personal attack."

"But your dad made you come home, didn't he?"

Caden nodded. "That doesn't matter to Gabe. He just sees me encroaching on his turf and thinks we need to go to war."

My heart ached for him. I couldn't imagine being at odds with my brothers the way he was. Sure, they annoyed the crud out of me, meddled and interfered, and were ridiculously overprotective, but I knew it came from a place of love. I had no idea how Caden's family had become so twisted.

"Do your parents see it?" I asked quietly.

A muscle in his jaw ticked. "Yeah. It upsets my mom, but I get the sense my dad likes it."

My stomach twisted, and I moved on instinct, reaching out and taking Caden's hand. My fingers grazed his calluses as I squeezed. "I'm so sorry."

He stared down at our joined hands. "I keep thinking that if the hotels are in a good enough spot, my dad will let up, and we can be a family again. But it's never enough for him."

I gripped Caden's hand tighter. "Family is supposed to support each other no matter what's going on."

"I think the only one who did that was Clara."

The cracks in my heart deepened, fracturing muscle and tissue. "She'd want you to be happy."

Caden swallowed, his Adam's apple bobbing. "She'd want us to be a family."

I was quiet for a moment, and then I said what I'd wanted to for so long. "She wouldn't want you to bleed yourself dry for people who don't give a damn about you."

Caden's gaze jerked up. "You cursed."

I shrugged. "Sometimes, you need those words for emphasis."

He stared into my eyes. "I can't give up. Not yet. Not on The Peaks. Not on the foundation."

"You're slowly killing yourself." I'd seen it over the years in my brief glimpses of Caden. The mischief had gone out of his eyes.

The banter and troublemaking were forced. He didn't have the same life in him. "I hate it."

Gold fire lit in those hazel eyes. "How do you see everything?"

"Because I've known you almost all my life." And I'd paid far too close attention.

Caden's thumb brushed back and forth across my hand. The motion pulled me toward him. Closer and closer. Each millimeter tempting fate.

His eyes burned brighter, his gaze zeroing in on my lips.

My heart hammered against my ribs. Just a breath away.

An owl hooted, and Caden jerked back, dropping my hand as if he'd been burned. He snatched up his Coke and took a long drink, not meeting my eyes.

My face flamed as my stomach pitched. I scrambled to my feet. "I forgot I have to prep for a trip for later this week. I'm going to eat while I work. There are blankets and pillows in the hall closet."

I didn't wait for an answer. I took my pizza and soda and booked it to my bedroom. But the image of Caden jerking away was burned into my brain. Just another reminder that he would never want me the way I craved him. The sooner I accepted that truth, the sooner I could move on.

Chapter Eleven

Caden

I WANTED TO TAKE ONE OF THOSE KNIVES OUT OF THE DUMMY and jab it into my thigh. That would've been less painful than seeing the hurt in Grae's eyes. Pain that I had put there because I was reckless.

My control used to be better, but that was when almost three thousand miles had separated Grae and me. When I could hide away in my New York City fortress and only head home a couple of times a year. Now, I saw her all the time. Couldn't help but breathe her in—that scent of honeysuckle with a bite, just like Grae herself. And then there was the way she understood me. How she got straight to the root of any situation and knew how it would affect me.

There were a million reasons to stay away. But I'd always been greedy when it came to Grae Hartley. Only now, I was playing with fire. A flame that had the potential to leave us both with third-degree burns.

I forced myself to finish my pizza, even though I had no appetite. I cleaned up my plate and wrapped the leftovers, placing them in the fridge. Then I listened. At first, there was nothing. Then I heard Grae moving around her room. A second later, the door opened.

I braced for her to come out. Tried to steel myself against her beauty. But she never appeared. Another door closed, and a second later, I heard the sound of a shower.

A stream of curses flew through my mind, and the sea of images I swam in was enough to send me straight to hell.

Grae stepping under the spray. Her hands, slick with soap, gliding over her skin. Me stepping into the shower with her. Fingers flexing on her hips. Me pounding into her.

Hell.

I crossed to my duffel and pulled out my laptop and earbuds. Popping them in, I turned on a playlist loud enough to drown out the water, then opened my email. But all I saw were images of Grae.

The scent of coffee teased my nose, and I rolled over onto my back with a groan. A muscle twinged. I blinked against the morning light. This couch was not meant for sleeping.

"Coffee?" Grae asked from the kitchen.

My gaze sought her of its own volition, but I regretted it the second I saw her. Grae was in silvery-gray silk sleep shorts and a matching tank top with slender straps that ghosted over her petite form. My back teeth ground together. "What are you wearing?"

She glanced down. "My pajamas."

"*That's* what you sleep in?"

She shrugged. "It's cozy."

That was not *cozy.* That would haunt my damn dreams for all eternity. My cock pressed against my joggers, and I muttered a curse, sitting up. "I need to go."

"Whatever," she mumbled, heading out of the kitchen.

Hell. I was making everything worse. I stood, gathered my

bag, and straightened the cushions on the couch. Then I headed for the door, arming the alarm and locking the door handle so it would catch when I closed it.

I strode to my SUV like the hounds of hell were on my heels. And maybe they were. That image of Grae was more than I could take.

Cracking my neck, I climbed behind the wheel. I needed a stiff shot of whiskey. But seeing as it was seven a.m., I'd have to settle for the strongest cup of coffee I could find.

I headed for The Brew, pulling into a spot a few stores down. I slid out of my SUV and headed for the quaint coffee shop. The space reminded me of Grae—all colorful with mismatched décor. And it had a vitality that was so similar to hers.

A bell jingled as I opened the door. The space was already about half-full of locals getting a fix before work and tourists heading out for their outdoor adventures.

My eyes burned as I got in line. I'd slept like crap, tossing and turning, haunted by dreams of Grae. What had I been thinking suggesting this ruse?

"You look rough, man."

I turned at the sound of Nash's voice. He ambled toward me, Maddie at his side. "Gee, thanks."

He chuckled. "What did you get up to last night? One too many beers?"

Maddie pressed her lips together to keep from laughing. "I doubt it was that."

Nash's gaze snapped to his fiancée. "What do you—?"

He cut his sentence off and then made a gagging noise. "I think I just lost my appetite."

The laugh finally escaped Maddie as she patted Nash's chest. "You never lose your appetite." She glanced my way. "What did you and Grae do last night?"

"Just remember I'm her brother, and there are things I never need to know," Nash growled.

I choked on a laugh. "Noted." I turned to Maddie. "Gigi decimated some mannequin named Bob, and then we ate pizza."

Maddie grinned. "Was she pissed at you? She only brings out Bob when she's really mad. She offered to put Nash's face on it for me a couple of months ago."

Nash reared back. "You wanted to throw knives at me?"

Maddie's eyes danced with humor. "Let's be honest. You played indifferent for a long time, mister. Made me think you only ever saw me as a friend. You deserved a few knives."

Nash wrapped her in his arms and brushed his lips across hers. "But it was worth the wait, wasn't it?"

She melted into him. "A million times over."

My heart rate jacked up, panic gripping my chest. I cleared my throat. "Please, don't make me vomit before I've had my coffee."

Nash shook his head. "Just you wait. You'll be worse than me in no time."

Panic dug its claws in deeper. That would never happen. Couldn't. I knew what it was like to lose someone who meant everything to me. I'd barely survived. The only option was to have places you didn't let people into and impenetrable walls.

Maddie's smile widened. "This is going to be fun to watch."

"Enough already," I grumbled. "What are you two doing today?"

Nash inclined his head toward the station. "I'm on duty."

"I've got a puppy training class at our place and then two private clients," Maddie answered. "What about you?"

I slid out my phone, trying to remind myself what was on my docket today. An email from my father glared at me from my inbox.

I want your first assessment report on resort operations by the end of the week.

No, *How are you?* Or, *Love, Dad.* Of course not. That wasn't how Harrison Shaw operated. I couldn't remember the last time my father had hugged me. I didn't think he'd even touched me other than to shake my hand at business meetings since Clara died.

"Everything okay?"

Nash's voice brought me out of my spiral. "Yeah, just a lot going on at the resort. Gala season."

It wasn't a lie. I had at least a dozen emails about that, as well.

Nash frowned. "Everything good with the fam?"

I chuckled. "Is it ever?"

"If you need to talk, blow off steam, whatever, you know I'm always here."

A burn lit in my chest. "I know, man. Thanks." But I couldn't get myself to open up to him. Not like I used to. Even though I knew he loved me like a brother, I couldn't break down the walls I'd built.

"Your mom sent us invitations to the gala," Maddie said. "It was so thoughtful of her."

My brows rose at that. It was a good sign, her being invested in something again. "She's excited you're back and that we're all in each other's lives again."

A mischievous smile stretched across Maddie's face. "And that you're dating Grae…"

"That, too." Guilt pricked at me. How would she feel when Grae and I broke up? I hoped it would be enough for her to see me back in the dating game. She'd think I was normal for a while. Maybe I could find some woman in New York willing to pose as a girlfriend a couple of years from now, too.

The idea made my stomach sour. Because no one would ever hold a candle to Grae.

Chapter Twelve

Grae

NOEL'S CHAIR SQUEAKED AS HE LEANED BACK. I COULD feel his eyes on me, probing. I kept my gaze on the printout of my guest list for my next hike. Each roster gave me ages, health risks, experience, and where they were from. I liked to memorize that before heading out.

Today's afternoon hike wasn't a long one, just two miles to a beautiful waterfall and then back to the trailhead. None of the people on the list should have any issues unless they'd lied like my last group.

Noel's gaze kept boring into me.

"Yes?" I asked without looking up.

"How's the pipe?"

My brows pulled together for the briefest moment before I remembered yesterday's cover story. "Oh, it's fine now. Everything was just a mess."

Eddie flicked a paperclip at me from his desk. "And how's lover boy?"

I sent him a withering stare. "I don't know. How's your right hand?"

Noel choked on a laugh.

Eddie just grinned. "I love it when you talk dirty to me."

"You're hopeless."

"But you love me anyway."

I laughed, leaning back in my chair. "I do. And what does that say about me?"

"That you have shit taste in men," Jordan said, striding into the room and handing Eddie a stack of papers. "Your rafting trip for tomorrow."

"That's harsh, boss man," Eddie grumbled.

I grinned as I looked up at Jordan. "But I stick around you so you might have just insulted yourself."

Noel's lips twitched.

Jordan rolled his eyes. "I've known you longer than all these fools. I'm the original. They're just the imitations."

It was true enough. Jordan's dad and mine had been friends since childhood. Even though he was several years older, he'd been present in my life since the day my parents brought me home from the hospital.

"How could I insult the OG?"

"Damn straight."

The screen door to the office squeaked, and I looked up to see Wren. I grinned. "What are you doing here?"

There was mischief in her hazel eyes as she lifted an insulated bag. "Can't a girl bring her bestie lunch?"

"With that look on your face, I'm pretty sure the answer should be no."

She burst out laughing. "But you're going to come with me anyway."

I glanced at Jordan. "It okay if I head out for a bit?"

He jerked his chin in a nod. "Of course. Your group gets here at one-thirty."

"I'll be back by one."

Eddie grinned at Wren. "Don't you want to invite a poor, hungry boy to join you?"

Wren's lips twitched. "Sorry, buddy, this is girl-talk time."

"I can do girl talk for whatever smells amazing in that bag."

Wren chuckled. "Sorry, just enough for two."

Eddie pouted.

I ruffled his hair as I stood. "I'll pick you up a sandwich on my way back."

He grinned up at me. "Have I told you lately that I love you?"

I snorted. "I guess that comes in handy since our band of misfits is stuck together for life."

Noel held out his hand for a fist bump. "You know it."

Touching my knuckles to his, I turned to head for my best friend. The words *girl talk* had me on edge. If anyone could see through my act with Caden, it would be Roan or Wren. And my bestie had a look in her eyes that said she was ready for an interrogation.

She wrapped an arm around my shoulders and led me out of the office. "Want to go down to the lake?"

"Sure."

She released me, and we moved in that direction, the breeze wrapping us in the scents of pine and a hint of lake water. I glanced her way. "Aren't you working today?"

Wren nodded. "Abel's covering for me while we have lunch."

"Any crazy calls yet?"

Wren had the best stories from working as a dispatcher at the police station.

Her lips twitched. "You might want to check on Roan later."

I winced. "What now?"

"Marion Simpson keeps feeding that bear, no matter how many times he tells her it's dangerous. He had to tranq it again, and she cursed him up and down for *'hurting her Yogi.'* The neighbors are getting pissed."

Roan could handle an angry bear way better than he could deal with people. He would definitely need a beer tonight.

Wren guided us toward a spot under a tree away from the more crowded areas. "I picked up sandwiches from the meat market. Hope that works."

She handed me one, and I grinned at *turkey club* scrawled on the paper. "My favorite."

"I'll get you to try something new sometime."

"But if you try something new and don't like it, you're just pissed you didn't get the thing you know you love."

Wren unwrapped her egg salad sandwich. "Or you could find something you love even more."

"Says the girl who ended up back with her childhood sweetheart."

Wren's face went all soft, and I made a gagging noise.

"You and my brother are a little much sometimes."

She laughed. "I'm not even going to apologize."

"Can we just try to keep it away from eating times?" I asked as I adjusted my insulin pump.

"Fine. Let's talk about your love life."

I froze, my sandwich halfway to my mouth. "What do you want to know?"

Wren just stared at me. "My best friend got together with a guy she's known practically all her life, she doesn't even bother to tell me, and now she's asking what I want to know? How about everything?"

I winced. "Sorry. It really was spur of the moment. I wasn't expecting it to happen."

Wren opened her chips. "Me either. The last I heard, you were about ready to fry him over an open flame."

"I don't know if it was that bad."

Wren gaped at me. "I had to stop you from dumping a drink over his head at family dinner."

"He was being annoying," I defended.

"But what I want to know is how we got from annoying to banging in a matter of weeks."

I worried my thumbnail with my forefinger. God, I was such

an asshole. Wren and I didn't lie to each other. We shared practically everything. The only thing I'd ever held back was the depth of my feelings for Caden. It had felt like that magic feeling between us might vanish if I spoke about it.

"G?" she pressed.

I stared down at my sandwich. "It's fake."

Wren was silent for a moment. "What's fake?"

"Caden and me."

Her eyes flared wide. "I knew I was missing a part of the story. I thought maybe you guys had been hooking up for a while, and the fighting was just some weird kind of foreplay."

I choked on a sip of soda and started coughing. "Definitely not foreplay."

Wren studied me, looking for answers I probably didn't have. "Why play lovebirds?"

I toyed with the tab on my soda can. "Rance wouldn't leave me alone, and it was starting to freak me out. Caden's dad is on his case about growing up and appearing settled down."

"What do you mean freaking you out?" Wren's voice filled with anxiety that immediately made me feel guilty. A guy who had been obsessed with her growing up had fixated on her so badly that he and two friends had attacked her, one shooting her in the chest and almost killing her.

I reached out and squeezed her hand. "Nothing like that. He just isn't getting that a relationship isn't in our cards. I thought if he saw me moving on, he would let it go."

Wren relaxed a little. "How's that working?"

"I think it is. He didn't text yesterday. I'm calling that a win."

She huffed out a breath. "Men. Such fragile egos."

I choked on a laugh. "So true."

Wren picked at her bread. "Are you sure this is a good idea?"

I took a bite of my turkey club to buy time, but I couldn't taste my favorite sandwich. "It's the simplest option. He'll be gone after the gala, and we'll come up with some amicable breakup story."

"But you care about him."

I stilled. "Of course, I do. He's Nash's best friend. I've known him forever."

Wren pinned me with a stare. "Grae, I may have missed it growing up, but I see it now. You're good at covering, but I know you. There are times I see you looking at him like your heart is breaking."

I swallowed against the lump in my throat. "It's probably just me trying not to murder him."

"G..."

I bit the inside of my cheek.

"It's me. How many times did you hold me while I bawled after Holt left? You and Gran forced me out of bed, made me eat, and made sure I *survived*. You saw me at my very worst. You know you can trust me."

My eyes burned. "I loved him."

Wren took my hand, squeezing it in silent encouragement.

"I don't know when it happened. It just always felt like he got me. That we understood each other in a way no one else could."

"Looking back, you two disappeared at the same time a lot."

A sad smile played on my lips. "We had this spot. If either of us was working something out in our heads, we went there. A lot of times, we'd find each other. Just talk it out—whatever was going on. After he lost Clara, we went a lot more. He was just going through so much..."

"And you were there for him."

I nodded. "I tried to be. He was shutting down, and it killed me. But he still let me in. Things changed after I got sick. He pulled away. Started putting up walls."

Tears filled my eyes, one slipping out and tracking down my cheek. "He never came to our spot again. Every time I went there, it killed something inside me that he wasn't there. I had no idea what'd happened. If I'd done something. If it was stuff with his family. Caden was physically present, but *my* Caden? He was just gone."

Wren pulled me into a hard hug. "I'm so sorry. I wish you would've told me."

"I didn't want anyone to know. I was so embarrassed. I thought we'd be together one day. That he was just waiting until we were older. I had all these childish dreams, and they just went up in smoke."

She pulled back but kept hold of my hands. "But now you're fake-dating the guy you were in love with for years…"

I gave her a smile that I knew looked like a grimace. "Seemed like a good idea at the time."

Wren barked out a laugh. "G…"

"I know. But I hoped having him in my life again would make me realize that we weren't right for each other after all. That the childhood image I had in my head would be shattered, and I could finally move on."

"How's that going for you?"

I sighed, leaning back against the tree. "Sometimes, I want to kill him. Other times, I want to jump him." But he clearly didn't feel the second half of that equation. Last night was more proof of that.

"Sounds super healthy."

I groaned. "It was such a dumb idea, but now we're in it, and I'm not going to bail on him because of a stupid childhood crush."

Wren worried her bottom lip. "I don't want *you* to end up crushed at the end of this."

"Trust me. That's not high on my list either."

"You could just have a fake breakup now. Maybe it's been enough already to get Rance off your case. Or I could have Holt talk to him—"

"No! I don't want my brothers involved. You know how they are. They'll probably pummel Rance and insist on coming on any date I ever have from now on."

Wren frowned. "They're not that bad."

I arched a brow. "Do you remember when Bobby stood me up for Homecoming?"

Wren winced. "We found him duct taped to the flagpole in his underwear on Monday."

"And someone would just happen to let the air out of his tires every month or so for the rest of the year. Not to mention the fact that they tried to make me take Lawson to prom." I sighed. "I know they love me, but sometimes that love is stifling. Living life means getting hurt now and then."

"I won't tell Holt. I promise. But are you sure you can handle the hurt that could come with dating Caden, fake or not?"

A lead weight settled in my stomach. I wasn't sure at all. I just had to hope that all this time with Caden would burn him out of my system for good.

Chapter Thirteen

Grae

THE SCREEN DOOR SLAPPED AGAINST THE FRAME AS I strode back into the office.

Eddie looked up from his computer. "How was it?"

I slid my backpack off my shoulder and let it fall to the floor next to my desk. "Perfect."

It had been one of those afternoons that reminded me why I loved this job so much. The group was small, just two families on vacation together from back east. Their kids were all middle and high school-aged and in awe of their first taste of the Pacific Northwest mountains.

They'd been interested in learning about the vegetation and animal life, and no one had lied about their fitness level. Add in the ideal weather and flowers in bloom, and you had the perfect afternoon.

Eddie leaned back in his chair. "Kind of hard to believe that we get to do this for a living, huh?"

"It really is."

Jordan peeked out of his office and shot me a grin. "Your tip came through on the website. Twenty-five percent."

Eddie let out a low whistle. "Damn, girl, you're on fire."

"They were great. If they book again, I call dibs."

Jordan chuckled. "I'm sure they'll request you."

My phone buzzed in my pocket, and I slid it out. An alert flashed from my glucose monitor. I'd tried to estimate the right combo of sugar, carbs, and fat I'd need to stay in a good range from the hike, but it wasn't an exact science, and now I was trending down.

Jordan moved in closer. "Everything okay?"

I nodded, quickly sliding my phone back into my pocket. "Yeah, just need to eat a little something."

He frowned. "You've been pushing hard lately. You need more days off?"

I fought the urge to snap at him and instead strode to the fridge and grabbed one of my mini orange juices. "I'm good. This is me managing."

I downed the juice, then pulled peanut butter and crackers out of my desk drawer and started munching.

Jordan frowned as if he wasn't sure he believed me.

Eddie swiped a cracker from my stack. "Come on, J-man. Grae's a badass. We don't need to worry about her."

He held out his hand for a fist bump.

I grinned as I touched my knuckles to his. Eddie never treated me any differently because I had Type 1, and I loved that about him. But he also sometimes forgot that I needed to be cautious. He was a throw-caution-to-the-wind and jump-off-a-mountain sort.

He'd been that way since he lost his fiancée, Megan, in a car accident a few years ago. He tried to live life to the fullest because he was one of the few who understood it could all be easily ripped away. It was one of the things that bonded us. The understanding of how fragile life was. For some, it meant living carefully. For us, it meant living *fully*.

Jordan's hand landed on my shoulder, and he squeezed. "Just want to make sure you're okay."

A little of my annoyance melted away. "I know. But I'm fine. Promise."

He gave my shoulder one more squeeze and then headed back to his office.

"He's such a buzzkill sometimes," Eddie muttered.

"He meddles because he cares."

Eddie leaned over, resting his hand on my shoulder, his eyes going comically earnest. "I just want to make sure you're okay."

I shoved him off. "Oh, shut it."

He chuckled. "You want to go grab a beer?"

I shook my head. "I want a shower, leftover pizza, and bed."

"Aw, man. Come on. I'll get you fresh pizza."

"Bribery will work another time." Because nights out with Eddie almost always ended up going way later than intended.

"I'll hold you to that."

I packed up the rest of my stuff and headed for the door. I paused as I opened it, looking over my shoulder and pinning Eddie with a stare. "Make sure you get your beauty rest."

He chuckled. "Any more beauty, and the women of Cedar Ridge will be powerless against me."

I just shook my head as I stepped outside. It was still plenty light out, and the walk home would do my muscles good—a light stretch after the hike. I might go for a bubble bath instead of a shower.

Tourists were out in full force, heading to early dinners or enjoying the extended sunlight at the lake. Kids laughed and screamed as they chased one another. Even as hectic as things could get during the summer, I couldn't imagine living anywhere else. Cedar Ridge had a kind of magic I'd never experienced in any other place I'd visited, near or far.

My phone buzzed in my pocket again, and I pulled it out.

Caden: *How did everything go today? Any issues?*

I stared at the message. How long had it been since his name had flashed on my screen? I couldn't even remember. Just seeing the curve of the letters had my heart rate ratcheting up. But as I read the message, I frowned. It was a simple proof of life check.

It might not make sense to some people why that grated so much. Not until you lived through the aftermath of being diagnosed with a life-altering disease. It was as if I was no longer anything but someone who might die from low or high blood sugar. The people in my life couldn't see anything but that. It didn't matter if I was happy or sad, just that my blood sugar was within range.

I thought about not responding and then decided that would be a jerk move. Caden was trying to help. He cared in his way, even if it wasn't how he used to. I had to make peace with that.

Me: *All good.*

I slid my phone back into my pocket, heading away from downtown and into the picturesque neighborhoods surrounding it. Craftsman cottages were painted in cheerful colors and surrounded by gardens with brightly colored blooms. The rest of my siblings lived far out of town, and that had its appeal, but I loved having a true neighborhood around me.

Turning onto my street, I caught sight of a figure jogging toward me. Each step that brought him closer had a weight settling heavier in my stomach. Rance could take a million and one jogging paths, but he just *had* to choose the one that led him by my house.

His pace slowed as he approached. "Hey."

I forced a polite smile. "Hi."

"Just getting off work?"

I nodded.

Rance jogged in place in front of me. "I'm heading home to shower and then meet Sarah, Dave, and a few others for a bite. Want to come?"

That was the group that had gotten me into this mess in the

first place. We'd all been in the same wider friend group through high school. I wasn't as close to them as I was to Wren and Maddie, but we hung out socially a fair bit. With Rance's attention, that felt awkward now.

"I'm pretty wiped. I'm going to call it an early night."

He frowned. "You haven't been hanging much lately. Is it because of Caden?"

I pressed my thumbnail into the pad of my forefinger to keep my temper in check. "I've been working a lot. But he's my boyfriend. I'm going to spend time with him."

Rance's jaw worked back and forth. "He doesn't deserve you."

"He's a good guy," I snapped. Caden might have hurt me in the past, but he would do anything for the people in his life.

"He's a player."

I bit the inside of my cheek. I didn't want to think about any women who might litter Caden's past; it hurt too much.

Rance dipped his head. "Even if you don't want anything with me, you deserve a hell of a lot better than him. He's going to screw with your head and then ditch you."

Something in me snapped. I was so sick of people trying to tell me what I should and shouldn't do. That I didn't know what was best for my own life.

"You don't know a damn thing about him. And the truth is, you don't know me either. Caden's in my life because I want him to be. If it doesn't work out, I'll deal. But I don't need your opinion or anyone else's."

I darted around him and stormed toward my house. But something deep inside me told me I was lying to myself.

Caden Shaw had the power to ruin me. And I knew it.

Chapter Fourteen

Caden

I STRODE INTO THE LODGE, GREETING PEOPLE AS I PASSED. THE meeting with Juliana, the stable manager, had been both a relief and infuriating. Gabe undermined her at every turn, so she didn't have enough staff for popular programming.

I knew him. Gabe was doing this to get his precious polo and do away with the trail rides and horsemanship classes. But people didn't come to a mountain resort in the West for polo; they came for a ranch-like experience.

Turning down a side hallway, I headed toward my office, slowing my pace as my brother approached.

"Well, look what the cat dragged in. Partying too late with that tight piece of ass last night?" Gabe sniped.

My back molars gnashed together as I struggled to ignore his comment. Letting him bait me the other day had been a mistake. The more Gabe knew something was a trigger for me, the more he went for it.

I kept my face a blank mask. "Actually, I'm just returning from a meeting with Juliana."

Annoyance flickered across Gabe's expression. "Why are you wasting your time there? We'll be getting rid of her altogether soon."

"The stables aren't getting the support they need, but I'll make sure that changes. Juliana and I came up with a lot of great ideas. Horseback camping trips, a camp for kids, maybe even having a horse whisperer come and speak."

A muscle in Gabe's cheek fluttered. "Dad likes my polo idea."

"Polo is for the Hamptons or Florida, not here. The stables have always been the heart of this place, and we don't want to lose that."

I couldn't handle losing it. Not when it was one of Clara's favorite places. *"Don't you just feel at peace here? It's like a little bit of heaven right here on Earth."*

Gabe's eyes narrowed. "How the hell would you know what's important to The Peaks? You're never here."

He said it as if it were my choice. As if I'd bailed on my family.

"Dad sent me back east. It wasn't my choice."

Gabe scoffed. "Sure. Like you didn't prime him for that because you knew I wanted the New York properties."

My eyes flared. I'd always thought Gabe had wanted The Peaks because he knew how important it was to our father. I'd had no idea he wanted to be in New York. "I didn't know. I thought you were happy here."

He rolled his eyes. "Bumfuck middle of nowhere versus Manhattan? Like that's a choice. Don't play all innocent and '*I care about you.*' I know it's an act. Dad's going to give me control when he retires, and I'm not letting you fuck that up."

Gabe took off, shoulder-checking me as he passed.

I didn't move for a moment. Couldn't. It was as if the weight of all the distance and mistrust between my brother and me settled over me. I'd hoped that things would ease with time. Get better. But I wasn't so sure this could be fixed.

My hand slipped into my pocket, seeking the little piece of metal that always grounded me. The way I'd once let Grae ground me in tumultuous times.

"Everything okay, sir?"

I blinked, taking in the bellhop. "Yes. Sorry. Just lost in my thoughts."

He smiled at me. "I know how that is. Just let me know if you need anything."

I nodded and headed in the direction of my office. Jalen was at his desk, fingers flying across the keys, but he paused as I approached. He winced. "The meeting went that bad?"

I shook my head. "Run-in with Gabe. The meeting was good."

A mixture of empathy and concern filled Jalen's face. "You going to be okay?"

"I'll deal. There's not really another choice, is there?"

Jalen's mouth pressed into a firm line, but he nodded, not speaking whatever was on his mind.

"I'm going to get some things in place for staffing at the stables. Can you pull up their budget for me?"

"I'll send it to your email."

"Thanks." I headed into my office, shutting the door behind me.

As I sank into my chair, I sighed. It wasn't even lunchtime, and I was exhausted. I pulled my phone out of my pocket and stared down at the screen, reading Grae's text for the millionth time. *"All good."* They were the same two words that had been there since last night. But they pissed me off. They were a brush-off.

My back teeth ground together. The urge to reply and try to tease more information out of her ate at me. But I knew why she'd put the walls of polite indifference back into place. That one moment of almost giving in to the thing I wanted more than my next breath and then pushing her away.

The pull to take it all back, show up at her door, and lose myself in her mouth and body was so strong. And that was exactly why I resisted. The ferocity of that pull was dangerous. Lethal.

I dropped the phone onto my desk, turning it over so I wasn't tempted. Instead, I opened my computer and got to work pulling employee applications, adjusting budgets, and sending possible new hires to Juliana.

A knock sounded on my door.

"Come in."

Jalen hurried in. "We've got a problem."

That familiar headache was gathering behind my eyes again. "What now?"

"Clive Jones is here."

I stiffened. My father hadn't said a word about him coming into town today. It made sense that he would want to scope out the facilities for his retreat, but my dad would've at least given us a heads-up. Clive and his financial clients were too important to Dad for him to risk anything but complete perfection.

"Is he meeting with Gabe?" I hated to admit it, but if he was, it was a smart move on Gabe's part. A face-to-face to see what Clive hoped to get out of the retreat.

Jalen looked worried. "Apparently, he's supposed to meet with both of you. He wants to hear the initial plans for the retreat. He said when he arrived that Gabe had confirmed the meeting via email."

The stream of curses that flew out of my mouth would've made a sailor blush.

Jalen handed me an iPad. "This has all the particulars of how many will be attending and what they need access to while they're here in terms of technology and meeting rooms. You're good at thinking on the fly. Read and walk."

I *was* good at thinking on the fly, but this was another level. I pushed to my feet, shoved my chair back, and headed for the door. "Where are we meeting?"

"Conference room."

"Let's go. I knew Gabe was pissed, but this is getting out of control."

Jalen sent me a sidelong look. "I would've quit a long time ago."

Unease settled in my gut as Grae's words about leaving and what Clara would want played in my head. But I didn't have time to think about that right now. Instead, I scanned the few pages about Clive's company and those who would be attending the retreat. The focus was on leadership and getting the heads of his various divisions to work together.

My mind spun, trying to come up with a cohesive plan in a matter of minutes. As I strode into the conference room, I found Gabe doing his best to charm Clive. He sent me a smirk. "So nice of you to join us, Caden."

I strode toward Clive and extended my hand. "Good to see you again. How was the helicopter ride from Portland?"

Clive sent me a warm smile, the deep brown skin around his eyes crinkling. "Smooth as always. How does it feel to be back at The Peaks?"

"These mountains always feel like home."

"There's nothing like that." He tapped the back of a chair. "I'm looking forward to the gala as well. It's such an important cause."

I swallowed the burn in my throat. "Thank you. It means a lot to us, as well. Clara brought out the best in us all. It's only fitting that she keep doing that now."

Clive's expression softened. "That's an incredible way to frame a loss."

Gabe cleared his throat, breaking the moment. "Let's have a seat. I've had the kitchen prepare a tasting menu so you can decide what you'd like served during the retreat."

Clive nodded. "Thank you. The food here is always impeccable. But I'll be honest. I need this event to go above and beyond. We're having some internal issues at Cornerstone, and I want this retreat to turn us around."

Gabe grinned. "Well, let's tell you what we have in mind. Caden, why don't you start?"

Asshole. I tried to ignore the fact that my brother was determined to throw me under the bus and focused on Clive. "Can you tell me what you think the biggest issue is with your leadership team?"

Clive leaned back in his chair, studying me thoughtfully. "Good question. As we've grown our financial services, my people stopped trusting each other somewhere along the line. I like that they're striving to be the best, but it's become incredibly cut-throat, and we're struggling because of it."

I nodded, giving myself a second to mull that over. It was so incredibly familiar, yet I hadn't found a solution for my family. "If that's the case, I think we need to do something a bit more unconventional."

Clive motioned for me to go on.

"We have four days, correct?"

"We do, and the gala's on the fifth."

"For the first two days you're here, I don't think we should have any shop talk."

Gabe had just taken a sip of coffee and started choking. "You've got to be kidding me. Who wastes that kind of time when you've got your entire international team together?"

Clive held up a hand. "Let me hear him out."

I leaned forward in my chair. "You need to remove those outside pressures and get to know each other again. You need your team to reinvest in one another. To see that each person's successes belong to the entire team. To do that, you need time, and to see each other as human beings, not just competitors."

Clive was quiet for a moment, tapping a finger against his water glass. Then a smile spread across his face. "I like it. Tell me how we do that."

"I was thinking we'd start at the barn. I know you're used to all the luxuries, but I'd like to do a camping trip."

Gabe sputtered something unintelligible, but I pressed on.

"No phones or devices. Just your team, the horses, our guides, and the great outdoors. Nothing will remove walls faster than that."

Clive chuckled. "You know, Caden, I think that might just be crazy enough to work."

I grinned back at him, but that grin died the moment I caught sight of Gabe. Because there was murder in my brother's eyes.

Chapter Fifteen

Grae

I FLIPPED MY PHONE BETWEEN MY FINGERS AS I LEANED against the outside of the cottage office, worry niggling at me. I'd texted Caden hours ago to see if he could go to family dinner this weekend to keep up our façade, but he hadn't responded. It was probably nothing; the man was practically running an empire, but still, something didn't feel right.

It didn't matter how much his rejection the other night had stung. I couldn't turn off my care for him. Flipping my phone right-side up, I unlocked it and pulled up an internet browser. I typed in *The Peaks* and hit call. Someone answered a second later.

"Good afternoon, you've reached The Peaks. How may I help you?"

"Hi. Can you please connect me to Caden Shaw's office?"

There was a brief pause. "May I say who's calling?"

"Sure, it's um, his girlfriend. Grae." I winced at the word *girlfriend*, but I was worried they might refuse to connect me otherwise.

"Oh, of course. One moment, please."

A second later, a male voice came across the line. "So, this is the famous girlfriend I keep hearing whispers about."

There was a warm, teasing quality to the man's voice that made me like him immediately. "Famous, huh?"

He chuckled. "You've got the staff in quite a tizzy that the un-gettable has finally been gotten."

If only they knew it was one big lie. "I'm not sure about that, but yes, I'm Grae."

"Grae, it's nice to meet you over the phone. I'm Jalen. I keep Caden's life from going off the rails."

I laughed. "I hope you're getting paid well for that."

His rich laugh boomed over the phone. "That I am. Now, what can I do for you?"

"I was hoping you might know where Caden is."

Jalen was quiet for a moment. Suddenly, I felt like a girlfriend checking up on the partner she suspected of cheating. "You don't have to tell me. I just wanted to make sure he was okay."

"I'm actually not sure where he is. Between you and me, he had a tough meeting this morning, and I think he needed to blow off some steam."

My chest tightened. "His dad or Gabe?"

"Gabe," Jalen said with a sigh.

"Thanks for the heads-up. If you see him, will you give me a call?" I asked.

"Sure thing."

Jalen took down my number, and we said our goodbyes. When I hung up, I stared at my phone, trying to decide where Caden might have gone. The truth was, I didn't have the first clue where he might try to find solace these days. I only knew where the Caden of years ago escaped to.

A little flicker of something that felt a lot like hope sprang to life in my chest. I opened the screen door and poked my head in. "I'm done for the day, so I'm taking off."

Noel looked up with a frown. "We were going to grab beers."

"Later this week? I've gotta check on something."

Eddie's brows pulled together. "Everything okay?"

I nodded. "It will be."

I didn't wait for more questions, just headed for the parking lot, thankful I'd driven this morning. Beeping my locks, I hopped in and started the engine.

My brain knew the route to where I was going so well, I didn't even have to think about it. Because I'd never stopped going there. Even if Caden had given up on our spot, I never had.

It only took me about fifteen minutes to get to the trailhead, then a ten-minute walk to the log that overlooked the creek. Each step made my heart beat faster. I stilled as I caught sight of the large form sitting with his back to me.

Caden was tall. Six foot three inches with broadly muscled shoulders. Yet, sitting there, he looked small. Almost like a little boy.

An ache took root in my chest. And it spurred my feet into motion.

Caden didn't look up as I approached, but I didn't let that stop me. I rounded the log and sat next to him, just like I'd done a million times before. I didn't say anything, just sat. He'd talk when he was ready.

I didn't know how much time passed before Caden finally uttered two words and then a sentence that nearly shattered me.

"It's broken. The kind that won't ever be fixed. But I just keep trying."

Grief dug its claws into my heart. "What happened?"

"Gabe scheduled a meeting with an incredibly important guest and didn't tell me about it. The meeting required hours of prep, but I had less than five minutes."

I studied the man next to me. "But you pulled it off."

Caden glanced over at me. "What makes you say that?"

I shrugged. "I know you. I know you thrive under pressure, and you understand people. What makes them tick. I bet you had the person pegged in two minutes and gave them everything they needed."

His lips twitched, but the hint of humor didn't reach his eyes. "It's a high, coming up with something on the spot like that, knowing the stakes, and making a stab in the dark, just hoping your instincts are right."

"And they were." There was no doubt in my mind.

Caden nodded, turning his gaze back to the water. "I should be happy. Celebrating."

"But Gabe ruined it."

"He hates me."

There was no emotion in Caden's voice. It was as if he were totally and completely defeated. I despised everything about it. There was no teasing or spark of life. Not even anger. Just nothingness.

And I couldn't fix it for him. I would've done anything to be able to. But all I could do was sit in it with him.

I leaned into Caden. He didn't move for a moment but then wrapped an arm around me. I nestled against his side and pressed a hand over his heart. "You're a good man."

The muscles tensed beneath my palm. "Don't."

"You're a good man."

Caden swallowed. "Gigi…"

"You are. The best. Always there for your mom. The best friend to Nash. Always jumping in when someone needs you."

He glanced down at me, our gazes locking. "I thought you wanted to murder me."

I shrugged. "Murder's my love language, remember?"

I headed toward The Brew as the early morning light filtered through the trees. I needed the most massive cup of coffee known to man. I'd tossed and turned all night, worrying about Caden. Hoping he was okay and hating that he didn't have the kind of familial support I did.

"G."

My head lifted to find Lawson walking out of the coffee shop and café. I grinned, crossing to him and throwing my arms around his waist.

His arms came around me in answer. "What's this for?"

"Just remembered how lucky I am to have you."

Lawson squeezed me a little tighter and dropped a kiss to the top of my head. "Everything okay? Caden isn't dicking you around, is he? I'll—"

I pinched his side. "Stop it. Caden's fine. Can't a girl just appreciate her overbearing big brother?"

Lawson chuckled. "I guess so."

"How are the boys?"

A look of fatigue filled Lawson's face. "Good. Just a lot right now."

"I can call off early today and pick up Charlie and Drew from camp."

Lawson shook his head. "No, I'm good. I'm just realizing I might need some full-time help come fall."

My brows lifted at that. "Seriously?"

He squeezed the back of his neck. "Charlie and Drew have a million and one activities they need to be carted around for, and as much as I'd love to leave Luke in charge, he hasn't exactly proven to be trustworthy lately."

I winced. My eldest nephew had taken my brother's car for a joyride without a license and now only communicated in grunts. It was a far cry from the happy-go-lucky kid of last year. "Is there anything I can do?"

"I wish." Lawson gave me another hug. "We'll get through it. It's just the ornery teenage years."

I hoped that was it. I was tempted to ask if it could be feelings coming up about their MIA mom, but Melody was a no-go zone for Lawson, so I kept my lips zipped. "Just let me know if you need a night off. And we have family dinner this weekend, so you'll get a little spell then."

"I'm good. Promise."

But Lawson didn't like to ask for help for any reason. The fact that he was thinking about hiring someone told me that things were not great in his world. I hated to sic our mom on him, but I might have to. She loved spending time with her grandkids, and Lawson needed a break.

"Okay. I need coffee, so I'm heading in."

Lawson gave me a wave as he moved down the street to the station, and I made a beeline for The Brew. The bell over the door tinkled as I entered, and Aspen looked up from the counter, her red hair gleaming in the morning light.

"Hey, G. You're in early."

"I've got a kayak trip this morning."

Aspen smiled. "That sounds heavenly. I need to sign Cady and me up for one of those."

"You don't need to sign up. I'll take you guys whenever you want."

"You don't have to do that."

"I'd love to. We could bring Charlie, too." My nephew and Aspen's daughter were as close as two friends could be.

Aspen chuckled. "You realize they won't stop chattering the entire day."

"That just means they'll keep each other entertained."

"Then we can have girl talk."

"Sounds like the perfect day to me."

Aspen held up her hand for a high five. "All right. What can I get you?"

"The largest black coffee you have and that bran muffin would be great."

She arched a brow. "Rough night?"

"I haven't been sleeping the best."

Worry lines creased Aspen's creamy complexion. "Everything okay?"

"Just busy."

A scoff sounded behind me. "Maybe if you stopped wasting time fucking my brother, you'd sleep a little better."

I whirled around to face Gabe Shaw. I hadn't even heard the bell. "Charming as always, I see."

Something about Gabe had always made my skin crawl. His gaze lingered in the wrong places, and he always moved in too close, just like now.

"Just calling it like I see it." Gabe's eyes roamed over me. "But I can't say I blame him. Looking damn good, Grae."

I fought the shiver that wanted to surface. "Do you want something?"

He grinned. "Just waiting for my coffee."

"Not here, you're not," Aspen said as she rounded the counter. "I'd like you to leave."

Gabe gaped at her. "You're kidding me."

She just met his stare head-on. "I don't want any of the customers feeling uncomfortable in this establishment. Your behavior is doing just that."

Gabe scoffed. "I'm joking. We're old friends. Right, Grae?"

"Just ignore him. He's not worth it," I told Aspen.

"It's not something I can ignore, and you shouldn't have to either. I'd like you to leave, Mr. Shaw. Or I'd be happy to call Chief Hartley and ask him to escort you off the premises."

Red crept up Gabe's throat. "Do you have any idea who you're messing with?"

"No, but I'm sure you'll tell me. Men like you always do. But it won't change anything."

Rage blazed in Gabe's eyes. "I was trying to throw the local businesses a few pity dollars, but I should've known better than to bother myself with trash." His gaze flicked to me. "Slumming it is more my brother's style."

He pivoted on his heel and stormed out of the coffee shop.

I turned to Aspen, and it was then that I saw she was shaking. I crossed quickly to her. "Are you okay?"

She attempted to give me a smile, but it was wobbly around the edges. "I'm fine. I just hate assholes like that."

I studied my friend, wondering if there was something deeper going on. I hadn't known Aspen long and didn't know her history, but I knew that she was kind, funny, and an amazing mother. Still, there was a deeply rooted fear in her, too. "You sure?"

She nodded. "Come on. Let me get you that coffee."

I watched her carefully as she poured my drink and got my muffin. I didn't miss the slight tremble in her hands, but that was the only thing that gave her away.

"Here you go. Shoot me a text so we can figure out our kayak day."

I handed her a twenty. "Sounds good. Let me know if Gabe gives you any trouble."

She waved me off. "It was you he was trying to rile. Keep an eye out."

My stomach twisted. "I will."

With a wave, I headed out into the sunshine and hopped into my SUV. The drive to the office was only a matter of blocks. Soon, I parked and headed inside.

I lowered myself into my chair and took out my bran muffin.

Eddie pouted. "You didn't get me anything?"

I grimaced. "Sorry, pal. I got distracted."

"How easily they forget us when they get fancy new boy-friends," he grumbled and then winced.

I arched a brow. "Late night?"

His lips twitched. "You missed out."

"I won't miss the hangover."

Noel chuckled. "Especially when he's on that ten-miler today."

Eddie took a swig of coffee. "Boot and rally, my friends. Boot and rally."

I scrunched up my nose. "That's disgusting."

"I have to agree," Jordan said as he strode in from the back. "But do whatever it takes because we've got a busy day."

He launched into our assignments for the day, and we started prepping gear bags. Poor Eddie looked a little green.

I shot him a grin. "Regretting that boot and rally plan?"

"Maybe a little." He leaned his head on my shoulder. "You'll nurse me back to health, right?"

I gave him a shove. "Do the crime, do the time."

He stuck out his tongue at me.

Noel smacked him upside the head. "Let's get these gear bags in the vans."

Eddie begrudgingly followed as Jordan headed back down the hall to his office.

I lost myself in a sea of paperwork until the screen door slapped against the frame.

Noel shook his head. "Eddie puked in the bushes."

I made a face. "I did not need to know that."

A second later, Eddie appeared. "Today is going to be brutal."

I pushed to my feet and grabbed a ginger ale from the fridge. "Drink this. It'll help settle your stomach."

Eddie lowered himself to the couch and took the offered soda. "Angel on Earth."

I snorted. "Hardly."

Shouts sounded from outside that had us all clambering to our feet and Jordan running out from the back office. We hurried outside and stopped dead in the parking lot. There, in the back corner, where I always parked so I could be in the shade, was my SUV. And it was engulfed in flames.

Chapter Sixteen

Caden

THE PHONE ON MY DESK RANG, AND I PICKED UP THE receiver. "Caden Shaw."

"Good to see you're at your desk early."

The sound of my father's voice wasn't ever something I wanted to start my day with, but at least he wasn't reaming me out.

"Morning, Dad."

"I spoke to Clive last night."

Of course, there was no greeting back. No asking how I was. Business and nothing else.

"Did he get home smoothly?" I asked.

"He did, and he was very impressed with your out-of-the-box thinking."

I stayed quiet, sensing a *but* coming.

"That was a risky move."

I slid my hand into my pocket, my fingers finding the smooth metal disc. It was a miracle the charm hadn't faded away into nothing. "I know, but he needed something new. I had an idea."

"You're lucky it paid off. He wants to go with your plan."

I grinned, but the win didn't feel as good as it should've because all I could think about was how pissed Gabe would be. "I'm glad he liked it."

Dad grunted.

"While I have you, I'm going to need some additional staff and funding for the stables. There's been a shift away from that part of the resort, and I think it's a mistake."

My father was quiet for a moment. "Why?"

"People don't come to the rugged mountains for polo; they come for a ranch-like experience. At The Peaks, they can have that but still go to a five-star spa and a Michelin-starred restaurant at the end of the day. We need to give them both."

"I see what you mean. Draft a proposal."

"It's already done. Sending it to your email now."

My father grunted again. "You're doing good. I was right to bring you back."

I hated the surge of pride I felt at his words. I didn't want them to matter anymore. But some part of me would always be that little boy who wanted his dad's approval. "Thank you."

"You still need to work on your image. You've damaged it with all your galivanting over the years. Look at your brother. You need to bring that new girlfriend of yours to events so people see you've changed. If that's even possible."

He said it as if I'd terrorized small children or something. I went on dates—if you could even call them that. Occasionally, those outings were photographed. But my father thought I'd committed treason just because I hadn't settled down like he wanted.

My back teeth gnashed together. "Grae's coming to the gala with me."

"Wouldn't hurt to have her show her face around the resort before then, too. You've got a lot to make up for."

He hung up without another word.

I kept the receiver to my ear for a moment, listening to the dial tone. There was never a compliment that wasn't followed by a slap. I had to remember that. Distance from my father might have helped me remain numb to him, but now that I was in his presence again, that wasn't so easy. And it was killing me.

My cell buzzed on the desk.

I set the receiver back in the cradle and picked up my device. A text flashed on the screen.

> **Nash:** *G's SUV caught on fire. We're at Vacation Adventures.*

I was on my feet in a flash, striding toward the door. I practically ran Jalen over as I stormed out.

"Shit. Everything okay?" he asked.

"I don't know. Reschedule today's meetings. I'll call if anything changes."

"Or if you need anything," Jalen called after me as I jogged down the hall.

On fire. Those two words circled my brain as I headed for my SUV. Nash would've said if Grae were hurt, wouldn't he? Icy claws of dread dug into my chest.

I hit Nash's contact on my phone as I climbed behind the wheel. It rang and rang with no answer. I cursed as I started the engine.

The tires squealed as I pulled out of the parking spot and headed for the resort exit. I nearly came out of my skin, waiting for the gates to open. The moment they did, I took off down the mountain road.

Memories battered at the walls of my mind. Grae passing out in my arms. Running down the mountain trail to my car. Racing her to the EMTs. Her face so pale. The doctor telling us they weren't sure if she would make it.

I shoved all of it from my mind. She was okay. She had to be.

I made the fifteen-minute drive into town in eight. I caught sight of fire trucks and police cars, but I didn't see Grae.

Squealing to a stop, I jumped out of my SUV and ran toward the four hulking forms I recognized as Grae's brothers. Their heads came up at the sound of my footsteps.

Roan was the only one who moved. It was a slight shift that allowed me to see Grae's petite form between them all. My chest seized.

I shoved through them, pulling her into my arms and gripping her tightly. I couldn't speak for a moment. It wasn't until I felt the rise and fall of her chest against my torso and the beat of her heart that I could form words. "Are you okay?"

My voice was barely recognizable, even to my ears. Raw, gritty, ravaged.

Grae's hands fisted in my shirt. "I'm fine. It was just my car. I don't know what happened."

I knew I needed to let her go for a million different reasons. But it was the last thing I wanted to do. I inhaled deeply, letting the scent of honeysuckle and spice fill my lungs. I held on to that as I let her go but shifted so my arm was around her shoulders. I told myself it was what a boyfriend would do, and that I was just playing the part. But I knew it was a damned lie.

"What do we know?" I clipped.

Lawson's gaze narrowed on me. "Firefighters just put it out. They're doing a cursory examination now."

"Who reported it?" I asked.

Nash motioned to a couple talking to another officer. "Tourists from Seattle. They were walking to breakfast when they saw it. They called it in and shouted for help."

"They see anyone lingering around?"

Holt shook his head. "The vehicle was fully engulfed by the time they saw it."

I cursed under my breath and glanced down at Grae. She was pale. Too pale. Fear put my chest in a stranglehold. "Do you need something to eat? Is your blood sugar okay?"

Grae blinked a few times and pulled out her phone, checking an app. "I'm fine."

"You're sure?"

She nodded, showing me the screen. "See? Right in range."

A little of that fear lessened but not enough. I leaned in closer, my lips grazing the shell of her ear. "We need to tell them about the break-in."

She squeezed my waist hard. "No. This could've been some freak vehicle malfunction. Just wait."

My jaw clenched. Holding this back was a bad idea. But when I registered the pleading in her eyes, I couldn't go against her wishes. So much had been taken out of Grae's control. She needed it now more than ever.

"What's going on with you two?" Lawson asked, suspicion lacing his tone.

Grae scowled at him. "Caden's worried. Just like you four were."

"Yeah, but—"

Lawson's words were cut off as Fire Chief Ramirez and Rance strode up. Rance made a beeline for Grae. He looked as if he might try to pull her out of my hold, but I shifted my body so that wasn't possible.

He glared at me, but then his expression gentled as he turned to Grae. "Are you okay?"

She nodded. "I'm fine."

"This could've been really bad. You're lucky the SUV didn't explode."

"Not helping, *Rance*," I gritted out. It was then that I realized he was still in civilian clothes. "Are you even on duty?"

He flushed. "I heard the call come in over the radio, so I came straight over."

Of course, he had.

Ramirez cleared his throat. "I'm glad you weren't injured, Grae."

"Thanks for putting out the fire, Chief," she said.

Lawson was all business, shifting seamlessly into police-chief mode. "What'd you find?"

"We found the remnants of what appear to be fireworks." Ramirez turned to Grae. "Did you have your window down?"

She nodded. "I always leave them cracked in the summer. It's not like there are many car thefts around here."

Holt groaned, pinching the bridge of his nose. "Seriously, G?"

"It gets hot. I don't want my car baking for hours while I'm at work," she defended.

Ramirez held up a hand. "I do the same thing. Unfortunately, it looks like someone used that as an invitation to drop some fireworks onto your driver's seat."

Nash frowned. "We had a call yesterday evening about someone setting off fireworks in trash cans."

The fire chief nodded. "One of the dumpsters actually caught fire, and we had to put it out."

"But this is an escalation," Lawson said.

Roan grunted. "Someone likes setting fires."

Grae shivered, and I pulled her tighter against me.

Rance's eyes narrowed at the action.

I ignored him. "Do you guys have any leads?"

Lawson sighed. "We're pretty sure it's teenagers. There's been an uptick in random vandalism with no rhyme or reason for the targets. It's been going on too long to be tourists. It has to be locals."

"You need to find them. Even if they are teenagers, someone could've been killed today." There was an edge to Holt's voice. He knew better than anyone the damage angry teens could do. He'd almost lost Wren because of it.

Ice slid through my veins as I held Grae tighter.

She looked up at me, worry in her blue eyes. "I'm okay."

"Holt's right. You could've been killed. What if the SUV *had* exploded?"

Grae's thumb stroked in rhythmic swipes across my abdominals. "It didn't."

A muscle fluttered under Lawson's eye. "I'm putting additional officers on foot patrol, days and nights. I'll put a handful in plain clothes so we've got a better chance of finding them."

That was something, at least.

Grae blew out a breath. "Do you guys need anything else from me? I'm supposed to take a group on a kayak trip in fifteen minutes."

I jerked back. "Are you serious?"

She shrugged. "I've got a job. It's not like sitting around here and crying over my car will help."

Jordan strode up to our huddle and squeezed her arm. "You sure you're up for that?"

Grae nodded. "It'll be good."

He studied her as if he wasn't quite so sure. "I'll come with you today. You've had a shock. I don't want you out there alone."

"You don't have to—"

Jordan cut her off with a look. "It's good for me to get out in the field every now and then."

Grae sighed. "Okay."

I glanced down at her. "You don't have to do this."

"I know. I want to."

I told myself to release her, to let go, but I couldn't get my arm to obey.

Grae stretched up on her tiptoes and pressed a kiss to the underside of my jaw. "I'll be fine. I promise."

My arm slid off her shoulders, but the action was agony. "Call if you need anything. I'll deal with your car."

"Thanks."

As I watched her walk away, it felt like someone had taken a meat cleaver to my rib cage. The moment she disappeared, I turned to Grae's brothers.

"We need these assholes found. And now."

Chapter Seventeen

Grae

EDDIE PULLED HIS TRUCK TO A STOP IN FRONT OF MY HOUSE and glanced over at me. "Want me to come in? We can order pizza and watch rom-coms…"

I chuckled. "Thanks, but I think I'm going to shower and hit the hay. It's been a long day."

Eddie nodded slowly. "Need a ride tomorrow?"

"I'll just walk."

He opened his mouth as if he might argue but snapped it closed when he saw my face. "You've always been there for me when I needed you. I just want to give you the same."

I wrapped my arms around Eddie in a tight hug. "I know. Thank you."

The guys had been great today, but the tiptoeing was driving me a little nuts. Jordan had been practically on top of me all morning on our kayak trip, asking if I was okay every five minutes. Noel brought me lunch and then stared at me until I ate every bite. Eddie just watched me as if he expected me to break.

I released him, grabbed my bag, and hopped out of the truck.

With a wave, I headed to the steps of my cottage, coming up short when I saw a large figure sitting on them.

Caden looked wrecked. Dark circles rimmed his eyes, and his hair was disheveled.

"Hey," I said softly.

"Hey."

"What are you doing here?"

He shrugged. "Didn't like the idea of you being alone tonight."

Crud. I didn't need that. The current acrobatics of my heart in my rib cage was proof enough. "You don't have to stay."

"I want to."

Another chest flip.

"Okay." I was a dumb girl. I should've insisted he leave. That I was fine on my own. The last time he was here had felt like a slow-motion car wreck. Instead, I reached out a hand and pulled Caden to his feet. "How do you feel about breakfast for dinner?"

He grinned, and the action sent a zap straight to my middle. "I feel great about it."

We headed inside, and I dumped my bag in the entryway. "I need to shower real quick. Make yourself at home."

Caden nodded a little awkwardly as if unsure what to do with himself now that he was here. Dang, it was adorable.

I hurried down the hall and away from the pull that was Caden. I grabbed sweats from my bedroom and took the fastest shower known to man, with the water set to frigid, hoping it would somehow pull me out of my stupid-girl state. When I made it back to the kitchen, I felt a little more in control.

Caden was perched on one of the stools at the counter. "Can I help?"

I shook my head. The last thing I needed was Caden trapped in my tiny kitchen with me, bumping into me, brushing up against me. "I'm good. How do you feel about veggie and cheese omelets?"

"I feel great about any food I don't have to make."

I chuckled and set to work chopping tomatoes, bell peppers, and onions. I sauteed them all in a pan and then set them aside next to some freshly grated cheese. I felt Caden's eyes on me the entire time. Each brush of his gaze made my skin burn hotter.

I didn't dare look at him, or I might spontaneously combust. Instead, I poured the egg mixture into two different pans. After a few moments, I spread the cheese and veggies in the center of both. I folded over the sides and flipped one and then the other.

"How'd you learn to do that?" Caden asked, his roughened tone skating over my skin and leaving a pleasant shiver.

My mouth curved. "My dad. He's the omelet master in our house."

"I forgot about that. Breakfasts were either omelets by your dad or waffles by your mom."

I slid the egg creations onto two plates and put them on the counter. Then, grabbing two sodas and silverware, I took the stool next to Caden. "I still can't do waffles as good as hers."

Caden bit into his omelet and moaned. "Well, you've got this down."

His words made warmth take root in my chest. There was something about taking care of someone that I loved. Maybe because so many people tried to take care of me because of my disease. "I'm glad you like it."

Caden devoured his meal in a dozen bites and then leaned back on his stool, watching me.

I took a sip of Diet Coke. "What?"

"I'm trying to figure out if you're really okay. You've gotten better at hiding your emotions."

My fingers tightened around my fork. I'd had lots of practice perfecting my mask of *everything's okay*. It was necessary when people constantly worried about you.

I looked up at Caden and found that some part of me wanted to tell him everything. Maybe it was because he'd been that person for me for so long. Maybe it was because I'd just been holding everything in for years.

"I freaking loved that car."

Caden stared at me for a moment and then burst out laughing. "The car? That's what got you the most upset?"

"It was a damn good SUV." It was one of those old-school Range Rovers that looked as if it belonged on safari. I'd spent way too much money having the engine completely rebuilt and the upholstery refurbished. Now, it was a total loss.

Caden reached over and tucked a strand of hair behind my ear. His fingers slid down to my neck, squeezing gently. "We can get you a new SUV." Emotion blazed in his eyes, making the gold in them spark to life. "But I couldn't take it if something happened to you."

Caden pulled to a stop in front of the Vacation Adventures cottage. He looked rough, and guilt pricked at me. Sleeping on my couch wasn't conducive to good rest.

"Can you do dinner with my family tonight?" he asked.

I straightened, a trickle of unease sliding through me at the prospect of being around Gabe. "Sure. What time?"

"I'll pick you up at six. My dad's on my case about showing my more respectable side around the resort."

I hated the flicker of hurt that flared to life in my chest. Loathed the part of me that yearned for Caden to simply want me there. With him. "What's the attire?"

Caden tapped the wheel. "Cocktail."

I nodded, grabbing my bag. "I'll be ready."

"Thanks."

I slid out of the vehicle without another word. I didn't want to give Caden a chance to see the hurt I knew lived in my eyes. Apparently, I was fully living the dumb-girl life right now.

I hurried into the office. Noel and Eddie were both sipping coffee, staring at me.

"I thought you were walking to work," Noel said.

I glanced at Eddie. "Reporting in on my whereabouts now?"

He held up a hand. "He wanted to make sure you had a ride if you needed one."

My shoulders slumped. "Sorry. I'm grumpy."

The corner of Eddie's mouth kicked up. "Trouble in paradise already?"

I stuck my tongue out at him. "No. I'm grumpy because my car is basically ash, and I don't want to deal with insurance or getting a new one."

"We can take you where you need to go until then," Noel offered.

"Thanks," I said, sliding into my chair.

The hinges on the screen door squeaked as it opened. When I looked up, I cringed. Rance strode inside and then handed me a bakery bag. "Thought you might need a pick-me-up."

I bit the inside of my cheek. "You didn't have to do that."

"That's what friends are for, right?"

I wanted to scream. Using the word *friends* meant I had no reason not to accept the gift when it was the last thing I wanted to do. "Thanks."

"No problem." Rance's expression grew earnest. "How are you holding up? I can hook up your SUV at my cousin's shop."

"Thanks, but I'm pretty sure it's totaled."

"I can go car shopping with you, then. I know that's a pain."

The bag crinkled as I gripped it tighter. "I'm good."

Annoyance flickered in Rance's eyes. "I'm just trying to help."

"And she said she's good," Noel said, an edge to his voice.

Rance's gaze snapped to him. "I'm her friend."

Eddie leaned back in his chair, making an exaggerated show of being relaxed. "If that's really the case, then you should listen to her. Stop bringing flowers. Stop bringing gifts. And fucking listen to her when she says no."

Rance flushed. "This isn't any of your business."

"You make it our business when you do it in front of all of us," Noel clipped. "It's getting old."

Rance's jaw went hard, and he jerked his gaze to me. "I was just trying to help."

"I know," I said quietly. "And I appreciate it. But I'm good. I think what would help the most right now would be some space."

Anger flashed in Rance's dark eyes. "Message received." He stormed out.

Why did I feel like this wasn't over?

Chapter Eighteen

Caden

MY FINGERS TAPPED AGAINST THE STEERING WHEEL AS I drove toward Grae's cottage. The twitchy sensation had been with me since the moment she'd stepped out of my SUV and disappeared into her office. It hadn't left for a second. Jalen had asked if I'd had too much coffee that morning or picked up a cocaine habit he should be concerned about.

The truth was worse. I cared. I always had, but that care was rooting itself deep now, spreading and taking over. It was becoming dangerous. Yet here I was, driving toward my greatest temptation's house.

I'd tried all day to rebuild the walls I knew were crumbling. To reinforce them with the strongest steel. As a reminder of why I needed to keep that emotional distance.

Clara's face flashed in my mind. Her head tipped back in laughter, green eyes shining, so carefree. And then another image. Her in that damned hospital bed, so tiny and frail, fading away...

I pounded my fist against the steering wheel. Physical pain was the only thing that could fight off those images. The only thing that could keep them at bay.

I pulled to the curb in front of Grae's house and stared at it. All the pots with their arrays of brightly colored blooms. She was in every detail. The rocks she'd painted with her nephews that were scattered across the garden beds. The little fairies and gnomes sprinkled around. The rockers where I knew she sat and watched the sun go down.

Those details would be the death of me. But still, I climbed out of my SUV and let them swallow me whole. I took the steps one at a time, trying to rein in the urge to get to Grae.

Reaching the front porch, I took a deep breath and rang the bell.

"Coming!"

There was a musical lilt to Grae's voice that had my gut tightening and that pull flaring to life again.

The door opened, and I froze. Grae had a beauty that shone every single day, in every state, no matter what she wore or how tired she was. But I wasn't used to seeing her like this.

She wore a pale pink silk dress with straps so thin and delicate they almost disappeared against her skin. The fabric hugged every curve, dipping low in the front and showing just a hint of cleavage that had my mouth going dry. My gaze tracked down her smooth, toned legs to the strappy shoes she wore that I couldn't help but picture hooked around my hips as I took her.

"Gigi…"

She bit her lip. "Is it okay? It's been a minute since I had to dress up for something."

"You're gorgeous."

This image would be burned into my brain for eternity. Her white-blond hair was curled in waves that framed her face, and she'd done something to her eyes that made them seem impossibly larger. So large I wanted to get lost in them and never come up for air.

Pink hit her cheeks. "Thanks. You don't look so bad yourself."

Her eyes tracked over my navy suit and down to my shoes.

I chuckled. "I guess we clean up okay." I glanced behind her. "You set the alarm?"

Grae turned, punching in a code and then stepping outside. She shut and locked the door, slipping her key into a tiny clutch. "Good to go."

I offered her my arm, not wanting her to traverse the steps in those shoes.

Her eyes flared. "Turning into a gentleman, are you?"

The corner of my mouth kicked up. "Never."

She laughed, and the sound wrapped around me, warming places that had felt cold for so long.

We made our way down the steps, and I helped Grae into the SUV. Rounding the vehicle, I climbed in and started the engine.

Grae toyed with the clasp of her clutch. "So, it's your parents and Gabe?"

"And Lena, his fiancée."

Grae's lips pursed at that.

"Not a fan?"

"I've only met her twice, but she doesn't really seem like someone I'd want to spend a lot of time with."

I chuckled. "You and me both."

Grae was quiet for a moment, staring intently at her bag.

"What's wrong?"

She worried the side of her thumbnail in a telltale sign of nerves. "I meant to tell you. I had a little run-in with Gabe at The Brew the other day."

I stiffened. "What happened?"

"He was an ass, and Aspen threw him out."

My jaw popped as I worked it back and forth. "What did he say?"

"Something about wasting time screwing you. Some other colorful things. I just wanted you to have a heads-up."

I glanced over at her. "You don't have to go tonight. I don't want you to have to be around him."

Grae reached over and took my hand, squeezing. "No. I want to. I don't want you to have to deal with them alone."

My ribs tightened around my lungs in a vise grip. How long had it been since someone had wanted to protect me? I couldn't even remember. "Gigi…"

"I want to. If you turn around, I'll kick your butt."

My lips twitched. "Wouldn't want you using those knives on me."

She grinned. "Just remember that."

We made the rest of the drive in silence. Instead of parking in the lot like I usually did, I pulled into valet. Two young guys hurried toward us, opening our doors.

"Good evening, Mr. Shaw. I'll keep her up front for you."

"Thank you, Matt."

I rounded the SUV and took Grae's hand, weaving my fingers through hers. It felt right—too right. But I didn't let go. I just kept playing with fire.

Two bellhops held the doors for us. I didn't miss how everyone's gaze, both women and men, traveled to Grae. I couldn't blame them. She had the kind of beauty that held you captive. But it wasn't just skin-deep. Her light radiated from somewhere in her very core. It pulled you in and didn't let go. She was an addiction, and you'd do anything for more.

I guided us toward an elevator and hit the button to go up. "We're eating at Skyline. I hope that's okay."

Grae nodded. "It's been a while since I've eaten there."

I glanced down at her outfit again. "Where's your pump?"

She laughed. "Geez, leave a girl a few secrets. It's under my dress. There's a little pocket."

A little of the panic eased. "Oh."

Grae shook her head. "I have been doing this a while."

"I know. I just…" I worried about her.

"I get it." She sighed. "Trust me when I say I'm used to people worrying."

There was a sadness in those words that made my chest ache. "It's because the people around you care."

"I know."

But there was defeat in her voice. I saw it then, how people's care had become stifling. I squeezed her hand.

Grae looked up at me as we stepped onto the elevator. "Let's make you look all respectable and shiz."

I couldn't help it, I laughed. "So respectable they won't know what to do with us."

She grinned. "I can't remember the last time I wore a dress."

My eyes raked over her. "You should do it more often."

Grae's cheeks pinked. "This outfit doesn't really work when hiking up a mountain."

"You'd definitely break an ankle in those heels."

The elevator dinged, and the doors opened to a large restaurant that took up the entirety of the top floor of the lodge. Floor-to-ceiling windows made it feel like you were hovering in mid-air over the mountains. The views were unparalleled.

The hostess broke into a wide smile with more than a hint of lust. "Mr. Shaw, it's so good to see you again." Her words held a familiar purr to them, even though I'd met her maybe twice.

"Good evening, Candace."

Her smile brightened at my use of her name. "Your family's already here. Let me take you to them."

I glanced down to see Grae glaring daggers at the woman.

I squeezed her hand, and she looked up at me.

"It's *soooo* good to see you again," Grae whispered mockingly.

I choked on a laugh. "Jealous, Gigi?"

She let out an adorable little huff. "I'm standing right here. It's rude."

My smile just grew wider.

Candace stopped just short of the table. "Here you are." She reached out, her hand lightly grazing my arm. "Please let me know if you need anything at all." Her eyes locked with mine. "*Anything.*"

I stepped out of her grasp, my gaze going hard. "I've got everything I want."

She blanched and scurried away.

Grae fought to keep her laughter under control. "Now I feel a little bad for her."

"She went too far."

Grae's gaze lifted to mine. "That happens a lot, doesn't it?"

I shrugged. "Sometimes. People find out you've got money and think you're the ticket to a free and easy life."

"But money doesn't magically erase all your problems."

I brushed a strand of hair away from her face. "No, it doesn't."

"Are you two going to keep creating a spectacle, or are you going to join your family for dinner?" Gabe snapped.

"Leave them be," my mom said, a smile in her voice. "They're happy."

Grae squeezed my hand as I guided her toward the table. I gave her the seat next to my mother, the friendliest face in the crowd. My father's expression was hard and impassive, while Lena looked as if she'd just sucked on a lemon, and Gabe appeared to be a cocktail or two in already.

I pulled out Grae's chair, helping her into it. She leaned over to give my mom a quick hug. "It's so good to see you. It's been too long."

My mom beamed. "You, too. When Caden told us you two were seeing each other, you can't imagine how happy I was."

Lena's nose scrunched up as if she smelled something bad.

"Grae," my dad greeted. "How are your parents?"

Grae sent him an easy smile, but I knew her well enough to see that it was forced. "They're good. My dad's getting back into the swing of things with search and rescue, and Mom's enjoying reaping the benefits of her summer garden."

Lena snorted. "Gardening, really? Don't you have staff for that?"

Grae turned to my brother's fiancée. "It's one of her favorite hobbies. She'd never give the task to someone else."

Lena placed a hand on Gabe's chest. "I'm so glad we don't have to worry about that."

Gabe stared hard at Grae, darkness swirling in his gaze. "And what about you, Grae? How are you spending your summer?"

She kept her smile light. "This is our busy season, so I've been out on the trails and the lakes quite a bit."

"It must be wonderful to spend so much of your time out-doors. The foundation keeps me pretty cooped up these days," my mom said.

"I do love an excuse to get out there and enjoy what's all around us."

My father cleared his throat. "What will you do about that job of yours as you and my son get more serious? Lena has devoted herself to supporting Gabe and making sure she's present when-ever he needs her."

Lena practically preened under his praise, and Gabe shot me a sharkish grin.

Grae's spine stiffened. "We support each other in all our en-deavors. But I'd never give up the things that make me happy to wait by the phone. Caden wouldn't want me to. When he needs me, we'll figure out a way for me to be here."

My hand landed just above Grae's knee, her skin silky-smooth beneath my palm. My thumb tracked in circles. "She's right. I love that she has a full life, all her own. She's worked incredibly hard for everything she's achieved."

"And that's beyond admirable," my mom said with a smile. "I'd love to go on one of your hikes someday."

"I'd be happy to take you anytime. Maybe you, Caden, and I could go next week on one of my days off."

My mother beamed. "I'd love that. Just tell me when and where, and I'll be there."

Grae and my mom lost themselves in planning, discuss-ing options for where we might go and some of Grae's favorite places in and around Cedar Ridge. My mother came alive in that conversation with Grae, becoming more animated than I'd seen her in years.

Gabe tipped back another swig of scotch, his eyes bloodshot.

Dad studied us both, his gaze finally zeroing in on me. "Have you talked to Clive about finalizing the retreat details?"

Gabe stiffened, his knuckles bleaching white as he gripped the glass tighter.

"We had a call yesterday. I'm getting more of the pieces into place."

"I can't believe you're signing off on this farce," Gabe clipped.

My dad arched a brow in his direction. "The client made their choice."

"And what happens when Caden's woo-woo, kumbaya plan doesn't work, and the retreat's a disaster? We could lose Clive's business for good."

My father's eyes flashed. "If that's the case, then retreat planning will fall to you from then on." He turned to me. "You take a risk; you have to know there could be a cost."

My jaw popped as it clenched.

Grae took my hand under the table, her delicate fingers weaving through mine. "And what happens when it's a tremendous success?"

She asked the question as if it were a foregone conclusion. That was the depth of her belief in me. I wasn't sure if I'd ever had that before. My mom loved me but steered away from any talk of business and achievements. Maybe because my father was so obsessed with them. Gabe certainly hadn't supported me. And my father seemed to relish my failures. Clara was the only one who'd ever really believed in me. Until Grae.

My throat tightened as I looked down at her. She met my father's stare dead-on, not cowed in the slightest.

He gave her a placating smile. "You seem so sure."

"I am. Caden has a way of seeing to the heart of people."

Gabe scoffed. "Heart has no place in business."

Grae shifted her focus to him. "If you know what makes people tick, not just what they want but what they *need*, you can create a solution that will go beyond any expectation they could've dreamed up."

My father leaned back in his chair. "She has a point." A grin spread across his face. "We'll just have to see which of my sons has what it takes to lead the company into the next generation."

Gabe's hold on his glass was so tight I thought it might shatter as a lead weight settled in my gut. My father wouldn't be happy until we destroyed each other.

We were quiet as I guided my SUV down the mountain roads toward town, both lost in our thoughts after a dinner that felt more like a battle. Gabe had launched snide blow after snide blow that I'd tried to ignore while my father watched the show with glee.

"Is it always like that?" Grae asked softly.

My fingers tightened on the wheel. "Pretty much."

"I don't know how you keep going back."

I wasn't sure anymore either. "I can't leave my mom to deal with them."

I felt Grae's gaze on me in the darkened vehicle. "She gets scattered when they start getting mean."

"It's her way of trying to shove down the pain of her family falling apart."

"I want to junk-punch your dad and brother."

I choked on a laugh. "I don't blame you."

Grae was quiet for a moment. "If you walked away from this, you could still have a relationship with your mom."

My ribs constricted. "I can't let go of The Peaks. Clara loved it too much. Always wanted to preserve it for generations to come. And I can't lose my role in helping Mom with the foundation. It's the one thing that gives the pain of Clara's loss purpose."

"Do you really think your dad would shut you out of Clara's foundation just because you left the company?"

"I wouldn't put it past him."

Grae sighed. "I hate how much he controls you."

"I don't love it either."

Her gaze bored into me. "Just think about looking elsewhere. Think about how it would feel to finally be free."

Freedom was such a foreign concept. One that wouldn't be in my grasp until my father died—probably not even then.

I reached over and laid my hand over Grae's. "I'll think about it."

I turned onto Grae's street and instantly hit the brakes. Lights on fire trucks and police cars flashed in the dark. People filled the street. And flames danced in the air.

"My house," Grae gasped.

It was completely engulfed in flames.

Chapter Nineteen

Grae

THIS WASN'T HAPPENING. THE IMAGE IN FRONT OF ME couldn't be real. Flames twisted and danced against the backdrop of an inky-black sky.

"My house," I whispered.

Caden quickly pulled to the side of the street and parked. The moment the SUV stopped, I jumped out, rushing toward the crowd. Caden cursed, jogging to catch up.

Clint, one of the officers who worked with Nash and Lawson, stepped into my path. "Whoa. You can't go up there."

"I-it's my house," I stammered as if that would explain it all. The home I'd worked so hard to build for myself. Growing up with wealth had given me so many advantages, but the combination of that and my Type 1 diagnosis had made me determined to stand on my own two feet. I'd worked my ass off to save up the deposit for this place. Even harder to afford to fix it up and decorate it. And now it was going up in smoke. Literally.

Caden wrapped an arm around me, but I could barely feel it.

"Let them do their job," he whispered.

I turned to him, tears stinging my eyes as I burrowed my face into his chest.

"What do you know?" he asked, his voice gruff.

"Not much," Clint said. "A neighbor called it in ten minutes ago."

Tires screeched, and doors slammed, but I didn't look up.

"Is she okay? She wasn't hurt, was she?" Lawson demanded.

"No," Caden said. "We weren't here. We were at dinner with my family."

"G," Nash said quietly, his hand rubbing my back.

I didn't want to look up. Didn't want anyone to see me cry.

Another door slammed. "What the hell is going on?" Holt barked.

"We don't know yet," Clint explained. "They're still trying to get the fire under control."

I swallowed my tears, forcing myself to straighten, but Caden didn't let me go. He kept one arm wrapped around my shoulders as I turned to face my brothers.

A mixture of worry and anger lined all their faces.

Lawson's gaze flicked up to the blaze. "Did you leave a curling iron on or something?"

I glared at him. "No. And they all have automatic shutoffs now anyway."

Caden squeezed my shoulder. "Let's wait until we hear from the fire chief. He'll know how this happened."

A truck peeled down the street, skidding to a stop. Roan jumped out and jogged toward us, panic in his expression. "You're okay?"

Guilt swamped me at the sight of his pale face. "I'm fine. I wasn't even here."

A muscle ticked in his jaw. "This isn't a coincidence. Your SUV and then your house?"

Caden's hold on me tightened as he looked down at me. "You need to tell them."

Pissed-off energy crackled in the air.

"Tell us what?" Lawson growled.

I swallowed hard. "The other day, I thought someone might've broken into my house."

"What?!" Nash snapped. "Why the hell didn't you call me?"

"I wasn't totally sure. The door was open when I got home, and a picture was moved, but I didn't realize anything was missing until later."

Caden's muscles hardened to granite. "You told me nothing was missing."

I bit the inside of my cheek. "I thought it was a prank."

"What was missing?" Holt gritted out.

I stared at the pavement. "A set of pajamas from my hamper."

Curses filled the air around me.

"Why didn't you tell me?" Caden asked, his voice tight.

"I didn't want you to freak out."

"The question is, why the hell didn't you tell *me* what happened?" Nash snarled at Caden. "You're supposed to be my best friend. This is my fucking sister. I deserved to know."

"Hey," I snapped, shoving Nash's chest. "This is my life. My choice about who knows what. You want to be pissed at someone, be pissed at me."

"Oh, don't worry. We are," Lawson clipped.

Holt held up a hand. "Let's all take a breath. Start from the beginning."

I worried my thumbnail with my forefinger. There was no getting around it now. I told them about hearing someone outside my window and about the break-in. We went over the vehicle fire and the events of tonight.

Holt's brows pinched. "Has anyone been paying you unwanted attention?"

I swallowed hard, glancing at the firefighters who had now extinguished the blaze. "I went on a couple of dates with Rance. He didn't seem to get the message that it wasn't going to work out."

"Why didn't you say anything?" Lawson growled. "I would've talked to him."

"Because I don't want you fighting my battles. I wanted to handle it myself, and I have. He backed off."

"Unless he just torched your house," Nash muttered.

My stomach twisted.

Roan moved in closer. "Anyone else? Not just overt advances, but someone getting too close? Making you uncomfortable?"

I glanced up at Caden.

"Who?" he asked, his voice rough.

"Gabe," I confessed. "He's always made me uncomfortable, but in the coffee shop the other day, it was more. He was angry."

A muscle in Caden's cheek popped. "He couldn't have done this. He was at dinner with us."

Relief swept through me. The idea that Caden's brother might have set fire to my house was almost too much to bear. I took a deep breath. "This could all be a coincidence. Maybe bad wiring caused this."

Holt pulled out his phone. "She's right, but I'm going to have my team at Anchor run a risk assessment. If there's something to find, they'll get it."

"You don't have to do that—"

Holt cut me off with a look. "You're my sister. I'm still part owner of a security company. Do you seriously think I won't use every resource I have to keep you safe?"

"Grae!"

Rance strode toward me, still in his fire gear. "You're okay?"

I nodded. "Fine. How bad is it?"

He winced. "Not a total loss, but your bedroom is pretty much gone."

Tears burned the backs of my eyes.

Lawson glared at Rance. "Heard you've been giving my sister some trouble. I'm going to need to ask you a few questions."

Rance paled. "What? No. She and I are friends."

"That's not what I heard. I heard you weren't happy that she didn't want to keep dating you. Maybe you're one of those firefighters who has become a little too obsessed with fire."

Anger flared in Rance's eyes as he shot me a scowl. "She wanted to date this asshole, so I backed off. I was trying to be her friend, but obviously, even that isn't worth it." He turned his focus back to Lawson. "You want to talk to me? Call my union rep." Then he stalked off.

"Seriously, Law?" I snapped.

His jaw worked back and forth. "I needed to see his reaction in the moment."

"And now you won't be able to talk to him at all," Caden grumbled.

Lawson glared at him. "If you would've told us what was going on, maybe things wouldn't have gotten this far."

"Just stop!" I yelled. "Please, just stop."

"All right," Holt said, his voice going soft. "Let's get you somewhere safe for the night so you can rest. You can come stay with Wren and me."

But I didn't want to stay with any of my brothers. Not when they were in this heightened state and pissed the hell off at me and everyone else. I'd never hear the end of it.

Caden's voice cut through the night. "She's going to stay with me."

Chapter Twenty

Grae

MY HEART LURCHED. STAY WITH CADEN? AT HIS HOUSE? Where I'd be drowning in his scent and a million other reminders of all the things I couldn't have?

My brothers scowled at him.

"She should stay with one of us," Nash snapped.

"Or at Mom and Dad's," Lawson added.

"How about *I* decide where I stay because I'm an adult with a mind of my own?"

Caden squeezed my arm. "Where do you want to go?"

My gaze lifted to his, and I lost myself in the gold flecks of his hazel eyes. I was still fully living that dumb-girl life. "With you. Can I stay with you?"

He dropped a kiss to the top of my head. "Of course."

My brothers didn't say a word.

I looked up at the still-smoking house. "They probably won't let me get anything from inside, huh?"

Lawson shook his head. "They'll have to assess the structure first."

My shoulders slumped.

"I've got stuff at my place you can borrow for now," Caden said.

"I can get some clothes from Mads and drop them off tomorrow morning," Nash offered. "See if they can grab her insulin from the fridge."

Maddie was at least a couple of inches taller than me, but the items would hold me over until I could buy some new things. And I could always get some more insulin at the pharmacy tomorrow.

"Thanks," I said quietly.

"Come on," Caden said. "Let's get you home."

Home. I wasn't sure I had that anymore. Between someone lurking outside, the break-in, and now the fire, my house didn't feel so much like a home.

I let Caden guide me back to his SUV. I didn't say a word as he helped me up and into the vehicle or as he started the engine. We were completely silent as we made our way back to The Peaks. Even the guard at the gate seemed to get that we weren't up for chitchat.

Caden's SUV wound around the darkened roads of the resort until he pulled up to a house I'd never seen before. I knew he'd had one built, of course, but I'd never laid eyes on it until this moment.

Even in the dark, I saw it was gorgeous—a blend of modern and rustic, wood and glass. But the windows on the front had been treated with something that kept you from being able to see inside.

Caden pulled to a stop in the circular drive. Jumping out, he rounded the SUV and opened my door. I took his offered hand and slid out of the passenger seat.

He didn't release me like I expected. Caden kept a hold of my hand until we reached the door. He unlocked it and ushered me inside, moving to disarm the alarm.

I hovered in the hallway. The place was beautiful but stark. Everything was clean lines; not a pillow out of place. But there wasn't a whole lot of *life* in the space.

"It's gorgeous," I said.

Caden's gaze flicked to me. "Thanks."

I searched the space for any hint of him but couldn't find one anywhere.

"What do you need? Food? A drink? Sleep?"

I turned back to Caden. "Can I take a bath?"

The corner of his mouth kicked up. "Of course. Come on."

He led me down a hallway with countless rooms I didn't have time to peek into. "Here's a guest suite you can use. It's right across the hall from my room." He moved into the large space and to an en suite bathroom.

I nearly gasped as I took it in. The place was massive, with an oval tub under a window that I could've swum laps in.

Caden opened a cabinet under the sink. "My housekeeper stocks toiletries. I think there's some bubble bath under here. Take whatever you want. I'll leave a T-shirt and some sweats on the bed for you to sleep in."

I looked up at him. "Thank you. For everything."

Caden's Adam's apple bobbed as he swallowed. "Of course."

Then he disappeared out the door, shutting it behind him.

I slipped off my heels. The cool marble tile was a balm to my aching feet. I crossed to the cabinet and pawed through it until I found some rose bubble bath.

Starting the water, I poured in the soap and waited for the tub to fill. I shed my dress and underwear, letting them fall in a pile on the floor. Then I capped my insulin port and set the pump on the counter. I opened my clutch and pulled out my earbuds and phone. There were several texts I studiously ignored. Instead, I turned on my relaxation playlist.

The songs were a blend of instrumental tunes that I could lose myself in and were just what I needed. Turning off the water, I stepped into the bath. The heat had me nearly moaning as I sank into it.

I tipped my head back and closed my eyes, trying to think about anything but the night's events. Instead, I got lost in my mind and took myself on a hike to one of my favorite spots. Then I planned the perfect trek for me, Caden, and his mom.

The door to the bathroom opened, and I shrieked, my arms flying over my chest. "What the hell?"

Caden's broad form ate up the space, his gaze flying to the ceiling. "You weren't answering. I thought maybe you'd drowned."

"Turn around," I gritted out.

The second he did, I popped out my earbuds. "I was listening to music."

"You're probably going to have hearing loss if you were listening that loud."

"Will you hand me a towel?" I grumbled.

Caden pulled one of the expertly rolled towels from the shelf in front of him. He extended it behind him without turning.

I pulled the plug and stepped out of the water. It had already gone lukewarm. I must've been here longer than I thought. I took the towel from Caden, quickly drying myself, and then wrapped it around my body.

"Okay."

Caden slowly turned. His eyes tracked over every inch of me. The towel was huge, but I suddenly felt as if I were standing in front of him in nothing but lingerie. He took one step toward me. And then another.

I swallowed hard. He'd lost his suit jacket and had his sleeves rolled up, exposing those toned forearms.

"Are you okay?"

There was an edge to Caden's voice that had my belly tightening.

"Honestly?"

"Always."

"It feels like my life is falling apart," I admitted.

Caden stepped closer, the heat of his body wrapping around me. He reached up, tucking a strand of hair that had escaped my bun behind my ear. "We're going to fix it."

"I don't know if the house is fixable. It doesn't feel like my safe place anymore."

He frowned, his hand dipping to my neck and resting there. "Then we'll build you a new safe haven. A new home."

I scoffed. "The billionaire *would* say that."

Caden shrugged. "It has its perks sometimes." The gold in his eyes flared brighter. "Things are replaceable. *You* aren't."

His head dipped. He pressed a kiss to my temple. Then a kiss below my ear. My breath hitched. A kiss to the corner of my mouth.

The gold in his eyes was on fire when he pulled back. "I don't know what I'd do if something happened to you."

My lungs constricted. I couldn't inhale.

And then Caden was simply gone. There one second and vanished the next.

What the hell had just happened?

Chapter Twenty-One

Caden

MY FISTS SLAMMED INTO THE HEAVY BAG OVER AND over again as sweat trailed down my torso. Usually, this release would be enough, but it wasn't even coming close this morning. I threw a hook, followed by an uppercut, sending the bag swinging back and making the chain rattle.

"What demons are you exorcising?"

I whirled at the sound of Nash's voice. "How'd you get in here?"

He rolled his eyes. "You gave me an extra key and the code, remember?"

"Regretting that right about now," I mumbled.

He snorted. "You look like shit."

"You don't look so great either."

"My sister's house burned to a crisp last night. What do you expect?"

I grunted in response, my hands tightening in the boxing gloves.

"How about sparring with something that hits back?" Nash challenged.

I arched a brow. "You've let yourself go soft, man. Not sure you're up for that."

He scowled at me. "Let's see who's soft."

Nash crossed to the gear cabinet and pulled out a set of wrist wraps and gloves. In a matter of minutes, he was ready to go. "Maybe I can knock your piss-poor mood out of you."

"Whatever."

We moved to the center of my gym, where I'd taped off a ring. We touched gloves and circled each other. Starting with testing jabs, we reacquainted ourselves with each other—it had been a while since we'd sparred.

"How's Grae?" Nash asked, bouncing on the balls of his feet.

"Fine. She was still sleeping when I got up."

A muscle in his cheek ticked. He'd thought I'd left her in my bed. In reality, I'd poked my head into the guest room before heading down to the gym.

Nash threw a hook shot to my ribs. I turned my body to avoid the worst of the blow and sent a jab to his chin but pulled back on my force at the last second.

Nash shoved me with his gloved fists. "Don't hold back, or you're not gonna get this out of your system."

I hit him with an uppercut to the solar plexus.

He grunted and hit me with another hook, this one to my jaw. "That's more like it."

The blow stung and set off something in me. We traded blow after blow until my muscles burned and my chest heaved. I blamed my lazy defense on my fatigue when Nash's fist connected with my cheek, and my head snapped back.

"Shit! Sorry." Nash halted as I pulled off a glove and felt my face.

That would leave a mark.

I shook my head. "It's okay. I was getting lazy."

Nash studied me for a moment. "You gonna tell me what's got you spiraling? It's more than the fire."

I ground my teeth together. Nash didn't see me quite as clearly as Grae did, but we'd been friends for most of our lives. He saw enough.

"It was a long night, that's all. A lot of shit has been going down."

Nash shoved me. "Shit you should've told me about."

"Gigi didn't want me to. I wasn't going to betray her. Not even to you."

He let out a growl. "It's more than that. You've been locking me out. You tell me some of what's going on but not enough to let me actually be there for you. Something's been eating you up these past few years, and it hurts like hell that you won't trust me with it."

I ripped off my gloves. "It's not about trust."

"The hell it's not. When I was a mess over Maddie, I came to you. Told you shit I'd never confessed to anyone else."

Raw guilt clawed at my insides. "I know."

"So, tell me what the hell is going on with you."

I threw my gloves against the wall, sending a photograph crashing to the floor. "I can't care about her."

Nash stilled. "Can't care about who?"

My gut hollowed out as if I hadn't eaten in weeks. "You know who."

Nash's nostrils flared as he struggled for composure. "But you do care about her."

"I can't." Panic raced through my veins, leaving fire in its wake.

"Why not? I wasn't crazy about the idea in the beginning, but it's clear you two are good for each other. You get one another in a way I'm not sure anyone else does."

Bile surged up my throat, and I swallowed it down. "I can't care about her and lose her. I can't."

Nash stilled. "Caden…"

"I've been down that road. It broke something in me. I don't know that I'm built to let someone in like that ever again." Especially someone who was already at risk like Grae. Her diabetes meant any one of a million different factors could send her over the edge.

Nash stared at me, breathing hard. "I can't imagine what you went through losing Clara—"

"Don't," I clipped.

"You have to talk about this. About her. This, the shit with your family, it's destroying you. And if you're not careful, it'll ruin the best thing to ever happen to you."

That invisible vise tightened around my rib cage again. I felt trapped. I couldn't let myself go there with Grae, but I couldn't let *her* go either. No matter what direction I moved in, petrifying fear awaited.

My lungs burned as black spots danced in front of my vision.

The ambulance sirens blared as we took each turn as quickly as possible, but my ears had grown numb to it over the past twenty minutes. My body had lost all feeling as I sat contorted in my seat in the front of the rig.

I couldn't risk taking my eyes off Grae. As if my gaze not faltering was somehow keeping her alive. Breathing. But barely.

She'd turned a color that almost matched her name, and all I could think about was how Clara had looked as she passed. The way her hand had gone limp in mine when she ceased to be.

I bit the inside of my cheek until I tasted blood. Grae couldn't die. The Universe wouldn't be that cruel.

"Heart rate's dropping," the EMT in the back yelled.

"What does that mean?" I asked, panic gripping my voice in a stranglehold.

The EMT next to me pressed his foot down on the accelerator. "That we have to move."

My breath caught in my lungs as a series of beeps sounded, and the EMT in the back cursed as she pulled things out of drawers.

"Almost there," the guy next to me said.

Tires screeched as he turned into the hospital parking lot. He gunned it to the emergency room, skidding to a stop.

An alert sounded from the back.

"She's coding," the woman shouted.

The back doors of the ambulance flew open to people with scrubs. "Get her to trauma three."

The EMT climbed right on top of the gurney as they rolled it out and began chest compressions as a doctor covered Grae's mouth with something.

I stumbled out of the ambulance, running after them. A woman stepped in front of me as we reached a set of double doors. "You can't go back there. I'm sorry."

"I'm with her. She's my—" I couldn't finish that sentence. My what? My friend? That didn't come close to cutting it. Grae was my whole world.

The dark skin around the woman's eyes crinkled in empathy. "The doctors need to work on her."

"Please." My voice cracked, tears filling my eyes. "I need to know she's okay."

The woman squeezed my shoulder. "Let me try to get an update for you. Wait here."

I stepped to the side of the wide hallway as she disappeared. The chaos of the emergency room was just background noise. The only thing I heard was the pounding of my heart and the roaring of blood in my ears.

It felt like an eternity until the woman reappeared, but it might've only been minutes. Her face was a blank mask. "Are you family?"

"Yes," I croaked. The Hartleys were more family to me than anyone else.

"Doctors are working on her now."

"Grae," I told the woman. "Her name is Grae."

"They're working on Grae now. Her heart stopped, but they were able to get it beating again. We're stabilizing her, and then we'll run tests to figure out what's going on."

Her heart. The thing that kept Gigi alive. Breathing.

Everything hurt. It was the kind of agony I never wanted to experience again.

The nurse cleared her throat. "We had to take this off Grae. Maybe you could keep it safe?"

She took my hand and placed a necklace in it. I stared down at the piece of jewelry. The present I'd given Grae on her thirteenth birthday. The sterling silver disc had a compass imprinted on it.

Because that was always what she'd been for me. The one person who could help me find my way. And now, I might lose her.

"Shit, Caden. Breathe. You're going to pass out."

But I couldn't. Couldn't get my lungs to obey. The vise was too tight.

"Follow me. Shallow at first."

I could just make out Nash through the haze. He raised and lowered his hand in tiny movements. I tried to track them and get my body to follow.

There was nothing at first but a burning fire in my lungs. Then the smallest hint of reprieve came—a brief burst of oxygen.

"That's it. Nice and easy."

My breaths slowly deepened until the black spots abated. I collapsed onto the bench behind me, my chest still aching.

Nash stared down at me.

I didn't say anything, couldn't. I couldn't even force myself to look at him.

"Caden…"

"It's nothing."

He gripped my shoulder, squeezing. "That wasn't fucking nothing. That was you having a panic attack and almost passing out."

I shoved to my feet, unwinding the wraps from my hands. "I've just been under a lot of stress, and last night didn't help."

"You need to talk to someone. If it's not me, then maybe a therapist."

My gut tightened. "I don't need to see a shrink."

"Then talk to Grae."

I stilled, the wraps wadded up in my hands. She'd always been my person. The one whose feet I laid my burdens at. The one who understood me best. Maybe that was why my head was so screwed up now. Because I didn't let myself fully have her anymore. "I'll think about it."

A muscle in Nash's jaw ticked. "Don't hurt her."

I tossed the wraps into the hamper.

"If you can't get your head on straight, if you're not willing to try, then you need to let her go."

Pain swept through me, a vicious flood taking out everything in its path. The idea of walking away from Grae and not having her in my life, even in this limited capacity, was almost too much for me to take. Even though I knew I should, I didn't think I was strong enough.

"Tell me you hear me," Nash gritted out.

"I hear you."

He clapped me on the shoulder. "I'm always here for you. Whatever you need. If you decide you can trust me."

Guilt churned low in my gut. "I'm sorry, I—"

"Don't apologize. Just know I'm here whenever you're ready. And don't make my sister collateral damage."

I jerked my head in a nod.

We put away our gear and headed up the stairs.

Music sounded from the kitchen; some oldies tune that was all sunshine and rainbows…the opposite of my current mood.

We followed the sound and the scent of something delicious. As we came into the room, I stopped short. Grae wore a pair of my basketball shorts that looked more like pants and a T-shirt that could've been a dress. Her hips swung back and forth as she sang loudly and off-key about walking on sunshine as she pulled something out of the oven.

Setting the casserole dish on the stove, she turned around and shrieked. Her hand flew to her chest. "Geez, make a little noise when you enter a room, would you?"

Grae's eyes narrowed on my face, and then her gaze snapped to her brother. "What the honeysuckle is wrong with you?"

Chapter Twenty-Two

Grae

CADEN'S CHEEK WAS ALREADY TURNING COLORS, AND I knew exactly who was responsible. I stalked over to Nash and gave him a hard shove. "Seriously?"

He stumbled back. "What did I do?"

"Punched Caden in the face from the looks of it."

Nash winced, sending Caden an apologetic look. "I'm sorry, man. I didn't mean to get you so good."

"So you *did* mean to get him?"

"We were sparring." Nash tried to excuse himself.

I held up a hand. "I don't want to hear it. If you're pissed that I'm staying here, talk to me about it. Don't punch Caden."

An arm came around me, and Caden pulled me into him. His chest was still damp with sweat, but he smelled like damned spring rain. "I'm okay, Gigi. We were just burning off some energy."

I looked up at him, searching. There were shadows in his eyes, ones I was desperate to know the source of. "He shouldn't be hitting you in the face."

"Caden socked me in the jaw," Nash muttered.

"Shut up," I snapped at him. "Don't think I won't tell Maddie what you did."

Caden choked on a laugh. "You don't mess around."

"No. I don't." I sighed. "Come on. Let's get some ice on that. Sit."

Caden obeyed, taking a seat at the massive kitchen island. Nash followed suit.

I searched through the freezer and finally found a gel ice pack. Wrapping it in a thin towel, I handed it to Caden. "Keep this on your cheek for twenty minutes."

The corner of his mouth kicked up. "Yes, Nurse Hartley."

I rolled my eyes and moved back to the stove. "I made tomato and mozzarella quiche."

"That sounds amazing," Caden said.

"Got enough for one more?" Nash asked hopefully.

I sent him a scathing look. "I should make you watch us eat it."

Nash pouted. "But you'd never do that because you know it's my favorite, and you love me."

I scoffed. "Everything's your favorite."

"I've got a good appetite. I think I'm still growing."

Caden snorted.

I dished slices of quiche and some sliced oranges onto three plates. "Water, milk, or OJ?"

"Water," they answered at the same time.

I poured three tall glasses and carried them over to the island. I took the stool next to Caden, giving myself some distance from Nash. I didn't trust myself not to deck my brother.

He gave me those puppy dog eyes. "Thank you, G. You're my favorite sister, and I love you the most."

"I'm your only sister."

He shrugged as he dug into the quiche. "Even if I had a dozen sisters, you'd still be my favorite."

"Don't talk with your mouth full," I scolded.

"It's a compliment to the chef," Nash said around another mouthful of food.

Caden grinned as he swallowed a bite. "This really is amazing. Thank you."

Warmth swept through me. "Thanks. It's nice to have someone other than me to cook for."

"You can always cook for me," Nash mumbled.

I shook my head. "I don't know how Maddie puts up with you."

"I'm generous with my sexual favors as payment."

I gagged. "I do *not* need to know about that."

Caden chuckled. "Maybe not breakfast talk, Nash."

A phone rang, and Nash slid his cell out of his pocket. "Speak of the devil." He tapped his screen as he slid off the stool and headed into the living room. "Hey, Mads."

I adjusted my insulin pump and then took a bite of quiche, but my gaze pulled to Caden. It was more than the shadows in his eyes; dark circles rimmed them, too. "What's wrong?"

He looked up. "Nothing."

I didn't look away, calling BS on his denial. "You look like you didn't sleep, you and Nash both look like you went ten rounds, and there's something in your eyes."

Caden reached for his water and took a sip, but he didn't answer.

"Tell me what's going on."

He spun his glass in circles. "You always see more than everyone else."

I saw *him* more than everyone else. Because I'd made a study of Caden Shaw since before I understood why. "You've had my back these past few weeks when I really needed someone. Let me have yours."

Caden's gaze lifted to mine, and I saw so much pain there that it nearly stole my breath. "I'm fucked in the head, Gigi."

My heart jerked. "You are not."

He chuckled, but there was no humor in it. "I am. Between my family and losing Clara, I don't handle things the way a normal person would. I don't do relationships for a reason. I don't let people past a certain boundary because I know it would destroy me if I lost them."

My heart thudded against my ribs. "Because you're scared."

"I'm not scared. I'm fucking petrified. I can't even let Nash in."

Pain flared in my chest as I looked at Caden. He'd been alone for so long. It was his doing, but at the same time, it wasn't his fault. I couldn't imagine how lonely he must've been. "You can change it. Choose a different path."

Caden shook his head, his focus dropping to his plate. "It's not that simple."

"I'm not saying it'll be easy, but I'm saying you have a choice. Choose to take just one step down a different path."

I knew what I was asking for without even saying the words. I was asking him to give me back some of what I had lost. But also more. Because I felt that pull between Caden and me. I knew now that it wasn't just in my head—it was too raw and real for it to be on me alone.

Caden's eyes lifted again. "Gigi…"

The doorbell rang.

I mentally cursed as Caden jerked straight.

"I'll get it." He strode out of the kitchen like the hounds of hell were on his heels.

What had I been thinking? Caden could have fixed things between us a million and one times, but he never had. I had to stop chasing after the glimmer of something he wasn't willing to fight for. Maybe this fake relationship would bring our friendship back, but it would never be more than that.

Caden reappeared in the kitchen with Lawson. I straightened. "Hey, Law."

He crossed to me and wrapped me in a hug. "You doing okay?"

I nodded. "I'm fine."

"I thought you were taking the kids out on the lake today," Nash said as he strode farther into the kitchen.

"Pushed it to tomorrow. I got a call from Ramirez this morning."

My stomach tightened. "Do they know what caused the fire?"

Lawson leaned a hip against the island. "It's all very preliminary. It will take a couple of weeks for the official findings."

"But he suspects something." Caden's voice had gone cold, emotionless.

Lawson nodded. "They traced the path of the fire, and it looks as if an accelerant was used."

Nash cursed, but Caden went unnaturally still.

"Someone tried to burn down my house." I couldn't disguise the tremor in my voice. I hated that little glimpse of weakness, but there was nothing I could do about it.

Strong arms came around me, cocooning me. Caden's body was so much larger than mine. It felt as if he could shield me from just about anything. And the heat coming off him in waves soothed something inside me.

"It looks that way," Lawson said. "Is there anyone who might be angry with you other than Rance or Gabe?"

I shook my head. "I don't think so. I mean, I'm sure I've pissed people off, but this is way too extreme for cutting someone off in traffic or getting the last muffin at The Brew."

Lawson nodded. "Holt has his team looking into things, but he wants you to consider a security detail."

"No," I clipped. "I'm not having a stranger follow me around."

Nash sent me a sympathetic look. "I know it feels invasive, but someone set your house on fire. What if you had been home?"

"They did it when I wasn't home," I argued.

Caden stiffened. "You set your alarm before you left. They shouldn't have been able to get in."

A muscle below Lawson's eye fluttered. "No, they shouldn't have. But they did. Which means whoever we're dealing with knows their way around a security system."

Caden's hold on me tightened. "She'll be safe here. No one gets onto the premises without being on an approved list, and I've got a state-of-the-art security system. I use Halo, the company out of Sutter Lake that Holt recommended."

Lawson nodded slowly. "That's a good start." He turned to me. "You need to be careful. No going places alone, especially at night."

The walls felt as if they were closing in around me, my freedom disappearing in front of my eyes. "I'll be careful. I promise."

"Is there any chance there could be trace evidence at the scene?" Caden asked.

"We've got a team going through it now," Lawson said.

"I hope that team doesn't include Rance," Nash grumbled.

Lawson shook his head. "It doesn't. I asked that he not be assigned to work any of the investigation side of this."

My stomach cramped. Just another reason for Rance to hate me. Great.

Lawson dipped his head to meet my gaze. "This is serious, Grae. Whoever this is, they're escalating. And they may not stop with the destruction of property next time."

I heard what he wasn't saying. That next time, they could hurt *me*.

Chapter Twenty-Three

Grae

I FLIPPED A PANCAKE ON THE GRIDDLE, HUMMING TO MYSELF as I did. For someone who didn't cook, Caden had a surprisingly stocked kitchen. We'd settled into a routine of sorts over the last week. I made breakfast every morning, then Caden drove me to work and went to his office. He'd pick me up at the end of the day, and we'd get takeout. Then we'd watch a movie or some bad TV and finally head to our respective bedrooms.

Caden was attentive and warm, but he'd erected a wall between us. That no-go zone I'd asked him to take down. The answer to that had clearly been: No.

I tried not to think about how much that hurt. How much I wished things were different. I had two choices. I could walk away altogether or take what he was able to give.

I saw now that it wasn't even what Caden *wanted* to give or not give. It was about what he was physically able to do. And if this was it, I'd take every last piece. I'd have him in my life as a friend. With time, I'd let go of my hope for anything more.

Footsteps sounded behind me, but I didn't turn around.

"Are those chocolate chip pancakes?"

The childlike hope in Caden's voice made me grin.

"With homemade whipped cream."

"I'm going to get spoiled with these breakfasts."

"Like you weren't already spoiled," I huffed.

He chuckled. "You have a point there."

I slid pancakes onto two plates and handed him one. "How's the retreat prep going?"

Caden crossed to the island, and we both sat. "Good. I hired a new staff at the stables. And yesterday, I went with the team to check out the camping spot. I think it'll be perfect."

"I'd love to see these high-powered CEOs on a camping trip."

"It definitely could be a good hidden-camera show."

I took a sip of my coffee. "You should do a day hike to the falls when they're up there. You could have their first team-building session when they reach the peak."

Caden glanced at me. "That's a great idea. Their defenses will be down if they're tired."

"Exactly."

He leaned back in his stool. "Maybe you should come work for me."

I laughed. "I think we would kill each other."

Caden grinned. "Hey, we've been cohabitating for over a week, and there hasn't been a single attempted murder."

I snorted. "That just goes to show my incredible restraint."

Caden shook his head, but a smile still played on his lips. "So, what's on your docket today?"

"I'm taking a group on the Cedar Line trail this afternoon."

He stiffened. "I thought you were staying at the office."

I toyed with the edge of my napkin. After everything that had happened, Jordan had thought it might be good for me to stick close to town, and Caden and my brothers had agreed. "It's been a week. Nothing else has happened. I need to get back to my life. And it's not like I'll be alone. I'm taking a group of eight people with me."

Caden's knuckles bleached white as his hold on his fork tightened. "I don't think it's a good idea."

I turned to face him. "This is my job. Jordan can't bench me forever. And I miss being out on the trails, teaching people about the area. If I don't get back to it, I'm going to go stir-crazy."

"You'll have your sat phone?"

"Of course. And a Taser and bear spray."

Caden's jaw worked back and forth. "Who's the group?"

"It's a family from the Midwest."

Caden didn't look convinced.

I gave him my best smile. "Would it help if I told you the dad is a former Navy SEAL?"

Caden's eyes flared. "Seriously?"

"We get bios on all of our guests so we know their fitness level and outdoor experience. I think I'll be good to go."

Caden stared at me for a moment, something unreadable in that gaze. "I just don't want anything to happen to you."

My traitorous heart ricocheted around in my chest. "I'll be good."

"Call me as soon as you get back?"

"I promise."

Jordan frowned at me. "I think I should come with you, too."

I was going to scream. "I'll be fine. I've got all my gear, and they're an easy group."

Noel glared in my direction. "He's right. It's not worth the risk."

"You guys sound like Caden," I grumbled.

Eddie smirked. "Lover boy not stoked about you going out on your own?"

"It helped that a former Navy SEAL will be on the trip."

Eddie's brows rose. "Really?"

"Yup."

Jordan sighed. "I guess that does make things a little better. But I still think I should come."

"You need to work out the scheduling for next week," I told him.

"I'll go," Eddie offered.

Jordan looked unsure.

"I only had the sunrise kayak trip. I've got nothing else for the day. Wouldn't mind getting out into the field."

"You don't have to do that. You must be exhausted," I said.

He grinned at me. "I'll sleep when I'm dead."

"You guys. I'm going to be fine. Navy SEAL, remember?"

A muscle ticked in Jordan's jaw. "Fine, but I'm going with you on the kayak trip tomorrow because there's no Navy SEAL on that one."

I blew out a breath but nodded. There was no use arguing. And I was tired of fighting these battles.

A door slammed outside.

Eddie stood. "Looks like the tour group is here. Let's get them loaded up."

Jordan and I greeted the family while Eddie and Noel loaded the equipment. It was actually two families—a group of aunts, uncles, and cousins—and they were thrilled to be in Cedar Ridge.

I chatted up two girls hoping to see a bear while Jordan gave our gear one last once-over. He turned back to me. "I think you're good to go."

I grinned at our group. "Let's hit the mountain."

The hike was exactly what I needed, and the normalcy of leading a group up the mountain was, too. I could forget the break-in, the fire…everything. I got lost in teaching the group about our surroundings and chatting with them about their lives back home.

By the time we were coming down and headed back to the trailhead, I felt like a part of their family.

Kathy, one of the moms, smiled at me. "Well, if you ever make it out to Missouri, we can take you on a hike."

Her husband, Mike, the infamous Navy SEAL, chuckled. "We don't have views quite like this one, though."

"It's pretty incredible to wake up to these mountains every day," I admitted. And it didn't hurt to be reminded of that.

Their youngest girl, Cindy, slipped her hand into mine. "I wanna lead hikes when I grow up. I could do this every day."

Kathy laughed. "You'll have to study hard in all your science classes. Think of all the plants Grae taught us about."

Cindy frowned for a moment and then nodded. "I can do it."

Mike grinned. "If my girl gets an A in science because of you, we're sending you a medal."

I laughed as we reached the trailhead. "Sometimes, you just have to see the practical applications of those annoying classes."

My steps faltered as we crossed the parking lot. Something about the passenger van wasn't right. And that was when I saw it. Every single tire had been slashed, and someone had smashed each window. But no one had touched any of the other vehicles in the lot. Only mine.

Chapter Twenty-Four

Caden

"WHAT'S GOING ON WITH YOU TODAY?" JALEN ASKED from his perch opposite my desk as we went over the final details for Clive's retreat and the silent auction items for The Clara Foundation gala.

I grimaced at my phone. I'd been twitchy all morning, hating the idea of Grae out on a trip alone. The only thing that had kept me from going with her was knowing how much having control of her life meant to her. "I'm fine."

Jalen arched a brow in challenge.

I fought the urge to squirm in my seat. "I'm waiting to hear that Grae's back from her hiking trip."

A grin spread across his face.

"Shut up," I mumbled.

Jalen's smile only widened. "It's good to see you like this. *She's* good for you."

His words only made me feel twitchier, as if my skin were too tight for my body.

A little of the amusement left Jalen's face. "It doesn't make you weak to care about someone."

Everything in me stilled. "I know that."

"Do you? Because from where I've been sitting for the past six years, you've done just about everything imaginable to keep people at arm's length."

I started to argue, but Jalen held up a hand to stop me.

"Don't get me wrong. You're friendly—warm, even. But there's an invisible wall that you don't let people pass. It's not healthy. You need to let people in."

I was quiet for a moment, letting the words land. I hadn't realized how much I'd been hurting the people around me by keeping them out. But after the conversation I'd had with Nash and now Jalen, it was obvious I was doing damage. "I'm sorry."

It was all I could say. I wasn't about to make a promise to change when I didn't know if that was possible. Sometime over the years, it had become ingrained in me to keep people out. And the idea of lowering those boundaries had panic eating at me.

"You don't have to apologize. I'm just happy to see that Grae is getting through."

Fear spiked in my gut, but I shoved it down, forcing a grin. "Don't go marrying me off just yet. This is new."

Jalen chuckled. "Just promise I can help plan the wedding."

I shook my head. He was hopeless.

My phone buzzed on my desk, and I swiped it up, hoping it was Grae. Instead, I saw Nash's name on the screen. I tapped accept. "Hey, man."

"Caden."

The lack of humor in his voice had my spine snapping straight. "What's wrong?"

"Grae's fine."

Those words offered the opposite of comfort. Instead, ice slid through my veins. "What happened?" I gritted out.

"I'm at the trailhead. Someone broke into the Vacation

Adventures van while they were on the hike. Smashed the windows. Slashed the tires."

I was already on my feet, striding out of my office. This wasn't a break-in; it was someone who was pissed the hell off. "I'm on my way. You're with her?"

"She's good. I promise. Pissed off more than anything."

That wasn't enough. I needed to see Grae with my own eyes, wrap my arms around her, and feel her heart beating against my chest. I picked up to a jog as I made my way through the lobby. "I'll be there in ten. Don't leave her alone."

A million thoughts flew through my mind as I ran to my SUV and climbed inside. Was this asshole lying in wait? Was he watching?

"You know I won't. See you in a few."

I hung up and started the engine. Images of Grae filled my mind as I took off. Memories of a lifetime together. But there were too many holes in it. Gaps that I had put there because I'd been so desperate to keep her out. Because I'd been a coward.

I floored it down the mountain road until I hit the turnoff I knew led to the trailhead. To Grae. I made the trip in nearly half the time it should've taken.

Gravel flew as I hit the brakes in the parking lot. I jumped out of my SUV and stalked toward the cluster of people.

A tall, broad man immediately clocked me and shifted so he stood in front of Grae. The move had Grae looking up. She whispered something to him, and he stepped aside.

The crowd parted, seeming to sense the feral energy swirling around me. Then I was in Grae's space, hauling her into my arms and holding her tightly.

She wrapped her arms around me, seeming to get that I needed this. "Hey. I'm okay. I promise. The only one that got hurt was Betsy."

I pulled back a fraction. "Betsy?"

One side of Grae's mouth kicked up. "The van."

I pulled her back to me. "It's not funny."

"I know." She ran a hand up and down my back. "I joke when the schnitzel hits the fan."

As I held Grae against me, I realized that I was trembling. It didn't matter how many walls I'd put up or how much I'd tried to reinforce them while the two of us had played this risky game of pretend. She'd snuck behind my defenses, and there wasn't a damn thing I could do about it.

A throat cleared, and I forced myself to release my hold on Grae.

Lawson studied us, an unreadable look on his face. "G, you had some things in the back of the van?"

She nodded. "A gear bag with extras of things and my pack that I don't bring on the hikes. It has a change of clothes in case of rain, some extra food, stuff like that."

He handed her a pair of gloves. "I want you to go through them and make sure nothing is missing."

"Sure." Grae donned the gloves, and I followed her as she headed to the van the crime scene techs were processing.

My gut tightened as I took in the sight in front of us. Glass was everywhere. The van's paneling even had some dents. I glanced at Lawson. "This is someone who is seriously pissed off."

A muscle beneath his eye fluttered. "I'd guess it was someone out of their mind on drugs, but there were two other vehicles in the parking lot that weren't touched."

Dread swept through me like an insidious inky cloud. "This was targeted."

"We have to assume so."

Nash gave me a chin lift as we approached.

"Thanks for calling," I said.

"Of course." His eyes tracked his sister as she moved to the crime scene techs with the two bags. "This isn't good."

Lawson shook his head. "I'd say this is likely a reaction to whoever this is, having their access to Grae removed. She's staying with Caden and is behind gates this asshole can't get past. He's angry."

My dread morphed into nausea. "What does that mean?"

"We need to hope he screwed up. Maybe he left some prints behind," Lawson said.

"You going to talk to Rance?" I growled.

Lawson nodded. "As soon as I leave here. But we can't only focus on him."

"We're going to interview everyone in Grae's life. See if they've noticed anyone hanging around that shouldn't be or anyone who has been unnaturally focused on her," Nash added.

That muscle under Lawson's eye fluttered again. "Not sure what the end game is with this. Are they trying to scare her? Just want her attention in some sort of sick way?"

My jaw worked back and forth. "You should talk to Gabe. I know he has an alibi for the fire at her house, but I'm not sure about the car fire."

"I will," Lawson assured me. "But you need to brace. He's not going to like it, and he could take that out on you."

"I'm used to my brother's wrath."

Lawson clapped me on the shoulder. "I'm sorry, man."

Grae straightened as she looked at the contents of her bag, her face going pale. I was moving before I consciously decided to. "What's wrong?"

Her pale blond hair swirled around her face as she looked up at me. "I had an extra change of clothes in this bag."

I looked down at the items spread out on a sheet of plastic. "They're right there, aren't they?"

Grae swallowed hard. "My underwear. They're gone."

Grae sat on the couch, her hands wrapped around a mug of tea. I paced back and forth in my living room as Lawson and Holt discussed our options.

"I can have a four-man team here by tomorrow," Holt said. "They can keep a low profile."

Grae shook her head. "I don't want a bunch of bodyguards."

"G," Nash urged.

"No. I'm staying in a gated estate. I'll agree not to go anywhere alone, but I'm not getting bodyguards."

My muscles wound so tight they felt like stone, but I couldn't stop moving. "What did Rance say?" I asked Lawson.

He sighed. "He said he was fishing this morning. Another guy saw his car at the lake, but no one actually saw *him*."

"I can't imagine him doing this," Grae whispered.

Holt turned to his sister. "This is an obsession. Someone who is mentally ill. And some people are really good at hiding that sort of thing."

She leaned forward, setting down her tea and dropping her head into her hands. "This is making me look at everyone differently. Even strangers on the street. I wonder if they're the ones doing this."

I strode to the couch, dropped next to Grae, and rubbed a hand up and down her back. "We're going to find them. You'll get your life back."

Her head lifted. "I don't want to feel like a prisoner."

I heard the words Grae didn't say. That she'd already felt like that for too long. She'd worked so hard to prove to her family that she could handle her illness and her life despite her diagnosis. Now, she felt like she was losing that. "You're not a prisoner."

"We just want to make sure you're safe," Lawson said.

"But at what cost?" Grae asked.

Holt sighed. "Okay. We hold off on a security team for now, but I want to put cameras at your work. I'll talk to Jordan about it. And no leading trips on your own."

Grae's shoulders slumped. "Okay."

Holt pushed to his feet. "I'm going to put these pieces into place and then go talk to Mom and Dad. They're freaked."

Grae winced. "I told them I was fine."

Lawson shook his head. "Would you be okay if this were happening to your daughter?"

"No," she mumbled.

"Give them a little grace."

Grae sighed and leaned back in her seat. "I'll call them again later."

Lawson nodded, and then he, Nash, and Holt headed for the door. I followed them out of the living room, and they stopped short in the entryway.

Lawson turned, pinning me with a hard stare. "Tell me you've got her."

My heart thudded against my ribs. Did I have Grae? I'd barely kept her alive all those years ago, had almost lost her.

Nash gave Lawson a shove. "Don't be an ass. He's doing everything he can."

"I want to hear him say it," Lawson growled.

"I'd trade my life for hers in a heartbeat." The words were out of my mouth before I could stop them. But they were the raw truth. I'd give everything I had to make sure I didn't fail Grae.

Lawson, Holt, and Nash stilled. Lawson studied me for a moment and then nodded. "Okay."

Nash hovered in the entryway as Lawson and Holt headed for their vehicles. "You gonna be all right?"

I jerked my head in a nod but wasn't sure if the action was a lie.

"Call me if you need anything."

"I will."

He pulled me into a hard hug. "I've got your back. Always."

A burn lit my chest as I released Nash and watched him walk to his SUV. He cared. And I'd been locking him out.

Closing the door, I flipped the deadbolt and set the alarm. I walked back toward the living room. I nearly tripped as I took in Grae on my massive sectional. She looked so small as she stared out my back windows into the surrounding forest. The look on her face was almost as if she'd given up.

That familiar vise tightened around my ribs as I thought about how determined this asshole was to hurt her. "Are you okay?"

Grae stood, picking up her now-empty mug. "I'm fine."

But there was no emotion in the words.

She crossed to the kitchen, rinsed her mug, and set it in the sink.

"Maybe you should lie down. Rest for a little bit."

Grae whirled on me. "I'm not breaking."

"I'm not saying you are. Just that you need to take care of yourself—"

She shoved at my chest, forcing me back a step. "I'm not weak. I'm not going to crumble."

"I know—"

"Do you? Because you sometimes look at me like you expect me to fall apart in front of your eyes. But you, of all people, should know better than that. I didn't break when I got Type 1. Or when you walked out of my life and broke my damn heart. And I'm not going to break because some asshole is trying to scare me."

Grae's chest rose and fell with each word, but I was frozen to the spot. All I could hear was *"broke my damn heart"* over and over in my head.

My body reacted before my brain. I moved so fast I couldn't have stopped myself if I'd tried. I was steps away, and then I was on Grae. My hands tangled in her hair as I pulled her face to mine.

The moment my lips met hers with crushing hunger, every wall I'd tried so desperately to keep up crumbled to dust. There was no doubt in my mind now. I knew I was ruined. But I didn't give a damn.

Chapter Twenty-Five

Grae

C ADEN TOOK MY MOUTH WITH A FERAL NEED THAT HAD heat licking through my veins. It burned. But that pain only stoked the pleasure coursing through me.

His tongue stroked mine in demanding bursts, and I gave as good as I got. I nipped his bottom lip, silently asking for more. For all of him.

Caden growled into my mouth as he lifted me, and I wrapped my legs around his waist. Then he was moving, striding out of the kitchen and down the hallway. I couldn't be bothered to try to see where he was headed; I just hoped it was toward a bed.

Each step ignited delicious friction against my core. I deepened the kiss, needing to drown in the heady warmth that was Caden.

He shoved open a door, and it hit the wall. A second later, he was lowering me to the floor.

The scent of him surrounded me as my feet hit the hardwood. I'd never been able to pin down exactly what it consisted of, just that it had always felt like home. Smelling it now, after so long, had a burn flaring in the back of my throat.

Caden pulled back, his eyes locking with mine. I saw gold fire in those depths. I didn't know how he'd kept that need hidden for all these years.

"Tell me I can have you."

My heart thudded against my ribs. "Yes."

Caden's fingers were on the hem of my tank, pulling it up and over my head. Then he stilled, his gaze tracking over my skin, the swell of my breasts in my bra, my bare stomach. His hand went to my pump. "I don't want to hurt you."

My fingers moved to the port site, unclipping the pump tube and capping it. "You won't."

Caden dropped to his knees then, and his lips skimmed across my belly, making me shiver. He trailed kisses around my port. "So strong."

That burn in my throat was back.

Caden's fingers hooked into my shorts and underwear, pulling them down in one swift motion. A startled gasp escaped my lips as he stared at the apex of my thighs. "So damn pretty."

He ran his thumb down my center, and my legs trembled.

He lifted one leg out of my shorts, taking my sock off at the same time, then removed the other.

"Spread your legs."

I squirmed in place. "Caden…"

That gold fire flashed as he looked up at me. "Don't hide from me. I want all of you."

I swallowed hard, moving my legs farther apart.

Caden's tongue flicked out, parting my core, and I gasped. There was no easing into things with Caden; he simply took. Each swipe of his tongue drove me higher. Two fingers slid inside me as his tongue circled my clit.

My fingers dug into his shoulders, and I worried I'd collapse. Caden's fingers curled, pressing against a spot that had my walls clamping down around him.

"Uh-uh-uh. Not yet." The words sent phantom vibrations across that bundle of nerves. Caden's hand pumped in and out of me in a rhythm that had me skirting around the edges of where I wanted to be.

"Please," I breathed.

"What do you need, Gigi?"

"More."

He chuckled against my clit, that tongue circling but stopping just shy of where I needed him. "More of what?"

I looked down at Caden, his face between my thighs. The image had that invisible cord inside me spinning and pulling impossibly tighter. "More of you."

His eyes flashed gold again. It was all he needed. Caden's fingers curled again, and his lips closed around that bundle of nerves as his tongue pressed down.

Everything around me fractured in a spiral of light and color. My legs shook so hard Caden's arm came around them, holding me up as he took and took. Wave after wave of sensation swept through me. Just as I thought I was wrung out, another crested, nearly taking me under.

Finally, Caden eased me back onto the mattress, his fingers slipping from my body. He stood, looked down at me, and licked those fingers clean.

"Can't imagine anything sweeter."

My eyes flared wide, and I pushed to sitting, reaching for his shirt.

Caden grinned. "Need something, Gigi?"

I yanked his button-down out of his slacks. "This. Off."

He chuckled. "Happy to oblige."

Caden's fingers worked the buttons from the top, and I went from the bottom. When we met in the middle, he tore off the shirt. My hands immediately moved to his belt, unbuckling it and pulling it free.

He stepped out of my grasp, kicking off his shoes and shucking his pants and boxer briefs. And then he was standing in front of me, nothing but air between us.

I couldn't help but drink him in. I'd imagined this moment

for too long, yet it was better than anything my brain could've dreamed up. Lightly tanned skin pulled taut over cut muscle. My eyes tracked over defined shoulders to a chest with just a dusting of hair. Then down to ridges of abdominals and a V of muscle I wanted to trace with my tongue.

Caden's cock jerked as I stared at it. He growled. "You're gonna make me come like a teenager."

My gaze jumped to his face as he stalked toward me. He bent, his fingers latching onto my sports bra. "Need to feel all of you."

Caden pulled the bra over my head, sending it flying. And then he was pushing me back to the bed, covering my body with his. "Shit. Condom."

My fingers dug into his shoulders. "I'm on the pill."

He stilled, his eyes searching mine. "I had a checkup right before I came back, and I haven't been with anyone since. You're sure?"

I nodded. I didn't want anything between us. I had no idea what this meant for Caden and me, but if I only had this stolen moment with him, this one glimmer of everything, I wanted to experience it all. "I'm sure."

Caden's eyes blazed as his hand cupped my cheek, stroking along my jaw. "Gigi…"

My legs wrapped around him, and he bumped against my entrance. Everything in me cried out for him. For everything he could possibly give me.

Caden slid inside on one long glide. My mouth fell open on a silent gasp. I'd never felt fuller—and in the best way. It was just shy of pain, yet somehow perfect.

I held on to Caden as I adjusted to his size, his feel, to all of him.

"Gigi," he whispered again.

"More."

I didn't have to tell Caden twice. He began moving, first in shallow, testing thrusts and then deeper. My hips rose to meet him. Something about the two of us coming together was completely unique—a path that would only ever be ours.

Our bodies spoke to each other in a secret language no one else would ever understand. With hands and mouths and so much more.

My back arched as Caden thrust deeper. My walls trembled. "Caden…"

I wasn't sure what I was asking for or if I simply needed to call his name, to tell myself this was real.

It unleashed something otherworldly in him. He picked up speed, shifting his angle so I had no choice but to sail over the edge with him. Caden arched into me on a shout, emptying himself into me in a cascade of sensation.

I clung to him, grasped every ounce of pleasure, never wanting to let go.

Caden's forehead came to rest against mine as we struggled for breath. "Gigi…"

Panic gripped me as he pulled back a fraction, his eyes searching mine. I braced for what might come. For him to tell me that this had been a mistake.

"I can't stay away from you anymore. I tried. I tried so damn hard it killed something inside of me. But I can't do it anymore."

"Why?" I whispered.

Fear flashed in those gorgeous hazel eyes. "I couldn't stand the thought of losing you."

My fingers tightened around his biceps. "I'm right here. I've always been right here. I thought you didn't want me."

Caden shook his head, and I saw so much pain in his eyes. "I've wanted you for longer than I ever should've. I tried to hide it, to shove it down. But only one person has ever owned me. You."

Chapter Twenty-Six

Caden

I KEPT ONE HAND ON THE STEERING WHEEL AND THE OTHER on Grae's thigh. I couldn't seem to stop touching her. Maybe it was because I'd held myself back for so long. Perhaps it was because she had some drug humming just below her skin. The reason didn't matter.

Grae tipped her head back against the seat as my thumb swept back and forth across her skin. It was as smooth as silk. I could lose myself in the feel of it.

I glanced over at her. "I can still turn around."

"I don't think missing work for sex is really a valid excuse," she murmured, a smile playing on her lips.

"I think it's an incredibly valid excuse."

Grae snorted. "Men."

"Hey, I'm going to have to deal with blue balls all day."

She arched a brow. "We had sex twice this morning. And I got you off in the shower."

I shifted in my seat. "It's that damn shower image that will have me in blue ball land."

Grae choked on a laugh. "Sorry?"

I stopped at a traffic light and leaned over to kiss her. "No, you're not."

God, that taste. I wanted nothing else on my tongue.

Grae moaned into my mouth.

A honk sounded, and we broke apart.

I glared at the car behind us with out-of-state plates—impatient tourists.

"Whoops," Grae muttered.

I pulled up to Vacation Adventures and put my SUV in park. "Walk me through today again?"

She searched my eyes, a hint of worry there. "I'm taking out a kayak group, but Jordan is coming with me, and we leave right from here. It's only a two-hour trip. Otherwise, I'll be in the office."

"And someone will be with you the whole time?" I pressed.

"Law talked to Jordan. They've both made it clear that I won't be alone other than to pee."

"It's not something to joke about."

Grae leaned across the console and brushed her lips against mine. "Humor is how I cope, remember?"

I kissed her again. "And Roan's picking you up?"

"Yup. I'll call you if that changes."

I forced myself to release her and leaned back in my seat. "Check in, okay? It'll make me feel better."

"I can do that. You just focus on the retreat and the gala. People will be arriving soon."

Grae was right. I needed my head in the game. Jalen and I needed to go over a million details. "I've got it covered."

She grinned as she slid out of my SUV. "I know you do. But I won't mind getting the play-by-play of when you make Gabe eat his words."

I chuckled. "I'll see if Jalen can get a video."

Grae waved and headed into the office. I waited until I saw her safely talking to Noel before I pulled onto the street. Even knowing they were looking out for her, driving away was brutal. As if I were leaving all my internal organs outside my body. But I forced myself to do it anyway.

Our event planner, Erika, moved around one of the four tables in the great hall. "This is option one. I'm calling it our traditional look."

The settings were exactly what you'd expect for a gala: gleaming silver, crystal glassware, and white china. Boring and expected.

"This is exactly what we need," Gabe said, nodding at her.

Erika gave him a polite smile. "I'm glad you like it, but we've got three other options for you to consider."

Gabe scowled. "If you want to waste our time, fine."

"Now, Gabe," Mom chided. "Erika has put a lot of work into this. Let's see what else she's come up with."

Erika smiled at my mom. "Over here is more of an art deco look."

That table had a black-and-white motif with pops of color. It was more interesting, but I didn't think it fit with the feel of the resort.

"This would be fun, and Clara did love bright colors," Mom said wistfully. "But it might be more fitting for our Miami property."

Erika nodded. "I can see that."

My phone buzzed, and I pulled it out of my pocket. A photo filled the screen. It was a selfie of Grae in her kayak.

Gigi: *No attempted kidnappings by any otters to report.*

I shook my head, but a grin played on my lips.

"That wouldn't be Grae, would it?" Pleasure swirled in my mom's voice.

I looked up from my phone. "How'd you know?"

"Because you only ever smile like that when she's around."

My eyes flared.

Mom shrugged. "I've always known she's been special to you.

I'm just glad you two finally figured out whatever was keeping you apart."

"Can we quit wasting time over this? You're acting like Caden finally getting into a relationship is the second coming."

My mom frowned at him. "I don't think being happy for your brother is wasting time."

"He's just going to fuck it up. Caden doesn't take anything seriously. So don't go planning the wedding now."

Mom's hands began a nervous flutter at her sides. "Gabriel…"

"Show us the next damn table," he snapped.

Erika jumped at his tone. "O-of course. This is what I call our natural look. I thought it might be nice to bring in elements of our setting with the tablescapes. We've got watercolor napkins in the lake's colors, rustic wood name cards, and pops of greens for the forest."

I cleared my throat. "This fits Clara to a T. Maybe we can get prints of some informal shots of Clara around The Peaks. It'll remind people why they're giving."

"That's a wonderful idea, Caden," Mom said. "I've got plenty of shots I'd love to use."

"Of course, you'd go with his idea," Gabe scoffed. "Dad'll hate it."

I took Mom's hand and squeezed. "It's okay."

"It's not," she whispered. "I don't see why you two can't get along."

Guilt dug in its claws. "He's just stressed with work. I'm not taking it personally."

"Are you two going to keep whispering, or can we actually get some work done?" Gabe clipped.

Mom's hand trembled in mine.

"Enough, Gabe," I barked.

He scoffed. "Stop acting like you're the chosen son. I'm sick of it. You're not better than me. I've been here working my ass off while you've been living it up in New York."

"I was working," I gritted out.

"Bullshit."

"Stop it," Mom cried, tears filling her eyes. "Just stop it."

Before either of us could get another word out, she tore out of the great room.

I whirled on Gabe. "I know you hate my guts, and that's fine. But around her, you can at least fucking pretend. She's already lost a daughter. It kills her that we aren't some big, happy family."

Gabe laughed, but it was ice-cold. "You don't give a damn about her. You just want to play the dutiful son so you can get control of The Peaks."

"I think you're talking about yourself there."

Gabe gave me a hard shove. "I care about the legacy of this family. Unlike you. If you get control of this resort, you'll ruin it like you do everything else."

Without another word, he stormed out of the great room.

I straightened my suit jacket as I turned back to our events planner. "I'm sorry, Erika."

Empathy filled her expression. "I'm sorry for you, too."

Blood roared in my ears. How had it come to this? Was it simple greed, or had something else set him against me? But I knew one thing for sure: I'd seen true hatred pulsing in my brother's eyes.

Chapter Twenty-Seven

Grae

"THANKS FOR PICKING ME UP," I SAID AS I DROPPED MY backpack onto the floorboard of Roan's truck and buckled my seat belt.

He simply grunted and started the engine.

I glanced over at my second eldest brother. I'd become an expert in reading his facial expressions over the years. I had to be when his words were so few and far between. "What's wrong?"

Roan kept his eyes on the road as he pulled into traffic. He didn't say anything for a few moments. That was the thing about Roan. When he *did* speak, he chose his words carefully. "Worried about you."

My heart clenched. *Crud.* I hadn't thought about how all of this might be affecting Roan. While he had the gruffest exterior of all my brothers, he was the most sensitive. Maybe because he was such an observer of the world and took everything on his shoulders, but he was an empath through and through.

"I'm okay," I said softly. "I'm being careful. And staying with

Caden means I'm behind a ridiculously over-the-top security system."

The Peaks not only had guarded gates but also people patrolling the grounds. They had to when their guests ranged from billionaires to celebrities to world dignitaries.

Roan's gaze flicked to me. "How's that going?"

My mouth curved. "You want to talk about my boyfriend?"

He grumbled something indiscernible under his breath.

I just laughed. Roan wanting to have girl talk wasn't something I was used to. "It's good. Really good."

I couldn't keep the smile out of my voice.

Roan slowed at a stop sign, studying me more carefully. "He going to stick around?"

My stomach tightened at the question. "We haven't gotten that far. We're taking things one day at a time."

Roan grunted. "Don't want you getting hurt."

"Relationships pretty much guarantee you're going to get hurt at some point. That's life."

"Don't get why people put themselves in that situation," he mumbled. "Dumb."

I stared at my brother. He was so kind—gentler than anyone would ever expect—and it broke my heart that he was so dead set on not allowing anyone into his life.

"Sometimes, I think how much we open ourselves to potential pain is the same amount we make ourselves available to joy. You can't have one without the other."

Roan's grip on the wheel tightened as he turned onto the road that led to The Peaks. "I've got plenty of joy."

But I wasn't so sure about that. It wasn't that Roan didn't have good things. He did. He had our family, a job he loved, and a house that was his haven. But I couldn't imagine that he wasn't lonely. And that made an ache settle deep in my chest.

Roan slowed at the gatehouse as a security guard stepped out.

"Welcome to The Peaks. Are you a registered guest?" the guard asked.

I leaned across the cab of Roan's truck. "I'm staying with Caden Shaw." I handed him my ID.

"Ms. Hartley. Welcome back." His gaze flicked to Roan. "I'll need your ID, as well, sir. Just to make sure you're on the list."

Roan grunted and handed him his driver's license.

The man referenced a tablet and then nodded. "Please, go right ahead."

The gate instantly began to open.

Roan scoffed as he rolled up his window.

"Shut up," I mumbled.

"Too fancy."

"It's a resort," I defended.

Roan just shook his head and kept driving.

A couple of minutes later, he was pulling up to Caden's house. He put his truck in park and then shocked me by pulling me into a hug. "Please, be careful."

I swallowed the lump in my throat as I hugged Roan back. "I am. I promise."

A second later, Roan released me. "Call me if you need me."

"I will." I grabbed my bag and slid out of the truck.

Making my way up the steps, I pulled out the key Caden had given me, then unlocked the door and stepped inside. "It's me."

The alarm beeped, and I hurried to punch in the code. I shut the door behind me, locking it and rearming the security system.

"Caden?"

There was no answer, but I'd seen his G-Wagon in the drive, so I knew he was home. Maybe he was getting a workout in downstairs.

I headed down the hall and into the living room, pulling up short.

Caden sat on the large sectional, staring out the back windows. His expression held nothing but defeat and maybe a healthy dose of grief.

Everything in me constricted. "Caden?"

He turned to face me, lines of strain around his eyes. "Hey, Gigi."

I crossed the room, sinking onto the sofa and letting my bag fall to the floor. "What happened?"

Caden shook his head. "Nothing. Nothing new, anyway."

Anger stoked deep in my belly. "Your dad or your brother?"

"Gabe. Started shit during a meeting with the event planner. Mom got so upset she ran off crying."

God, I wanted to junk-punch that man. "I'm sorry."

"I don't think I can keep doing this. I think my being here is only making things worse."

My breath caught in my throat. "You want to leave?"

Caden looked at me then. "It's the last thing I want to do."

I swallowed down my panic and took his hand. "Do you think it's time to consider finding another job?"

It killed me to say it because I knew the chances of that job allowing him to stay in Cedar Ridge were slim to none. And what would that mean for us?

Caden's hand tightened around mine. "I've fought for this for so long. To make my dad proud. To make Clara proud."

My thumb traced an infinity symbol on the back of his hand. "You know Clara would be proud of you. But that's not because of anything you've done with any hotel. It's because of the man you are. Kind, loyal, caring."

Caden's fingers pulsed around mine.

I took a deep breath. "But I don't think you'll ever get that from your father. You could save the world from nuclear disaster, and he'd still find fault in you."

A sad smile pulled at Caden's lips. "Am I a superhero now?"

"You know what I mean. He lives to pick you apart, and it kills me that you let him."

Caden's jaw hardened. "I keep thinking if I try hard enough, if I become more of the man he expects me to be—"

"Screw that!" I snapped. "That just means you'd become like

him, and that's not a very good person. You're better than he'll ever be, and I don't want you to lose that."

Caden shifted, framing my face in his hands. "You make me want to be a better man."

I closed the distance between us, brushing my lips across his. "You don't need to be better. You're already the best."

He wrapped his arms around me. "I'll start looking to see what else is out there."

I swallowed against the dryness in my throat. "Good."

"We'll find a way, Gigi. I'm not going to lose you when I just got you."

I burrowed into his hold. "I don't want to lose you either."

The beeping sound pulled me from sleep, and I shifted in Caden's hold, groaning.

"What time is it?" he grumbled.

I sat up and reached for my phone. An alert from my glucose monitor flashed on the screen. *Crud.*

I swung my feet over the side of the bed.

Caden sat, instantly on alert. "What's wrong?"

"My blood sugar's trending down. I need to get some juice."

He quickly got to his feet.

"You don't need to get up with me."

Worry filled his eyes. "Of course, I do."

I pressed my thumbnail into the pad of my forefinger to keep from snapping at him. "I'm used to this. It's no big thing."

But Caden still followed me into the kitchen. My phone alerted again as my blood sugar dipped lower. I picked up my pace, grabbing the orange juice from the fridge.

Caden was waiting with a glass, and I filled it.

"What can I do?" he asked, concern lacing his words.

"Can you grab me a protein bar?"

He nodded, disappearing into the pantry.

I chugged the juice.

Caden unwrapped the bar and handed it to me. "What will this do?"

I took a bite and chewed. "I need the instant jolt of the sugar in the juice, but this will help slow the absorption because there's fat and protein."

My alarm went off again, and I muttered a non-curse.

He gripped the edge of the counter. "Maybe we should go to the hospital."

I shook my head. "This happens sometimes. Hopefully, I can get it in check."

"Hopefully?" Caden gritted out.

I winced. "Occasionally, I get into a cycle that's harder to break. But I've got the pump for a reason."

"But it's clearly not doing its job," he growled.

I took another bite of the protein bar. "It is. My body just gets out of whack sometimes."

A muscle along Caden's jaw ticked. "What do we do now?"

"We?"

Annoyance flickered in those hazel eyes. "You and me. We're a team. I'm not leaving you to deal with this alone."

Pressure built behind my eyes. That was exactly how I'd dealt with my disease for most of my life. Alone. Because when I let people in, they tended to hover and try to take over, thinking they knew best. But here Caden was, simply wanting to help. To support me however he could.

I cleared my throat. "Now we go back to bed."

He looked somewhat skeptical.

"My alarm will wake me up if I need to do anything. Maybe grab another bar just in case?"

Caden nodded and dipped into the pantry again. He re-emerged with the entire box, and I couldn't help but laugh.

He shrugged. "Better safe than sorry."

I poured myself another glass of juice in case I needed it, and we headed back to his bedroom.

We climbed into bed, and Caden pulled me into his arms. It was then that I felt the tremble in his muscles. I looked up at him. "Are you okay?"

He stared down at me, so much emotion in his eyes. "Nothing can happen to you."

The thread of panic in those words set me on edge. "I'll be fine."

Caden held me tighter. "Promise me."

"I promise." But I wasn't sure those words were truly mine to give.

Chapter Twenty-Eight

Caden

I WATCHED GRAE AS SHE POURED CEREAL INTO A BOWL. There was no off-key singing along to a song playing on her phone. No dancing around the kitchen while she made an elaborate breakfast. She moved slowly, and I didn't miss the dark circles rimming her eyes.

It was no wonder. We'd been up a dozen different times last night with her glucose monitor.

"Do you need to call your doctor today?" I asked.

She shook her head. "If it happens again this week, I will. But this kind of thing happens every so often."

My gut twisted as if some prize fighter were going ten rounds with it. While Grae had gotten a short burst of sleep last night, I'd made the mistake of googling what could happen if a diabetic's blood sugar got too low. They were at risk for seizures, a coma, and even death in some cases.

My palms started to sweat, and I gripped my coffee mug harder. "I can call off work today, and we can rest."

"No. You've got retreat stuff, and I need to go to work."

I stiffened. "You've had almost no sleep, and you look like crap."

"Gee, thanks."

"You know what I mean. It's obvious you don't feel well."

Grae turned on her stool so she faced me. "I've dealt with this before. I know my limits. I won't take a group out today, but I can sit at a desk and do admin work. I'll make sure I'm eating what I need to, and I'll go to bed early tonight."

My back teeth ground together.

She reached up and pressed a palm to my cheek. "Trust me to know my limits. Please."

There was a desperation in her voice that had me giving in. I wrapped my arms around her, resting my chin on her head. "This isn't easy for me."

"I know." Grief laced each word. "Am I hurting you?"

I held her tighter. "No. This isn't on you. I just can't take the idea of something happening to you."

Grae pulled back. "But something *is* going to happen to me. That's life. You can't protect me from everything that might come my way."

I struggled to keep my grip on her gentle.

"But you can walk with me through it. Just like I'll walk with you."

I tucked a strand of hair behind her ear and squeezed her neck. "Okay."

Grae leaned forward, resting her head on my chest. "Thank you."

I forced myself to release her and turn the conversation to lighter things. We talked about Grae's plan to take Aspen and her daughter, Cady, on a kayaking trip. And then I suggested we could take Cady and Charlie camping overnight with the horses. We lost ourselves in that planning for a while. It was easy and normal, but I felt the shadows at the edges of my mind taunting me.

The ride into town was mostly quiet, and each mile that

passed twisted my insides tighter. The idea of just dropping Grae off and leaving her killed me.

I pulled into a parking spot outside the Vacation Adventures cottage and slid out of my SUV. I rounded the vehicle and opened Grae's door.

She took my hand. "You don't have to come in."

I dropped a kiss to the top of her head. "Let me be a gentleman."

Grae's brow rose. "Gentleman, huh?"

I grinned. "In public, at least."

She snorted but took my hand anyway.

I'd never been one for public displays of affection like this, but Grae was different. I wanted to touch her anytime I could. Wanted the world to know that she was mine and I was hers. I led us toward the building and held open the screen door for her.

"G!" Eddie greeted around a mouthful of breakfast burrito.

Noel lifted his chin at her, but his eyes narrowed on me.

Jordan looked up from pouring a mug of coffee, concern filling his eyes. "You okay? You don't look so hot."

"Long night," Grae mumbled.

"You need to take it easy today?" he pressed.

"Probably not a bad idea." She glanced at Noel. "Can you take my hike today?"

He nodded. "Of course." His gaze shifted to me. "Need to take better care of her."

I stiffened.

"Noel," Grae snapped. "It's not his job. And there's not much I can do when my blood sugar alarms are going off all night."

Noel snapped his mouth closed.

"Awkward," Eddie singsonged.

Jordan cleared his throat. "You can work the books with me today."

"Sure," she muttered.

I pulled Grae into my arms, brushing the hair from her face.

"Call me if you need anything. If you get tired, I can come and pick you up."

"Okay."

I took her mouth in a long, slow kiss. "See you tonight."

Grae's eyes were just a little hazy. "Tonight."

As I released her, I noticed everyone's focus was on us. Jordan looked annoyed, Noel appeared pissed the hell off, and Eddie looked like he'd just tasted something bad. But I didn't give a damn. They needed to get used to me being around because I was here to stay.

I gave Grae one more quick kiss and headed outside toward my vehicle. Just as I reached it, my phone dinged.

> **Nash:** *Saw your SUV at Vacation Adventures. Time for a coffee?*

I glanced at my watch.

> **Me:** *A quick one. The Brew?*

> **Nash:** *I'm already here.*

I hopped behind the wheel and drove the three blocks to the coffee shop. Since it was early, parking wasn't too bad, but there was already a decent crowd inside.

Nash flagged me down from a table in the corner, and I headed his way.

"I already ordered you an Americano."

"Thanks, man." I slid into the empty chair. "Any updates from forensics?"

He shook his head. "So far, nothing. It's starting to look like the perp wore gloves."

I slid my hand into my pocket, my fingers working over the worn charm. "That means premeditation."

"At least to a certain degree. Or this guy is just always prepared."

"You think he travels with a kit?"

Nash shrugged. "Could be the case. And if so—"

"He's done this before," I finished for him.

Nash nodded.

I cursed. "How the hell are we supposed to find this creep?"

"We have to hope he starts to get sloppy."

But what harm could he do before that happened?

Aspen's red hair caught my eye as she made her way through the tables with a tray of drinks. She stopped at the table next to ours, setting down two mugs and a couple of scones for the couple there. "Here you go," she said with a smile.

"Thank you." The woman stared at her for a moment. "It's crazy. You look just like that woman who got murdered in Mississippi. The one whose husband went down for it. But lots of folks think he didn't really do it—"

"Sally," her husband clipped.

"What? She does."

Aspen had gone an unnatural shade of white.

"Sorry," the man said. "She's got a crazy true crime obsession. She thinks everyone could be a serial killer."

Sally glared at her husband. "They could be anywhere."

Aspen forced a laugh. "It's okay."

But I didn't miss the tremble in the tray as she moved to our table. "Hey, Caden."

"You okay?" I asked.

That unnatural smile widened. "Of course. Here are your coffees. Just flag me down if you need something else."

She was gone before Nash or I could get out another word.

"Caden?"

I turned at Nash's voice. "Sorry. What'd you say?"

"How was Grae last night?"

Memories of those alarms going off and Grae's pale face filled my mind.

Nash straightened. "That bad?"

I shook my head. "She had low blood sugar for a lot of the night."

Nash cursed. "Those nights are rough."

I gripped my coffee mug. "They happen a lot?"

"I don't know about now since she keeps that stuff pretty close to the vest, but growing up, they would happen every so often. Scared the hell out of our parents."

"Scared the hell out of me," I admitted.

Nash studied me for a moment. "You dealing with this okay?"

I glanced out the window to the water across the street. "I'm dealing."

I had to. Because I wouldn't lose Grae. Not again.

Chapter Twenty-Nine

Grae

I LEANED BACK IN MY CHAIR, STARING AT MY COMPUTER. THE letters had all started to blur together. My brain was mush. I liked to call it a hypo-hangover. There was fatigue, of course, but the worst was the brain fog. As if everything were coming at you in slow motion.

Footsteps sounded behind me, and I looked up.

Jordan lowered himself into Eddie's empty desk chair. "How are you holding up?"

"Good," I lied as I straightened.

Jordan simply stared at me.

I sighed. "I feel a little out of it."

"You don't have to be here. You know you can always call out if you need a day or two to recuperate."

"I know. But if I'd stayed home, I would've been climbing the walls. It's better to be here and busy. I'll get good sleep tonight and be back to normal tomorrow."

Jordan's mouth pressed into a firm line, but he nodded. "As long as you're sure."

"I am."

I expected him to get up and go back to his office then, but he didn't. Instead, Jordan picked up a pen and began spinning it between his fingers.

"Is everything okay?"

He clicked the pen a few times. "I know this might be crossing a line…"

"But?"

He sighed. "Caden seems pretty intense around you."

I studied Jordan for a moment. It might've been crossing a line if he were simply my boss, but we'd been friends for as long as I could remember, and I could feel his genuine worry. "I think it's just that things have been intense in general."

He nodded. "Law have any idea who might be behind this?"

"Not that he's told me. I think they're still waiting for test results on a lot of evidence to come back." He was always complaining about how slow the county labs could be.

Jordan flipped the pen between his fingers in a staccato motion.

I just waited. I'd known him long enough to know that he was working up to something. He'd say it when he was good and ready.

"I don't think this thing with Caden is a good idea."

I bit the inside of my cheek. "Okay."

Jordan stilled the pen. "Okay?"

I shrugged. "I'm not going to try to convince you otherwise. You obviously have an opinion about him that's different than mine."

Jordan's jaw hardened. "He's a player, Grae. In more ways than one. He'll be gone from here in a matter of weeks, and then where will you be?"

"I'm not trying to be a jerk, but that's for us to figure out. I don't need to defend my relationship to you or anyone else."

"I just don't want you to get hurt."

"And I might. Heck, I probably will. But that's *my* choice."

Jordan's fingers tightened around the pen. "I'm not saying it isn't. I just want you to be careful."

The hinges on the screen door squeaked, and I looked up.

Wren stepped inside, her gaze ping-ponging between Jordan and me. "Sorry, am I interrupting?"

I pushed to my feet. "Not at all." I crossed to my friend and gave her a hug. "What are you doing here?"

"Just wanted to check on you. See if you wanted to grab lunch."

"Sure, I'm about due for a break."

"You're not supposed to go anywhere alone," Jordan argued.

I sent him a withering stare. "I'm not. I'm going with Wren. In broad daylight."

"I said I'd keep an eye on you—"

"I've got her back," Wren interjected. "We'll just go down the block to Dockside."

"Fine," Jordan clipped, shoving out of the chair and stalking toward his office.

Wren let out a low whistle. "What the hell was that about?"

I shook my head. "Let me grab my wallet, and I'll tell you on the way."

I got what I needed from my backpack and followed Wren out of the cottage.

She linked her arm through mine. "I feel like we need a *Little Women* night."

"We might," I said with a laugh. We'd watched the movie so many times we knew the thing by heart.

"Spill, girl."

I sighed. "Jordan thinks this thing with Caden is a bad idea."

She glanced at me. "So he has no idea it's all pretend?"

I rolled my lips together, and Wren stilled.

"It's not fake?" she squeaked.

"Things might have changed…"

"Start talking," Wren commanded.

A laugh burst out of me at the image of my bestie with her slight pregnancy bump in opposition to her commanding tone. "Okay, okay."

So, I told her everything. From how things had slowly started to shift, to the combustible night Caden and I had shared, to his admission of always having had feelings for me, to him staying up with me all night.

Wren sighed as she slid into one side of the booth at Dockside. "I won't lie. It's damn romantic."

My cheeks heated. "I've never felt anything like what it was with him."

Wren grinned. "You two have stored up some serious heat."

Jeanie strode up to our table. "If it isn't two of my favorite girls. What can I get for you today?"

Wren's hand went to her belly. "I've got a serious craving for a cheeseburger and a chocolate milkshake."

"Well, we gotta give that little babe everything they want," Jeanie said with a grin. "What about you, Grae?"

"I'll have the same. But a strawberry milkshake, please."

"You got a bun in the oven, too?" she asked.

I'd just taken a sip of water and started choking.

Jeanie cackled as she thumped me on the back. "Not quite ready for motherhood yet?"

"Not quite," I rasped.

"I'll get these right out to you," she said as she strode away.

Wren pressed her lips together to keep from laughing.

"It's not funny. That could get around town in two seconds, and Caden would lose his mind."

The humor slipped from Wren's face. "He doesn't want kids?"

I toyed with the edge of my napkin. "I don't know if he does or not. This is all pretty new."

Wren nodded, but a hint of worry had made it into her expression. "And Jordan's worried you're going to get hurt."

I leaned back against the seat. "Everyone having an opinion about my love life is starting to drive me batty."

"It's because people care about you."

"It's more than that."

Wren frowned. "What do you mean?"

I tore off a corner of my napkin, shredding it into tiny pieces.

"Ever since I was diagnosed with Type 1, people have this need to protect me from everything. I know it comes from a good place, but it makes me feel like they think I'm weak."

"That's the last thing I think you are," Wren said quietly.

I didn't say anything.

She sobered. "But I've made you feel that way."

I shrugged. "Sometimes. I feel like people question every decision I make."

"I'm sorry, G. I think when we almost lose someone, when we know they're at continued risk, we want to do everything we can to protect them. But I didn't consider what that might feel like to you."

"I'm not trying to make you feel bad—"

Wren held up a hand to stop me. "No. I need to know this stuff because I can't change anything if I don't know it's happening. I know how trapped I felt when Holt wanted to basically call out the National Guard to protect me. I don't want you to feel that way."

Just hearing Wren say that she got it, that she didn't want to make me feel weak, helped. "Thank you."

She reached across the table and took my hand, squeezing it. "I trust you. You have a great sense about people. All you have to do with Caden is follow your heart."

My eyes started to burn. "You jerky little B. If you make me cry in a public place, it'll totally ruin my rep."

Wren burst out laughing. "No tears. But I do want all the sexy details…"

I grinned. "That I can give you."

We dissolved into all the epic girl talk I needed—the kind where I felt her excitement for me. There might have been a few squeals that brought eyes to us, but I couldn't find it in me to care.

We paid our bill and headed out of Dockside and into the sunshine.

Wren hooked her arm through mine. "I'm happy for you, G. I've never seen you like this about a guy."

"I've never felt this way about anyone before."

A smile spread across her face. "You deserve this."

A shadow crossed in front of us, drawing my gaze.

Rance's hulking form towered over us as he scowled at me. "Call off your fucking brother."

My spine snapped straight. I didn't think I'd ever heard Rance curse before. "What are you talking about?"

His teeth ground together. "Don't act like you don't know. Lawson showed up at the station to question me. Do you know how bad that made me look?"

"I didn't know. But he's questioning pretty much anyone I have a history with."

Rance scoffed. "Trust me. I'm regretting that now."

"I'm sorry, but—"

"I don't want your damn sorries. I want you to quit fucking up my life. Just remember, two can play that game." And with that, he stalked away.

Chapter Thirty

Caden

I LOWERED MYSELF ONTO THE BED, WATCHING GRAE'S CHEST rise and fall. I'd picked her up around four, and she'd disappeared into our room to nap a couple of hours ago. *Our room.* I liked thinking of it that way. I had the sudden urge to make the whole damn house ours. To blend everything that was hers and mine.

Leaning against the pillows, I sighed. I wasn't even sure if I'd be living here if I quit working for my father.

My gut churned. I knew how much Grae loved Cedar Ridge. Not only the place but also the home she'd built with her family. I wasn't about to pull her away from that. I'd just have to find a way to stay.

Grae's eyes fluttered open. "Hey."

"Hey yourself."

She reached up, rubbing a spot between my brows. "What's with the worry lines?"

"Just thinking."

"About?"

"Nothing important."

She frowned.

"Nash texted." I hurried to divert her. "He wanted to know if we wanted to meet him and Maddie at Dockside for food and music."

Grae's eyes brightened at that, and she sat up. "That sounds like fun."

"You're not too tired? You were sleeping pretty hard."

She leaned forward and brushed her lips across mine. "All rested now."

I growled against her lips. "I don't know. Maybe we need to stay in bed for the rest of the night just to be sure."

Grae laughed and leapt off the mattress. "Nope. I want to dance!"

I chuckled as she disappeared into my bathroom. This could be trouble…

Heels sounded on the hardwood floor, and I looked up from my phone. My muscles wound tight as I drank Grae in. Her pale blond hair framed her face in loose waves that I wanted to tangle my fingers in. Her eyes were rimmed in something that made the blue impossibly brighter.

But the dress she wore had me nearly swallowing my tongue. It was some sort of halter deal that tied behind her neck, dipping low in the front and giving me a peek of her cleavage. It hugged her body in all the right places, stopping at mid-thigh. And then she had to cap it all off with a pair of cowboy boots.

"Where did you get that?" I croaked.

She eyed me carefully. "I had some stuff at my parents'. Nash brought it over when he came by the other day."

I closed the distance between us, my hands skimming down her sides. The pale pink material was silky to the touch. "Are you trying to kill me?"

A smile curved Grae's lips. "Maybe…"

She stretched up onto her tiptoes and brushed her lips against mine. "Let's go, or we'll be late."

I groaned as Grae ended the connection, walking toward the front door. The view from behind was even worse. The dress dipped low, exposing her gorgeous back. I mentally began reciting football stats and started after her.

The drive into town was quick since tourist traffic had eased up for the day. Grae played DJ, switching from one station to another. I parked in the lot next to Dockside and climbed out of my SUV. By the time I'd rounded the vehicle, Grae was already opening her door.

I held out a hand to her, and she took it with a smile. "I think this is our first date."

I stilled for a moment. "I'm an ass."

She frowned. "What are you talking about?"

I tugged her against me, brushing the hair out of her face. "I haven't even taken you on a proper date."

"I don't care about that stuff."

I bent my head, taking her mouth in a slow kiss. "You deserve the world, Gigi. To be taken to dinners, on trips, to drown in flowers."

Grae's fingers wove through mine. "I don't need fancy. I just need you."

I stared down at her, seeing nothing but the truth in her eyes. "You really mean that, don't you?"

Her lips twitched. "I've been waiting for you for a long time, Caden Shaw. I just want to enjoy having you."

Something lurched deep in my chest. It let loose a fierce wave of panic, but I shoved it down. Instead, I wrapped an arm around Grae and guided her toward the restaurant. "You've got me."

By the time we reached the front door, I could already hear the music pouring out into the night. It sounded like some cover band, but they weren't half-bad. The bouncer gave me a chin lift and smiled at Grae. "Have fun, you two."

We stepped inside. The place was packed with a mix of tourists and locals. Some were eating, more were drinking, and the dance floor was already full. I caught sight of Rance and some other guys on the fire crew and inwardly groaned. We did not need drama tonight.

"In the back corner," Grae said over the music, oblivious to Rance's presence. And maybe that was for the best.

I followed the incline of her head to see Holt, Wren, Nash, and Maddie taking up a table. I maneuvered us through the crowd, keeping an eye on everyone who passed.

Grae slowed at a table. "Looks like triple trouble."

Eddie grinned. "You know it."

Noel took a long pull of his beer. "Lookin' good, G."

"Thank you, sir," she said with a mock curtsy.

"Hey," Jordan greeted, but I didn't miss how his eyes hardened a fraction as he took me in.

Nash waved to us from his table, and Grae turned back to her friends. "Gotta go, boys. See you on the dance floor?"

Eddie did some sort of bizarre shimmy shake. "You can't handle my moves."

Grae burst out laughing, and I wanted to drown in the sound.

"No one can handle your moves. They're an assault on the eyeballs," Noel said with a shake of his head.

Eddie scowled at him, and they began bickering as I led Grae toward the table that her brother had secured.

"We ordered for the table," Nash said, chomping down on a nacho.

Maddie rolled her eyes. "What he means is that he had no patience, so *he* ordered for the table."

Holt chuckled. "But if Nash is good at one thing, it's ordering food."

Wren elbowed her fiancé. "Like you're any different. You were already scoping out the dessert menu."

He shrugged. "They have pie."

Grae laughed and slid into the empty chair next to Maddie. "Some things never change."

I sat next to Grae as a waitress hurried over to us. "Can I get you two anything to drink?"

Grae smiled at her. "Water and a margarita, please."

"I'll have a beer, whatever is local and on tap."

The waitress nodded and took off again.

"Is it usually this packed when they have a band?" I asked.

Nash nodded as he ate another nacho. "During the summer, always."

I leaned back in my chair, resting my hand on Grae's thigh. "Maybe I need to think about getting some bands up at The Peaks."

Grae glanced up at me. "That's a great idea. You could even do some more low-key concerts out on the grass with that amazing view."

My brows rose. "Maybe I need to hire you."

She laughed and shook her head. "I'm too busy as it is." She turned to Wren. "How are you feeling?"

Wren's hand went to the tiny swell of her belly. "I actually feel really good. The morning sickness has pretty much passed."

Maddie grinned at Grae. "We need to start planning her shower."

Grae clapped her hands and let out a squeal. "I can't freaking wait."

They lost themselves in talk of baby shower themes and food options, and I just watched Grae. I could've done it for hours. Joy radiated out of her in waves. Everything about the night was so normal. The kind of life I'd been missing for so long.

"You love her."

I stilled at the sound of Holt's voice and tried to beat back the panic his words caused. "She's an amazing woman." It wasn't an admission, but I knew the truth deep down. I'd been gone for Grae for most of my life.

Holt took a sip of his beer. "I wasn't sure about you two."

"I don't blame you." I'd never been serious about a woman before. Had never been willing to take that risk. But with Grae, it was as if I didn't have a choice. She had burrowed deep before I had the chance to fight her off.

"Don't feel that way anymore."

I studied Grae's brother. "Why not?"

He was quiet for a moment. "It's how you look at her. How you move around her. You're always aware of where she is in the room. Like you're prepared to jump in front of a bullet at the drop of a hat. Like you'd do anything just to see her smile. How could I not want that for my sister?"

Everything hurt. The kind of pain you knew had been living in you for years but was just being exposed for the first time. It was what I would've wanted for Clara.

I swallowed hard. "Thanks, man."

"Fucking piece of shit!"

The rage in Gabe's tone had me lurching to my feet.

He stumbled as he shoved me hard. "You just can't stop fucking up my life, can you?"

Holt and Nash were by my side in a flash.

"What the hell are you talking about?" I snapped.

Gabe's eyes were bloodshot, his gait unsteady. He was clearly trashed or high. Maybe both.

That bloodshot gaze cut to Nash. "Set your pig friends on me. Do you know what it could do to my reputation to have cops showing up at my damned office?"

I stiffened.

Nash didn't show even a flicker of reaction. "We're talking to everyone who's had a run-in with Grae lately. You're the one making a scene now."

Gabe whirled on me. "I know this is you. You think Dad will get wind of it and turn more control over to you."

"I have nothing to do with an official police investigation, Gabe."

"The hell, you don't. Nash and Lawson are in your back pocket. Ditched us and practically moved in with them in high school. I know it's you." His rage-filled gaze snapped to Grae. "You think I'm going to lose my birthright over a piece of ass like you?"

I shoved Gabe hard, making him stumble. "Get the hell out of here before I do something I'll regret."

I didn't have time to react. For someone inebriated, Gabe moved surprisingly fast. His fist struck out, connecting with my jaw with a vicious snap.

Nash was on him in a flash, pulling Gabe's hands behind his back as Holt helped. "That's assault. Want me to arrest him?"

I shook my head, holding my jaw. "Just get him out of here."

"You sure about that?" Nash pressed.

"In his goddamned back pocket!" Gabe yelled.

"Just get him gone."

People were staring now.

Nash jerked his chin in a nod, and he and Holt forced Gabe through the crowd.

Grae's hand slid into mine. "Come on."

I didn't have time to argue or ask questions. She tugged me through the throng of people looking at us like we were the best soap opera they'd seen in years.

Grae led me down a hall and through double doors into a kitchen. "Hey, Cam. Got any ice?"

A large cook took one look at me and motioned to a machine. "Towel's in that drawer there."

Grae grabbed a towel, filled it with ice, and then motioned for me to follow her. She slipped into a back office and closed the door behind us. A second later, I had cool ice pressed to my jaw.

"I'm so sorry," she whispered.

"It's not your fault."

My voice was empty. Completely devoid of emotion.

"Caden…" Grae pulled me down onto a small couch in the space, keeping the ice pressed to my jaw.

"He's got so much hate in him. And I don't have the first clue why."

Grae ran her hand through my hair, and I leaned in to her touch. "It's because you're so good."

I blinked at her.

A sad smile spread across her face. "You care so deeply about others. You always have. You looked after Clara, are an amazing friend, and an incredible son. Seeing all that just makes Gabe see what he isn't."

I felt a burn deep in my chest at how Grae saw me. Growing up the way I had, there were times when all I saw as I looked at my life was failure. Knowing it was the last thing she saw…it healed something inside me.

I let out a long breath. "I don't think Gabe gives a crap about that stuff."

"Maybe not. But he cares that others see it in you. Even your dad, who's the worst, has a begrudging respect for you. And you light up your mom's whole world. He hates that."

I collapsed back into the couch. "I don't get why we can't just celebrate each other's wins. Hell, we're working for the same company. We're a part of the same damned family."

"Because Gabe sees everything as a competition."

I slid a hand along Grae's jaw and under her hair. "I don't like that he's fixating on you."

She leaned in to my touch. "I can handle Gabe. He's an entitled butthole, nothing more."

My lips twitched. "Butthole, huh?"

"He's not even worth a dollar in the swear jar."

I leaned my forehead against Grae's, breathing her in. Then I shifted, hauling her onto my lap. I needed to feel her body pressed against mine. To remember that while my world was falling apart, I still had her.

Grae curled against me, keeping my ice pack in place. I didn't know how long we stayed like that, but the ice finally began to melt, and Grae set it in a champagne bucket on a side table. Then she studied me carefully. "You okay?"

"Do I have you?"

"Always."

"Then I'm okay."

The door to the office flew open, and Nash filled the entryway. "We have a problem."

A million curses flew through my head. "What now?"

A look of pissed-off concern flashed across his face. "There's another fire."

Chapter Thirty-One

Grae

FEAR PULSED THROUGH ME. "WHERE?" I ASKED, SCRAMBLING off Caden's lap.

Nash glanced at Caden before looking back at me as if he didn't want to answer.

"Where?" I demanded.

"Vacation Adventures."

Caden cursed as he stood. "When?"

"The call just went out," Nash said. "Got a text from Law. He's already there."

I grabbed for Caden's hand, needing the reassurance of his touch. "We have to go. I need to see how bad."

Worry streaked across Caden's face. "It could be a coincidence."

"Do you really think so?" I asked.

He cursed again. "No. Come on."

Nash led us to the hall, where Holt, Wren, and Maddie were already waiting.

Maddie wrapped me in a hug. "You okay?"

"Not really."

Wren rubbed a hand up and down my back. "Let's see what's what. Maybe it's not as bad as we think."

My stomach roiled as a million and one different possibilities ran through my head, but I nodded.

Holt motioned to a back door, and we filed out of it. Caden wrapped an arm around me as we rounded the building to Main Street. Sirens sounded from down the street, and the air had a faint glow.

We all picked up our pace. But when the Vacation Adventures building came into view, I gasped. The entire structure was completely engulfed in flames.

"Oh my God," Wren whispered.

"It's all my fault."

My words were barely audible, but Caden heard them. He wrapped me in his arms. "This isn't on you."

But it was. If I didn't work there, none of this would've happened. I burrowed into Caden's chest. "This is Jordan's livelihood."

He'd worked so hard to build his business. Now, because of me, it was all going up in smoke.

Caden's arms tightened around me. "We'll help him rebuild. I'm sure he has insurance."

But it was more than that. Someone was trying to destroy my life one piece at a time, and I was terrified of what they might do next.

"Grae!"

My head lifted as Noel and Eddie jogged over to us. Both their eyes were wide.

"What the hell is going on?" Eddie asked.

"We're not sure yet," Caden answered for me.

"Where's Jordan?" I croaked.

Noel inclined his head toward a group of officers. Jordan was talking to Lawson and looking supremely pissed off. I guessed angry was better than sad, but I was sure grief would hit him later.

Firefighters surrounded the building, spraying more water on the blaze.

Noel eyed Caden and me. "Do they know what started it?"

Holt shook his head. "We don't know anything yet. Nash just went to try and get some more info. I'm texting my team to check the footage from the cameras I put in and see if we got anything."

I glanced over to see Nash talking with Clint, but I doubted they had anything to share.

"This is insane," Eddie muttered.

A muscle ticked in Caden's cheek. "You need to talk to my brother. We had a run-in tonight."

Nausea swept through me. If Gabe did this, Caden would hold himself responsible.

No one said anything else as we watched the firefighters battle the blaze. They got it under control remarkably fast, but the damage had been done. Even though the structure still stood, it would surprise me if it wasn't a complete loss.

Jordan ambled toward us, looking lost. My stomach dropped.

I stepped out of Caden's hold and crossed to him. "I'm so sorry."

Jordan wrapped me in a hug, holding on tightly. "I can't believe this happened."

I swallowed hard. "It might be my fault."

Jordan reared back, his gaze cutting to my face. "You think this is the same person who set your house on fire?"

"How could it not be?"

Jordan gripped my shoulders. "This isn't your fault."

I bit the inside of my cheek. "If I didn't work here, it probably wouldn't have happened."

He ducked his head. "Grae. We've known each other for pretty much our entire lives. Do you really think I'd hold you accountable for something like this?"

"No, but—"

"Good. Because I never would. This could all be an accident. Some faulty wiring or something. Let's not borrow trouble just yet."

I sighed. Hoping for that felt ridiculous at this point, but I didn't want to argue with him. "Okay."

He released me, turning toward the building as firefighters made their way inside. "This is going to be a shit show."

"You know I'll help however I can. Pull extra hours to go through whatever they can salvage. Anything."

Jordan glanced down at me. "I know. You've always got my back."

"Always."

Caden stepped up behind me, wrapping an arm around my chest. "I'm sorry, man."

Jordan's jaw hardened, but he nodded. "Thanks."

Eddie and Noel joined us. Eddie winced as he took in the wreckage. "This blows, boss."

"You call the insurance company yet?" Noel asked. "They'll cover it, right?"

Jordan nodded. "Someone's coming out in the morning. We'll just have to wait and see how much damage was done."

My stomach churned. How many memories did this cottage hold for me? Too many to count. It had been my first job out of school, the one where I proved to myself and my family that I could stand on my own two feet. We'd shared a million laughs here, and even a few tears.

A firefighter emerged from the building and strode across the parking lot to Lawson, holding something that looked like a box. He and Lawson shared a handful of words as Lawson snapped on gloves and took out an evidence bag.

The firefighter opened the box, and Lawson stared inside for a handful of moments. Then there was a flurry of movement— more police officers and a crime scene tech.

My stomach hollowed out as dread pooled there.

None of us said anything as Lawson looked up, locking eyes with me. His expression was unreadable, but he started toward our group. His steps were heavy, slow. Each one had my heart racing faster.

Lawson came to a stop in front of Caden and me.

"What is it?" I whispered.

A muscle below his eye fluttered. "One of the firefighters found a fireproof box sitting on your desk."

"What? I don't have one of those."

Lawson nodded. "He thought it was odd, so he opened it. This was inside."

Lawson held up a clear evidence bag. Inside was a photo.

It took a moment for me to place the image. It was of Caden and me walking back from that first lunch at Dockside. But someone had scratched out Caden's face. And in bright red letters it read:

YOU DON'T BELONG TO HIM.

Chapter Thirty-Two

Caden

I WRAPPED A BLANKET AROUND GRAE'S SHOULDERS. SHE looked so damn small sitting on my couch. She hadn't said a word on the way home. Not when all four of her brothers had descended, along with her parents. They'd talked over and around her, all fighting about what they thought might be best for Grae.

"Baby, don't you think you should move back in with Dad and me?" Kerry asked.

"I think she should stay with my team in Portland. Whoever this is had enough foresight to spray paint the damned camera I installed," Holt argued. "She should go stay in one of Anchor's safe houses."

My gut tightened at the idea of Grae going anywhere without me.

"If she leaves, the stalker could go to ground," Nash said. "We should keep her here but in protective custody."

I lowered myself to the couch and took Grae's hand, squeezing.

Her eyes came to me. They were bloodshot and had shadows in them that I hadn't seen in years.

"What do you want to do?" I asked.

Grae blinked at me as if shocked that anyone would ask her that. "Huh?"

"What would make you feel safe?"

She stared into my eyes. "I want to stay here. With you."

"Then that's what we'll do."

Everyone erupted, and the arguing started all over again.

"Enough!" I barked. "I know you all love Grae, but the last thing she needs right now is you guys fighting like cats and dogs."

"She's our sister," Lawson growled.

"Yeah, your sister. Not your property. She's an adult with a mind of her own. And she's one of the smartest and strongest people I've ever known. But it looks like you've all forgotten that."

Everyone went silent.

I sighed, squeezing the back of my neck. "The thing that I always loved about your family is how you were always there for each other, no matter what came your way. But that doesn't mean you get to steamroll Grae in the process."

Nathan clapped me on the shoulder. "You're right." He looked at his daughter. "I'm sorry, Pumpkin. You know it comes from a place of care."

"I know," she whispered.

He winced. "But it probably feels pretty overbearing."

Grae didn't agree or disagree, but he had his answer.

Nathan released his hold on me. "Let's clear out and let Grae and Caden get some sleep. We can talk about a plan tomorrow."

"Dad," Holt argued.

"No," Nathan said, finality in his tone. "You taught me some valuable lessons when you came home. I'm trying to do a better job of seeing what my kids need from me. And right now, Grae needs support."

Lawson scowled at Nathan. "I'm positioning two officers outside."

"That's fine," I said, trying to make peace. Grae wouldn't have to see them, and she wouldn't have to leave.

He turned that scowl in my direction. "You're not law enforcement, Caden."

"I know that. But I would do *anything* for your sister, and I think you know that."

Grae stiffened next to me, her muscles going hard as stone.

Lawson's jaw worked back and forth, but he didn't argue.

Roan crossed to his sister, bent, and kissed her head. "Stay safe."

There was a fury brimming just beneath his surface that had concern flashing through me. But he turned and left before I could say a word.

Kerry hugged her daughter. "I'm sorry, baby. I just worry about you. It's hard to turn that off, even when you're grown."

Grae hugged her back. "I know."

"Call if you need anything," Nathan said, ushering Kerry out.

Lawson sent another glare in my direction and followed them.

Grae looked at Holt. "Go home to your pregnant fiancée, who is probably worried sick about you."

Guilt flashed across his face. "I could stay tonight…"

"No. You're going home. We'll talk tomorrow."

He sighed and then bent to hug her. "Please, be careful."

Grae returned the embrace. "I'm not leaving this locked and guarded house. I'll be fine."

"Okay. Call me if anything happens."

"I'll light the bat signal."

Holt shook his head, but I saw a hint of amusement in his expression as he headed to the door.

The only one left was Nash. He leaned forward in the overstuffed chair, resting his elbows on his knees. "We've been screwing everything up, haven't we, G?"

Grae's eyes widened. "What d'you mean?"

"You hate telling us anything about what's going on with your Type 1. You didn't tell us Rance was bothering you. You just let us fight about *your* damned life without saying a thing. We've been suffocating you for years."

Tears glistened in her eyes. "You love me."

"But that's no reason to make you miserable."

"I'm not miserable."

I took Grae's hand and squeezed, sending her silent encouragement.

She glanced at me and then looked at her brother. "Sometimes, it's a little much. But I know it comes from a place of love, so I try to deal with it."

Nash ran a hand through his blond hair. "But dealing with it means hiding things from us because you feel like you have no other choice."

"Sometimes," Grae admitted.

"I'm so damn sorry. I should've seen it before now. But I swear to you that things will be different."

She swallowed. "It'd be nice to feel like I don't have to hide things from you."

"Teammates. Not taking over. That sound good?" Nash asked.

"That sounds good."

Nash grinned and shook his head. "Anyone who comes at you has to deal with a knife-wielding badass. So, really, it should be you protecting me."

I chuckled. "You've got a point there."

Nash stood and looked my way. "Thanks for seeing my sister for who she really is. And for making sure the rest of us see it, too."

I got to my feet and pulled him in for a back-slapping hug. "It's impossible not to. She burns way too brightly."

I followed Nash to the front door. Opening it, I took in the police cruiser in my drive and the two officers seated inside.

Nash paused in the entryway. "She's lucky to have you."

I stilled. "I'm the lucky one."

"You both are." He glanced out toward his SUV. "I'll talk to our brothers and get them to back off a little. But it won't be easy. We're all used to protecting her. It was always our job."

"No one's saying you can't now. Just that *she* has to be a part of it. Don't steal her power."

Nash nodded. "I see it now. I really do. I'm just pissed as hell that it took me this long."

I met his gaze. "What matters is that you see it now and are willing to change things. Not every family is. It just shows how amazing yours is."

He studied me for a moment. "You know you're a part of that, right? Family isn't always blood. Sometimes, it's the people we choose to walk beside. And that has always been you, brother."

My throat constricted as I struggled to swallow. "Love you, man."

"Love you, too. Brother for life."

His words meant more than Nash would ever know.

I cleared my throat. "Now, get out of here before I go back to Grae crying. She'll use her knives on you."

Nash barked out a laugh. "Can't risk that." He headed down the steps. "Call if you need anything."

I gave him a wave and then closed and locked the door. Setting the alarm, I headed back into the living room.

Grae was right where I'd left her, but silent tears tracked down her face, glistening in the low light.

The sight was a sucker punch to the gut. I crossed the room in five long strides, picking her up and cradling her in my lap. "Gigi…"

Her breath hitched between silent sobs. "Do you know that I love it when you call me that?"

I held her tighter against me. "I thought you hated it."

I'd started using the nickname when we were little, but sometime after I'd put up that wall between us, she'd started biting my head off every time I said it.

"Love it," she hiccupped. "But it killed before, too."

A burn lit deep in my chest.

"It reminded me of everything I'd lost."

I nuzzled her neck. "I'm so sorry."

"But I have it back now. I have more than I ever thought I

would. But I can't help but wonder if I'm being the most selfish person on the planet."

I reared back. "Why the hell would you think you're selfish?"

"You saw that picture, Caden. Whoever this is hates that we're together. They've burned entire buildings. What happens when that isn't enough? Everyone's so worried about me, but it's *you* they should be worried about."

I pulled Grae against my chest, holding her tightly. "I'm going to be fine."

"You don't know that." Grae's voice trembled with each word. "I can't lose you. Can't be the reason something happens to you."

Fear spiked deep, clawing at my insides. "Don't even think about walking away from me," I growled.

She shook her head against my chest. "I can't. Maybe I'm too weak, after all. Maybe you're just my kryptonite." She pulled back, her watery eyes locking with mine. "Promise me you won't leave me."

I framed her face in my hands. "I promise."

I just hoped she could give me the same.

Chapter Thirty-Three

Caden

"IF YOU RUIN THIS VIEWING, I REALLY AM GOING TO USE you as my next knife dummy."

Grae pinned Nash with a stare so cold I believed her. But the whole image just made me want to laugh because while she was glaring at her brother, she was wearing a unicorn onesie complete with a horn and fuzzy rainbow socks.

Maddie let out a low whistle as she kicked her own rainbow-colored feet up onto the coffee table. "I'd watch out, Nash. G and Wren take their *Little Women* viewings *very* seriously."

Wren hauled a bowl of popcorn onto her lap. "Do you remember when you interrupted Beth's death scene last time?"

Nash eyed the bowl of popcorn warily. "She beaned me with a bowl just like that one."

Grae snorted, flopping onto the couch next to her two fellow unicorns. "You deserved it."

His gaze narrowed on her. "You could've given me a concussion."

"Two words. Beth's. Death. You don't mess with that."

"She's right, Nash Bash," Wren said, popping a piece of popcorn into her mouth.

Nash gaped at her and then turned wide eyes to his fiancée. "You aren't going to defend me?"

Maddie held up both hands. "I'm staying out of this. I'm just here for the popcorn."

Grae snickered.

"Oh, shut up," he clipped.

My phone dinged, and I slid it out of my pocket.

> **Jalen:** *Your dad wants you and Gabe in his office in fifteen.*

I grimaced at the screen.

"What's wrong?" Grae asked.

I quickly smoothed my expression. "Nothing. Just work stuff."

She frowned. "You can go into the office if you need to. It's not like I'm alone. I've even got Barney Fife over there."

Nash glared at her. "Hey."

"I don't need to go in." My dad could deal without me for a single day. I'd already sent him an email to let him know why I wouldn't be in, but of course, he didn't give a damn.

Grae stood and crossed to me. She wrapped her arms around my neck and stretched up onto her tiptoes. "Go get some work done. You'll feel better. And *Little Women* makes you cry anyway."

"It does not."

Her lips twitched. "Oh, I forgot, you had something in your eye."

Nash snorted.

"It was allergy season," I argued.

Grae stole whatever else I was about to say with a long kiss. "Go, work. I'll reward you later."

I grinned down at her. "Never made out with a unicorn before."

Nash made a gagging noise. "Get out of here before you ruin my movie snack appetite."

"Never gonna happen," Maddie shot back at him.

I brushed the hair out of Grae's face. "You sure?"

She nodded. "I'll be fine."

"Okay, I'll be back before the movie's over."

"Take your time. We'll be here."

I kissed Grae once more and then released her, glancing at Nash. "You'll stay?"

"There are snacks. What do you think?"

I shook my head and grabbed my keys from the counter.

Just as I reached the door, I paused. The idea of leaving her after everything that had happened felt beyond wrong.

Grae had flopped onto the couch, her head tipping back in laughter at something Wren said. Looking at her now, you'd never know there was anything wrong. That just last night, someone had set her place of work on fire because they were angry at her.

Movement caught my attention as Nash stood. His gaze locked with mine. *"Go,"* he mouthed. *"I've got her."*

I swallowed the apprehension and nodded, heading out the door. Two new police officers were in a different cruiser. I waved to them as I got into my SUV.

It only took me a matter of minutes to make it to the lodge. Annoyance flickered somewhere deep as I made my way inside. Sometimes, it seemed as if my father liked to yank my chain just to see if he still had control. To demand something of me as a test and nothing more.

I wound through the halls until I made it to his office. His secretary stood the moment she saw me. "Mr. Shaw. Your father and brother are already inside. Please, go in."

I nodded, not bothering to thank her because it would've been a lie. This was the last place I wanted to be.

Opening one of the double doors, I stepped inside. My dad and brother were in the sitting area, Dad in one of the leather club chairs, and Gabe on the sofa. Gabe looked more than a little rough. His eyes were bloodshot and rimmed in dark circles, and his complexion was a few shades paler than normal.

"Nice of you to finally join us," my father clipped.

My gaze cut to him as I crossed to a chair and sat. "I sent you an email. There was an incident last night, and I needed to be home with Grae."

Gabe stiffened. "What *incident*?"

My eyes narrowed on him, assessing. I couldn't tell if he thought that I'd shared his explosion with our father or if he was nosing around about the fire. "Someone set Cedar Ridge Vacation Adventures on fire and left a threat for Grae inside."

Dad took a sip of his coffee. "You're going to face a number of personal issues during your life, but I need to trust that this job will remain your priority."

Gabe shifted in his seat. "She's been nothing but drama since you got involved with her."

"I think *you're* the one we should be worried about. Where'd you go after you got booted out of Dockside last night anyway?" If he had started that fire, if he was the one terrorizing Grae... Fury surged and swirled inside me.

Redness crept up Gabe's throat.

"What's he talking about?" Dad snapped.

The scathing look Gabe sent me told me he'd like to gut me where I sat. "Nothing. Caden just has his little law enforcement friends stirring up trouble."

My jaw turned to granite as I stared my brother down, struggling not to throttle him.

Dad's grip on his coffee cup tightened. "You two need to grow up. I don't know where I failed in raising you, but I won't have your immature games ruining my business."

I struggled to keep my breathing even. Where he'd failed? Just about every way I could imagine, starting with viewing us as pawns instead of sons.

"You both have important projects right now. Caden has Clive's retreat, and Gabe has the VIP brunch leading up to the gala. After those are completed, I'll be doing an assessment of your responsibilities."

My fingers dug into the arms of the chair. "Meaning?"

A cold smile played on my father's lips. "Whoever has the most success with their endeavors will get first pick of the properties they'd like to manage."

The coffee I'd downed earlier sat heavy in my gut. Of course, my father would turn this into a competition.

Gabe grinned. "I can't wait to take control of the New York properties. But I think I'll keep The Peaks, too, just to make sure Caden doesn't run it into the ground."

Anger flared like hot lava sweeping through me. Gabe didn't give a damn about The Peaks. But he knew I did. Knew it meant everything to me because it was Clara's favorite place in the world. He would burn it to the ground just to ruin something I loved.

Dad chuckled. "Now that's the kind of confidence I like to see."

I pushed to my feet. "Is that all?"

Any hint of amusement fled his face. "Watch your tone, son."

The urge to deck him was so strong I nearly gave in. "I've clearly got lots to prepare for with this death match you're so keen on."

Dad's chuckle was back. "Maybe I should take bets."

I didn't laugh.

He waved me off. "Get out of here. Just remember, I'll be watching."

I strode out of the office without looking back, rage pulsing through me. I was so distracted I nearly mowed someone over. My hands went to the woman's arms to steady her. "I'm so sorry—"

"Caden, are you okay?" my mom asked, straightening.

I stared at the only person who still felt like family. "I don't know if I can keep doing this."

Panic lit her features. "Doing what?"

"Working for him."

My mom's fingers dug into my arms. "I know he's more hardened. Losing Clara hurt him more than he lets on, but—"

"He's always been hard," I argued. "But it's more than that now. It's like he's determined to tear us all down to his level."

Her hands began to flutter in a staccato beat. "I'll talk to him. I can fix it. Just don't do anything rash."

"Mom…"

"It would kill me not to have you around. Not to have you as a part of our family business. Please, just let me try."

I wrapped her in a hug. "Okay."

But I knew that agreement would be selling a piece of my soul to the devil.

Chapter Thirty-Four

Grae

I STARED DOWN AT MY PHONE AS THE SCENERY WHIZZED BY my car window. Nothing from Caden. My thumbnail dug into the pad of my forefinger.

Something was wrong. It had been for days. At first, I'd thought it was the fire at Vacation Adventures, but now I wasn't so sure. It was as if he was building that invisible wall between us again. Just the thought had nausea roiling through me.

"Whatcha thinking about so hard back there?" Eddie asked from Noel's front passenger seat.

"Nothing." I slid my phone back into my backpack. Caden was wrapping up Clive's retreat; maybe business had him distant.

Noel grunted as if to call bullshit.

Eddie took pity on me and changed the subject. "Want to see if we can lose the po-po just for fun?"

I glanced out the back window to see my now-typical tail. Two officers at all times. Outside Caden's house. Following me to work. Staying outside our makeshift offices at Jordan's place. Following me home.

"Somehow, I don't think starting a police chase is the relaxing end to a long day I'm looking for."

Eddie sent me a grin through the rearview mirror. "Live a little, G. I think you need some fun in your life."

"You say fun. The cops say jail time."

Noel snorted.

A little of the humor slipped from Eddie's face. "Honestly, you doing okay?"

My heart squeezed at the concern in his voice. Sometimes, I forgot that he and Noel could take life seriously. As much as they both lived for the next thrill, we'd been through a lot together. When Noel's brother was arrested for dealing and flipped his world upside down. When Eddie's fiancée, Megan, had been killed in a car accident. A Type 1 scare I'd had on the job. None of our lives had been perfect, but we were always there for one another.

I leaned against the seat. "It's been a long few weeks."

"Understatement," Noel said as he turned onto the road that led to The Peaks.

"Lawson say if they've found anything yet?" Eddie asked.

I shook my head. "Nothing other than proof that the second fire was arson, too."

Noel scrubbed a hand over his face. "Whoever this is knows what they're doing."

A shiver passed through me at that knowledge.

Noel slowed to a stop at the guard station, and a familiar guy stepped out. He caught sight of me in the back seat and waved. "Welcome back, Ms. Hartley." He shifted his gaze to my friends. "I'll just need to see some ID before I can let you in."

Eddie raised his eyebrows.

"Caden put you both on the list," I mumbled.

They handed the security guard their drivers' licenses. A few seconds later, he nodded. "Head on in."

"Thanks," I said with a smile.

Noel eased his car through the gates as they opened. "Fancy pants."

"It's a resort," I grumbled.

I gave him directions to Caden's place, and as we pulled up to it, he and Eddie both let out low whistles.

"No wonder you came around to the douchebag," Noel mumbled.

I smacked him upside the head. "Don't be an ass."

"She's totally gonna put salt in your coffee," Eddie warned. "You should know by now that our G can't be bought."

"Thank you," I huffed.

Noel scowled. "I'm just saying a place like this doesn't hurt."

I grabbed my backpack. "Thanks for the ride."

I slid out of the car before either of them could say anything else or before I bit someone's head off. Everyone just had to have an opinion about Caden and me.

The squad car pulled in just as I made my way up the front steps. Unlocking the door, I stepped inside and disarmed the alarm. "I'm back."

The word *home* was on the tip of my tongue, but I bit it back. Caden's place had been feeling a little less homey lately.

"In the kitchen," he called, but I heard that same emptiness in his voice—a void that had my insides twisting.

I locked the door and reset the alarm, then walked in the direction of Caden's voice. I found him sitting at the kitchen island, staring at his computer.

"Hey," I greeted.

"Hey," he echoed, not looking up.

I bit the inside of my cheek. "How was your day?"

"Good."

Annoyance stirred somewhere deep. "Got anything more than a one-word answer?"

Caden turned on his stool, his gaze finally coming to me. "What do you mean?"

I dropped my bag onto the kitchen floor. "You've been doing

this keeping-me-at-arm's-length act for the past three days, and it's starting to both freak me out and piss me off."

Guilt flashed in those gorgeous hazel eyes. "I wasn't trying—"

I stepped between his legs and pressed a finger to his lips. "I don't need excuses. Just tell me what's going on."

Caden dropped his head to my shoulder, nuzzling my neck and breathing me in.

Something in me eased at the tenderness of the gesture. The edge of that panic subsided, and I wrapped my arms around him. "Talk to me."

Caden's heart thumped against my chest. "I feel like I hurt someone no matter what direction I move in."

My arms tightened around him. "Like who?"

"My mom, mostly. I ran into her after my meeting with Gabe and my dad the other day. I told her I wasn't sure I could keep working for him."

I straightened. That seemed like a good thing to me, but the look on his face told me it wasn't.

Caden squeezed the back of his neck. "She begged me not to quit and to let her try to fix things."

"Hasn't she tried before?" I knew Jocelyn Shaw well enough to know that she would've tried anything to keep her family together.

He nodded. "I've never talked to her about quitting before, but I know she's talked to my dad about how he treats Gabe and me. But it's useless. Every time I try to have an honest conversation, he brushes me off or mocks me for wanting to talk about *feelings*."

Anger flickered to life somewhere low. "It's not fair for her to ask you to stay in a toxic situation."

"I think she worries she'll lose me if I leave the company. I hate the idea of hurting her, and I hate the idea of walking away from Clara's favorite place on Earth and leaving it to Gabe. He'll ruin it just to spite me."

"Clara doesn't live in The Peaks. She lives here." I pressed a palm against Caden's chest. "You carry her with you every single day."

His Adam's apple bobbed as he swallowed. "I feel like I'd be betraying her if I leave."

"She wouldn't want you to be miserable for any reason. She'd want you to go out and live your life to the fullest. To be happy."

Caden's hands came to rest on my hips, pulling me closer. "It feels like I'll lose a piece of her."

"You won't. I'll make sure of it. We'll keep her memory alive every day. There are a million other spots in and around Cedar Ridge where I have memories of her, so I know you do, too."

"The secret spot at the lake…"

I grinned. "She was the first one off those cliffs and into the water."

Caden chuckled. "How a ten-year-old talked more shit than Law, I'll never know."

"She put you all to shame."

His fingers tightened on my hips. "You always have this way of easing the worst of it. How do you do that?"

"Because I see you. Even when you try to hide from me, I see you."

Caden traced a finger over my lips. "I don't want to hide anymore."

"Good." I closed my mouth around his finger and sucked deeply.

"Gigi…"

I nipped his fingertip.

He growled, pulling his finger from between my teeth and lifting me onto the counter.

I let out a surprised shriek as Caden shoved his computer aside and hooked his hands into my tank top.

He lifted it up and over my head, letting it fall to the floor and moving to my bra. "Missed you."

"And whose fault is that?"

As my bra joined my shirt, Caden's head bent, and he latched on to my nipple.

My mouth fell open in a stuttered gasp.

"I think I should make it up to you then…" His teeth grazed the peak, making me shudder.

"That sounds like a good plan to me," I said between pants.

Caden's hand moved between my legs, stroking me through my shorts.

I arched into his touch, wanting to be closer, wanting all of him.

"So damn pretty," he murmured against my skin. "Look how you flush pink every time I touch you. Love watching that skin change colors."

My breaths came faster as I gripped his shoulders.

Caden's fingers deftly unhooked my insulin pump from my shorts and set it on the counter. Then he pulled my shorts and panties free in one jerk.

I loosed a startled sound as my bare backside hit the marble counter.

Caden sent me a quelling look as he let my shorts and flip-flops fall to the floor. "Let's play a game."

Everything in me twisted and tightened in desire. For Caden. And whatever he would give me.

"Think you can be a good girl and stay very still?"

My heart ricocheted around in my rib cage. "Yes," I breathed.

A devilish grin spread across his face. "That's what I like to hear."

Gold sparked in those hazel eyes. "Hands behind you. Grip the counter."

I swallowed hard but did as he instructed. The move thrust my breasts higher, and Caden tracked them with his gaze.

Caden moved the stool so it was right in front of me, the legs grating against the hardwood with a sound that echoed off the walls. Then his hands were on my knees, pushing them apart.

I bit the inside of my cheek to keep from trying to shut them again, but I couldn't stop myself from squirming.

Caden's hands tightened on me, his eyes flaring. "Punishment or reward? What will it be?"

Blood roared in my ears. "Both."

He chuckled. "Greedy. I like it."

Four fingers whipped out, smacking my bare thigh. "That's for moving when I told you not to."

The sharp sting quickly melted into a smoky heat. Wetness pooled between my thighs.

Caden's grin widened. "Liked that?"

I nodded.

He sat on the stool and leaned forward, his lips trailing up my thigh. He kissed and licked the spot where his fingers had been.

As he climbed higher, I gripped the counter harder. It took everything in me not to move.

"Such a good girl," he whispered between my thighs.

The vibrations from his lips spread to my core, and I shuddered.

"I think you deserve a reward."

Caden slid two fingers inside me, and the air left my lungs in a whoosh of relief. He curled those digits in lazy strokes that nearly drove me insane.

"Please…" The word was out of my mouth before I could stop it.

"What do you need, Gigi?"

"More," I breathed.

Fingers slapped against my thigh again. "Be specific."

"Your mouth," I squeaked.

Caden grinned. "My favorite dessert."

His head dropped to between my legs, and his tongue circled my clit.

I cried out, the edge of the marble biting into my palms.

"Love those sounds," he growled against my core.

A third finger slid inside as Caden's lips closed around that bundle of nerves at the same time his tongue pressed down.

There was no warning. I simply shattered. The lights around me flickered, and nonsensical noises slipped from my lips. All I could do was hold on to the counter and ride each wave of sensation. Caden's fingers wrung more and more from me. Whenever

I thought I was done, he somehow sent me cascading over the edge again.

By the time the final wave passed, my muscles shook, and I struggled to catch my breath. Caden grabbed my insulin pump and lifted me off the counter, cradling me in his arms as he strode down the hall.

"Wait," I mumbled. "What about you?"

"That was just for you. My apology for shutting you out."

My brows lifted. "If that's the apology, shut me out anytime."

Caden laughed, and that warmth swirled around me. "Noted."

That gold in his eyes sparked again as he looked down at me, and I swore I saw love there. I wanted to say those three little words so badly it hurt. But I held them back. Because some part of me feared that no matter how good things were between Caden and me, that might send him running for the hills...

Chapter Thirty-Five

Caden

"Tell me again," Grae demanded, practically bouncing in the passenger seat.

My lips twitched. "Clive said it was the best executive retreat he has ever been on, and he wants me to plan the one for next year."

She let out a squeal and stamped her feet against the floorboards of the SUV. "I told you."

I glanced Grae's way for a moment. "You did." I forced my gaze back to the road. "I really liked doing it, too. Thinking about how to break down people's walls so they can connect."

"Maybe that's something you could turn into a full-time gig. Helping people get back to their roots."

"Maybe." It had been a rush to think that way and make sure everything was executed perfectly. And I'd been wracking my brain for options that would keep me in Cedar Ridge if I did leave my parents' company.

Grae squeezed my hand. "You'll figure it out."

My thumb tracked back and forth across the back of her hand. "*We'll* figure it out."

She grinned at me. "I like being a team with you."

"So do I."

"And you're team chauffeur?" Grae teased as I made the turn onto Main Street. "I do have a brand-new SUV now. And you should really be prepping for the gala tonight."

"I like driving you," I said, lifting her hand to my lips.

"Don't turn me on before I have to go to work," she grumbled.

"Maybe I want you thinking about me all day long."

Grae shifted in her seat. "If I have to suffer, then so do you. I'm going to text you the dirtiest things I can think of so you have blue balls right along with me."

I choked on a laugh. "Vicious."

"And don't you forget it."

I followed Main Street to the edge of town where Jordan's house stood. I pulled to a stop in front of the two-story Craftsman just a couple of blocks from Grae's old place. Sliding out of my SUV, I rounded the hood and opened her door.

"I see the gentleman is back in full force this morning."

I arched a brow. "And what was I before?"

Her eyes danced with mischief. "I'd say last night you were a little bit of a devil."

I hauled her to me, kissing her deeply. "I think you liked the devil."

Grae bit her bottom lip. "I wouldn't mind a repeat performance."

"I'll certainly never look at that counter the same way again."

She laughed and wrapped her legs around me, brushing the hair out of my face. "You're fun, Caden Shaw."

A throat cleared behind us, and Grae dropped from her spider monkey hold.

Ramirez, the fire chief, stood on Jordan's front porch, and Rance stood next to him, glaring daggers at us.

Grae squirmed in place, and I took her hand, tracing comforting circles on her skin.

"Grae," Ramirez said with a nod.

"Sorry. I didn't see you there," Grae mumbled.

Rance scoffed. "Sure you didn't."

Ramirez sent him a quelling look. "We wanted to stop by and let you know that your house has been cleared as of last night. I apologize that processing it took so long."

"What does that mean? I can go inside?"

Ramirez nodded. "I can recommend a couple of local fire restoration companies. The majority of the actual fire damage is in the bedroom, but I'm afraid there's smoke and water damage throughout."

"Is it safe to enter?" I asked.

"Yes. We've done a structural assessment. But it's a mess, and there could be damaged items you could hurt yourself on, so I would leave the rehab to the professionals," Ramirez urged.

I shifted to look at Grae. "Do you want to take a look and call someone before work?"

"Did you not hear us?" Rance clipped. "You need to leave it to the professionals. But you probably think you can handle anything."

My gaze cut to him. "I wasn't suggesting we try to fix anything. But we need to get an idea of the damage to tell the fire restoration company."

My voice was calm and even, but anger flickered deep down. Rance was acting like a spoiled toddler who hadn't gotten the toy he wanted.

Lawson had questioned him after the office fire. Patrons at Dockside had seen him at the bar most of the night, but no one could give an exact recounting of the time because they'd been too distracted by the band and spending time with friends. Lawson had also tried to have another conversation with Gabe, but my brother had told him to go through his lawyer from now on.

Ramirez squeezed Rance's shoulder. "There's no harm in them having a look."

"Whatever," Rance said, shaking off the hold and stalking toward a truck on the street.

Ramirez let out a sigh. "I'm sorry about that. I should've told him to wait in the car. I thought maybe his temper had cooled."

"It's okay," Grae said. "I know things are a little awkward right now."

Ramirez nodded. "Look, I know Law talked to him about these fires, but that's not Rance. No matter how mad he is, he wouldn't do something like this."

Grae bit her lip. "I can't see it either. Even though he hates me right now, I've never seen him knowingly hurt another person. My brother is just covering all his bases because it's his job, and we have no idea who this is."

Ramirez's shoulders relaxed a fraction. "It's good to hear you feel that way. I'm so sorry this is happening. I want to catch this asshole as much as you do, so let me know if there's anything I can do."

"I will. Thank you for everything."

He gave me a chin lift and headed for the truck.

I studied Grae for a moment. "You really don't think it's Rance?"

Grae sighed. "I just don't see it. Maybe it's because I've known him for so long, but I just don't."

I wrapped her in a hug. That was Grae through and through, always seeing the best in people.

"Is Captain America gone yet?" A voice came from inside the screen door.

I chuckled as Eddie popped his head out. "Captain America?"

He rolled his eyes. "Rance has become a piece of work. He thinks he's God's gift to anyone in danger. He came in and basically started lecturing us all on fire safety."

Grae groaned. "I'm sorry."

Jordan came through the door and patted her shoulder. "Not your fault."

Noel followed. "I don't know. If I had to listen to another story about how he prevented imminent disaster, I might start blaming you."

Grae grimaced. "I'll bring coffee tomorrow to make up for it."

Eddie looked instantly hopeful. "And scones?"

"You drive a hard bargain, but yes."

The amusement fled Jordan's face. "Your house is cleared?"

Grae nodded. "Do you mind if I walk over really quick and check it out?"

"Of course not. We'll come with you."

"You don't have to—"

"We'll come with you," Jordan insisted.

I wrapped an arm around Grae's shoulders. "Come on. Let's get it over with, and then you can get to work."

She nodded again, but I saw the apprehension in her eyes.

"Whatever it is, we'll deal with it. We're a team, remember?"

"Okay," Grae breathed. She stretched up onto her tiptoes and brushed her mouth against mine. "Thank you."

"Always."

Eddie made a gagging noise. "Can we cut the ooey-gooey stuff short?"

Grae reached up and flicked his ear.

"Hey! That hurt," he whined.

Jordan just shook his head. "Children, let's get this show on the road."

We headed down the walkway, and the squad car that had followed us rolled down its window. Clint stuck his head out. "Where are you headed?"

"They cleared Grae's house, so we need to take a quick look. Then we're heading back."

He nodded and climbed out of the car.

"You don't have to come," Grae assured him.

He gave her an indulgent smile. "G, your brothers would have my balls if I started slacking."

She huffed out a breath. "Fine. School field trip I guess."

Clint laughed. "You'll be real happy when this is over, and you have some alone time again."

"You have no idea," she grumbled.

We made our way the two blocks to Grae's cottage. It didn't look that bad from the outside, but I wanted to eat those words the moment we made our way inside. The scent of smoke still clung to the walls, and soot and water damage were everywhere.

Noel let out a low whistle. "Shit, G."

She slowly walked through the living area to the hallway, grief making itself at home in her expression. "I can't imagine it ever smelling right again."

I took her hand and squeezed. "We'll figure it out."

I'd pay any price to make sure she felt at home wherever she wanted to be.

Grae headed in the direction of her bedroom. "I need to see the worst. Just get it over with."

"Okay." We'd rip off the Band-Aid and then start the healing process.

Black streaks coated the walls as we approached what was left of her door. When we got to the entryway, Grae pulled up short, gasping.

It took me a moment to realize what I was seeing. Black-and-white photos covered the space. Ones of Grae. Of the two of us. Intimate ones of her changing, of us embracing. And coating all of them was what looked like blood.

Chapter Thirty-Six

Grae

"I T'S ANIMAL BLOOD," LAWSON SAID, LEANING AGAINST the counter in Caden's kitchen.

The dark circles under his eyes had gotten worse over the past two weeks, and guilt pricked at me.

"What type?" Roan asked, barely restrained rage coating his words.

"Don't know that yet, just that it isn't human."

I burrowed deeper into Caden's hold. At least there was that. But it didn't make me feel a whole heck of a lot better that Bambi or some other innocent creature had lost their life just so whoever this was could terrify me.

"Can you part with one of the photos?" Holt asked.

The gang was all here again. My four brothers. My parents. Even Wren and Maddie had come. I'd forced Jordan, Noel, and Eddie to go back to our makeshift office, not wanting them to miss even more work because of me.

Just thinking about the photos made me shudder. Private

moments where I'd had no idea someone watched, let alone pho-tographed me.

Lawson eyed Holt. "What are you thinking?"

"My team can run it through our private lab and see what we can find out about the paper and the printer."

Lawson pursed his lips and then nodded. "You can do that. You're technically a consultant, after all."

"Yeah, that whole dollar retainer you pay me really comes in handy."

Nash slapped him on the back. "Your nosy ass just wanted in on the action."

"It's true," Wren agreed, rubbing her belly. "He gets bored. And when he gets bored, he gets in my way."

"Hey," Holt protested.

She shrugged but did so while grinning. "It's the truth."

Lawson turned to me. "I'd like to call my friend, Anson, and go through the case with him. He used to work as a profiler for the FBI."

Nash shot him a questioning look. "Last time you called him, he told you to F off."

Lawson's jaw tightened. "His time with the bureau didn't ex-actly end well, but I think he'll help if he knows my sister's at risk." Lawson glanced my way. "Is that all right?"

My fingers twisted in Caden's shirt. "You're asking me?"

His gaze flicked to Nash. "It's been made clear to me that I might have been doing my fair share of steamrolling." Apology flickered in his eyes. "I don't want to make you feel like your life isn't yours, G. It's just hard to turn off the big-brother thing, even when I might need to."

I slipped out of Caden's hold and crossed to Lawson, throw-ing my arms around him and squeezing tightly. "I always want you to be my big brother."

"Nash said we were suffocating you."

"Maybe a little. I just want to feel like we're fighting all our bat-tles together, not that you're fighting mine *for* me."

Lawson rubbed a hand up and down my back. "I get that. And I'm sorry I made you feel that way. I just—"

"You're a protector. It's hard for you to turn that off, even if it's just to pause to include someone else in the plan."

He released me, nodding. "I've gotten used to running the show."

"That makes sense. But I really appreciate you asking me on this one. I think having your friend take a look at the case is smart. Go ahead. And if he needs any more information from me, just let me know."

Surprise lit Lawson's expression, and I laughed. "I can be pretty agreeable when you work *with* me."

"It's a Christmas miracle," Nash said with a grin.

I elbowed him in the gut.

Lawson just shook his head, but that hint of amusement quickly slid from his face. "I had the crime scene techs take shots of all the photos. I'm going to need your help with creating a timeline of everything."

"Is that really necessary?" my mom asked, a hint of panic making its way into her tone. "She shouldn't have to look at them."

Dad squeezed her shoulder. "Kerry..."

"I can handle it," I assured her. It would probably give me nightmares, but I wouldn't waste the opportunity to show my brothers that I was stronger than they realized.

"This could be the break we've been waiting for," Holt said.

Caden wrapped an arm around my chest, pulling me back into him again as if he needed my body against his. "What are you thinking?"

Holt shifted on his feet. "We've been hoping the unsub would get mad enough to make a mistake. Removing Grae from his orbit has done that. If she can tell us when these photos were taken, we'll have a list of times he wouldn't have had an alibi. We'll cross a lot of people off our list that way."

"And we know they must have been placed between last night when the scene was cleared and this morning," Lawson added.

Caden's fingers stroked my arms in a calming rhythm. "Anyone could've seen the fire department taking down the crime scene tape and known no one would be on the premises."

Nash nodded. "It's true. Our best hope is to figure out a timeline from the photos. We've got officers setting up a room at the station with all of them on display."

I shivered again, and Caden pulled me tighter against him. He dipped his head, his lips skimming my ear. "I'll be with you every step of the way."

"If you can come down tomorrow, that would be great," Lawson said.

"Sure. But we have the gala tonight."

"You don't have to go," Caden said. "You've been through a lot—"

I turned in his arms. "I'm going. This is for Clara. And I'm not letting you deal with your family alone."

"Gigi…" He brushed the hair from my face.

"I'm going, and that's final."

"Don't argue with her, brother," Nash said. "She's stubborn as an ox."

I stuck out my tongue at him. "I'm going to take that as a compliment."

"We'll be there, too," Maddie assured me.

"You're all welcome," Caden said. "But I'm afraid it's black tie, so you'll have to dress up."

Maddie grinned. "I love an excuse to see my man in a tux."

Nash's eyes heated as he pulled her into his arms. "Got a James Bond fantasy, Mads?"

"Maybe…"

"We'll go, too," Wren offered.

Holt nodded. "That way, you'll have extra backup."

Roan's jaw went tight. "I'll wait outside."

Guilt pricked at me. "You don't have to. We'll have plenty of people around."

"I'll be outside," he insisted.

"Okay," I acquiesced.

Lawson pulled out his phone. "I'll have your usual two-man detail on the premises in case more support's needed."

"We have security working the event, as well," Caden added. "I've briefed them on the situation."

Maddie grinned at Wren and me. "You know what this calls for, right?"

"Uncomfortable shoes?" I suggested.

She rolled her eyes. "Spa day!"

Chapter Thirty-Seven

Caden

JALEN MADE HIS WAY ACROSS THE GREAT ROOM AS I WENT over last-minute details with Erika. The space had come together beautifully. It was a blend of rustic beauty and the elegance our hotels were known for, with a dose of authenticity courtesy of the snapshots of Clara.

"You were right about the place settings," she said with a smile. "It feels like we've brought a touch of the outdoors in but elevated it. And the photographs really make the décor meaningful."

"Thank you for all the hard work you've put into this. None of this would've come together without you."

She beamed. "Thank you, Caden. This is the fun part."

Jalen cleared his throat, and I turned to face him. "How are the girls doing at the spa?"

He grinned. "I like them. I have half a mind to blow off my responsibilities for the day and join them."

I chuckled. "I should warn you. They have a thing for watching *Little Women* on repeat, and they'll do bodily harm if you interrupt Beth's death scene."

Jalen let out an exaggerated gasp, his hand flying to his chest. "I would never. That's sacrilege."

"Then you guys will get along just fine." My hand dipped into my pocket, fingers touching the charm that had become my talisman. "There haven't been any issues?"

He shook his head. "The two police officers have been joining in on the fun—one waiting outside Grae's treatment room and the other in the spa lobby. I've got the ladies set up in a suite upstairs where they can get ready. I'll send up food and drinks once they're done at the spa. And the items you requested will be waiting."

I clapped him on the shoulder. "Thank you for everything."

A beaming smile spread across Jalen's face. "I know you didn't ask, but I love her for you."

That burning sensation was back in my chest, but it held a pleasure I couldn't deny. "I'm damned lucky."

"That you are." Jalen shifted on his feet, uneasiness entering his expression.

My stomach dropped. "What's wrong?"

"For you? Nothing."

"For someone else?" I surmised.

Jalen pressed his lips together and nodded. "You know how I mentioned I'd cultivated a few different sources around the hotel?"

"Your network has always been vast."

He flicked imaginary locks over his shoulder. "Thank you."

"Jalen…"

He nodded quickly. "Your brother's morning event was a disaster."

My brows pulled together. "What do you mean?"

Gabe had overseen a welcome brunch for our VIP gala guests. It was a time for them to hobnob before the main event and ease into the festivities.

"I heard from one of the waitresses working the brunch that he got the numbers completely wrong. There wasn't enough food, and they had to pull booze from the restaurant upstairs. Gabe was late and looked completely hungover. People were not happy."

My gut churned. What the hell was going on with my brother? He'd overindulged occasionally in the past but never like this. It was as if he were unraveling before my eyes, and I didn't have the first clue why.

"Does my father know?" Even calling him that felt wrong. Harrison Shaw hadn't done anything *fatherly* in more years than I could count.

Jalen winced. "He was at the brunch."

"Hell," I muttered.

"I'd never seen smoke come out of someone's ears until this morning."

I could only imagine.

"On the bright side," Jalen said, "I might have overheard Clive singing your praises to your father. He said the company retreat was the best he's ever been on."

It should've felt like a win, but I felt nauseated. "I need to go do something."

Jalen blinked. "Everything okay?"

"It will be." I started toward the exit. "Do you know where my mom is?"

"I saw her getting her hair done at the spa earlier, but she said she was heading home."

I nodded. "Thanks."

I headed down the hallway and nearly collided with Gabe.

"Watch where you're going," he barked.

My gaze tracked over him. This wasn't a Gabe I recognized. His suit was rumpled, his hair disheveled. "Are you okay?"

He scoffed. "Like you give a fuck."

"For better or worse, I do. And something's obviously wrong."

Rage flared in his brown eyes. "You can drop the saint act. No one's around to see it."

"Asking my brother if he's all right isn't an act."

Gabe's jaw hardened to granite. "Always the perfect fucking son. Do me a favor and just stay the hell out of my life."

He checked my shoulder hard as he passed.

I stood there for a moment, wondering for the millionth time how we'd gotten here. Maybe the *why* didn't matter. It wouldn't change where we were. But that knowledge had grief settling deep in my bones.

I forced myself to start walking again, making my way through the lodge and outside to the parking lot. Jumping into my SUV, I headed for my parents' house, hoping my father would be holed up in his office and not at home.

The drive took less than five minutes, and I breathed a sigh of relief when I didn't see my dad's Maserati out front. I parked in the circular drive and headed up the front walk.

The door was locked, so I rang the bell. A second later, I heard footsteps. The door swung open, and my mom smiled. "Caden, I wasn't expecting you. I thought you'd be tied up with gala business all day."

I stepped into the entryway and gave her a quick hug. "I needed to talk to you about something."

Concern flashed in her features. "Come in. We can sit in the library."

That room had always been my mother's domain. When life got hard, she escaped into her books and shut the world out for as long as possible.

She led me through the hallways I'd raced Clara down as a child. There were a million memories from growing up in this house, but only a fraction of them were good.

As I stepped into the library, the familiar lavender scent enveloped me. My mom gestured me toward a sitting area by the large window. The furniture there was more comfortable than what my father required in the living room. It was the kind you could sink into and stay all day.

I took a seat on one side of the couch, my mother on the other. I let out a deep breath and took her hand. "I'm going to leave the company after the gala. I'll tell Dad tomorrow."

My mom stilled. "Caden. I talked to him. I think he'll try harder—"

"Mom."

She quieted, and I squeezed her hand.

"It's not healthy. Not for any of us."

My mom's eyes began filling with tears.

That sight had always cowed me in the past. Her grief was the thing that had me staying in a situation that had become beyond destructive. But I couldn't do it anymore.

"I've tried so hard to fix things," I said. "Put up with Dad's cruelty because I knew we were all dealing with the pain of losing Clara in our own ways. I didn't want to hurt you by walking away from a company your family built. Didn't want to betray Clara by leaving her most beloved place in the hands of people who didn't truly care about it."

Mom's breath hitched as tears tracked down her cheeks. "You could never betray your sister. She loved you more than anyone else in the world."

"I see that now. Clara would want us all to be happy. And we're the furthest thing from it. This is toxic, and it's slowly killing all of us. I can't sit by and watch it happen anymore."

My mom's tears came harder. "I'm so sorry. I didn't realize it had gotten so bad." She shook her head. "No. I didn't *want* to see, so I looked the other way."

I squeezed her hand again. "I love you. I'll always be here for you. But I can't have Gabe and Dad in my life anymore. Maybe one day, with some distance and perspective, and if things truly change."

"But they're your family," she said between hiccupped cries.

"Maybe by blood. But Grae has shown me what family and love are truly supposed to be. And it's not this."

My mom stared at me for a moment, taking in my words, my expression, and reading my truth. She pulled me into a hard hug. "You deserve to be happy. You've always had the best heart I've ever known."

"Thank you." My voice cracked as relief spread through me.

Mom released me. "You love her."

"It scares the hell out of me, but I do."

She smiled. "If it scares you, it just means it's important."

Something about that shifted the way I thought about my fear. "I like thinking about it that way."

My mom pushed to her feet. "Hold on."

She crossed to her antique rolltop desk. As a kid, I'd played on the floor while she wrote countless letters at that desk. She fished a key out of the top drawer, unlocked the bottom one, then dug around for something.

A few seconds later, my mom walked back toward me. She placed a small, navy velvet box in front of me. "This was my grandmother's. She and my grandfather had the kind of love story that could fill the pages of one of these books. Maybe it would be a good start to your and Grae's love story."

I slowly picked up the box and opened it. The ring gleamed in the afternoon sunlight. It was a large oval diamond surrounded by an intricate antique setting.

I waited for the panic to hit, but it didn't come. And it was then that I realized a part of me had always known I'd marry Grae Hartley someday. But I was ready for that day to be now.

Chapter Thirty-Eight

Grae

WREN LET OUT A LOW WHISTLE AS JALEN OPENED THE door to a massive suite. "Grae, I think you dating a guy who owns a fancy-ass resort might have its perks."

Maddie grinned as she hurried inside. "I was Team Caden the moment he got us a spa day."

"Good to know you're both easily bought," I said, following them into the suite.

Jalen chuckled as he motioned my police detail inside. "A late lunch will be delivered any moment now, along with some champagne."

I took in the space around us and stilled. There were flowers everywhere. Countless bouquets of…wildflowers. I swallowed hard. "Did Caden do this?" I whispered.

Jalen smiled. "He wanted you to have a relaxing afternoon in the perfect setting while you got ready."

I crossed to the largest bouquet and plucked out a card with my name scrawled across the outside.

Gigi,

There isn't a time I see a wildflower and don't think of you. Thank you for always seeing me. For always having my back. I'm the luckiest man in the world to have you in my life.

Caden

"Oh my God. That's so sweet."

I whirled on Wren and smacked her nose with the card. "Nosy much?"

She grinned. "You're my best friend. It's not like you wouldn't have told me."

"I wanna read it." Maddie grabbed the card from my hand.

"Hey!"

"Awwww. Totally swoon-worthy."

Jalen laughed. "I knew I liked you guys." His eyes twinkled. "There's more waiting for you in the primary bedroom."

"More?" I squeaked.

"Come on." Maddie grabbed my hand and hauled me toward the room.

As we stepped inside, we froze again. There weren't just more flowers; beyond that was a rack with six different breathtaking gowns hanging from it.

"Caden wanted to make sure you had something to wear that would make you feel beautiful," Jalen said.

Tears burned the backs of my eyes. I'd told him I had an old prom dress I could probably squeeze into from my parents' house, but he'd wanted me to feel comfortable tonight. Confident.

"And there's something else on the bed," Jalen added.

"Holy crap, G," Wren whispered. "He isn't messing around."

I walked to the bed on shaky legs. Three red leather boxes lay on top of the mattress with a card. I grabbed the card first.

Gigi,

I couldn't be prouder to walk into a room with you at my side. A little something to show you how much you shine.

Caden

I swallowed hard as I opened the first box—a pair of delicate diamond earrings. They looked like falling snowflakes that would catch the light. The second box housed a classic diamond tennis bracelet. And the third, a necklace that was the most beautiful thing I'd ever seen. It had the same snowflake resemblance as the earrings and would settle along my collarbone.

"He didn't have to do this," I whispered, tears filling my eyes. My hand reached up, touching the spot where the simple compass necklace used to lay. Now, I'd be able to wear something of Caden's again. And that couldn't have felt more right.

Wren wrapped an arm around me. "Don't you know Caden well enough by now? He did this because he *wanted* to."

Caden hadn't said those three little words yet, but he didn't need to. They were in his eyes. In his every action. And I felt them down to my bones.

My hands skimmed over the pale blue fabric of my gown. The silk hugged my curves, dipping low in the front with a lace overlay on my cleavage. The diamonds at my ears, throat, and wrist glimmered in the light.

"Are you ready?" Wren called from the living area. "The boys are on their way up."

I let out a shaky breath and forced myself to leave the haven of the bathroom. Maddie let out a wolf whistle as I made my way to the living room. "Damn, girl, you were right to go with the blue. You look like an ice princess."

Wren beamed at me, waving a hand in front of her face. "You look too beautiful. I'm going to cry."

Her reaction was exactly what I needed, and I burst out laughing. I crossed to my bestie and placed a hand on her tiny belly. "It's not me making you cry, it's this little one."

"You're both jerks," she muttered.

Clint chuckled from his spot on the couch. "Hormones, man. I'll never forget how my sister cried at the drop of a hat while she was pregnant."

A knock sounded on the door, and then it opened. Holt, Nash, and Caden entered, but I only had eyes for Caden. He wore a navy tux that fit him like a dream and somehow made the green of his eyes impossibly brighter.

The moment his gaze zeroed in on me, he stilled. That gold in his hazel eyes sparked, and then he ate up the space between us. The rest of the world melted away as his hands found my face, drawing me in.

"You're the most beautiful thing I've ever seen."

My breath hitched. "Thank you for making me feel that. The dresses, the jewelry, the spa."

Caden's lips brushed mine. "Don't you know by now? I'd do anything for you."

"Hey, no making out with our sister in front of us," Nash grumbled.

Maddie smacked him. "Don't ruin their moment. Caden gave G the most romantic day of her life."

Holt arched a brow. "You putting us to shame, Caden?"

Wren grinned. "He definitely is."

My cheeks heated, but I took Caden's hand. "Maybe we should go downstairs."

Nash chuckled. "Always hated being the center of attention."

Caden's fingers wove through mine. "You sure you're ready for this?"

I nodded. "Let's go charm the pants off some stuffy, rich people."

Wren snorted and shook her head. "You know *you're* rich, right?"

"But I'm not stuffy," I argued as we filed out of the hotel suite.

Holt dropped a kiss to her head. "I hate to break it to you, Cricket, but you're rich now, too. We *are* getting married."

Wren's lips twitched. "Oh, I know. I'm just using you for your money. That and the hot sex."

Caden choked on a laugh. "Harsh."

Holt hit the elevator button. "I'll take what I can get."

Nash clapped him on the shoulder. "Smart man."

We climbed into the elevator, taking it to the lobby. We followed the flow of impeccably dressed guests headed toward the gala. As we stepped inside, I gasped. "Caden, this is gorgeous."

He squeezed my hand. "Erika did an amazing job. I think it feels like it really fits the space."

"It's like a magical forest," Wren muttered as she took it in.

"Not too shabby, brother," Nash admitted.

"Thanks. Now, let's get some drinks," Caden said.

He flagged down a cocktail waitress, and we all placed our orders.

Lena grinned like a shark as she strode toward our group. I had to admit she looked beautiful, but it was only skin-deep.

Caden tensed, his arm tightening around me.

"Caden," she purred, patting his chest. "You look so handsome."

He stepped back, taking me with him. "Lena."

She pouted. "Always so uptight."

"Maybe if you didn't make him feel incredibly uncomfortable, he wouldn't be so tense around you." My voice stayed sickly sweet, but my eyes were hard.

Lena's jaw went slack. "I would never."

Nash snorted. "Please, you've been hitting on him for years.

You think your poor ole fiancé doesn't see, too? I feel bad for Gabe, and I hate that prick."

Lena's face reddened. "I don't need to listen to these crass insults." She turned and stormed off.

Maddie let out a low whistle. "She's something."

I glanced up at Caden. "You okay?"

He sighed. "Fine. Maybe she'll be embarrassed enough to finally leave me alone."

We could all hope.

A hand gently patted my arm, and I turned.

Jocelyn Shaw sent me a wavering smile. "Grae, you look stunning."

I wrapped my arms around Caden's mom in a hug. "So do you. That dress is perfection."

She ran a hand down the garment as I released her. "Thank you. Can I steal you for a moment?"

I looked at Caden, who sent his mom a questioning look.

She laughed. "I promise not to tell her any embarrassing childhood stories."

"Mom…" he warned.

I waved him off and then looped an arm through hers. "Don't let him intimidate you. I want to hear *all* the embarrassing stories."

Jocelyn laughed as we walked out onto the balcony, where it was a bit quieter. "You're good for him."

"I hope so because he's good for me."

A sad smile spread across her face. "I haven't done a very good job protecting that goodness."

I stilled at the balcony's edge, not saying anything.

"I wanted to thank you for protecting him…the way I should've. Caden told me you've helped him see how much the situation with his dad and brother is hurting him."

"He didn't want to cause you pain. Any of you. But I hate what it puts him through."

Jocelyn patted my arm. "You were right. And so is Caden. I

didn't want to see how destructive it had all become, but it's hurting all of us. We need to face it. I'm *going* to face it."

I squeezed her hand. "That's incredibly brave."

She smiled at me. "It's nice to find a little bit of that bravery again. I'd forgotten I had it."

"We all forget sometimes. It helps to have people who remind us."

"You're that for Caden. You always have been."

My heart clenched in a squeeze that straddled the line between pleasure and pain. "It's an honor."

Jocelyn glanced over her shoulder. "I'd better let you get back to him. He's got that worried look on his face."

I laughed. "Okay. Maybe we could get lunch one day this week. Just the two of us."

"I'd love that."

"Me, too."

I left Jocelyn on the balcony and headed in Caden's direction. He met me halfway. "Is everything okay?"

"Your mom is pretty amazing."

He lifted a brow in question.

"She's stronger than you think."

Caden glanced over my shoulder at his mother, who was now talking to another woman. "It's good to hear that."

"Caden," a man I didn't recognize called out.

We were pulled into conversation after conversation until my bladder protested. I squeezed Caden's arm. "I'll be right back."

"I'll go with you."

I shook my head. "Clint's right there." I gestured to the man in the corner. "He'll keep an eye on me."

"Okay." He pressed a kiss to the corner of my mouth. "Don't stay away too long."

I grinned and headed toward the hallway. Clint fell into step behind me. "Where are we headed?"

"I'm going to the little girls' room. I don't think you're allowed."

He chuckled. "I'll just wait in the hallway."

"Sounds like a plan."

The first bathroom I came to was packed, so we walked farther down the hall until I found a blissfully empty one. Stepping inside, my ears rang from the silence after a good hour of loud conversation.

I quickly did my business and washed my hands. Taking a deep breath, I braced for more mingling.

As I stepped out into the hallway, I frowned. Clint wasn't anywhere to be seen. I started in the direction of the gala, my head swiveling.

I heard a groan, and my steps faltered. A hand grabbed my hair and pulled hard, yanking me backward. I tried to scream, but it was too late.

Chapter Thirty-Nine

Caden

NASH STRODE OVER AND HANDED ME A BEER AS I SAID goodbye to Clive. "Looks like everything is going pretty damn smoothly."

My gaze tracked over the crowd as I leaned against the balcony railing and took a sip. "Even the old man can't be pissed about this one."

Nash eyed me carefully. "Do you honestly care what he thinks?"

"A part of me always will. He's my dad, even if he hasn't acted like it much lately."

Nash grunted in agreement.

"I'm quitting."

His brows lifted. "Seriously?"

"Told my mom today. I'll tell him tomorrow once the dust from the event has settled."

"What brought that on? You've been entrenched in the family business for as long as I can remember. Never even considered working elsewhere."

"Your sister showed me what family can be," I admitted.

A smile spread across Nash's face. "You're a goner."

"I think I always have been."

A little of that smile slipped. "If you quit the company, what are you going to do for work? It's not like there are a bunch of hotel conglomerates in Cedar Ridge."

"I'd never make Gigi leave. She loves it here. Her family's here."

"But what about you? She's not the only one who deserves to be happy where she is."

I'd always loved what I did. All the moving pieces, the constant new challenges, but a job was only one piece of the puzzle of life. And that piece paled in comparison to a life with Grae. "I'll figure something out. Maybe I'll consult. I've thought about going into the vacation rental game. Cabins and lodges on the mountain. Maybe organize retreats out of them, as well."

"There's always a market for that if you can find the real estate to buy. It's getting harder and harder."

"I have my ways."

Nash chuckled. "I don't doubt that."

I slid my hand into my pocket, feeling for the charm. "I need to tell you something."

Nash shifted, leaning a hip against the balcony railing. "Okay."

"I'm going to ask Grae to marry me."

I waited for shock or maybe even anger, but Nash simply stared at me.

"Was there a question in there?" he asked, taking a sip of his beer.

My lips twitched. "I was expecting some sort of reaction. Want to punch me?"

Nash shook his head and grinned. "You're one of my closest friends. You're a good man. And you love my sister like crazy. Why would I be anything but thrilled?"

My chest burned. "Thanks, man."

He pulled me in for a back-slapping hug. "You've always been a part of our family. This will just make it official."

My throat constricted, and I swallowed to clear it. "Means the world. Gonna talk to your mom and dad. Tell them my plans."

A devilish grin spread across Nash's face. "But not ask permission?"

"Nothing on this planet could stop me from asking Grae to be my wife."

Nash let out a low whistle. "Law's gonna shit a brick; his baby sister getting married."

I winced. It was clear that Lawson was the brother who struggled the most with letting her go, but the strides he'd made earlier today told me he'd get there.

"Make sure I'm there when you tell him. If he decks you, I wanna get it on video."

I barked out a laugh. "Gee, thanks."

"We can put a still on the family Christmas card."

"Nothing says Christmas cheer like a punch to the jaw."

Nash lifted his beer. "Deck the halls."

Movement caught my attention, and I saw my father headed in our direction. I'd carefully avoided him all day, but he looked determined now.

"This being the last one of these has to make it easier," Nash said, picking up on my father's approach.

"I guess so."

"Want me to stay or leave you to it?" he asked.

"Probably better if you leave." It was always better when my father didn't have an audience.

"Just give me the sign if you need me."

I gave Nash a chin lift. "Thank you. For everything. You've always had my back."

He slapped my shoulder. "And that will never change."

I knew it, too. And that was one of the greatest gifts.

Nash made a beeline for Maddie, who was chatting with Wren and Holt, avoiding my father's path. I didn't blame him.

A handful of seconds later, Dad made his approach. "Caden," he clipped.

"Dad," I greeted.

"What the hell is going on with your brother?"

I fought the urge to groan. "Your guess is as good as mine."

My father's eyes narrowed on me. "He's been like this ever since you got back. I know you've done something."

Anger flared from somewhere deep, a place that had lain dormant for over a decade. "Have you ever considered that this might be on you?"

Dad reared back. "What are you talking about?"

"Oh, maybe the fact that you've taken joy in pitting us against each other since we could walk? Or that you've made it clear that we're both the world's greatest disappointments to you?"

A muscle ticked in his jaw. "I've made sure you're strong. That you can handle what life throws at you."

"You've torn us apart, piece by piece. And when we get the hell away from you, what are you going to be left with? Your bitterness and cruelty. Sounds like a pretty pathetic life to me."

Redness crept up my father's throat. "You'd better watch your tongue—"

"No. I've been doing that for far too long. I'm done. The way you act is beyond wrong. I'm not going to put up with it anymore."

"What the hell are you talking about?"

"I quit, Dad. I'm not going to work for the company anymore."

My father's jaw went slack as he gaped at me. "You can't be serious."

God, it felt good to say. As if the weight of a dozen men had been lifted from my shoulders. Or maybe just the burden of a tyrant of a father. "I'm dead serious. I'll stay on for my two weeks' notice, but then I'm gone."

Coldness crept into my father's expression. "This is that girl's doing. She was always trouble. I should've known she'd mess up your life."

"This is me, finally waking up after years of abuse," I snapped.

He scoffed. "Like your life has been so hard. I've given you everything."

"Except for the one thing I needed. The knowledge that you gave a damn about me."

My father laughed, but it was an ugly sound. "And you think *Grae* does? All she wants is your money and status."

He was grasping at straws, and I knew it, but her name on his lips had me searching the room anyway, unease settling over me when I didn't see her anywhere. She'd gone to the restroom twenty minutes ago. She should've been back by now.

I shoved past my father.

"Hey! I'm not done talking to you," he snapped.

But I didn't give a damn. I needed to find Grae. Now.

Chapter Forty

Grae

WHITE-HOT PAIN FLARED IN MY SCALP AS SOMEONE yanked me back, hard, into a room. The door slammed behind me. A hand went over my mouth, making it hard to breathe. I squirmed and clawed, trying to break free.

"Fucking bitch!" the man spat.

I knew that voice.

My stomach roiled as I fought harder to get out of Gabe's hold. My fingernails dug into his arm, and he cursed, throwing me to the floor.

My head clipped the edge of a chair, and flares of light danced in front of my eyes.

"Serves you right," he spat.

I blinked rapidly, trying to clear my vision. It took a count of ten for Gabe to come back into focus. It was then that I saw Clint's fallen form in the corner of the room.

Fear grabbed hold, digging in its icy claws. I had to get out of here, needed to run. To get help. I cursed myself for finding a bathroom in an empty hallway too far away for people to hear me scream.

"Don't even think about it," Gabe snarled. He pulled something from his waistband.

There was a flash of metal in the lights of the meeting room, but it took my mind several precious seconds to recognize it as a gun. My heart hammered against my ribs, my breaths coming quicker.

"What? Nothing to say now? You always had such a smart mouth."

I swallowed hard, trying to assess the situation the best I could. I took in Gabe, clad in his tux, gun pointed straight at me. More than just the weapon was wrong. Gabe's face was clammy with sweat, his hair matted to his face, his eyes wild.

"What do you want, Gabe?" I tried to keep my voice as even as possible, even though everything in me shook.

He snorted. "You're just like him. Think you're better than everyone."

"Like who?" But I knew. Gabe had always looked at Caden with distaste, but that had morphed into true hatred over the years. I just didn't know why.

Gabe's chest rose and fell in ragged breaths. "He thinks he can take everything from me."

"Caden doesn't want to take anything from you."

"Don't say his name!" Gabe snapped, his grip on the gun tightening.

"He's trying to steal the hotels, Lena, our parents. Everything."

My fingers dug into the carpet beneath me as I gauged my options for making a run for it. "He's leaving the company." I didn't know that for sure, not yet, but maybe it would buy me some time.

Gabe stilled. "Bullshit."

I shook my head. "It's true. He's miserable working for your father."

Gabe chewed on the side of his lip as he mulled that over.

While he was distracted, I slipped off my strappy heels. If I had to run, I wasn't going to do it in stilettos.

"You're lying," Gabe clipped, stalking toward me.

"I-I'm not. We've talked about it. He hates what your father has put you both through."

Gabe reached down, grabbed my hair, and hauled me up. "Don't insult my father."

That pain in my scalp bloomed bright again. "I'm sorry."

He gripped me tighter, pressing the gun into my side. "No, you're not. You're just the same. Trying to act like you care while you steal it all."

I needed to calm Gabe and fast. Keep him talking. But how did you talk someone down who was clearly in the throes of some sort of breakdown? "Why do you think he wants to steal from you?"

Rage bloomed in Gabe's eyes, and I knew I'd made a grave mistake.

"He thinks it's his!" Gabe bellowed.

I knew I had to move, and fast. My knee came up in one swift action, finding its target between Gabe's legs.

He hollered in pain, his grip on my hair loosening.

I took my opening, running for the door as fast as my legs would carry me. But it wasn't enough. I should've known better. It was hard to compete with a fuel like hatred.

Just steps from the door, Gabe caught hold of my dress, the fabric ripping. Then he got my hair again, yanking me back. But he didn't stop there. He threw me against the wall with vicious force.

The room spun around me, and my legs went weak.

Gabe's hand closed around my throat, squeezing hard. "He thinks he can take from me? I'm going to take from him."

I clawed at Gabe's arm, but he didn't even seem to notice.

"Might fuck you first. Really make him pay."

Panic shot through me, and I fought with everything I had, but it wasn't enough. Black spots danced in front of my vision.

The door flew open, banging against the wall.

Gabe's hold on me fell away, and I collapsed to the floor, coughing and trying to suck in air.

Some part of my brain recognized Caden, fury in those hazel eyes I'd never seen before. He was on his brother in three long strides, his fist lashing out and connecting with Gabe's cheek. But Gabe didn't go down. Instead, he struck with a vicious uppercut to Caden's ribs, his hand with the gun rising and going for Caden's face.

Caden ducked the worst of it, realizing now what his brother held in his hand. Caden tackled Gabe to the floor. They grappled, both trying to get control of the weapon.

I screamed with everything I had in me, but Gabe's assault had already turned my voice raw. I tried harder, silently pleading for more sound to come out.

It was no use.

Then all I could hear was sound. The crack of a bullet. And everything went still.

Chapter Forty-One

Caden

THE SHOT RANG IN MY EARS, BUT I DIDN'T WASTE A second. The moment the bullet hit the wall and distracted Gabe, I put all my strength into a punch to his temple. Gabe slumped to the floor in a heap.

I clambered for the gun, making sure the safety was on before sliding it into my waistband. My gaze instantly searched for Grae. She struggled to her knees, panic in her eyes, and I was already moving.

I hauled her into my arms. "Where are you hurt?"

The sight of her torn dress and the red marks on her throat had panic surging through me. "Did he…?" I couldn't even finish that sentence.

Grae shook her head, then winced. "No," she croaked.

I pulled her into me. "Where does it hurt?"

"Just my throat. My head."

"Gigi…" It was all I could say. That one word held a million silent apologies.

Shouts sounded, and half a dozen people filed into the room:

Nash, Holt, security, and Clint's partner. But I kept hold of Grae. I couldn't let her go. Not for a single second.

"What the hell happened?" Holt barked.

"Gabe," I choked. "He attacked her."

Nash and Holt were on Gabe in a flash. He started to come to as Nash pulled a set of handcuffs from his tux pocket. It took my brother a few moments to realize what was happening. He flailed and cursed, trying to deck Holt, but Nash got his hands behind his back and began reading him his rights.

Security and Officer Adams rushed over to Clint. Adams had her radio out and called for backup and an ambulance.

I still didn't let go of Grae.

Her heart hammered against my torso. I tried to let each beat reassure me. She was alive, breathing. But all it did was tell me how terrified she'd been. And it was all my fault.

Doc closed her medical bag. "Lots of tea with honey. Maybe some ice cream. That will all help your throat." She handed Grae a bottle of pills. "These are for if the pain gets too bad. Do you think you'll need something to help you sleep?"

There was sympathy in Doc's gaze, and I was grateful that she'd been willing to drop everything and make a house call when Grae had refused to go to the hospital.

"I'll be okay," Grae assured the doctor, her voice still a bit raspy.

I swallowed against the tightness in my throat, trying to clear it, but it was no use.

Doc studied Grae for a moment and then nodded. "I want to see you for a recheck the day after tomorrow, okay?"

I nodded. "I can bring her in."

"I'll have my office call you and let you know what time."

I extended a hand to Doc. "Thank you. For everything."

"I'm happy to help however I can." She turned back to Grae and handed her a card. "This is a local therapist. She's good. I think it would be smart to talk to her."

Grae took the card but didn't say a word.

I'd make sure she called. But it killed something in me that she had to. All because of my brother.

When Nash and Holt hauled Gabe outside to put him in a squad car, he'd been railing about how he was going to kill me and that I would pay if it was the last thing he did. The sheer fury in him was unlike anything I'd ever seen.

My mom had lost it when she saw the aftermath. She was so hysterical the EMTs had been forced to sedate her. Lena had freaked out on the cops, telling them they had it all wrong and that she planned to sue them.

My father had simply stared in dumbfounded shock.

Doc lifted her bag and glanced at me. "Call my cell if there are any issues."

"I will." I wouldn't hesitate, not with Grae. I walked Doc to the front door and waited until she was in her car and pulling away before I returned to Grae.

She sat on my sectional, a blanket wrapped around her. I crossed to her, sitting on the coffee table so I could take her in fully. "What do you need?"

Grae blinked at me a few times. "Nothing."

"More water? Some tea? Ice cream?"

"Caden," she said softly.

"I can run you a bath. Sit with you." I wasn't about to let her go into a tub alone when there was a slight chance that she could have a concussion.

Grae took my hands in hers. "Caden," she said again.

"Do you want something to eat so you can take some of those meds?"

"Stop it and talk to me."

Everything in me constricted, making it hard to swallow, difficult to even breathe. "I don't know what you want me to say."

Grae's blue eyes pierced me. "Tell me what you're feeling."

I pushed to my feet, needing to move. I felt as though the sensations gathering in my chest would burn me alive if I stayed still. "It doesn't matter what I'm feeling."

Grae didn't move, but her eyes tracked me. "It matters to me."

"He hurt you," I growled.

"Yes. But I'm okay, and he's in a jail cell."

Grae was so calm. As if she hadn't been brutally attacked and almost strangled. Even now, those red marks on her neck were darkening. They'd turn purple before long, proof of what my brother had put her through.

"I left you alone, and he hurt you."

Grae stood then, letting the blanket fall to the couch. She slowly crossed to me. "I wasn't alone. I had Clint. And I told you to stay."

I shook my head with vicious ferocity. "I shouldn't have listened."

Grae pressed a hand to my chest. "You didn't know."

"I should've." The words hurt to say. I'd known my brother was furious at me. Knew that he saw Grae as my weakness. I somehow knew he would mess with her to get at me, but I had no idea he would take it this far.

Grae pressed her palms to my cheeks. "This isn't your fault."

But it was.

I stared down at the woman I loved with everything I had. "How can you even bear to look at me?"

Chapter Forty-Two

Grae

MY HEART CRACKED INTO A MILLION LITTLE PIECES at Caden's words, each shard so tiny I wasn't sure I'd ever be able to put it back together again. Not the way it was.

What had happened tonight would change us both forever. But Caden was paying the highest price.

My thumbs swept across his cheeks. "Do you know what I see when I look at you?"

Caden was silent, but his eyes flared.

"The man who's always there when I need him the most. The person who gets me better than anyone else. Someone who's kind and loyal and will do anything for the people he loves."

"I failed you," he croaked.

I let one hand trail down his face to the back of his neck and squeezed. "I'm standing in front of you. Breathing. Living. Because you came. And it's not the first time you saved my life. You always show up when I really need you."

The corner of my mouth kicked up. "You even let me maul you when I was trying to escape a bad date."

"Gigi…"

"I will only ever see the best things when I look at you. I'll only ever see the truth."

Caden searched my eyes. "How?"

"Because you've always been that glimmer of light for me. A beacon of hope. Even when I didn't want you to be."

Caden brushed the hair out of my face, his fingers tangling in the strands. "You shine so brightly it terrified me. Worried if I ever lost you, my world would go black."

"But I'm right here. No matter what happens, we always seem to find our way back to each other."

The gold in Caden's eyes burned bright. "Love you, Gigi. I always have. Every moment we were side by side. Every moment we were apart. I think the times I pushed you away…I only loved you more."

My breath hitched, everything in me pulling taut. "I love you, too. Even when I didn't want to, I couldn't burn you out of me. You were always there."

Caden's hand slid along my jaw, tipping my head back. "I'm so sorry I hurt you. I'm sorry I was a coward."

"Losing each other just makes us appreciate this more." I stretched up onto my tiptoes, bringing my mouth to his. I poured everything I didn't have the words for into the kiss. Because what I felt for Caden went beyond love. It was something indescribable. Something I could only paint with my body against his.

"Gigi…" he whispered against my lips. "You need to rest."

"I need *you*."

It was the simple truth. I needed to feel him. To reassure myself that we were okay, still here, and would always find our way back to each other.

Caden stared down at me, his eyes searching. And then he hoisted me into his arms.

My legs encircled his waist, holding tightly. As if I needed to guarantee that I wouldn't lose him.

Caden strode down the hall toward his bedroom, but I didn't let that stop me. My lips trailed over his neck, and when my teeth grazed his ear, he let out a growl that made me grin.

A second later, Caden lowered me to the mattress, his fingers coming to the T-shirt I wore. His movements were so incredibly gentle as he lifted it over my head and sent it sailing to the floor. His eyes flared. "No bra?"

I shrugged. "We were going to bed."

Caden's gaze dipped to the baggy sweats I wore. His hand trailed up my thigh, to the very core of me. "And here?"

My eyes danced. "Why don't you find out?"

His fingers unhooked my insulin pump and then latched on to the waistband of my sweats. He pulled them off in one swift move. That muscle in his jaw flexed. "Gigi..."

"I don't like sleeping in underwear."

Caden's fingers dipped between my legs, stroking. "It does make for easy access."

"I'm all for practicality," I said between pants.

He grinned as a finger teased my opening. "Good to know."

"Caden," I whispered.

"Tell me what you want, Gigi."

"I want you. Inside me. Filling me. Need all of you."

Caden's hand was gone, and he was stripping out of his tux faster than I could blink. He lowered himself so he hovered over me. "I'll always give you what you need." His eyes locked with mine as my legs encircled his hips. "Tell me you're sure."

"Never been more sure of anything."

It was all Caden needed. He slid inside on a slow glide. Usually, when Caden took me, there was a hint of feral need. But not now. Caden took his time with each thrust as if he wanted to make sure I felt every possible sensation.

My fingers dug into his shoulders, my back arching. My hips

rose to meet his, finding the path that was ours alone. But I didn't lose Caden's eyes for a single second.

I saw it all before he said a single word.

"Love you, Gigi."

Those words I'd craved for so long sent me spiraling over the edge. My walls clamped around Caden, and he came on a shout, his forehead pressing against mine as he thrust deeply.

We stayed like that, locked together, until both of us caught our breath. When Caden slid from my body, I wanted to weep at the loss. But he pulled me against him and wrapped me in his arms. His body cocooned mine in a way that said he'd always be with me.

Caden shifted again, pulling open the drawer on his night-stand. The light was so low I couldn't see what he was grasping for but then he was back again. His lips ghosted over my hair.

"I told my parents I'm leaving the company."

I stilled then and turned in his hold. "You did?"

He nodded. "Mom was supportive. Dad was pissed."

I wasn't surprised. "I'm glad your mom handled it well."

Caden's fingers trailed up and down my arm. "You've made me see what family should be. What it means to truly love someone."

My heart picked up speed. "You've always known. You just needed someone to have your back while you fought for that."

Caden's lips brushed mine. "And you've been that for me. Never had a fiercer defender."

"And you always will," I promised.

"Build that family with me. One that always supports and defends. One that loves with everything we have."

"Caden," I whispered.

He held up a ring that glinted in the low light. "I know the timing's shit, and I should wait to sweep you off your feet with a million flowers or a helicopter tour or a fancy dinner, but I don't want to waste another second living without you. I want you in my bed, in our home, by my side. I want to make babies with you and grow old and gray."

I couldn't hold back. I jumped on him.

Caden let out a grunt as I straddled him.

"Yes!" Tears cascaded down my cheeks as I kissed him. "Yes. Yes. Yes."

His mouth curved against mine as he slid the ring onto my finger. "Think we could get married tomorrow?"

Chapter Forty-Three

Grae

CADEN TUGGED ME AWAY FROM THE FRIDGE AND INTO HIS arms.

"Hey," I protested. "I need to make us breakfast. I thought you were *starving*."

He grinned as he lifted my hand and pressed a kiss to my ring. "Just needed a good morning."

I stared at the diamond catching the light and throwing a series of rainbows around the kitchen. The ring was absolutely breathtaking, and I loved that it had carried his grandparents through over sixty years of marriage.

I brushed my lips across Caden's. "Pretty sure you already said good morning twice and then a third time in the shower."

He chuckled. "Better do it a fourth time just to make sure—"

His phone rang, cutting him off. Caden cursed. "Cockblock."

I laughed. "Might be a good thing. Wouldn't want either of us to pull a muscle."

Caden shook his head as he moved to answer his cell. "We're going to have to start a training regimen."

I choked on a laugh as he pressed the phone to his ear. "Caden."

There was a pause.

"Sure, she can come through. Just give her a map to my place."

I glanced at Caden in question as he ended the call. "Who?"

"Aspen. She probably wants to check on you."

Guilt pricked at me. "I should've texted and let her know I was all right."

Caden brushed his lips across mine. "You've had a lot going on. I bet Maddie brought her up to speed."

I nodded, letting myself melt into his hold. "Things are going to be crazy for a while."

"They will. But we'll handle it together."

"I like the sound of that."

The doorbell rang, and Caden released me. "I'll get it."

I busied myself with making coffee as if that would some-how normalize things. Muted voices sounded from the front of the house, and then I heard footsteps. A second later, Aspen appeared. Her skin was even paler than usual, and worry lined her face. "Grae…you're okay?"

I hurried toward my friend and pulled her into a hug. "I'm totally fine."

I met Caden's eyes over her shoulder, and we shared a con-cerned look. I gave Aspen one more squeeze and then released her.

"It was my day to take Cady and Charlie to camp. Lawson told me what happened when I picked up Charlie. I just needed to see with my own eyes that you were okay."

"I am. I promise."

Aspen's gaze zeroed in on my throat, and she blanched. "I'm so sorry, G."

I took her hand, squeezing hard. "It looks way worse than it is. I've always bruised super easily."

That much was true. Thankfully, my voice was mostly back to normal.

"They arrested him?" Aspen pressed.

I nodded. "He's in jail."

Though I didn't know for how long. Gabe had all the money in the world for a good lawyer. The thought made me shiver. At least with Lawson and Nash working at the station, I'd get a heads-up if they released him on bail.

Aspen looked down at our joined hands, and her eyes widened. "Wait, is that…?" Her words trailed off as if she were scared to even say them.

I laughed. "It's been a somewhat eventful twenty-four hours."

A little of the tension running through Aspen melted away, and her eyes shone. "This is just the thing to soothe the hurts. I'm so happy for you."

She pulled me into another hug.

"Thanks," I mumbled into her hair.

Aspen straightened, released me, and tried to brush away the tears. "Here I am, barging in on you, and it's the morning after you got engaged. I'll just be on my way. But let me know if you need anything. I can bring over dinner or anything at all."

"You don't have to go," I assured her.

Aspen shook her head, the tears still coming. "I need to get to work anyway. I'll see you later."

She scampered down the hall before Caden or I could stop her, and the door slammed in her wake.

I glanced at Caden. "That was extreme, right?"

He nodded, his brow furrowing. "She was jumpy at The Brew the other day, too. I wonder if something's going on."

I stared down the hallway. "I hope not."

My phone rang on the kitchen island, and I crossed to it. Lawson's name flashed on the screen. I picked it up and hit accept. "Hey."

"How are you feeling?"

"Pretty good, actually." I glanced down at the ring on my finger, smiling at everything it meant. But I wasn't about to tell my brother over the phone. This was an in-person reveal.

"Good. Doc checked you out?"

"Last night. And I'm going back for a recheck tomorrow, but she wasn't overly concerned about anything."

Caden sent me a look that called *bullshit*. But I just rolled my eyes.

"No concussion?" Lawson pressed.

"She didn't think so."

"Okay, but Caden's keeping an eye on you?"

I smiled down at the counter. "Yes, Caden's taking good care of me." I paused for a second, the smile slipping. "How are things at the station?"

Lawson knew what I was asking without me saying the words. "Caden there, too?"

"Yeah."

"Put me on speaker. I can bring you both up to speed."

I pulled the phone away from my ear and hit the speaker icon. "Okay."

"I'm not point on the case since you're my sister, but I've had the team keep me up to date."

I bit the inside of my cheek. "I'm sorry you're off the case."

"I should've taken a step back before now, but I wanted to help."

Caden wrapped an arm around me. "Tell me you've got him."

"The evidence is piling up," Lawson said. "The crime scene team has been going through all the evidence we have, and they found a timing device in a closet at Grae's house."

A muscle in Caden's jaw ticked. "Meaning someone wouldn't have had to be physically present to set a fire?"

"Correct." Lawson blew out an audible breath. "And we've been working on a timeline for everything else. He doesn't have an alibi for any of it."

I looked up at Caden. "Not even his fiancée?"

"Nope. Seems she gives him a pretty long leash. Didn't care if he didn't come home as long as he paid the credit card bills," Lawson grumbled.

Caden stared down at me. "I'm so sorry, Gigi."

My fingers dug into his waist. "We've been over this. His actions aren't on you."

"She's right," Lawson agreed. "You've been hurt by Gabe's actions just as much. Now you have to take the time to put the betrayal behind you and heal."

Lawson was speaking from an experience that had marked him, but I wasn't sure he'd ever fully healed. I just hoped Caden could.

I stretched up onto my tiptoes and kissed him. "It's you and me. Remember what we're building."

Caden's eyes softened, and he wrapped his other arm around me. "You and me."

Lawson coughed. "Please don't start making out. I've been through enough in the past twenty-four hours."

I choked on a laugh. "Then get off the phone so you don't have to hear it."

"Yeah, yeah. Can you come down to the station to give a more formal statement this afternoon?"

"No problem."

"Thank you. Love you, G," Lawson said, his voice gruff.

"Love you, too." I clicked off and stared up at Caden.

"You okay?"

He nodded. "I need to go talk to my parents."

I hated that he did but knew it would be better to get it over with. "Do you want me to come with you?"

Caden shook his head. "I'll make it as quick as possible, and then we can go pick up some breakfast."

"I'll be here waiting."

He kissed me long and slow, the kind that reminded me what we were fighting for. "Love you, Gigi."

"I'll never get tired of hearing it."

Caden kissed the tip of my nose. "I'll remember that."

I slipped out of his hold. "Go before I make you stay."

"Okay." Caden grabbed his keys and headed down the hallway. "Lock the door behind me and set the alarm."

I almost argued with him that we didn't need to worry about that anymore, but with everything Caden had been through lately, I simply followed him to the door.

"I won't be long," he said as he headed down the walk.

"Take all the time you need," I called.

As Caden slid into his SUV, I closed the door and locked it. Then I set the alarm. I made my way back to the kitchen, and as my ring caught the light, I smiled, my insides warming. Caden Shaw was going to be my husband.

I let out a full-blown, giddy squeal and then dissolved into laughter. Then I decided to make chocolate chip muffins. I set to work pulling ingredients from the pantry, humming while I did so.

Just as I opened the fridge, the doorbell rang. I closed the door and headed down the hallway. Peeking through the peephole, I grinned at the familiar face and disarmed the alarm.

I opened the door to the morning sunshine. "Hey—"

I didn't get another word out because something hit me in the middle. Blinding pain ricocheted through me, making my muscles spasm and then give out altogether. I crumpled to the floor, and as darkness closed in around me, it was Caden's name on my lips.

Chapter Forty-Four

Caden

I PULLED TO A STOP IN FRONT OF MY PARENTS' HOME, IDLING for a moment before putting my SUV in park. This house held so many memories. The good. The bad. And everything in between. But it was time to let it all go.

Turning off the engine, I slid out of my SUV and headed up the front path. I hesitated for a moment and then rang the bell.

There was nothing at first, and then footsteps came from inside. They echoed, making the space inside sound as empty as it was. The door opened slowly, and my mother appeared.

She wasn't dressed nearly as formally as usual. Instead, she wore casual joggers and a T-shirt with a slouchy cardigan wrapped around her. But it was her eyes that worried me. They were empty, bleak.

"Caden," Mom said softly.

I stepped into the entryway and wrapped her in a gentle hug. "Hey, Mom." I didn't bother asking if she was okay. I knew she was a wreck. There was no other option.

"How is Grae doing?"

I released my mom and stepped back. "She's doing a lot better this morning."

"That's good." Mom's voice shook on the words.

"I wanted to come and talk to you and Dad. Check on you."

She nodded, but the movement was jerky. "He's in the living room."

Mom started walking without waiting for an answer from me, leading the way down the hall and into the living room.

My father sat in his usual leather chair. He had a newspaper in his hands, but he wasn't looking at it. Instead, his focus was on the back windows as he stared into the forest.

He looked up at the sound of our footsteps. At least a dozen emotions flitted across his expression at the sight of me, but they moved too quickly for me to pin any of them down. "Caden."

There was no warmth in his voice at my name, no affection, only clinical coolness.

"Dad. I wanted to check on you and Mom. See if you needed anything."

A muscle in his jaw flexed. "You can start by getting that woman to drop any charges she might be planning against Gabe."

Every muscle in my body turned to granite. "He tried to kill her."

My father scoffed. "Hardly. They had a little tussle. It was nothing."

"There are finger marks around Grae's throat. He tried to strangle her. He had a damned gun," I gritted out.

Mom let out a sound of distress, but I didn't back down. Couldn't. My father had to see what he'd wrought.

"The police said he doesn't have an alibi for any of the incidents that have happened to Grae."

My mom started to cry softly.

Dad threw the newspaper to the floor. "His drinking has gotten out of control. I'll send him to rehab, but this family doesn't need our name dragged through the mud. The company doesn't need it."

There it was. My father didn't give a damn about Gabe. Or me.

Or the fact that an innocent woman had almost been killed. All he cared about was his precious reputation. His company.

"Enough," Mom whispered.

"You and Grae will retract your statements, and we'll make sure the rest of the witnesses sign nondisclosure agreements," my father continued.

"I said enough!" Mom snapped.

Dad jerked back. "Jocelyn."

Tears still glistened in her eyes, but there was something else there now, too. An anger I'd never seen in her before. "I've stood by for too long. Let you twist this family into something I don't even recognize anymore."

My father gaped at her. "What are you talking about?"

"I thought I loved you once. But the way you've torn apart our boys, treated them with nothing but cruelty and cold calculation…I'll hate you for the rest of my days."

Dad pushed to his feet, redness creeping up his neck. "I won't allow you to talk to me this way. This is my house—"

"That's where you're wrong, Harrison."

He froze. "What the hell are you talking about?"

Mom clasped her hands in front of her and met my father's stare. "The land this resort is built on has been in my family for generations. Every building on it belongs to *me*."

Dad's jaw went slack, and then fury flared in his eyes. "Fine. You want The Peaks, you're welcome to it. You'll drive it into the ground in less than a month."

"Not just The Peaks," she said calmly.

A vein in my father's neck bulged, but he didn't say a word.

"I called an emergency meeting of the board this morning. We've all decided that you are no longer equipped to lead this company. You're being replaced. We've given you a generous severance package, but you'll be leaving."

"You fucking bitch!"

My father lunged, but I stepped in front of him, shoving him back with enough force that he stumbled into that damn chair he loved so much.

"Don't," I growled. "You don't touch her. You don't even speak to her."

Dad shoved up to standing. "You'll pay for this."

He grabbed his keys from the side table and stormed out of the house, slamming the door behind him.

My mom let out a shaky breath. "That went better than I thought."

I turned to face her. "Mom…why?"

"It was time." She gave me a sad smile. "My great-grandfather started this company. I wasn't about to let Harrison ruin it. I just wish I hadn't let him hurt you and Gabe so badly. I've made so many mistakes…"

I pulled her into a hug and felt her trembling. "We're going to be okay."

She pulled back a fraction. "Interested in running a hotel conglomerate?"

That startled a laugh out of me. "Honestly? Not really. But I would love to run The Peaks."

A genuine smile spread across my mother's face. "We'd love to have you."

I squeezed her hands. "I think you should come stay with Grae and me for a few days while you sort all this out with Dad."

She shook her head. "I already have my lawyer filing for divorce. When your father tries to come back onto the property, he'll find that he's not permitted on the premises. I'll box up his belongings and send them wherever he wants."

I studied her for a long moment. "You're sure about this?"

Mom gripped my hand tighter. "A part of me died with Clara. I was so scared that if I lost anything else, the rest of me would go, too. I was so desperate to hold on to my family that I couldn't see it was killing us all."

"I'm so sorry."

"I'm the one who's sorry." She took a deep breath. "There's something I need to tell you."

A lead weight settled in my stomach. "Okay."

"Gabe is adopted."

Shock swept through me. "What?"

"For a long time, I thought I couldn't have children. Your father wasn't happy about it."

I wanted to deck my dad for making my mother feel worse about something that must have been incredibly painful already.

Mom released my hand and toyed with the hem of her cardigan. "We decided to go the adoption route. Your father demanded it be kept a secret. He didn't want anyone to know that Gabe wasn't his blood."

She fingered a button on her sweater while she lost herself in the memory. "I went along with it because I wanted a child so badly. And after Gabe came along, it all seemed worth it. Imagine my surprise when I got pregnant with you and then Clara."

"Gabe found out, didn't he?" I asked, the pieces coming together.

My mother nodded. "When he was in middle school."

I tried to remember when Gabe had changed, when our relationship had shifted. It was when he was in seventh grade. I'd thought he was just over having a younger brother and sister tagging along, but it was so much more.

"He became fixated. It didn't matter how much I reassured him that he was ours; he always felt less than." A tear slid down her cheek. "I failed him."

I hugged my mom tightly. "You didn't fail him. There's a sickness in him that you couldn't heal."

"I never thought he would hurt you and Grae."

"I know. But we're okay. And the three of us will heal. Together."

My mom pulled back, her eyes still full of tears. "Together?"

I smiled down at her. "I think it's time we build the family we were always meant to have. Don't you?"

Her mouth curved. "I'd like that."

I stayed with my mother for another hour, making sure she was truly okay. When I was sure of that, I headed for my SUV, calling security on the way. My mom had already brought them up to speed. My father had left the property and wouldn't be welcomed back.

I shook my head as I turned into my driveway. Never in a million years had I thought this morning would turn out the way it had. I parked my SUV and climbed out, heading up the front walk.

My steps faltered as I took in the entryway. The door was slightly ajar.

Panic lit inside me, surging through my system with a vicious burn.

"Grae," I called, shoving open the door and heading inside.

There was no answer.

I strode through the house, searching from room to room. She wasn't in any of them. I pulled out my phone and hit her contact, my heart hammering against my ribs.

A ring trilled from the kitchen. I moved in that direction.

Grae's phone sat on the island. But she was nowhere to be found.

Chapter Forty-Five

Grae

I GROANED AS I ROLLED OVER. MY MUSCLES FLARED WITH A deep ache as if I'd been caught in an especially vicious wave and knocked against a few dozen rocks.

My eyelids fluttered, and light burst through my vision in flashes that made my head pound. What the heck had happened? I tried to search my memory. Had I had a rough blood sugar night? Too much to drink?

And then the memory I'd been searching for slammed into me. The face I'd always recognized as a friend. The jab of a Taser. Going down.

I shot up to sitting, and the world swam in a blur around me as I tried to get my bearings. Bile crept up my throat. The room I was in was bare. I sat on a mattress on the floor with blankets and pillows, but the space had nothing else.

Struggling to my feet, I hurried over to the door. My hand stilled on the knob, and I listened. I didn't hear anything outside. I turned it—locked.

I let a dozen very real curses fly and then turned around. There were two windows in the room, and I quickly crossed to the nearest one. I took in my surroundings. I appeared to be on the second story of a cabin surrounded by woods. But there was an overhang just outside this window. It covered a porch. If I could get out onto it, I could lower myself to the ground without risking too much injury.

Studying the window, I unlocked it and shoved all my weight into opening it. Nothing moved. I tried again—still nothing.

I straightened and set to work examining the pane. That was when I saw the tiny flashes of silver. Nailheads. He'd nailed the window shut, planned for this.

Tears stung my eyes as pressure built in my head. This couldn't be real. It had to be a nightmare that I would surely wake up from.

A beep at my hip sounded, and I glanced down. A warning from my insulin pump.

I let another curse fly. I'd meant to change it out last night, but I'd been distracted by Caden and his proposal and losing myself with him all night long. I'd completely forgotten about it this morning. This was so bad.

The sound of a key in a lock had me spinning around to face the door, hands fisted in preparation.

The door opened, and Eddie filled the space. He grinned that same easy smile he always gave me, as if nothing was wrong. "Good, you're up. You were out for like an hour."

I blinked a few times as if that would somehow right the situation in front of me. "What's going on?"

He extended a bottle of water to me. "Thirsty?"

I didn't take it. He could've injected it with drugs for all I knew.

Eddie shrugged, opened it, and took a sip. "What do you think of the new digs?"

I'd been to Eddie's apartment in town more times than I could count. He'd always said he liked being in the middle of things. This place was none of that.

"Why?" I croaked.

Eddie's expression went stormy. "You can't be trusted out there anymore."

My heart picked up speed. "Can't be trusted to do what?"

"You're mine. You always have been."

"Eddie…we're *friends*."

Rage flared in those familiar amber eyes. "You're mine. You promised me."

Confusion swept through me. "I promised you?"

"You promised after Megan died. Promised you'd always be there."

"And I have been…as your *friend*."

Fury burst through Eddie, and he slammed the water bottle against the wall. "No! You told me you loved me."

I froze, fear pulsing deep. I'd told Eddie, Noel, and Jordan that I loved them countless times, but I didn't mean it like that.

"You get coffee and treats just for me. You take care of me. You make sure I eat and sleep. You said we'd always be together. You promised. But you broke that promise." He snarled. "You can't be trusted. Gotta keep you here until you remember."

My mouth went dry. Eddie's mind had twisted. Maybe from the trauma of losing Megan, but maybe not. Maybe it had always been this way.

"I can't stay here, Eddie. I need to go to work. See my family. I need my insulin." My pump beeped as if to punctuate my point.

Eddie glared at the device at my hip. "You don't need that. You're strong without it. You always have been."

That panic was back. "If I don't have my insulin, I'll die."

"You will not," he growled. "That's the people in your life trying to control you. I see it. How annoyed you get when they ask about it. When they say you can't handle things."

Blood roared in my ears. Eddie had taken me without any preparation for the things I needed to stay alive. I glanced down at my pump. It was already running on empty. How long did I have before I started feeling the effects? Maybe an hour if I was lucky.

"Eddie, please. At least get me some insulin. You can sneak into my house. There's still some in the fridge."

"That's not your house!" he screamed. "This is your house. You're home now. With me. We're going to be happy here. You and me. I'll take care of you."

"Were you the one at my house? Outside my window?" It hurt to ask, but I had to know. Had each and every occurrence been Eddie and not Gabe?

Eddie's jaw tightened. "I just wanted to make sure you were safe. I miss you when we aren't together."

My eyes burned; the urge to cry was so strong. "Did you take my pajamas?"

"I needed to feel close to you." His voice had gone almost childlike, and it turned my insides. But that innocent tone disappeared as anger flashed in his eyes. "But then you had to let him touch you."

I swallowed as my mouth went dry. "Eddie…"

"He shouldn't be touching you, *ever*!" His voice vibrated with fury as he started pacing. "I had to set the fires then. They help me let out my anger so I don't hurt you. I don't want to hurt you, even when you make me mad."

"The pictures?" I croaked.

Eddie turned those furious eyes in my direction. "You had to know that it wasn't okay. That you couldn't be with him." He tapped his fingers against his legs as he paced. "You'll learn. Once you realize we're meant to be, everything can go back to normal. Once you realize you were always meant to be mine."

"I'm not yours," I whispered.

He charged, shoving me hard against the wall. "You're mine! Say it!"

He slammed me against the wall again, making my ears ring and my head spin.

"I'm yours," I croaked.

Eddie shoved his forearm across my throat, making it hard to breathe. "I don't believe you."

"Can't. Breathe."

He released his hold on me and threw me onto the mattress, beginning to pace. "She lies. He changed her."

"Eddie, please. Just let me go. I won't tell anyone." Tears burned my eyes.

"Liar!" He flew at me, pinning me to the mattress. His eyes flared as they zeroed in on my hand. On the ring. "It's all been lies, hasn't it? You're just like the rest of them. Can't be trusted. Never as good as my Megan."

"I'm sorry," I wheezed, terror pulsing through me.

"You're not. But you will be. Because I'm going to make you burn."

Chapter Forty-Six

Caden

I PACED BACK AND FORTH ACROSS MY DRIVEWAY AS COUNTLESS law enforcement officers and crime scene techs milled about. Lawson and Nash had made it here in record time after I called, and Roan and Holt hadn't been far behind. But no one had a clue where Grae was. Gabe was still in jail, and the only person he'd been allowed to talk to was his lawyer. He couldn't have done this.

Pulling out my phone, I called my head of security for the third time. "Where are you?"

"On my way, sir. I had to get the security camera footage loaded onto a laptop. I still haven't been able to get in touch with the guard who was on duty."

"Hurry up," I gritted out and hung up.

Rage swelled, too much for me to contain. I grabbed one of the folding chairs and sent it flying into my side yard with a curse.

The flurry of people stilled and stared at me.

Nash crossed to me in three long strides. "You need to keep it together."

"I can't lose her," I said through heaving breaths.

"We're not going to."

"I just got her back." My throat tightened, burning with the emotion I couldn't let free.

Nash dropped his hands to my shoulders and squeezed. "And you're gonna build that big, beautiful life together."

My teeth ground together. "Asked her to marry me last night."

Pain lanced through Nash's eyes, but he quickly covered it. "She shoot you down?"

A strangled laugh escaped my throat. "Got my ring on her finger."

"Mom's gonna freak. She's been dreaming about Grae's wedding from the moment the doctor told her she was finally having a girl."

My ribs constricted in a painful squeeze. I could see that day—Grae walking down the aisle toward me, wildflowers in her hair, a secret smile playing on her lips, those blue eyes shining. "Gonna be a hell of a wedding."

A resort SUV pulled into my drive, and my head of security jumped out. Dennis rushed over to the table we had set up. "The footage is ready to go."

Holt opened the laptop and hit a few keys. "We look for familiar faces first. If we don't see anyone we know, we run every single person who came through."

We all nodded in agreement as the tape played on fast-forward. Holt paused on each face. They were mostly guests I didn't recognize. No one tripped my trigger.

Then Holt paused the tape again.

Nash cursed. Lawson pulled out his phone. Roan looked like he wanted to kill someone. I froze. My blood went cold as Eddie's face filled the screen.

"Jerry," Lawson clipped into his phone. "Need you to look up property records for an Edward Pierson."

Lawson lowered his phone and put it on speaker.

"Just a second," Jerry said, and the sound of typing came across the line. "He's got an apartment in town."

"Not there," I snapped. There was no way he was keeping Grae above a shop.

"Keep looking," Lawson ordered. "Any other properties he has ties to?"

"Gonna need a minute," Jerry muttered.

Grae might not have that minute. My hands fisted so hard my knuckles cracked.

Jerry's typing ceased. "That's weird."

"What?" I growled.

"This property was purchased by an LLC, but he's tied to the corporation."

My gaze shot to Nash, and we shared a look. Someone didn't try to hide the identity of their ownership unless they were famous or up to no good.

"I'll be damned," Jerry muttered.

"Tell us," Lawson snapped.

"According to the state, Edward Pierson is the sole owner of that LLC. Place on North Arrow Leaf Trail. Just sent you the address, Law."

Everything in me stilled. My muscles wound tight, strangling the bones beneath. Eddie. The coworker Grae had sat next to for years—her friend.

"We need to move. Now," I ground out.

Clint strode up, rocking a shiner from the night before. "You know you guys can't go. We're calling in SWAT. Give us an hour, and we'll go."

An hour? Anything could happen in an hour. He was delusional if he thought I was waiting while some maniac hurt Grae.

I didn't waste my time arguing. I simply turned on my heel and started toward my SUV.

Clint called my name, but I ignored him, picking up to a jog.

"Let's take my SUV," Holt called. "I've got gear, and it's not an official vehicle."

I didn't need to be told twice. I changed direction and headed for his SUV, climbing into the passenger seat. Lawson, Nash, and

Roan threw vests into the back and piled into the rear seats. Holt was off before anyone could say a word. "Got a gun safe and a few vests in the back."

Lawson glanced at Nash. "We could lose our badges over this."

"You think I give a fuck?" he snapped.

Lawson jerked his head in a nod.

Holt glanced at me. "This guy trip your trigger?"

I shook my head. "Not once. Seemed like a goofball who cared about Grae. Harmless."

But I'd been wrong. Just like I'd been wrong about my brother.

Holt turned onto a road that would take us to Eddie's hidden property.

I replayed every interaction I'd had with the man, trying to read anything from them. I came up empty.

"Caden, I need you to take the rear when we get there. You're not trained," Lawson warned.

"Fine." I didn't give a damn who went first as long as we got to Grae.

Her face flashed in my mind. The way she tipped her head back when a laugh caught her off guard. How her eyes sparked when I was inside her. The gentleness when she told me she loved me. I couldn't lose her.

"Oh, shit."

My gaze snapped to Holt. "What?"

He pointed over the trees ahead. "Smoke."

Chapter Forty-Seven

Grae

I POUNDED MY FISTS AGAINST THE LOCKED DOOR. "EDDIE!"

My insulin pump beeped again, and my vision blurred. *Crap.* This was beyond bad.

My nose twitched, the scent of something tickling it, and I froze. Smoke.

He didn't. There was no way. But I'd seen the unhinged fury in Eddie's eyes when he told me I'd burn. He was making good on that promise.

I pounded harder on the wood, screaming his name, but there was nothing.

Smoke seeped under the door, and I scrambled back. I knew the gray cloud would kill me far sooner the flames would. I had to get out of here, and I needed to do it now.

My gaze jumped around the room, looking for something, *anything* that might help me break free. But Eddie had prepped my cell well. There was only the mattress and blankets, a couple of pillows, and the discarded water bottle. I'd given in and drunk every last drop; I was so thirsty.

I glanced back at the bed, zeroing in on the wool blanket. Then I looked at the window. Crossing to it, I tapped the glass. It was an older cabin, so the glass was thick, but this was my only hope.

I coughed as the smoke thickened in the room, my eyes burning. Hurrying to the mattress, I yanked off the blanket and wrapped it around my arm. I went back to the window and turned so I was facing away from the glass. I hauled my arm back and brought it down with all the force I could muster, but my entire limb felt like it weighed a hundred pounds.

Pain streaked from my elbow up my arm, but the cracking sound was music to my ears. I brought my arm up and did it again. This time, the glass shattered.

Pieces fell to the floor, leaving a jagged frame in place. I covered the sharp edges and windowsill with the blanket and hoisted myself up. As I pushed through the opening, glass scraped against my back. I ignored it and kept pushing through.

I pulled fresh air into my lungs, coughing harder as I climbed out onto the overhang. Slowly, I scooted toward the edge and glanced over. My vision swam as I surveyed the drop. It was farther than I'd originally thought, but I had no choice.

Lying back, I flipped onto my belly and slid down the overhang until I hung off the side, my legs dangling. Flames danced inside the cabin, crackling and popping with angry fierceness. I said a silent prayer and released my hold.

I dropped the five feet, landing in a heap in the dirt with a muffled cry of pain. I stayed still for a moment and tried to survey the damage. Pain radiated through me, but I didn't think I'd broken anything.

A shout sounded, and my head snapped up. I caught sight of Eddie standing to the side of the cabin, surveying his work. Fury flashed in his amber eyes, spurring me to my feet.

I wanted to stick to the road and avoid getting lost in woods I wasn't familiar with, but I didn't have a choice. I needed cover and a chance to hide. So, I dashed for the trees, my muscles burning and stomach cramping. Even with the dose of adrenaline, my body felt heavy, and my mouth was like a desert.

Eddie screamed in rage. He yelled nonsensical things about promises and me needing to burn.

Tears stung my face as branches tore at my skin, but I just kept running.

My foot caught on a root, and I went down hard. I didn't even register the pain this time, just scrambled upright to keep running. But it was too late.

A hand caught my T-shirt, yanking me back against a hard chest. "You think you can betray me and walk away?" Eddie bellowed.

"Please," I wheezed.

Dark spots danced in front of my vision, and the world tilted sideways.

Eddie pressed a blade against my neck. "I wanted to watch you burn, but maybe I'll just watch the blood drain from you instead."

"D-don't. I'll do whatever you want. Please."

Images of Caden's face flashed in my mind. The tender way he looked at me when it was just the two of us. The way that gold flashed and danced in his eyes when he wanted me. The mischievous smile I could watch for hours. I'd just found him again. I couldn't lose him.

The blade pressed harder against my neck, and I cried out.

"Don't move, Eddie," Lawson called, stepping through the trees.

I nearly wept with relief at the sight of my brother.

Eddie's other hand grabbed me by the hair. "This is my property. Mine. You're not allowed here."

"Let her go," Nash said, making his presence known to our right.

Eddie whirled. "Get out!"

The blade pricked my neck, and I cried out again.

"Hey, just take it easy," Lawson said.

Movement to our left caught my attention, and my tears did

come then. They silently tracked down my cheeks as Caden stepped into view. His face had gone pale, but feral fury pulsed in those hazel eyes.

Eddie caught the movement, too, backing up, the knife still pressed to my throat. "You can't be here! No, no, no! She's not yours. She's mine. She'll always be mine."

"Let her go," Lawson warned.

My eyes didn't leave Caden. "I love you," I called.

"No!" Eddie screamed, pressing the knife harder against my neck.

Two shots sounded, and then I fell.

Chapter Forty-Eight

Caden

THE FIRST CRACK OF A BULLET PIERCED THE AIR, AND I was already running. The second crack and I was almost to Grae. But she was already falling.

I dropped to the ground next to her, my hands hovering over her body, not wanting to hurt her.

Some part of me was aware of Lawson and Roan checking Eddie for a pulse next to us.

"Caden," Grae croaked.

"I'm right here. Where does it hurt?"

She had a slice across her neck. It wasn't deep, but it was terrifying, nonetheless. Scratches decorated her arms in angry patches of red. And her eyes were unfocused.

"Everywhere," she rasped.

"We need to get her to Doc," I snapped at Nash and Holt.

Holt jerked his head in a nod.

Lawson looked up from Eddie's fallen form. "He's gone."

There wasn't a single part of me that was sad about that.

Law looked at Grae, worry etching itself deep in his expression. "I'll stay with the body and wait for reinforcements."

"I'll stay with you," Roan added.

I leaned over Grae, brushing the hair from her face and pressing my forehead to hers. "I'm going to pick you up."

"Mm-kay."

Her voice sounded far away, and panic lit through me. Her insulin pump beeped, and that panic turned to terror.

Holt bent, fumbling with the pump. "It's out of insulin. She must be spiking."

This couldn't be happening. I couldn't lose her. Not again.

My arms slipped under Grae's body, and she cried out in pain. I froze, my gaze jerking to Nash.

His jaw was so tight he likely cracked a molar. "We have to do it."

I moved then, Grae's moans slicing deep as I lifted her into my arms and stood. Her head rolled into my chest. "Gigi."

"Mmm?" she mumbled.

"Need you to stay with me. Open those blues."

Grae fought to open her eyes. "Feel funny."

My steps came faster. "I know, but we're gonna get you some help."

"Love you, Caden," she whispered, then her head went completely slack.

"Gigi!" I gave her a slight shake as I picked up to a run.

But there was no response. There was nothing at all.

The waiting room was full to bursting. Kerry and Nathan sat clutching each other's hands. Lawson stared down at his phone, most likely getting updates from Aspen, who was watching the kids. Maddie clasped Nash's hand, trailing her fingers over his arm in a comforting pattern. Holt had his arm wrapped around a red-eyed Wren. Roan glared at the wall opposite him. Jordan and Noel sat quietly, both pale with shock from the news about Eddie.

The grief and anxiety were palpable. The emotions swirled around the room, grating against my skin and making me twitchy.

I pushed to my feet, unable to take it anymore. I strode out of the waiting room and into the hall. I couldn't leave, but I couldn't stay either. So, I paced. Up and down the hall, counting the linoleum tiles as I went. Blue. White. Blue. White.

Grae's face flashed in my mind: her skin unnaturally pale and clammy, her breaths shallow.

Memories slammed against the walls I'd tried so hard to keep up—memories from all those years ago when I'd almost lost her.

"Caden?"

I turned at the sound of a familiar voice. "Mom?"

She hurried over to me, wrapping me in a hug. "How is she? Have you heard anything?"

I shook my head. "The doctors are still working on her."

Mom released her hug but took my hands. She searched my eyes, clearly not liking what she saw there. "I'm so sorry."

My ribs twisted in a painful vise. "I don't think I can take this."

She squeezed my hands. "You can and you will. You'll stay strong for Grae until she can be strong for herself."

"It's my greatest fear."

Mom's brows pinched. "What is?"

"That I'd lose her the way I lost Clara." It was the first time I'd truly given voice to the thoughts that'd tormented me for so long. I knew why I'd stayed away from Grae after her diagnosis. It had felt too precarious to remain close. But it hadn't done me any good. Because Grae had already buried herself deep. So deep no amount of time or distance would ever get her out.

"Oh, Caden," my mom said, pulling me into another hug. But, this time, she didn't let go. "I knew it marked you."

"It marked all of us."

Her hand rubbed up and down my back in a way she hadn't done in years. "We can't let losing her keep twisting us up and forcing us into making all the wrong decisions. Clara would never want that."

"I know," I rasped.

"Loving people means exposing ourselves to the worst kind of pain."

My arms jerked around her.

"But it also gives us the greatest beauty we'll ever experience. Can you honestly tell me you'd trade even one second with Grae to escape this pain?"

I pulled back, meeting my mom's eyes. "No."

She squeezed my arms. "Because you love her."

"I wasted so much time trying to keep her out." My words were barely audible, just a faint, raw whisper.

My mom pinned me with a stare. "But you aren't going to waste any more."

"I asked her to marry me."

Mom beamed, her eyes going glassy. "I can't wait to plan that wedding."

That startled a laugh out of me—the last sound I would've expected. "You and Kerry both."

Footsteps sounded in the hall, and I turned to see a man in scrubs heading toward the waiting room. I instantly moved in that direction.

He stepped inside, looking around the space. "Grae Hartley's family?"

Everyone instantly stood.

"I'm Dr. Jones. I've been taking care of Grae."

"How is she?" Kerry croaked.

He turned his focus on Grae's mother. "She's stable but hasn't regained consciousness. She had several superficial wounds that we cleaned and stitched, but the greater issue right now is that she has been in ketoacidosis."

Kerry let out a strangled sound, pressing into her husband's side.

"We've got her blood sugar back in range. Now, we just have to wait for her to wake up. We'll have more information then."

"Can I see her?" I said the words before I even knew I'd thought them.

The doctor turned to me. "We can have one or two people in the room at a time. It's up to you who goes first."

Kerry sent me a wobbly smile. "She'd want to wake up to you."

That burn was back in my chest. "Thank you."

The two words were barely audible, but the sentiment was there.

The doctor nodded and motioned me out of the waiting room. I followed him down the hall to a bank of elevators.

"We have her in ICU currently so we can keep a close eye on her, but she's breathing on her own."

I wanted that to reassure me, but the truth was I was too damn terrified, so I simply nodded.

When the elevator doors opened on another floor, Dr. Jones led me down another hall, punching a code into two double doors. He guided me through a maze of rooms until he stopped outside an open door. "Talk to her. It might help."

I swallowed, trying to clear the lump in my throat, and then I moved inside. The smell of antiseptic nearly took me out at the knees. Memories of countless days spent with Clara as she underwent treatment. Memories of sleepless nights by Grae's bedside. But I forced my feet forward.

The sight of Grae did me in. Her body looked so tiny in the massive hospital bed. Her face so pale. She had gauze wrapped around her neck, and wires protruded from beneath her hospital gown.

But I didn't let myself stop. Not until I sank into the chair next to her bed.

I gingerly took her hand in mine, lifting it and pressing my lips to her skin. "I'm right here, Gigi. I'm not going anywhere."

It was a vow. An oath.

The tears came as I watched her chest rise and fall. I didn't try to stop them; each one held all the love I felt for the woman beside me. I let them fall onto our joined hands, hoping they'd magically bring her back to me.

I slid my hand into my pocket and pulled out the necklace I'd carried with me for eleven years. Ever since the EMTs had taken it off Grae to place paddles on her chest and shock her back to life. I laid it over our joined hands. Some part of me believed holding on to it for so long had brought her back to me once. I just needed it to do it again.

My lips ghosted over her hand. "Need you, Gigi. Please, don't leave me."

Chapter Forty-Nine

Grae

THE FAINT BEEPING SOUND GRATED AGAINST MY EARS.
"Turn it off," I grumbled.

I tried to turn over, but pain ricocheted through me in angry pulses.

"Take it easy, Gigi," a rough voice warned as warm, gentle hands gripped my shoulders, shifting me back to the mattress.

I blinked rapidly at the sound, wanting more of it. Light filled my vision, almost hurting my eyes.

"There she is."

Caden's face came into focus in snapshots. Brief glimmers of the man I loved with everything I had. But he looked rough. Thick stubble covered his jaw. Dark circles rimmed his eyes. His hair was a mess as if he'd run his fingers through it a hundred times.

"What's wrong?" I croaked.

His hand came to my face, thumb stroking back and forth across my cheekbone. "You gave us a scare. Your pump ran out of insulin, and you went into ketoacidosis. You were in a coma for over twenty-four hours."

Everything came back to me in short bursts. Opening the door. The Taser. The cabin. The fire. My body jerked, making a fresh wave of pain cascade through me. "Eddie."

Caden kept one hand on my cheek and the other curved around mine, squeezing. "He's gone. You're safe."

"Gone?"

Caden nodded.

Tears filled my eyes, spilling over. Not for the person who'd terrorized me but for the friend I'd lost. "His mind got so twisted."

Caden leaned over me, pressing his forehead to mine. "I know."

"Why?" I rasped.

"Not sure we'll ever completely understand." Caden straightened, searching my face. "Police found some journals. After Megan died, it was like he fixated on you. Needed you to keep going. But that need turned dark, obsessive."

My chest grew tight, and I gripped Caden's hand tighter. "I didn't see it."

"I know. No one did." Pain flashed in Caden's face. "I'm so sorry I left you alone."

My hand jerked in his. "This isn't your fault."

"Wouldn't have happened if I hadn't left."

"Don't be an idiot," I snapped.

His brows lifted.

"If it hadn't happened right then, Eddie would've found another time. It was impossible for you to be with me twenty-four-seven."

"Might be proving you wrong these next few months," he muttered.

I lifted a hand to Caden's face, his stubble pricking my palm. "Please, don't take this on."

"I was terrified," he whispered.

A burn lit along my sternum. "I'm so sorry."

Caden's eyes glistened with unshed tears. "Losing Clara broke something in me. I was so terrified to lose someone else, I didn't let anyone close. Didn't truly let them in."

My heart broke for the boy who'd lost his sister, his partner in crime, his best friend. My heart broke for the man who still carried those scars.

"But when you were fading away in front of me, all I could think about was the time I'd wasted trying to keep you away."

My hand slid down Caden's neck and pulled him close. "But we aren't wasting time anymore."

His eyes searched mine. "Never again. Don't want to waste a single second."

"Think we could get the hospital chaplain to marry us right here?"

Caden grinned. "Pretty sure your mom and mine would murder us both."

A laugh burst out of me, and it felt so damn good. "You might have a point there."

"Never gonna get tired of that sound, you laughing. Missed it so damn much."

My nose stung. "Caden…"

He slipped his hand into his pocket and pulled something free. "I need to give you something back."

My brows pulled together. "What?"

Caden dropped a tiny silver charm connected to a delicate chain onto the blanket.

I gasped as I scooped it up. "My necklace?" I stared down at the tiny compass I'd loved so much, hardly believing it was real.

His throat worked as he swallowed. "The nurse gave it to me when we brought you into the hospital all those years ago. I held it the entire time they worked on you. Every moment you were in the coma. It was like my talisman. I thought if I just held onto it, you'd be okay."

My eyes burned, and pressure built behind them. "Caden."

"Even when I walked away, I had this with me in my pocket every single day. It made me feel close to you."

A few tears slipped free, and Caden brushed them away.

"Sometimes, it feels like the necklace brought me back to you.

You've always been my guiding force. My internal compass showing me the way. And now, I have to give yours back to you."

He bent and fastened the necklace around my throat. I looked up into his eyes. "I couldn't love you more."

Caden dipped his head, his lips brushing mine. "I can't wait to marry you." His mouth teased, and he slid the ring the doctors must have taken off back on. "Make babies with you." His tongue stroked. "Build a beautiful life."

"Sick. No kissing my sister in front of me," Nash groused as he strode into my hospital room.

Caden pulled back, glaring at Nash. "You're the one who didn't knock."

"It's a damned hospital. I shouldn't have to worry about walking in on you getting it on with my baby sister."

Roan's lips twitched as he stepped into the room. "If that rock on her hand is anything to go by, I think we'll have to get used to it." He crossed to me, wrapping me in a gentle hug. "I'm so glad you're okay."

"Thanks, big brother," I whispered.

"Rock?" my mom squeaked from the doorway, her gaze flying from me to Caden and back again.

Nash grabbed my hand, holding it up to the light. "I'll be damned. She did say yes." He grinned at Caden. "Good job, man." Then he scowled. "You still aren't allowed to kiss her in front of me."

Epilogue

Grae
ONE MONTH LATER

"**D**on't lift that," Caden barked.

I slowly set the box on the hatch of his SUV and turned to face my fiancé. "Caden…"

"You're still healing."

I blew out a breath, making the hair around my face flutter. "The doctor said I'm good to go. *Two weeks* ago."

"He said you still needed to take it easy," Caden argued.

"*If* I felt tired or was in pain. I'm neither."

The handful of stitches on my back and neck had come out during that visit, and the bruises on my throat had faded so much they were nearly nonexistent. I felt remarkably good, all things considered.

Caden crossed to me, brushing the hair out of my face and wrapping his arms around me. "Just let me take care of you for a little while longer."

I melted at the pleading in his voice. Things hadn't been easy since my kidnapping. Caden had been on edge, rechecking the locks on the doors and windows every night before bed and checking my blood sugar levels more often than I did.

I pressed a palm to his chest, relishing the feeling of the steady beat there. "I'm okay."

Caden dropped his forehead to mine. "You had a nightmare last night."

I shifted in his hold. "But you got me through it."

He pulled back. "Want to tell me what stirred things up?"

I'd had a few nightmares while in the hospital, and Caden had gotten me through each one. He'd climbed into that hospital bed and held me until I could go back to sleep. The nightmares had faded once we got home, but they'd kicked up again last night.

"I don't know if I want to go back to work at Vacation Adventures," I admitted.

Jordan had told me to take all the time I needed, but ever since I'd gotten the all-clear from Doc, I'd been thinking about it more. There were just too many painful memories. I couldn't sit at a desk that should've been next to Eddie's. I couldn't be forced to relive a million different memories but question them all.

Caden stilled, staring down at me. "Okay."

"You don't think that makes me a coward? Not to mention a horrible friend for leaving Jordan high and dry?"

Caden traced the ridges of my spine with his fingertips. "I think you're the strongest person I know. And the kindest. How many times have you had Jordan and Noel over here, just making sure they know you don't blame them? Making sure the three of you heal together."

They'd been to the house at least five times in the past two weeks alone. Jordan had been especially apologetic, both for not seeing what Eddie was hiding and for doubting Caden. Seeing how wrecked Caden had been at the hospital had made Jordan and Noel realize just how much he loved me. They might have even started to *like* him. And they weren't the only ones; even Rance had found a moment to apologize to us both.

I toyed with the hem of Caden's T-shirt. "I don't want to hurt them, but I think I need to start fresh."

"They love you. They'll understand."

Warmth curled around me. Caden always knew just what I needed to hear. "Gonna have to figure out what to do with my life."

I loved leading trips in the wilderness around Cedar Ridge. Losing that would be a blow.

Caden's gaze shifted, and my eyes narrowed on him. "What?"

He shrugged. "I might have an idea."

"Spill."

He grinned. "Always so impatient."

I tweaked his nipple. "Stop toying with me."

"Ow! Geez, you're vicious," Caden said, rubbing his chest.

"Could've gone for my knives instead."

Caden chuckled. "Point taken." He shifted on his feet. "What would you think about coming to work at The Peaks?"

My eyes flared. "Work for you?"

Caden had been leveled with more than his fair share of work now that Gabe was in prison, and his father had officially been ousted from the company. But he'd never brought up the idea of me coming to work for him before.

"*With* me," he clarified. "We could transform The Peaks into what it always should've been: a family place. One where people can reconnect with their loved ones and themselves. You've always been great at using nature to help people do that."

Tears stung my eyes. It was the ultimate compliment. It was what I always hoped to bring people when I took them up on the mountain or out on the lake. I couldn't imagine anything more special than doing that alongside Caden.

"Okay," I whispered.

His brows flew up. "Okay?"

I laughed. "You don't have to be quite so shocked."

Caden wrapped his arms around me. "I just thought I'd have more of a fight on my hands."

"I've gotta let you have your way now and then. It'll keep you on your toes."

He shook his head but grinned down at me. "Can't imagine being happier than I am right now."

I stretched up onto my tiptoes, brushing my lips against his. "What about when my family gets here any minute, and I turn your house into complete chaos?"

The fire restoration company had finally gone through my place, boxing up everything that wasn't too badly damaged by the fire, and everyone was helping me officially move into Caden's house today. It hadn't been a total loss, but it would take some serious work before I could sell it.

Caden kissed the tip of my nose. "Worth it."

Honking sounded, and Nash rolled down his window. "Stop kissing my sister in front of me."

Maddie smacked his chest.

"Maybe we could get him a muzzle," Caden muttered.

I couldn't hold in my laugh as I reached up to finger the necklace Caden had returned to me after eleven years. The fact that he'd kept it with him for all that time was a greater gift than he'd ever know.

A parade of vehicles filed into our driveway, and my brothers, parents, Maddie, and Wren piled out, all grabbing boxes and starting for the house.

"Where should we put these?" Holt called.

"Just pile them in the living room for now," I answered. "I'll figure out where to put it all later."

Caden winced, and I grinned as I patted his chest. "Just remember, you're the one who asked me to marry you. Gonna mess up your organized existence."

He kissed me long and slow. "I think I've needed that all along."

A car door slammed, and I looked up to see Jocelyn walking away from her Mercedes with a wide smile. "I brought sustenance."

Her transformation over the past month had been nothing short of miraculous. Casting off Harrison and taking control of her life had been just the ticket. She'd been absorbed into the fabric of my family as if she'd always been there, joining in on family dinners and game nights. And most surprising of all, she'd taken control of the family company instead of hiring someone else to take the helm. The new job had made her come alive at a time she desperately needed it.

I crossed to Jocelyn and gave her a big hug. "Thank you so much for helping."

"Wouldn't miss it for the world. And I brought some new samples to go over with you and your mom."

Caden groaned. He was already losing it over the wedding talk.

Jocelyn shot her son a warning look. "Don't you even start with me, young man."

I choked on a laugh.

Nash grinned at Caden. "You'd better watch your step if she's young-manning you already."

Caden grimaced but didn't argue. "What can I get out of your car?" he grumbled.

"Now that's better," Jocelyn huffed.

We made quick work of unloading all the vehicles, me sticking to only the lightest items. Then we descended on the feast that Jocelyn had brought. We devoured it while sitting on our back deck, the sun streaming down around us.

Caden leaned over and pressed a kiss to my temple. "Need anything else to drink?"

"I'll take another diet."

"You got it." He squeezed the back of my neck, disappearing into the house.

Roan lowered himself into Caden's empty seat. "How are you feeling?"

I smiled at my brother. "Good. I don't think I've ever been this happy."

A softness filtered into Roan's eyes, one I rarely saw. "I'm glad, G."

I stared back at him. "Want this kind of happiness for you, too."

Roan's face closed down, and I cursed myself. I knew I shouldn't have said anything, but I couldn't help it. With all this joy swimming around in me, I had to want it for the people I loved most, too.

His gaze shifted to the trees. "Some people aren't built for that. Part of them is too broken."

My heart cracked at his words. "Nothing's too broken about you."

Roan shook his head, standing. He bent and kissed the top of my head. "Enjoy your happy."

I watched him wind through our small crowd and disappear down the porch steps into the forest where he'd always felt more at home.

"Everything okay?" Caden said, sliding back into his chair.

I forced my gaze back to him. "I'm worried about Roan. He's pulling away more and more."

Caden looked to where Roan had disappeared. "He's been through a lot."

I nodded. "I just wish I could fix things for him. Take some of that burden."

Caden turned to me, his eyes gentling. "Kindest heart I've ever known."

I leaned into him. "Just want him to be happy. To heal."

Caden framed my face in his hands. "Miracles happen. You're living proof of that. Helped heal pain in me I thought would never mend."

Tears gathered in my eyes. "Caden."

He kissed the tip of my nose. "Love you, Gigi."

My lips curved as I sat back in my seat. "I'll never get tired of hearing those words."

"Good. Because you're going to hear them a lot."

I laughed, and it felt so dang good. The breeze picked up and carried the scent of roasted chicken our way. My stomach roiled. *Crap.*

I lurched to my feet and made a beeline for the bathroom. *Don't puke. Don't puke. Don't puke.*

My hands hugged the bathroom sink as I took deep breaths,

in through my nose and out through my mouth. Slowly, the nausea faded.

The door eased open, and Caden slipped inside, worry lining his face. "What's wrong?"

"Nothing. I just felt off for a second."

"Gigi…" he warned.

A million very real curse words flew through my head. "I had a plan."

Caden arched a brow.

"I wanted to tell you on our first night in our house, just the two of us."

"Tell me what?"

I swallowed hard, hoping like heck this news would make him happy. "I'm pregnant."

Caden's jaw went slack. "You're what?" he whispered.

"Pregnant. Preggers. Knocked up."

"You're on the pill."

I lifted my shoulders and let them drop. "I wasn't really good about taking them in the hospital, and then when we got home…"

Well, we hadn't wasted any time.

Caden moved in closer, his hand going to my belly. "A baby?"

"I know we didn't plan—"

He cut off my words with a kiss. "Can't imagine anything better."

Tears filled my eyes. "Really?"

"Greatest gift I've ever been given: your love, this baby, our family."

"Stop it."

He pressed his forehead to mine. "Thanks for holding on for me."

Caden's face went blurry in front of me. But I still knew it like the back of my hand. Because he'd always lived in that secret place inside me, and I knew that would never change.

"Thanks for being worth it."

Acknowledgments

Now, for my favorite part of a book. The acknowledgments. I love the peek we get inside authors' worlds in this section. Because, let me tell you, it takes a village to get a book finished and out into the world.

First, in my writerly world. Sam, I'm not sure how I finished books before we found each other. Thank you for encouraging, cheerleading, brainstorming, and reading this first draft. I'm profoundly grateful for your friendship and the way you get my words and help me make them better. Rebecca and Amy, thank you for reading the early chapters and helping me make sure I got that first fake relationship kiss just right. Thank you for being there to listen to a million ideas (or spirals) and for cheering so hard for me at every turn. Laura and Willow, my little love chain. Thank you for making me laugh harder than anyone, supporting me through all the crazy ups and downs, and being lights in my world. Elsie, thank you for always talking all the things and making me cackle laugh through it all. Secret handshakes and immunity necklaces forever.

Second, in my non-writer world. My STS soul sisters: Hollis, Jael, and Paige, thank you for the gift of twenty years of your friendship and never-ending support. I love living life with you in every incarnation. And Paigey, sharing the writing journey with you has been such a bright spot in my days. You light my creativity on fire, and I'm incredibly grateful.

And to all my family and friends near and far. Thank you for supporting me on this crazy journey, even if you don't read "kissing books." But you get extra special bonus points if you picked up one of mine, even if that makes me turn the shade of a tomato when you tell me.

To my fearless beta readers: Crystal, Elle, Kelly, and Trisha, thank you for reading this book in its roughest form and helping me to make it the best it could possibly be!

The crew that helps bring my words to life and gets them out into the world is pretty darn epic. Thank you to Devyn, Margo, Chelle, Jaime, Julie, Hang, Stacey, and Jenn; Katie, Andi, and my team at Lyric; and Kimberly, Joy, and my team at Brower Literary. Your hard work is so appreciated!

To all the bloggers who have taken a chance on my words… THANK YOU! Your championing of my stories means more than I can say. And to my launch and ARC teams, thank you for your kindness and support, and for sharing my books with the world. An extra special thank you to Crystal who sails that ship so I can focus on the words.

Ladies of Catherine Cowles Reader Group, you're my favorite place to hang out on the internet! Thank you for your support, encouragement, and willingness to always dish about your latest book boyfriends. You're the freaking best!

Lastly, thank YOU! Yes, YOU. I'm so grateful you're reading this book and making my author dreams come true. I love you for that. A whole lot!

Also Available from
CATHERINE COWLES

The Lost & Found Series
Whispers of You
Echoes of You
Glimmers of You
Shadows of You
Ashes of You

The Tattered & Torn Series
Tattered Stars
Falling Embers
Hidden Waters
Shattered Sea
Fractured Sky

The Wrecked Series
Reckless Memories
Perfect Wreckage
Wrecked Palace
Reckless Refuge
Beneath the Wreckage

The Sutter Lake Series
Beautifully Broken Pieces
Beautifully Broken Life
Beautifully Broken Spirit
Beautifully Broken Control
Beautifully Broken Redemption

For a full list of up-to-date Catherine Cowles titles, please visit www.catherinecowles.com.

About
CATHERINE COWLES

Writer of words. Drinker of Diet Cokes. Lover of all things cute and furry. *USA Today* bestselling author Catherine Cowles has had her nose in a book since the time she could read and finally decided to write down some of her own stories. When she's not writing, she can be found exploring her home state of Oregon, listening to true crime podcasts, or searching for her next book boyfriend.

Stay Connected

You can find Catherine in all the usual bookish places…

Website:
catherinecowles.com

Facebook:
facebook.com/catherinecowlesauthor

Catherine Cowles Facebook Reader Group:
www.facebook.com/groups/CatherineCowlesReaderGroup

Instagram:
instagram.com/catherinecowlesauthor

Goodreads:
goodreads.com/catherinecowlesauthor

BookBub:
bookbub.com/profile/catherine-cowles

Amazon:
www.amazon.com/author/catherinecowles

Twitter:
twitter.com/catherinecowles

Pinterest:
pinterest.com/catherinecowlesauthor

Milton Keynes UK
Ingram Content Group UK Ltd.
UKHW040728010823
426141UK00004B/251